She struggled not to *miss my Carly-bear*—tex searching for his mistress' she studied their hundreds of messages it might explain why he cheated, because so far nothing made sense. She and Todd were happy together. *Weren't we?*

The only reason she didn't call and yell at him not to bother coming home was she needed to see his face when she asked why.

She noted the phone number. Ten simple digits to identify the woman Todd had been screwing for at least six months, based on their texts.

The folder trembled in her hand as she located the tab with the BioLarge team's contact information. She was being irrational, and yet it felt as if the paper might melt onto her fingertips. She wiped her palms across her skirt. It couldn't possibly be the…

Same Phone Number.

Praise for *THE EXIT STRATEGY*

"Timely and provocative with ripped from the headline themes, you'll want to rise up and cheer on Cameron's witty and ingeniously crafted characters. By the time you finish reading *THE EXIT STRATEGY*, Ryn and Carly will feel like the best friends you never had. A thoroughly satisfying read."

~Kerry Lonsdale, Wall Street Journal bestselling author

"A #MeToo story powered by real life, real hope, and an unlikely friendship. Cameron brings warmth and emotion to this Silicon Valley story of power, ambition, and friendship."

~Jennifer Klepper, USA Today bestselling author

"A rollicking read complete with lightning-fast pacing, witty prose, lovable characters. Unputdownable!"

~Samantha Vérant, author

"In the spirit of Katherine Center with Liane Moriarty-style twists. A rallying call for women to believe in themselves and join together. A thoroughly entertaining and gratifying debut."

~Leah De Cesare, author

"It's about friendship, feminism, standing up for yourself and how much stronger women are when we stick together. A must read."

~Alison Hammer, author

The Exit Strategy

by

Lainey Cameron

The Exit Strategy

Cover Art by *Diana Carlile*

The Wild Rose Press, Inc.
PO Box 708
Adams Basin, NY 14410-0708
Visit us at www.thewildrosepress.com

Publishing History
First Mainstream Women's Fiction Edition, 2020
Print ISBN 978-1-5092-3138-6
Digital ISBN 978-1-5092-3139-3

Published in the United States of America

Dedication

To my mum Irene—

Thanks for teaching me that women
don't need to fear their strength or minimize their voice,
and can be badass resilient, smart, caring, and
open-hearted—everything I needed to know in life.

Acknowledgments

Thanks to my inspiring, supportive husband Eric, without whom this book would not exist. You are everything to me, and everything Todd could never be.

This story is an ode to the women who taught me the power of female friendship: Nikki Fenton, Janet Hill, Kirsty Nicholson, Mary Poffenroth, Laura Taylor, Crystal Coleman, Leah White, and Brekke El (who gifted me the character name of Ryn).

I owe so much to the members of Women's Fiction Writers Association (WFWA). Through WFWA I met the team who made this book what it is: Margie Lawson, Kemlo Aki at Author Accelerator, and Tiffany Yates Martin, the best development editor. I'm also deeply grateful to Alison Hammer, Leah de Cesare, Mary Hawley, Jennifer Klepper, Elena Mikalsen, Sweta Vikram, Be Warne, the Fictionistas group, and so many writers, listed in the full acknowledgements on my website, for their acts of generosity.

To Jordan and Tiana, the rest of my awesome family, both in the UK and USA, my friends and cheerleaders, and everyone on my launch team: thank you! Your words sustain and uplift me.

I couldn't end without the hugest note of thanks to Judi Mobley, my insightful editor, Diana Carlile, cover designer, and their colleagues at The Wild Rose Press.

Chapter One

Ryn scrawled *seething* on a scrap of paper and crammed it into the Feelings Jar on her desk. She winced at the glare bouncing off the adjacent skyscrapers, streaming through the wall of windows into her office. The San Francisco weather gods apparently didn't get the memo. Dismal fog was the appropriate backdrop to discovering her husband's affair. Not sparkly damn sunshine.

She opened her valuation spreadsheet. Perhaps a focus on the data would calm the shit-storm rumbling inside her head. Pops' technique of stuffing unwanted emotions in a jar usually worked. But not this morning, and the meeting with BioLarge started in ten minutes. The promotion she'd been denied for two years depended on closing this deal. She refused to blow it because of an infidelity brain scramble.

The rows of numbers blurred, and she struggled to recall her negotiation points, as dozens of memories demanded re-examination.

Todd's golf trip last month. *With Her. His mistress.*

Two weeks ago, when his apartment development project required an extended stay in Nevada through the weekend. *With Her.*

Those loving texts when Ryn was out of town.

—*I can't manage one more hour without you. What time do you land?*—

Not so loving now. Just measuring how much longer he had. *With Her.*

She didn't know which hurt more, Todd lying or him finding this other woman—this *Carly*—so special she was worth risking a perfect partnership.

Ryn stood and shook out her hands. If more time remained, she'd redo her analysis, but her brain had been buzzing like this since yesterday. Thousands of micro-deceptions like memory popcorn, every burst a new realization of betrayal.

Keep it together, Ryn. She focused on the faded poster of John Wayne on a rearing horse opposite her desk, a gift from her oldest brother Jack, and tried to summon a happy memory of childhood on the ranch in Montana.

Eyes closed, she imagined the morning scent of impatient cattle trampling soggy grass. From horseback, she leaned and opened the barn gate for the squad of grumbling cows who blocked her way, nudging her stirrups with their wet noses. Behind them, Jack and Mom trotted across a field dotted with wild roses to catch up, Mom's head tilted back in laughter, her everyday teal and purple headscarf rippling.

Ryn opened her eyes and dug her teeth into her bottom lip. She couldn't even summon a real memory instead of wishful thinking. Life had never delivered sunshine and wildflowers. Before she became old enough to ride the morning cattle rounds, Mom died from that soul-sucker cancer, and Ryn had been exiled to live with Aunt Dusty.

She closed her laptop, giving up on any hope of adjusting her mood. At least here at Sentra Ventures she was indispensable, and the BioLarge team would arrive any minute.

Ryn opened her prep folder. With the remaining time she'd review the background of the last executive she asked to meet today. So far her negotiations were with Paul Alexander, this company's CEO, but funding a startup without evaluating the technical founder would be bad business. Annoying that, despite asking him twice, Paul claimed his co-owner was too busy with clinical trials to join their prior meetings.

Her fingers flipped to the section of the folder with management biographies.

A photo of Carly Santos, BioLarge's cofounder and chief scientist, smiled next to a biography full of patents and achievements.

Carly.

Ryn's skin prickled. Prickled like the moment you notice inconsistencies in a company's accounts. Or at night when you cross the road to avoid the man with the neck tattoo, and he follows you.

She studied the photo. Carly was a common enough name. There must be hundreds, thousands of women named Carly in the Bay Area.

Big doe eyes stared at her with a warmth that never showed in her photos. Ryn's steely pose in leadership shots had become an office joke, with the other partners pushing her to *smile just this once.* But grinning on demand wasn't how a woman got taken seriously in a world where testosterone dripped down the walls.

Ryn ran her finger along Carly's waves of chestnut brown hair and studied the dimples in her smile. Ms. Santos was gorgeous in an unassuming, wouldn't-steal-your-husband kind of way.

This woman, this professional, couldn't be Todd's

Carly.

That would be ridiculous. Spanish soap opera ridiculous. Trashy television ridiculous.

She leaned over her keyboard and searched for the file of texts downloaded from Todd's phone. She didn't regret hacking into his account. Not since yesterday afternoon when she'd listened to the impatient valley girl twang of the receptionist at his conference hotel.

"Again, I'm sorry, ma'am, to keep repeating myself, but no matter how many times you ask, I cannot arrange a surprise massage for a Mr. Runyan."

"Because he's not staying there?"

"Like I said, I cannot disclose information about our guests, but I also cannot arrange the gift you're asking for…"

Ryn rubbed her eyes, then pushed on her stomach, trying to still the slithers of every reaction she'd tailspun through since yesterday: starting with incredulity, then questioning her sanity, followed by checking his texts, and panic after she read the messages from Carly. As if the real Ryn, the one with everything under control who understood how life worked, exited stage left at the exact second she learned Todd lied about where he stayed.

"Soulmates have nothing on us," he joked the night before he left, after delivering her Nutella toast with a kiss while they worked together late at the dining table. "Ten years and still best friends." His fingertips caressed her shoulders and that sunbeam of a smile snuck across his face. "The sex ain't all bad, either."

He leaned over and closed her laptop in what had become a sign between them. No matter how hectic their work lives, they always made time for each other.

She struggled not to reread his—*Five reasons I miss my Carly-bear*—text on her computer while searching for his mistress's phone number. Perhaps if she studied their hundreds of messages it might explain why he cheated, because so far nothing made sense. She and Todd were happy together. *Weren't we?*

The only reason she didn't call and yell at him not to bother coming home was she needed to see his face when she asked why.

She noted the phone number. Ten simple digits to identify the woman Todd had been screwing for at least six months, based on their texts.

The folder trembled in her hand as she located the tab with the BioLarge team's contact information. She was being irrational, and yet it felt as if the paper might melt onto her fingertips. She wiped her palms across her skirt. It couldn't possibly be the…

Same Phone Number.

Carly Santos is Her. Todd's Carly-bear.

Ryn shoved the folder off the desk. Briefing notes, purple Post-its, and Carly's smug smile splayed across the hardwood.

The pounding of her pulse said fly into *fix-it* mode. She thrived on the adrenalin rush of gluing together broken agreements, resurrecting deals thought dead, smoothing over potential PR disasters. Strength in the face of crisis was part of why she had progressed to here, on the edge of becoming senior partner.

But she couldn't fix Todd's cheating.

Nor could she enter the conference room in two minutes and close the terms to fund his lover's company.

It wasn't too late to cancel. Even if Paul and Carly

sat fifty feet away in the lobby, she could claim a sudden conflict. She grabbed the phone to dial Keisha, their office manager, but paused, remembering her boss's glare in last week's meeting. Simon drummed his fingers on the table, his disapproval obvious as she presented her case for investment of three times the firm's normal amount in this company. Despite not getting his vote, she'd won over the other partners with her insistence they get in early because she predicted BioLarge would become the hottest company in health-tech.

Dread crawled up her calves. If she bailed now, Simon would jump at the chance to show her success record wasn't so flawless. Five years lost. She'd be back to defending her perfect results, plunged into the frustration of arguing the case for her inclusion in the senior team. Perhaps Simon would even use her failure as an excuse to delay her promotion a second time.

The photo of shameless Ms. Santos, the only apparent winner in this equation, taunted her from the floor.

No, worse than shameless. It couldn't be a simple co-incidence; Todd's mistress showing up here. Carly must know she was meeting Todd's wife.

Perhaps Todd encouraged her to pitch Ryn for money. Even coached her?

Ryn stumbled back from her desk to remove the photo on the floor from her line of sight. Sending his mistress to her office showed so little respect it froze the breath in her chest.

Suddenly she wasn't a renowned venture capitalist, but a terrified pre-teen, sure she'd suffocate after she failed to convince her father to let her return to live with him and her brothers. To the only place she'd ever known as home.

She remembered this cinch fastened inside her ribs, pulling tighter and tighter, crushing her lungs until no breath or hope remained. That day was a full year after Mom died, a year she spent most afternoons ugly crying into the haystacks in the barn until Pops suggested the Feelings Jar. *Write it down and close it inside.*

She glanced at the compact earthenware pot on her desk, then picked it up. This jar served her better than she'd ever admitted to her father. It made survival possible in an industry where, as a woman, the slightest raise in voice branded you an emotional wreck. On days when a colleague insulted her intelligence, she simply returned to her office, scratched out what she thought of them, stuffed it inside the jar, and strolled into the next session.

Perhaps if she took the pot with her now, it could serve as a mental crutch and let her fake her way through the meeting with Carly, until she came up with a better plan.

Heels clicked on marble in the corridor outside her office.

What an absurd idea. She was an admired venture capitalist, not an eleven-year-old kid who missed her brothers and mommy.

Keisha pushed open the stainless steel and smoked glass door. Her box braids swung as she turned right, taking in the papers and Post-it Notes on the floor, then spun left to where Ryn stood behind her desk clutching the jar, her back against the wall.

If her friend was shocked, her perfect eyebrows didn't rise to show it, but the softness of Keisha's tone contrasted with her usual efficiency. "Is everything okay?"

Ryn forced out a breath and replaced the pot. As the only two women in this office, she and Keisha had each other's backs. But she couldn't bear talking about Todd yet, even if Keisha might be the one person she'd trust to ask for help.

Keisha gathered the documents from the floor and placed them gently on the desk with a bemused smile. "I came to remind you we want photos of the BioLarge team. For the announcement, assuming we sign today."

Ryn whipped her gaze toward the bank of windows overlooking Coit Tower and the San Francisco skyline. If they weren't behind a wall of glass, she'd spit on the city below. No matter what happened with Todd, signing the paperwork today ensured the ongoing humiliation of facing Carly in board meetings. She needed to find another solution.

She ought to delay the meeting, but Ryn suspected her voice might break if she spoke. Instead she turned and nodded, blinking away the moisture blurring her vision.

Keisha cleared her throat as if to ask a question, but seeing Ryn's state, apparently thought better of it. "For now, I'll have your guests wait in the lobby. We can take the picture after the meeting—just let me know if you need anything." She pulled the door closed behind her.

Always keep it professional. Ryn had taught Keisha well since she convinced the firm to hire her a year ago.

She stroked the rough glaze of her Feelings Jar. Perhaps her idea of taking it into the conference room wasn't so foolish after all. Not if it helped her keep it together. The attendees wouldn't even know she brought it. She grabbed her briefcase, stuffed the jar inside, and surrounded it with papers.

If she maintained her cool without acknowledging who Carly was, Ryn could declare some terms needed further negotiation, avoid signing the paperwork, and buy herself time to find a way out of this catastrophe.

She reread her favorite quote along the bottom of the John Wayne poster. *Courage is being scared to death, but saddling up anyway.*

Most people couldn't put their emotions aside and pretend this was any other meeting, but six years of working at Sentra Ventures—refusing to let Simon's condescension undermine her confidence—had proved most types of humiliation could be endured in twenty-minute increments.

Time to saddle up. She gripped her desk with both hands and focused on the rearing horse until she no longer risked the weakness of tears, then flung the door open and strode toward the lobby.

She just prayed that, if Todd's mistress made any snide comments, she wouldn't succumb to temptation, grab the pot, lean across the conference table, and smash it over Carly's head.

Chapter Two

Carly blotted her lipstick using the reflection on the microwave while Sammy played with his Cheerios. She gauged whether he'd eaten enough to stave off the morning grouches. A good mom wouldn't send her five-year-old to school hungry, but if they didn't leave in fifteen minutes, she'd be late for the meeting with Ryn Brennan.

She leaned over the table and ruffled his corkscrew curls. "Eat a few more spoonfuls; then we'll get on the road, okay?"

"But Mommy, it's oggy."

She turned to grab the cereal box and angled her head toward the inside of the cupboard, so he didn't catch her chuckle. This newest word was only a day old in his vocabulary.

"Problem solved," she said, pouring a few more dry Cheerios into his bowl. "Not soggy anymore, li'l guy." No need to correct his pronunciation. Sammy learned new words so fast, these days. He'd locate the missing S by tomorrow.

An all-teeth grin spread across his flushed cheeks, and he slowly took a bite, watching for her response. She gave him a thumbs-up.

While he ate, she tugged on the sides of her maroon wrap dress. Her intended outfit, a less clingy skirt suit which better said Competent-Scientist-

Worthy-of-a-Multi-Million-Dollar-Investment, sat in the laundry hamper. Last night, while rehearsing her presentation in the bedroom mirror, she toppled a glass of wine and it spilled over the chair where she'd draped her suit and left the sample wedding invitations. Typical for her to be so clumsy. She opened the to-do list app on her phone and added—*order more samples*—. At least she and Todd had months before they planned to send them.

Still, ruining the suit was not a good omen. She couldn't afford to let her team down in today's meeting. Paul, her CEO and co-founder, admitted yesterday that if BioLarge didn't secure this funding, they'd need to reduce costs and lay off twenty employees. For luck, she touched her necklace, the small gold cross Uncle Remy gave her. Her friends wouldn't lose their jobs just because she messed up another presentation.

"Enough, Mommy?"

A quick check of Sammy's bowl showed he'd eaten a solid half. The chair scraped on laminate as she pulled him away from the table.

"Quick-quick. Show me how fast you can find your backpack and coat. And don't forget to brush your teeth."

He jumped to the floor and his grin lingered after he scampered from the room.

She glanced at the coffee table, piled with wedding magazines and the new catalog for playsets Todd brought last week. She couldn't wait to see how far the famous Sammy grin extended when they unveiled the special model with swings, a climbing net, and two slides the day they all moved in together.

Todd would be an amazing stepdad, the way he

thought of the small things that showed someone they were loved. Uncle Remy had been just as thoughtful.

She picked up the printout of her presentation from the hallway table, and repeated the opening line she'd chosen for the first slide, which contained hundreds of pictures of those who'd died from heart attacks which could have been prevented.

The implications of this cardiac diagnosis technology are vast. Once released it will save millions of lives.

Every time she looked at Remy's picture in the center of the page, her heart ached. He was the only family member who'd stuck with her. She remembered the day he placed this cross around her neck. *I love my brother and his wife, but they're wrong. You are not the sum of your mistakes. God doesn't forsake those who have sinned, and neither do I.*

Remy was why she persevered during the long slog to design and perfect this product. He didn't have to let her live in the apartment at the back of his house in Oakland for six years while she gained the high school diploma she'd missed after running away from home, and then her college degree. If only this type of diagnostic solution had existed earlier, he would have lived long enough to meet and adore Sammy.

She entered the bedroom and flashed the mirror a broad, confident, of-course-you-should-fund-our-company smile. The expression almost worked, except her eyes contained slivers of doubt.

Come on, Carly. Today of all days, are you going to let the confidence-suck demon win?

What would Todd say if she called and told him she was freaking out? He'd remind her to focus on the facts. Eight years ago, while completing her master's after Remy died, she invented this diagnostic solution. So explaining the technology didn't scare her. But the facts also said public speaking was not her thing.

Massive understatement. Her stomach back-flipped as she relived last year's investor meeting when she froze onstage. Paul stepped in and tried to save the presentation, but they failed to secure the funding.

In truth, giving presentations was as much her thing as playing a ukulele hanging upside down from a Ferris wheel. Naked.

She smiled at the mirror again, this time with a power pose. Feet wide, shoulders back, face relaxed, like you belong. *You got this.*

Sammy hurtled into the bedroom. He paused for a moment, then planted his feet, and mimicked the pose, hands on hips.

He jumped his legs together and stretched both skinny arms in front of his head. "Superman!"

Carly laughed and swept him into her arms. "Superman indeed."

He wriggled, so she set her mini-me on the floor. Same cheeks as hers that flushed in an instant, same dark coffee curls that, with the grace of hair products, she turned into waves most days. But his love of words and ability to talk for ten minutes without stopping were all his own.

She leaned and gave him one of those high-fives he lived for. Maybe one day she'd master the complicated side-bump—fist bump—high-five Todd invented with him, but for now she'd let it be their thing.

She grabbed his lunchbox, slipped on a jacket, and did one last check for sticky fingerprints on her dress.

All good. The puzzle pieces of life were finally falling into place.

With the warmth of his hand in hers, they swung out the door and down the concrete steps toward the car. Some days, no matter how well she planned, fate conspired to make her late, but today she would not let it happen. For once, she'd planned plenty of time for the kindergarten traffic snarl.

****

Carly hurried to keep pace with Paul who jogged across the marble lobby of the Sentra Ventures building. He didn't look back, which meant he was upset. Understandably. She'd made them late. Again.

She caught up with him at the elevator and leaned against the mirrored wall, savoring the silence while the doors shut.

Darned cupcakes.

She pictured the teacher's expression when Carly passed Sammy's hand into hers—at first surprised, then accusatory. Carly had completely blanked on today being her turn to supply the birthday cakes for class.

Only a heartless mother left children cakeless on their birthday week, but she knew better than to believe an emergency grocery store run actually took ten minutes. At the mega-intersection beside the school, she sat with the tray of pink-and-teal frosted confectionary on the backseat, begging the lights to change as the trip turned into twenty, then twenty-five minutes, then thirty.

Paul studied her from across the elevator, concern lines digging into his forehead. His gray suit, wrinkled as usual, reminded her of the crumpled shorts he wore when they snuck chardonnay into the Stanford library

14

during grad school. Since then, her friend had grown accustomed to the role of charismatic CEO, but still didn't know how to use an iron.

He stepped to her side and gave her an elbow nudge. "Ready to dazzle 'em? Don't worry, I know Ryn will love you."

She raised an eyebrow at him, surprised not to be on the receiving end of a dig at her lateness.

"Try and remember, the folks at Sentra, they're just like us." His face broke into the goofy sideways grin he always used to cheer her up. "Well, except for the money...and the shark teeth."

Carly pulled her dress away from her clammy armpit, under her jacket. She inspected the mirror and marble wall as the elevator climbed. Paul's jokes usually made her laugh, but shark teeth weren't far from true. The articles said Ryn Brennan had become one of the most successful women in the valley, an expert at selecting winning companies. To thrive in the male-dominated world of venture capital the woman must have held herself to a higher standard at every rung of the ladder. One tough cookie. Of all the audiences Carly had pitched, Ryn would likely be the most demanding.

Breathe, Carly, breathe. She slowed her inhales as she did during meditation on the deck each morning, before Sammy awoke.

"Carls, please relax. Trust me, the firm is already convinced. They just wanna meet our superstar chief inventor and scientist before we close the deal. And I'm here to support you."

She groaned. "So, they like me, we get the money. Continue the research, save lives. And if they don't?"

"Please don't go there. We've managed to secure funding at every stage so far. This isn't that different."

His lips pinched in a familiar frown. Paul had always believed in her, but lately he lacked patience for what he referred to as her 'three u' problem: unreasonable, unjustified, and unproductive self-doubt.

But this time she wasn't worrying for no reason. Carly smoothed the skirt of her dress and debated the best way to pose the question she fretted over since consulting a peer at another company. Paul would likely accuse her of being melodramatic, but apparently it wasn't unusual at this stage of funding to request an executive to leave. Ryn could say yes to funding BioLarge but insist on replacing Carly.

The science aspect of the job she understood better than anyone. But the executive role for the launch phase of a product this revolutionary required stage presence and expert market judgment. Getting this product to the world mattered the most, so if asked, would she sacrifice herself for the greater goal and leave her own company? God knows she'd already left behind a trail of terrible life decisions.

Paul's gaze lowered to where her hand tugged on the bottom of her sleeve.

"Thanks for covering it. You never know how folks will react."

She rubbed her arm through her jacket. It was difficult enough to be taken seriously as a female scientist, no matter what you'd achieved; more so with a gun, bleeding skull, and butterflies covering your entire arm.

By now, at thirty-five, she was proud of how she had pulled herself together, especially since Sammy's birth. But it still hurt to remember this tattoo wasn't the worst decision of her teen years. Try stealing from your parents' church fund and running away with a boyfriend at fifteen.

She wished she'd found the gumption to walk away from Kyle during the five long years that followed. Even after he fell into the hell of addiction, she believed her loyalty to a man, by then her husband, was noble, not one more mistake.

But fifteen years had passed since she left Kyle and turned up on Uncle Remy's doorstep. The people who stared at her tattoo as if she were about to open her briefcase and peddle them coke had zero justification to judge her so harshly. Not when these days her crummiest decisions involved a last-minute run for cupcakes.

The problem was that, in these Silicon Valley money meetings, impressions often mattered more than actual results.

"Paul, have Ryn or the other investors given you a sense of how they feel about our exec team?"

The corner of his eyes wrinkled. "You worried I won't make it?"

"No, not you, doofus. I talked with Ahmed—you know the co-founder of Medi-K?—last week. He said they replaced him after—"

The elevator dinged, and the doors swept open on the twenty-fourth floor: Sentra Ventures.

Pitch time.

****

The decor in the lobby of Sentra Ventures clearly resulted from an excess of cash, merged with a shortage of taste. The living plant wall was common in the fancier lobbies Carly had visited, but the layered Persian rugs clashed with Italian cherub statues on every shelf, and the Philippe Starck modern furniture didn't match any of it. *Aladdin's palace meets Miami Vice.*

She perched on an angular white seat and an assistant arrived with a tray of high-end sparkling water in six different flavors.

"I'm so sorry about the wait." The assistant—or maybe she was an office manager—made an attempt at a reassuring smile, but her eyes tightened on the edges and she rapidly backed away.

Carly's stomach switched into its familiar pre-presentation gentle wash cycle. She knew what happened next. One stumble over the words and the cycle accelerated; two and it went into full spin. Then her voice panic-froze, and everyone in the room wondered why she had suddenly stopped presenting, sometimes mid-sentence.

She unstuck her legs from the plastic edging of the chair and took a deep breath. She didn't have to face this alone. Paul was right here, and if she bombed, he could always step in and help.

She glanced at the living plant wall and focused on the calming sound of water, feeling an affinity with other anxious entrepreneurs who must have sat in this same spot. Like her, they would be seeking funds to continue businesses into which they'd already poured years of their lives. In her and Paul's case, seven years.

Their company would never have existed if it weren't for Paul. He first suggested to turn her master's project into reality. In their first year, working from coffee shops, it often seemed he believed in the possibility more than she did, but in year two, when they were both holding other full-time jobs, and Paul had two young kids, she picked up the mantle of cheerleading, and secured their first angel funding from a group of Stanford professors.

She let herself smile. In their coffee shop days, she wouldn't have believed they'd end up here; owners of a real company with almost a hundred employees, and a logo people recognized on the front of the building. And by next year, they'd be helping patients across the country.

"What?" Paul asked, likely bemused by her stealthy smile.

"Oh, nothing. Just reminiscing about how far we've come. What do you think the hold up is?"

He leaned in close to her shoulder, so the assistant didn't overhear. "I don't know, but it's weird. Maybe they're making a point by having us wait because we arrived late."

Carly turned away from the assistant and rolled her eyes, so only Paul could see. A power play hardly seemed like the right way to start a new business partnership.

Finally, a tall woman with a striking copper bob appeared from the corridor and strode across the lobby. An emerald scarf curved around her spotless ivory blouse, and she smiled in the way of a person who had everything together, as if her entire life were neatly clipped in place by that scarf pin.

Carly had met this type of woman at school parent meetings; those with little patience for people like her, who permanently ran late and struggled just to hold the basic threads of life together. She unstuck herself from the chair and stood, but Ryn didn't acknowledge her before shaking Paul's hand.

"Nice to see you again, Paul."

Carly must be right in thinking the lady had become one hardened cookie. And rude.

Paul pushed gently on Carly's back. "Let me introduce our chief scientist and my co-founder at BioLarge who—"

"I'm aware of who Ms. Santos is."

There was a snarl to Ryn's voice. Her gaze focused on Carly's feet and remained there for a few seconds before scanning up over her hips and across her breasts. The length of scrutiny felt almost as if she were checking Carly out.

Ryn still didn't look straight at her face. Instead, with a flash of a scowl, she pivoted and strode back across the lobby.

Carly's cheeks and chest burned. Her stomach swerved into a faster cycle. *What's so wrong that I didn't even merit a handshake?*

She inspected her skirt, her shoes. The wrap dress might be a little tight, and her black flats weren't exactly high fashion, but nothing deserved this type of snub.

Ryn had already covered half a long corridor, presumably headed toward their conference room. As they hustled to catch up, Carly raised her eyebrows at Paul. He returned an "I-dunno" shrug behind Ryn's back but didn't seem too concerned.

Best not to let herself be derailed by Ryn's lack of manners. She was likely just one of those matter-of-fact analytical types with no social skills, annoyed by the disruption to her carefully regimented schedule.

Although her scowl in the lobby didn't resemble you-made-me-late frustration. More like frosted fury.

In the conference room, an entire wall of floor-to-ceiling windows showcased a many-million-dollar panorama of San Francisco's skyscrapers and the bay. In the center, a monumental table of the made-from-one-tree variety dominated the space.

Carly wondered if the setting had been designed to impress or specifically to intimidate entrepreneurs like them, who could barely afford rented desks. Or windows.

At the far end of the slab of wood a man in a lime green polo shirt tapped on his phone. Two younger men wearing glasses, likely junior associates, also followed them into the room. Ryn had brought reinforcements.

Carly circled the table and sat on the same side as Paul, facing away from the distraction of the view. He gestured toward the man in the lime shirt, now opposite her. "Carly, meet Blake Cushings from Free Age Capital. He'll also be on our board, along with Ryn, once we close this funding round."

"Hello, Carly." From the way Blake's face reset into smile lines after his greeting, he would be a friendlier audience than Ryn Brennan. Carly reached to shake Blake's hand. Unfortunately, his firm was a smaller player in this deal where Ryn's firm would hopefully provide ninety percent of the money.

Before they finished shaking, a rapid *tak-tak-tak* started further along the table.

Carly turned to her left. Ryn sat beside Blake, clicking a ballpoint pen on the wood in short sharp bursts.

"We're already late and have limited time. Let's

get going."

Carly couldn't read Ryn's expression, because her gaze focused not on the group around the table, or the pen she click-clicked against the wood, but on the floor where she'd set her briefcase. Socially inept was an understatement.

Still, she got the message. Ryn was impatient to start.

Carly pulled her laptop from her bag, stood, and pushed open the screen. Below the edge of her sleeve, the jaw and teeth of the skull in her tattoo had become visible.

Perhaps this was the lady's problem. Ryn could be one of those people who jumped to instant judgment.

Carly steadied herself against the table. What did her counselor say in college? *You get to write your own story.* After his comments, she'd researched tattoo removal in her final year, but lasering a whole arm wasn't easy. Just like her past, it would still have been there, transformed into ghost scars. Instead, the counselor gave her the idea to revise, restart.

Before speaking, she visualized the butterflies that ran along her arm, weaving in and out of her history, a reminder of her own resilience. The first one she added to the skull and gun after completing her undergrad, representing renewal. A mark of pride in her persistence through college after leaving Kyle, even if it meant starting her waitressing shift at four a.m. every day, before her classes. In her thirties she added the five larger butterflies that covered most of the gun, each representing a year of Sammy's life. But the skull she decided to keep. She'd read an article which said Mexicans viewed them as a symbol of rebirth.

She released her grip on the edge of the table. The best approach to flash judgments like Ryn's was to counter hostility with pleasantness. Carly pasted on the smile of a small-town mayor running for reelection, picked up the cable, and connected her laptop.

"I'm thrilled with the opportunity to present our groundbreaking cardiac diagnosis solution today." She tapped a key to display her presentation on the giant wall screen, but nothing happened. The screen remained dark.

She wiggled the cables and pressed the key again. Still nothing.

Darn it. She looked toward Ryn for help. This was her conference room. She must know how the screen setup worked.

Ryn finally raised her head and met her gaze. A torrent of hostile energy smacked Carly from across the table. Ryn's eyes blazed bright, set deep with pure loathing.

Holy hell. Carly's stomach clicked into full-speed spin. She'd seen venom like this only once before: the day she finally walked out on Kyle.

Ryn's problem sure as heck wasn't about her tattoo.

She turned to ask Paul for help, but he conferred with Blake, his back toward her. *Great support, friend, thanks.*

Fine. She possessed enough technical smarts to work the screen herself. A quick scan of the tabletop revealed no remote control, so the power must need to be turned on at the wall.

She dodged two empty chairs while Ryn stared in silence. Carly slid her hands up the screen's sides.

Nothing on the left. Only volume on the right.

Ryn's gaze scorched her back. Carly swallowed once, then again, wishing she had brought one of the water bottles from the lobby.

She turned toward the room. Paul still chatted with Blake, and the two younger note-takers stared out the window, clearly bored.

Ryn opened her mouth as if to say something, then snatched a piece of paper, and scrawled a few words. She folded it in half and placed her manicured hand on top.

"Ms. Santos, do you require assistance?" Ryn's neutral tone was at odds with her fingernails digging into the note.

Her question drew Paul's attention from his conversation, and he noticed Carly standing by the screen. "Carly, what's going on?"

"The monitor, it's…not connected."

Paul raised his eyebrows at Ryn. "Are we missing something here? Is there a control panel, somewhere?"

"Indeed, there is." Ryn's expression held no emotion, a perfect model of business-meeting blank. "Right here." She opened a hidden section in the center of the table and turned on the screen.

What on earth? The woman seemed to enjoy watching Carly squirm. But then why switch in a nanosecond from obvious hatred to behaving as if nothing were unusual?

Carly returned to the table, hitting her thigh against an empty chair. She punched the same key and her slides displayed, like normal. She could almost believe she imagined Ryn's venomous look.

A familiar flush flamed up her neck and across her

cheeks. The slides not showing wasn't her fault, but she'd still looked as stupid as she felt in these rooms full of money people.

She pointed at the screen. "I intend to share an overview of the core technology involved in our cardiac care. The implication is vast millions of lives. Sorry, what I mean is, the implications of this cardiac diagnosis technology are vast, and it will save millions of lives."

For the next ten minutes, she kept her focus on Blake's and Paul's friendly faces as she presented. Paul advised her to share her passion for how older relatives would see their kids grow up, and it worked. She could talk for hours on why this technology deserved to be in the world.

Blake looked fascinated, nodding along, as did the young men, who typed notes. She took care not to let tears well up when she presented the second of the slides with Remy's last photo, looking so vibrant at the North Beach street festival the week before his heart attack.

After a few more pages she realized it must seem weird, the way she talked only to Blake and the young men, not the senior woman in the room, and she risked a glance toward the other end of the table.

Ryn still held the note between her fingertips as if waiting for the right moment.

Carly's heart accelerated as if Sammy had fallen down the stairs, banging his head on the way. She stammered her next sentence.

"So, um, the testing timing is, I mean was, a bit longer than, than what we anticipated because it's been challenging to find engineering talent, especially when it…" *Darn it.* She'd lost sight of her point.

Ryn leaned in and placed the note at Carly's left. "I may have a contact who can help." Again her tone sounded tempered, like a doctor breezing her way through a good news patient consult. But the glare at Carly as she withdrew her hand said her message was anything but benign.

Should she open it?

Carly's gaze bounced from the paper, to Ryn, then back to Paul, her throat raw like desert dust.

The room stayed silent, waiting for her to continue. No way she could read it discreetly while everyone watched her.

The note now sat next to her laptop. Bright white on lacquered wood. She wasn't sure she even wanted to know what it contained.

Everyone in the room continued to stare, likely wondering why she didn't continue her presentation. Carly cleared her throat. She'd entirely forgotten where she left off.

She looked toward Paul, and he saved her by asking a question of Blake. "Didn't I read an interview last week where you said the engineering shortage is particularly affecting health care start-ups?"

With Blake focused on answering, everyone's attention shifted to him. Except for Ryn. She nodded at the note as if daring Carly to open it.

She should find out Ryn's problem, see if it risked killing their deal. Carly bent over, unfolded the paper and peeked.

How dare you come here? To my office?

Carly jerked her head up. Ryn's eyes narrowed into intense green blazes. Her expression implied not only might she fly off the handle at any moment, but she could rip an entire door off its hinges and bludgeon Carly to death with it.

Carly took a stumble-step back from the table. *What have I done to her?*

Her heart pummeled her rib cage, powered by a rush of adrenaline telling her it was well past time to get the hell out of this room. Perhaps if she left, Paul might finish the presentation and still secure their funding?

The muscles in her throat tensed. A hangman's rope strangled whatever confidence she'd miraculously sourced just twenty minutes ago. She stuffed the note in her jacket pocket, stared at the polished wood floor, and begged the room to stay in focus. She didn't even know Ryn. Hadn't met, or so much as seen her, before today.

Paul coughed. "Is everything okay?"

She needed to answer and excuse herself, but the freeze had stolen her voice.

Carly sank into her seat and studied the grain of the table. This couldn't be more mortifying.

Ryn turned toward Paul with a humorless smile. "Turns out there are a few new issues with the terms I'd prefer to resolve over email. Let's just answer any questions and finish here for today." The crack in her tone reminded Carly of an Alaskan glacier calving off a wall of ice.

Blake posed a few questions and Paul answered. All Carly could do was wait until they left, share the note with Paul, and explain why she'd frozen.

As they walked toward the lobby after the meeting, she considered whether to pull Ryn aside, but she chatted with Paul the entire length of the corridor.

Perhaps Ryn had met Carly in the past and for some reason she didn't recognize her. Or Ryn could simply have mistaken Carly for someone else.

At Ryn's insistence, they all lined up against the living plant wall and her assistant took photographs. Standing by the Sentra logo looked like celebrating in front of the Oscars banner, not as if Carly had completed less than half her presentation. But did the photos mean Sentra still intended to fund them?

She glanced around the overstuffed lobby. A braver, more confident person might yank Ryn into the bathroom she'd seen in the corridor and insist on talking, but Carly didn't want to cause a scene.

As soon as they completed the photo session, Ryn crossed the lobby and stood by the far wall. She stared as Carly hit the elevator button, then watched, watched, watched, as the doors closed between them.

****

The elevator whooshed shut and Carly let her weight fall against the wall, her jagged breath leaving patterns on the mirror. She'd never attended a meeting where someone relished watching her fail, and she handled it terribly.

Paul touched her shoulder. "Are you okay? You didn't seem yourself in there."

"Are you kidding? What on earth just happened? I don't even know that woman, but she clearly has a problem with me. Didn't you notice how she glared the entire time?"

Paul rubbed a palm across his chin. "I give you it was pretty weird. And I understood we'd sign today. Why don't I call her later, see if something we said created a new issue or concern?"

Carly pulled Ryn's note from her pocket but kept her hand by her side. If they didn't secure this funding, her first team members would lose their jobs by next month. She'd never forgive herself if she and Ryn had a simple misunderstanding. Her own cowardice in not simply talking to Ryn could mean they ran out of cash before their diagnosis solution even made it to market and saved lives.

She closed her fingers and crumpled the note. "Why don't I reach out? I have no idea why, but I got a vibe her issue is with me. She might be more open to talking if it's only the two of us."

Carly recognized the tilt of Paul's head which meant he debated two sides of a decision. "Sure. Whatever."

Whatever? His response sounded so unlike Paul, who'd fought years for this company. She studied his face. Under the elevator lighting his skin had a yellowish tinge, as if he'd expended every ounce of energy. Was he being short because he felt exhausted or repressing anger because she torpedoed their pitch?

"Sorry, Carls, there's just a ton of stuff on my mind right now. Okay if I come to your place tomorrow before Sammy gets out of school? There's another topic we need to discuss, but it's best to talk away from the team."

"Of course." Carly offered up a smile, but her brain wrestled with what required an out-of-the-office meeting. They hadn't met at either of their homes in years, but she knew better than to push Paul before he wanted to talk.

A tense silence sat between them on the walk to the parking garage and throughout the drive from the city.

Usually, she loved this trip over the Golden Gate, but since they arrived, fog had settled on the bridge. Eerie shadows marked where its golden tips should have been.

When they descended the hill toward their office in Marin, she finally spoke. "Paul, what do we tell the team about the meeting?" Everyone expected them to return with a signed contract.

Paul continued to stare at the road, hands clamped on the steering wheel. "I don't know, Carly. Don't answer. Or tell them it went fine."

Carly tensed. Now she knew for sure something was wrong. Paul prided himself on open communication with their entire team.

Either she was correct that Ryn wanted to replace her, or Paul had a bigger problem on his mind. But what could be bigger than their funding being in jeopardy?

Chapter Three

The Macallan swirled in its crystal tumbler, radiant in the day's last light. Ryn stood on the maple floor of her dining room and watched the golden liquid spin. The same whisky she and Todd saved for special occasions.

She took a deep slug, then placed the glass on the table, next to her open laptop. Rifling Todd's pockets and rereading every message only confirmed her fears. After he arrived home tomorrow there would be no more special occasions because his affair was clearly about more than sex.

It wasn't only the 'L' word sprinkled throughout their text messages. Todd and Carly appeared to spend more evenings at Carly's house than at the upscale restaurants he so loved. Todd was handsome, stunning even, with those emerald eyes and captivating smile. He didn't have to pass entire hours stuck inside anyone's home just for sex. And from the texts, it seemed their affair spanned not six months, but more than two years.

Ryn took another swallow of whisky, controlling her desire to slam the tumbler through the glass table. Marriage had never been part of her plans. When Todd proposed for the first time, she proudly informed him that while she appreciated the offer, she didn't need a man to fix the closets or make her whole.

They'd met only three weeks before at the Forbes

31

Venture Capital 30 Under 30 awards ceremony. Her name had appeared on the list of up and comers in Silicon Valley and he peppered her with questions at the reception on her choice of investments. The conversation quickly transitioned to her love of horses, and Montana, and he listened, enthralled, as if no person were more interesting. Flattering, how he fell so fast, but she believed him to be joking with his marriage proposal four dates later.

Life was too short to make the same mistake as her mother. Mom enjoyed a burgeoning career as a travel photographer before she got pregnant with Jack and abandoned her globe-trotting life to settle for raising three kids in Montana. Ryn did not intend to give up everything she'd worked for to cater to a man who insisted she put his needs first. God knows, she did enough pandering in the office every day, surrounded by men who too often refused to take her seriously.

She ran a finger along the photos hanging on the living room wall and unhooked the beach shot from the Dominican Republic; an artsy black and white print that matched the others on the slate-gray walls.

She never imagined Todd would persist for over a year after his first proposal. She must have said no a hundred times before the night he arranged on this beach, their table circled by candles and scampering sand crabs. He plunged to one knee again, and brushed the sand off her hand. His eyes grew moist as he explained how he'd never want to steal her independence or turn her into his lesser half, but he could no longer stand the pain of rejection if his best friend didn't choose to be with him.

Todd wasn't a crier, but she saw his fear, the

anticipation of her saying no again, and she finally accepted what he kept assuring her. He didn't want the illusion of a perfect wife, a woman who'd accommodate him and sacrifice everything. He just wanted her: a works-too-hard, sometimes socially awkward, often-talks-too-loud real woman, flaws and all.

So why screw us up to be with Carly?

Cheating for sex would have made more sense. And hurt less.

She paced into the kitchen and grabbed the jar of Nutella from the cabinet, opened the patio door, and gazed at the view over Tiburon Harbor as the first spoonful of smooth, nutty chocolate caressed her taste buds. So far, her only conclusion was that Carly represented everything Ryn didn't. Warm, curvy, domestic. All Barefoot Contessa.

Ryn could eat this whole jar and it wouldn't add any curvature to her hard angles. Although it couldn't only be physical. Carly must be funny, too. Todd used to say Ryn's corny ranch jokes wouldn't even make cowboys laugh.

But even if she knew from the beginning she'd never qualify as a domestic goddess, it wasn't enough reason to give up on them after a decade. She and Todd were best friends, life partners. He accompanied her to networking events where she needed a confidence boost, and she cheered him through every deal and disappointment. And on their weekends away to Lake Tahoe and Sonoma County, she didn't play Ryn Brennan, stern venture capitalist, but got to be his best friend and nurturer. A free spirit, who spontaneously visited obscure wineries, and walked hand in hand on the beach.

Maybe she should stop being such a coward and just call him and hash it out?

She glanced around, looking for her phone. The throbbing in her head warned her calling was a dumb idea. For all she knew Todd was with Carly now, given he wasn't at the conference in Phoenix.

Screaming down the phone at them might release the tension keeping her breath ragged, but it wasn't her best move. She needed to see his face when she confronted him, to understand why he betrayed her.

She kept the whisky and paced outside across the deck. Fergus, her tabby cat, jumped from the roof and landed beside her. Ryn faltered and tripped, then caught her balance. She might be more drunk than she realized.

She sat on the rough deck, pulled Fergus close, and stroked behind his ears. He stayed for three seconds then pulled away, rejecting her in favor of the warmer house. *Et tu, Fergus?*

Tears stung in her eyes. This would be the time to cry, if only from frustration, but she wouldn't let it happen. She'd allow tears the moment she told Todd they were finished. She didn't know if he'd even fight to keep her.

She turned toward the bay. Between the wooden slats of the deck, seagulls squawked and squealed around the harbor far below. On the street outside, two of them fought, jumping in spasms, tearing more at each other than the carcass between them. Instinct over intelligence.

Her behavior today at Sentra hadn't been considerably more evolved. She shivered to think what Marilyn, her first venture boss, would make of her middle-school tactic of passing a note across the table.

"You're whip smart, but as a woman you can never let personal and professional overlap," Marilyn had told her more than once. "You're swimming with the sharks, kid. Learn to demand the respect of every man in the room, and never ever volunteer to make coffee."

Never let personal and professional overlap. She'd made a habit of following Marilyn's advice, so how did she forget it during the meeting with Carly? A massive underestimation of how fury apparently flushed her brain of all professional control.

She stood, her ears pounding again with the memory of how Carly stared at Ryn as if she were the one with a problem. Yes, continuing the meeting had been a mistake, but what Carly did was far worse. *Showing up at your lover's wife's office is brazen beyond belief.*

Ryn reentered the house, wavering against the kitchen wall. On second thought, she should damn well call the marriage-wrecker.

Todd wouldn't pick up if staying with his mistress, but Carly might answer. If he was actually with *Her* and not in Phoenix, Ryn could catch him in the act. No debate. No denials.

She spotted the phone on the coffee table, grabbed it, and plunked herself on the white leather sofa.

What would she say to Carly if Todd wasn't at her place? *Are you sleeping with my husband?* Ryn already knew they were.

For the first time, it occurred to her she and Todd didn't share a last name. Perhaps Carly knew she was cheating but not the identity of Todd's wife? No, it seemed highly unlikely after two whole years.

She cradled the phone, the burn of whisky still smoldering in her chest, debating whether to make the call or just continue drinking.

Chapter Four

Carly muted the ringer and returned her phone to the pocket of her cardigan. A number she didn't recognize, likely a telemarketer, wouldn't interrupt her favorite stabilizing part of the day.

She pulled the covers over her and Sammy's legs and they settled in and read his beloved book of the moment: the story of how a proud chicken and a scared donkey become friends.

His chubby fingers curled around the edges of the book. Carly readjusted on the bed, careful not to touch the pages. Since they visited Paul's daughters at their elementary school, her son had become adamant that big kids held their own books. They'd finished the second page when he sneezed.

He looked up at her, then sneezed a second and third time.

She leaned over and grabbed a tissue from the box by the bed. Sneezing like this in November meant his allergies were more likely caused by dust than pollen, but she already cleaned his room twice this week. If she knew how to reach his dad, she might call and ask if Kyle suffered from allergies as a kid and if so, what type.

"Oh no, Mommy." He held out the book, eyes walnut-wide with concern at the snot-covered page. "It's all soggy."

"It's okay, sweetheart, we can clean it."

She blew his nose, wiped the book, and ruffled his hair. Her future poet laureate. With these curls, add a beret and glasses and her five-year-old bookworm even looked like a poet.

As usual, he fell asleep before the last page. She extricated herself from the bed and stood a few moments and admired his flushed cheeks.

Hard to imagine only six years ago she was submerged in doubt over whether to bring this perfect little human into the world. Not only had she made the world's dumbest one-night slip, but with the worst timing: only a year into getting BioLarge off the ground.

She kissed Sammy's forehead and returned to the living room, where a handful of toy trucks lay strewn across the woven rainbow rug. Who'd have guessed that a pregnancy she considered punishment by an avenging God would be her chance to make one honorable, redeeming choice this lifetime. No matter what other mistakes she made in life or at work, Sammy was the sun that made her rise every morning.

Her laptop sat on the dining table, and she picked it up and settled on the sofa. Sure, it had been difficult raising an infant while launching a startup, but with help from Paul and her best friend and neighbor Dev, she'd made it work. BioLarge had come too far now, despite all their obstacles, to allow extra complications to stall them getting to market. She just needed to schedule a meeting with Ryn Brennan, and fix her problem.

She located Ryn's email address easily enough, and typed a subject line of "Follow-up," but stopped after her first sentence. Ryn's issue with her must be personal, so how to word it?

Thank you for taking time to meet with Paul and me today. I can tell by your note in our meeting you have an issue with me...

Scratch that.

I wanted to suggest we talk about the note you passed...

This didn't work either. Every version made her sound either loopy or paranoid, but she didn't imagine Ryn's attitude today. If looks could kill, Ryn's would have ground Carly to bitch dust.

What could she have against me?

Carly rose, lit two candles, breathed the scent of calming jasmine, and poured herself a glass of pinot.

She supposed it might be possible her ex, Kyle, conned or stole from Ryn. As far as Carly knew he hadn't returned to the Bay Area since their last contact five years ago, when she gave him a choice between getting clean or opting out of Sammy's life. And why would Ryn even come in contact with a person like him? Too far-fetched.

No, the vehemence of Ryn's hatred when Carly opened her note channeled a level of emotion reserved for child kidnappers and jilted spouses. Which meant other than mistaken identity, there were no logical options, because Sammy had left her stretch marks as reminders of a difficult pregnancy—and Todd's wife was dead.

The phone buzzed again in Carly's pocket. No one called more than once after eight o'clock at night other than telemarketers or debt collectors.

She answered the call this time. Might as well ask

to be removed from their list, or they'd keep bothering her.

"Carly?" A woman's voice, almost inaudible.

"Yes, can you please take me off your list?"

No sound other than breathing and what sounded like the clink of ice on glass.

Not a telemarketer, but a stalker? She re-checked the number—local area code—and moved her finger over the screen, preparing to hang up.

"It's Ryn. Ryn Brennan."

Carly froze in the middle of the living room, phone in one hand, wineglass in the other. This was a conversation she wanted, but not now. Not standing here in her pajama bottoms and ratty cardigan, with no clue what to ask this crazy woman. She'd assumed an opportunity to prepare before they talked.

"Em, hello, Ryn."

"We met today at Sentra."

"Yes, I remember." Carly heard the sharp edge to her own voice. Did Ryn imagine she'd forget?

Best let Ryn do the talking. The sooner she spilled the problem, the better Carly might understand how to handle it, especially if it was a mistake.

"What can I help you with?"

"How dare you come to my office?" Ryn's voice held the same ice-on-rage tone as this morning, but she overemphasized the start of each word, as if wanting to sound crisp. "And is…there…now?"

Carly moved toward the patio door to the outside deck for a better signal. "I'm sorry?"

"I asked, issh he there right now?"

Not a weak phone signal; Ryn slurred her words. Her company's top investor had drunk-dialed her?

Carly stared at the phone, debating whether the correct etiquette was to hang up. If Ryn had been drinking, she might not even remember this call by tomorrow.

Instead, she kept her tone soothing. "Ryn, I truly don't know what you're talking about. I think it would be best if we talk in the morning."

"Stop playing dumb. I've seen your texts. I'm asking if he's there."

"Ryn, I'm afraid you've got me mixed up with someone else."

"Oh fuck, you reaaally don't know who I am, do you?"

"Don't know what?" Carly put a finger to where the skin on her forehead pulsed. A doozy of a headache verged on hitting her hard.

"That I'm Todd's wife?"

Carly shook her head as if her ears were suddenly submerged. Her pulse surged, even as her brain slotted the pieces into place and reassured her. It had indeed been a mistake. For whatever reason, Ryn confused Carly's Todd with her own husband. Carly's fiancé was Todd Runyan, not Todd Brennan.

"Ryn, you've got the wrong person. I'm sorry about whatever's happening with your husband, but my Todd isn't married—I mean, his wife died many years ago."

A dog barked somewhere in Carly's apartment complex, quieted, then started again. She glanced at the screen to see if Ryn had hung up, but she was still there.

Ryn had to be wrong. Todd couldn't hide an entire other relationship. He didn't wear a wedding ring, and even if he took one off, there were no tan lines on his fingers. Some nights he stayed here. He couldn't stay over if he had a wife at home.

And married men cheated, but they didn't get engaged.

Although if anyone could make a monumental mistake about a man, she'd be that person. She'd misjudged Kyle not once, but twice.

"Again I'm asking you, is he God damned there?"

Carly's gaze flicked around her living room—Sammy's backpack hanging by the door, the pictures of him and Todd at the beach on the mantel—even though she knew it was stupid. Todd was in Phoenix.

The candles created jumpy shadows on the striped wallpaper. Ryn sounded so sure.

"Of course, he's not here. He's out of town. But he's also not married. We are. I mean…" *We're getting married.*

The wineglass shook in her hand. Todd didn't always stay over, but he visited her apartment practically every day he didn't travel. Any other Wednesday night he'd be on his way over with a list of movies to consider, and fried chicken.

Well, except for weeks like this one, when he left on an extended work trip for his real estate development projects.

And Sammy's preschool play last year, when he got stuck in Nevada closing a crucial deal.

And the holidays, when he needed to take care of his elderly family in Oklahoma.

The holidays are for those you love. A phrase her mother said all the time, back when Carly still had a family. She placed the glass on the table before it slipped through her fingers.

Images flashed at hell-speed. Days and weeks

Todd traveled. Every time he rescheduled a date. Every unexpected out-of-town meeting. "I'm sorry, work just keeps getting in the way, but for sure I'll be here on Halloween next year." *Oh God.*

She'd never even met Todd's family.

"He can't…I mean, I don't believe you."

"Ms. Santos, or should I call you Carly-bear?"

Carly-bear. Her vision blurred and the headache hit like a wrecking ball swinging from across the living room. A nickname Todd invented the day they visited the Santa Cruz boardwalk and played game after game, unsuccessful in their attempts to win Sammy a teddy. Todd proposed instead they drive into town and buy him one. Then, as they walked toward the parking area and the warmth of boardwalk lights flicked on around them, he swung her hand and said she was already his Carly-bear, the only good luck mascot he'd ever need.

"I'm not sure how you…unaware Todd Runyan is my husband."

She fell against the wall for support because everything spun. The phone fell from her hand and Ryn talked from the floor. "…my husband…your cheating…."

Carly sank, joining the phone on the woven rug, in part to stop the room revolving, and because she didn't know if she could stand and absorb the scale of Todd's deception. They'd been dating over two years. Their wedding was in six months.

She wrapped her arms around her knees and lowered her head.

Breathe, Carly. In. Out. In. Out

She wasn't getting married. They weren't moving to a new house with a yard. No standing at the kitchen window, Todd's arms wrapped around her, watching Sammy smile as he whooshed down the slide. No backyard at all.

Oh God, I'm the other woman.

Sure, before Sammy, she made humongous mistakes, but she was no longer Carly Santos, teenage runaway and ex-thief. Since then, she'd grown into Carly Santos, caring working-mom scientist. She'd battled to be better than someone's sordid mistress.

Ryn still ranted through the phone sitting next to Carly's pajama-clad legs. "...Shameless shhlut...get your own husband. Who are you...breaking up a marriage?"

Should she pick up the phone; try and explain she didn't know Todd was married? But then, Ryn had no reason to believe her. She'd been tricked into sleeping with the woman's husband for years.

She reached over and ended the call. Arms wrapped around her knees, she breathed into the darkness.

In some small recess of her mind she believed this wasn't real. When she looked up, she'd see television cameras, discover this was a big joke, and Todd would open the door with a bucket of fried chicken. He'd have written one of those beautiful apology cards he brought when he worked later than promised and missed the chance to hang out with her and his favorite little guy.

She released her knees and tilted her head back. The same white stucco covered the ceiling. And yet everything slowly disappeared, an Etch A Sketch of a perfect family someone shook too hard. No Sammy skipping down the aisle holding two rings tied with orange ribbons to a purple cushion. No cheering from the sidelines hand in hand with Todd when Sammy scored his first soccer goal. No chance to show her parents she'd created a complete family of her own.

She stared at a stain she'd never noticed on the rainbow rug, remembering the day she left Kyle at twenty-years old. After they argued and he flung her against the wall of their ant-infested room, she was too scared to leave that night. But the next morning, when cleaning carts lined up outside, providing more safety, she stood in the flimsy motel room door, and he laughed.

"Good luck making *smarter* decisions, Carly. Call me when you figure out the common denominator in your life's fuckups is you."

And now she'd chosen Todd. A cheating bastard. Only she could be dumb enough to fall for two men whose every word deceived.

She sat for what felt like hours, rocking back and forth, phantom shadows from the candles quivering on the walls, her mind trying to grasp at wisps of a future already lost.

How would she tell Sammy? Todd had been a stable presence in his life, coming over for movie nights and cookie-making sessions since Sammy was three—as long as he could remember. Sammy doted on Todd, the only father figure he'd known.

How on earth did she explain a cheating scumbag to a five-year-old, let alone justify why his mother—the person supposed to protect his feelings and safety—welcomed a man like that into their lives?

There must have been signs she missed, like perhaps their weekly date nights being on a Thursday. Todd said he preferred quieter evenings when the best restaurants weren't crazy-busy, and you received better service. Plus, it was easier to find a babysitter. But he must have planned to leave space on weekends for Ryn, *his wife*.

She scoured her memories for more signs she should have caught, like his father and mother being too elderly to travel. If there were more obvious red flags, in her naïveté she'd missed them.

She thought about going to bed, then reconsidered laying down right here on the rug. She couldn't bear to lie her head on the same pillowcase where she slept with him. Tomorrow she'd wash—or maybe burn—all her bedding.

In the evening Todd would return from Phoenix, but like hell did he get to reduce her to the role of sleazy mistress. She'd refuse to see him. Not tomorrow or ever again.

She traced the line of butterflies along her arm. So much for rebirth and second chances. She was cursed with continuing to make the same mistakes. Maybe her parents were right, once you chose the wrong track, the universe granted no forgiveness.

This morning she'd stupidly thought Ryn disliked this tattoo. For sure, now she would cancel their deal. Carly pushed on her forehead with both hands, and pictured the shame of explaining to Paul why they lost their funding.

The air stuck mid inhale, halfway down her throat.

Was this why he wanted to talk with her? Perhaps Ryn had already asked for Carly to be removed from BioLarge, but for a whole different reason than Carly imagined. She didn't even know, once she told Paul the truth, if he would be sympathetic. Before he met Myra, his current wife, he'd divorced because of his ex-wife's cheating.

And a CEO's first duty was to the company's future. No matter how much history she and Paul shared, if securing millions required asking for her resignation, might he agree to that trade-off?

She grabbed her sides and rocked harder. She'd been willing to consider sacrificing herself for the company this morning, but her plan of moving to a new house with Todd, where they'd share costs, had evaporated. She couldn't afford to lose her job now, too.

She never regretted investing in her future, but she still made monthly payments on both her undergrad and master's debt. And rents in the Bay Area were insane. Less than two months of paying for this apartment, without a job, would empty her savings account.

Sure, she had rebuilt her life from scratch once, working every waking hour to cover college fees and to pay back her parents the money she stole. For whole months, when short on cash, she survived on nothing but bread and tomatoes from the cheap Mexican supermarket. But she refused to raise Sammy that way.

She hauled herself to her feet, closed her eyes and took a breath. She wasn't perfect, but she didn't deserve this. Todd did not get to ruin her and Sammy's lives. Nor would he force her to quit on a company and medical solution she invested seven years developing.

She marched toward the wine in the fridge, poured a glass to the brim and downed half. Whatever it took, and no matter what Ryn demanded, tomorrow she intended to explain the situation and convince Paul that firing her was out of the question.

Chapter Five

Dawn light flooded Ryn's bedroom and her brain attempted to jackhammer out from inside her skull. She reached for her phone, which wasn't in its normal spot on the bedside table, then pulled a pillow over her head. She had an event outside the office this morning and didn't remember where.

She rose from the bed, shaded her eyes, and inched into the bathroom. Fergus darted in front of her, and she dodged him, slamming her hip into the granite counter. Pain radiated up and along her side.

He curled apologetically around her legs as she opened the cabinet and downed three Excedrin and six vitamins, followed by a large glass of water. Way to cope with crisis by drinking herself into a stupor.

Not such a fix-it hero now, are you, Ryn?

She tugged on her bathrobe and searched for the phone. At least Simon had meetings out of the office today. A good moment to call in one of those personal days she never used. Once the headache passed, she'd use the extra time and prepare for Todd's return tonight. Although what did she intend to prepare for, exactly? Her achievements proved her worth, and if Todd was fool enough to cheat, he didn't deserve her.

The living room blazed with raw light reflected from the harbor as she lifted cushions, and ran a hand along the back of the couch looking for her phone. How much had she drunk yesterday? She never lost control enough to forget to plug it in before going to bed.

She sank to the sofa as the memory of her conversation with Carly returned in full-bitch technicolor.

Last night she sat right here and called Carly a slut. The proud champion of women's entrepreneurship had called the owner of her star investment one of the worst words a woman could call another. She had behaved no better than those crass movies she loathed, where two women debased themselves waging war over a man who deserved neither of them.

Change of plan: first the salvation of coffee, then find the phone. Her bare feet slapped on hardwood as she walked toward the kitchen, passing her framed 30 Under 30 article on the wall.

She glanced at the Post-it Note stuck on the glass, a pain jagging deep in her chest. *Forty together will be even better.* Todd wrote the note six months ago while happy-drunk. He'd been delighted with the surprise party and whisky tasting she arranged for his fortieth birthday and he couldn't stop saying how only a perfect partner would know how to make him feel so loved.

And yet somehow perfect wasn't enough. She wasn't enough.

Well, screw him.

She reached the kitchen, started the coffee grinder, and put both hands over her ears, begging it to finish fast as more fragments of the call with Carly rattled around her head.

I don't believe you.

You've got the wrong person.

My Todd isn't married.

49

The way the line went dead after Ryn used Todd's surname.

Oh God, the meeting at Sentra. Carly had no idea Todd was married. What kind of person instantly assumed the worst of another woman? Ryn's call last night had blindsided her.

The grinder stopped, but each step—inserting the grounds, then water, depressing the plunger—brought back more snapshots of what a world-class bitch she'd been. The way she growled at Carly before they started their meeting, the note she passed, yelling over the phone.

The shock of finding out about Todd must have scrambled her thinking, because she didn't even stop and consider he might be lying to both of them.

Sunlight glinted on metal across the kitchen. Her phone sat on the opposite gray granite countertop, half-hidden behind the empty Nutella jar. She should call Carly to apologize. Wasn't that what a decent human would do?

She poured a mug and took a sip of coffee, hoping to rev herself up and make the call, then wished she hadn't. The shame of talking with his mistress, the walking manifestation that Ryn never mattered to Todd in the way he claimed, made her stomach queasy. The only viable plan for this morning; cancel her meetings and crawl back into bed.

She walked to the phone, opened her calendar, and groaned. Today was the panel on entrepreneurship she co-sponsored in Half Moon Bay with Kim. Bailing meant doing something Ryn never did—letting down one of the few people in this industry she considered a friend.

A glance at the kitchen clock confirmed if she left soon, she'd miss the conference's opening session, but still arrive before her panel started. She considered making toast, but another groundswell of nausea threatened to flood her system. She'd manage without. Judging from the empty Nutella jar, her bloodstream contained a week's worth of sugar.

She poured her coffee into a travel mug and closed the lid. On her way through the living room she snatched the Post-it from her 30 Under 30 article and crumpled it. Now they wouldn't even be together when she celebrated her own fortieth birthday in two years.

Fifteen minutes later, dressed in a black skirt and red blouse, she backed her SUV out of the driveway. Her workout bag and Nikes sat in their regular spot in the trunk. After the conference she'd run off the hangover and find the right words for Todd tonight. For now, she needed to put her cheating lowlife of a husband aside and do a passable job at the forum, even if this hangover felt like the coffee grinder still shredded the inside of her head.

****

The Ritz-Carlton perched on the edge of a cliff in Half Moon Bay, next to a golf course overlooking the roiling Pacific. Ryn reached the hotel's access road and her phone buzzed, flashing Simon's name across the screen.

She hadn't stopped and returned his last two calls for fear of arriving late at the panel, but this was the third time in thirty minutes. Seconds later two follow-up texts arrived.

—*Where are you?*—
—*Heard BioLarge didn't sign. Call me*—

It wasn't yet ten a.m. and Simon found out she didn't close the deal yesterday?

Gravel crunched under the SUV's tires as Ryn veered into a parking area beside the golf course. Sufficient time or not, her boss expected an answer. She placed the phone on the passenger seat and got out of the car. She needed a second to think.

The flags along the golf course flapped violently and she took deep breaths of salt-edged air, hoping to ease her headache enough to invent an excuse her boss might believe. If she learned anything from losing her last promotion, she couldn't risk providing a shred of justification for Simon to renege on his promises.

Two years ago she'd entered his office expecting to discuss when they'd announce her new position, but Simon stared at the table and mumbled.

I don't want you taking this the wrong way, Ryn, you're very valuable to the firm. But health care is an increasingly crowded market, so I've decided to launch Patrick's fund first.

Instead of her, Simon awarded leadership of Sentra's next fund—and the senior partner title that came with it—to his squirrel-brained brother-in-law.

She didn't know which had been worse, the sinking realization that perhaps he never intended to give her the promotion, or her arguments with Todd in the following weeks. A man with her investment record would have reached senior partner years ago, and to her the principle mattered more than the consolation money Simon offered her not to quit. But Todd's real estate firm wasn't cash flush back then. He accused her of just holding a grudge. Even if Simon couldn't promote her yet, the cut of investments he offered, worth three times her current salary, proved he understood her value.

The wind crossing the golf course whipped Ryn's hair across her eyes, where she stood next to her SUV. Most days she still questioned whether she made the right decision. By staying at Sentra she gave Simon a free pass to get away with nepotism. Once again, the boys' club had won.

At least her memory of that meeting gave her an idea to justify the delay in signing with BioLarge. Crowded markets always made Simon nervous: the same reason he claimed his brother-in-law's fund proposal was a safer bet. She would say she needed a few more days to better study the competition.

She checked Simon's newest text message before she prepared her response.—*I'm here, where the heck are you?*—

Simon being here made no sense. She typed a response.—*Here in Half Moon Bay?*—

He responded instantly.—*Yes, thought I'd see your session and get in round of golf*—

This couldn't be good. Driving an hour away from the office meant he was checking up on her. Perhaps he already suspected a bigger problem with yesterday's meeting than a delayed signature.

Ryn jumped in her car and drove the last quarter mile to the hotel.

She smoothed her windswept hair, passed through the hotel's grand entrance, and spotted Simon's beer-gut swagger heading toward her.

His jaw jutted over the rolls of flesh under his chin, and a red flush covered his cheeks. Hard to tell if he was annoyed or just breathless from stomping across the lobby.

"Blake said you didn't close the terms? I couldn't find you yesterday for a debrief."

Dammit. In her hungover state, she didn't consider he might call his country club buddy to get the inside scoop. Did Blake also see the note she passed to Carly?

Kim peeked out from a room across the lobby, and with relief, Ryn waved her over, ignoring how Kim's nose rose in distate when she recognized Simon.

Negotiation tactics 101, the art of diversion. Ryn's best strategy involved focusing her boss's thoughts somewhere else than the dynamics of yesterday's meeting.

As Kim crossed toward them, the slit in her black dress showed a few inches of ankle, and a green dragon roared up one arm. Ryn admired the dress. She'd never dare wear an outfit so striking yet feminine, but Kim—the only female owner of a sizable venture capital firm—inhabited a post-success, I don't-give-a-damn world. If crossed, she'd eat a peer like Simon for lunch with salt and Sriracha.

Here goes the distraction. "Kim, about today's panel. I'm thinking, given Simon is here in person, if we get any questions on the entrepreneurial gene controversy, maybe we let him answer for himself?"

Simon squirmed, and his gaze darted toward the front door, as if suddenly desperate to leave for the golf greens.

Ryn had just reminded him of the media disaster created by his offhand comment in a *New York Times* interview when asked why he didn't invest in more female entrepreneurs. *Who knows? I always make the best investments. Maybe women don't have the balls or the entrepreneurial gene, or perhaps it's the same thing?*

She'd made excuses for his statement at multiple forums like this over the last year, even if her cheeks burned with the shame of representing a boss who didn't know better than sounding like a frat-boy who forgot to grow up.

"Certainly, not necessary..." Simon mumbled.

Kim shook her head at him as if scolding a toddler. "You still haven't publicly apologized for that, dear? I can make space today if you'd like to admit you slept through the 'women are not the dumber gender' part of the middle school biology curriculum?"

Ryn sucked in a breath so fast both Simon and Kim turned and stared. She'd underestimated Kim's signature bluntness. The goal was to distract Simon from quizzing her on BioLarge, not rile him up so much he grasped the microphone and said something even dumber.

Kim continued without giving Simon time to form a comeback. "How's the new flagship deal coming along?" She nodded toward Ryn. "I still can't believe you scooped me."

Ryn offered her a smile. Without planning it, Kim had just provided a perfect opening to explain why the deal had been delayed. "Going great. We should close soon, but I'm too aware the medical devices market is turning into a boxing contest..." She explained her intent to look more thoroughly at competition before signing the final paperwork.

Simon crossed his arms as if ready to disagree, then uncrossed them and shrugged. From the way his gaze alternated between the conference room fifty feet away and the exit, he debated how long he could risk standing here before Kim physically pulled him inside and up onstage to answer questions. "Ryn, you know what you're doing. I was just thinking…it looks like it might rain later, and my back acts up if I sit in these sessions too long. I believe I'll go ahead and get a few holes in, while the weather holds."

"Yeah, I hear you. These all-day conferences can feel so lengthy. See you in the office tomorrow." Ryn grabbed Kim's dragon-covered arm and turned them toward the meeting room.

They entered the hall and she exhaled. She'd bought herself breathing space for a week or more on BioLarge, but she still needed a resolution to the Carly Santos dilemma.

The other speakers waited at the front, near the stage, already wearing microphones. Walking past thirty rows of people who'd come to hear her talk, the irony hit. Who was she to play role model on this panel for the female entrepreneurs in the room?

A hungover role model who ignored sexism when two years ago she should have sued the pants off Simon for discrimination. But if she'd done that, she wouldn't have worked another day in this industry, or be on the brink of becoming one of a handful of female senior partners.

She reached the first row and scanned the faces in the audience before she attached her microphone. They'd never imagine someone strong like Ryn letting her cheating husband interfere with her flagship investment. And like hell did she intend to allow that result from Todd's treachery. She wouldn't abandon her biggest deal and put her promotion at risk because of him.

As she climbed on stage, and smiled at the other panelists, it occurred to her that a more ruthless investor might push Carly Santos out of the company. It wasn't an unusual move for a Venture Capitalist to force out a founder, and Carly was a talented scientist. She'd find another job in a heartbeat. But that would be just as unethical as Simon giving Ryn's promotion to Patrick.

Sure, Ryn had a reputation for being tough, but she didn't sink to the level of prioritizing her own discomfort over someone else's career. She straightened her back and took her seat beside the other panelists. Instead, she'd have to close the deal but minimize her interactions with Carly. Perhaps she could suggest the science officer played too crucial a role to be caught up in long board meetings.

Ryn composed her face into a welcoming expression and prepared to answer the first question for the panel. One thing she knew for sure—if she ever had to sit in a room with Carly again, she needed a damn better plan than a Feelings Jar.

Chapter Six

Carly monitored the clock on the wall of the BioLarge conference room. Ten minutes until she needed to drive home and meet Paul at two o'clock. After this morning, she knew she wasn't being paranoid, because whenever she approached his desk, he'd waved her away and mouthed *This afternoon.*

She pushed back in her chair, struggling to keep her eyes open. Her team of five in this status meeting must think her uninterested, but the truth was she hadn't slept.

Yesterday after hanging up on Ryn, she spent the night surrounded by plush zebras and trucks on the floor of Sammy's bedroom. She needed to hear his breathing, his gentle snuffles, to believe she hadn't irreparably harmed her sweet, funny boy by welcoming a monster into their lives.

At five this morning, before Sammy woke, she meditated for fifteen minutes, then texted Todd three words—*I deserved better*—and immediately blocked his number.

She glanced again at the clock and stood up from the conference table. "Appreciate the detailed update, folks. Okay if I send you my feedback via email?"

Twenty minutes later she swung open the door of her apartment and every detail assaulted her.

A calendar marked with Todd's fake travel dates

hung on the kitchen wall. On the coffee table, fulfilled brides glowed on stacks of wedding magazine covers next to the catalog of playsets on which Sammy would never swing. The entire apartment looked as if fate took a big red marker to the real, whole family within her grasp, but left the fake props behind, to remind her what an idiot she'd been to fall for his charade.

She made the dark coffee Paul liked, ready for his arrival in ten minutes, then grabbed two large garbage bags from under the kitchen sink. If she had to throw out her self-respect, and grovel to keep her job, she refused to do so surrounded by the debris of her latest life disaster.

She ping-ponged from living room to bedroom, grabbing and stuffing symbols of aborted plans and counterfeit love into the bags.

In the center of the mantel sat her favorite photo. Todd and Sammy grinned triumphantly on Capitola Beach in July. They'd taken hours to construct the world's largest sand city, complete with a school and a statue, and named it Sammyville.

She'd posted it on her Facebook but couldn't tag Todd because he didn't have an account. Talk about an obvious sign she failed to see. Who didn't have Facebook these days? Todd may have played on her yearning for a perfect cereal-box family and echoed it with promises of a house in the suburbs and swing sets, but she was the one who'd chosen to believe his paper-thin lies.

A savvier woman would have seen through him. Sure, she googled Todd after their third date, but everything she found on Twitter concerned his real estate business. He said he preferred to connect with his non-work friends in real life. She'd even found it charming.

She ignored the phone ringing in the back pocket of her jeans, placed the picture in a drawer and took a long look before closing it. Too painful to throw this one away. Maybe with a pair of scissors she could save Sammy's half.

She pulled out her phone and switched it to vibrate. All morning, since she blocked Todd, it had rung nonstop from different unknown numbers. She hadn't listened to a single message. It didn't matter if he intended to leave Ryn or had some grand plan to make their fake future possible. She wouldn't risk letting herself be conned again by the liar.

It was mortifying, quite how stupid she'd been, and now she needed to admit the whole sordid story to Paul.

"Carly, it's me." Paul opened the door as he spoke. He wore jeans and sneakers, the sleeves of his crumpled shirt rolled up above his elbows. From the way his shoulders hunched, he was even more tired than her.

No, not tired, he looked defeated. Carly's stomach clenched. Perhaps Ryn had already withdrawn their promised funding.

She ushered him to the sofa. "Coffee?"

"Do you have any tea?" His gaze roved around the room, nervous in a way she wasn't used to seeing him.

She put on the kettle in the kitchen. When she turned back, Paul stood two feet away, across the breakfast bar that connected to the dining room.

Time to make her case. She faced him over the countertop. "Paul, I apologize for freezing during the presentation at Sentra, but I learned some stuff yesterday I need to share. I wasn't on my A-game, but I promise, I'm going to try and sort this out—"

"Wait a moment, Carls," His brows knitted and an emotion she couldn't calibrate flickered in his eyes. "We can always discuss improving your presentation skills, but that's not why I came here."

Paul's back straightened, and his voice had the same hardened tone as difficult personnel meetings, when he'd rehearsed and wanted to say the exact words he'd prepared. "If you don't mind, I'd prefer to go first. Can we talk about whatever you have to say, after?"

Her fingers tightened around the edge of the countertop. Her friend, the person with whom she'd battled through every tough startup moment, the only person she trusted enough to seek advice when deciding to keep Sammy, didn't even want to hear her side of the story?

She grasped the teapot hard to stop her hands from shaking as she poured Paul's tea, and brought it with her coffee to the living room. They'd founded BioLarge together as equal partners, but she'd provided the main engineering ideas. He didn't get to throw her off the company bus just because Ryn Brennan—the person providing new fuel—demanded her gone.

She handed Paul his mug.

"Please sit." He gestured at the spot next to him on the sofa.

When she sat, he took her hand. She jerked backward. If he intended to fire her, this was a novel approach, even for a friend.

"Carly, I need you to be brave and open minded. I should've told you before, but the truth is I haven't been feeling great for a few months, now."

Wait. She looked again at his expression and

61

Lainey Cameron

attempted to rewind her thoughts, his words. The regret in his eyes didn't match the set of his jaw. She studied his complexion, the same exhaustion she noticed in the elevator at Sentra. For weeks, the skin stretched taut around his eyes, and now she looked at him properly, he'd lost weight. She and Paul were friends, and she'd been so self-absorbed with Todd, and Sammy, and the engagement, she hadn't even noticed.

She took his hand and squeezed. *Tell me.*

"I finally went to the doctor and got the results last week. I have prostate cancer."

Carly wasn't sure if she gasped out loud or only felt the breath whoosh from her mouth. "How bad?" Her voice sounded squeaky, a toy with a dog's paws squeezing out every ounce of air.

"It's stage 3—but not all bad news. The success rate can be high, they say over ninety percent after radiation."

Can be high, not *is high.* She'd noticed his choice of words. As if Paul didn't quite believe it.

He moved closer on the sofa and pried her fingers from their vise grip on his hand.

"I recognize it's a ton to take in, but Myrna and I have been working together on a plan." His tone soothed. This was so Paul. He had cancer, and attempted to make it easier on her.

She pushed her mug away and hugged him hard, cycling through what his wife and the kids might need. Rides to the school, hospital. Cover parts of Paul's job at BioLarge. She could certainly ease his burden at work.

She leaned in to show he had her full attention. "How can I help?"

62

"So, Carly, that's just it, I have something big to ask. Myrna insists I take time off. And she's right. I can't be there for the needs of a hundred employees while I'm going through months of radiation treatment. I need to put my family first."

Myrna was right. Of course, Paul couldn't balance treatment and lead a company. They'd find an interim CEO, hopefully someone with stellar stage presence given the upcoming launch. Perhaps their finance officer, Oliver might fit? No, bad idea. He had zero people skills. It would have to be someone from outside. Once they started, Carly and the other exec team members could split the internal tasks, so the new CEO could focus on being the temporary external face of the company.

"It's important I hand the reins to someone I trust, who understands the science and has a passion for our mission…and I believe that right person is you."

She dug her fingers into the sofa but couldn't focus on his next words because his last ones made no sense. *He has to be kidding.* Sure, she understood the technical side, but leading the entire company? Their partnership worked because she brought the ideas and the science, while he made the big financial decisions.

She pictured Oliver's stare of disbelief in their last executive meeting when she proposed taking an extra two months to solidify their testing results and lighten the load on the team. "I'll explain offline to Carly what the term 'runway' means, and why running through our cash by paying the team for an extra sixty days without new funding could not only kill the company but may be the dumbest idea I've heard all year."

On second thought, in comparison to Oliver, who

addressed every employee with equal disdain, at least the team liked her. God forbid they hire an interim CEO like him.

"Paul, I see why you're suggesting I'd be an easy transition, but I'm worried about the public-facing stuff. The speeches, the interviews, etc."

Not to mention the Ryn Brennan factor. Ryn would definitely back out of funding them if the woman she'd called her husband's slutty mistress became CEO.

"I know the press work will likely be a struggle, Carly, but I wouldn't ask if I didn't think you could manage it. You did an amazing job leading us through a complex approvals process, and research is the heart of this company."

Flattering that he believed her the best fit, but it wouldn't take more than two decisions like her proposal in the exec meeting to wreck their future. Her mouth tasted as if she'd crammed it full of those sour apple candies Sammy so loved.

She took a couple of breaths and exorcised the self-doubt. This wasn't about her, but Paul. The team, her team, needed a leader they trusted. And if he considered her capable, then why couldn't she believe it herself?

She didn't exactly need the time she set aside for planning a wedding. A new challenge at work at least provided a distraction to avoid the emotional crater into which she already felt herself falling.

"Plus, the CEO role is more money, Carly. Can't hurt, and…"

Good point. Perhaps she might even save enough for a deposit on a small condo.

Although none of this solved the Ryn dilemma, because there would be no money to pay salaries if she didn't provide the next round of funding.

Paul was still talking. "...make sure we close the series before you take over, so you won't have to manage the process."

"Sorry?"

"The Sentra investment. Ryn Brennan called on my way here to assure me there's no cause for concern. She's still going to sign."

Ryn still intended to fund them? Only because she didn't know Carly might become the CEO who she'd work with.

"Plus, I suspect Ryn can be a great advisor for you in the new role."

As if. The woman was an anger grenade, waiting to detonate.

Carly studied Paul's face, debating whether to tell him. The skin under his eyes looked translucent. Stacking one more problem on him didn't seem fair, if she might still find a way to solve it herself.

She'd ask Dev first. Her best friend and neighbor was a serial entrepreneur with experience on start-up boards, and he already knew the Todd news. This morning when they'd seen each other on the landing he instantly sensed her agony. They couldn't talk with Sammy standing next to them, but she'd called Dev an hour later, from the path around the corner from her office, sobbing like a hot mess.

If anyone might advise her on how much of an issue working with Ryn posed and be brutally honest on whether Carly stood a chance of succeeding in the role, it was him.

"All I'm asking is to please consider it, Carly. Can you do that?" His tired eyes pleaded. "For me?"

She pulled hard on the underlayer of her curls and a few strands came away in her fingers. How could she not agree? If she was bold enough to found a company, she should summon the guts to lead it. Other than fear of working with Ryn, she didn't have a good excuse not to take the job.

"I'm inclined to say yes, but let me sleep on it and I'll answer for sure tomorrow. And please tell me what else I can do to help."

Paul stood, and she hugged him. If hugs could heal, she'd hold him all night.

As soon as she closed the door behind him, she unlocked her phone and texted Dev.

—*Can you swing by tonight? Need help. Advice*—

—*Home now. Want me to come over? Can be there in 20*—

She answered yes, then collapsed into the armchair. Paul could be underestimating the skills she lacked. An hour ago, she'd been convinced he intended to fire her. Not exactly the razor-sharp situational assessment required of an astute leader.

And she had no idea how to solve the Ryn problem. Even if she didn't cancel their deal, Carly would count herself lucky if Ryn didn't start their first board meeting with a slide introducing her as *Chief Slut*.

****

Carly made more tea and placed the pot and cups on the coffee table. A few minutes later, Dev joined her from across the concrete landing. Instead of his usual work attire of jeans and an ironed linen shirt, he wore sweats and a dirty gray T-shirt. Now she considered it, strange for him to be home mid-afternoon and not at one of his start-ups.

He covered the room in three long strides and grabbed her in a bear hug. "I am so so sorry. How are you holding up?"

Carly leaned into the hug. Since the day she moved into this apartment with Sammy still in his baby carrier, she'd been surprised how she and Dev became such fast friends. Only a few weeks after she first invited him over to watch a movie, he was making late night runs to the grocery store for baby supplies. Now, five years later, she couldn't imagine life without him.

He stepped back and glanced at the walls. "No insult and I know it's only a day old, but the blank patch decor doesn't really suit the place. Let's dig around for alternate photos to put up. Or I can bring you a few of me, your bestie, with the hot bod on the beach in Kerala?"

Dev flexed his lanky biceps in full body builder style and Carly shook her head at him and plunked down on the sofa. "Yeah, no thanks, buddy."

He chuckled and took a seat opposite her on the armchair. "Okay, okay." Dev made sweeping gestures with his hands. "So, this is the point where you tell me I should spend more time dating smart women and less hanging out at bars or the yoga studio with ladies I pretend are good enough for me, but are really after my money."

"And you tell me to make more time for myself and stop trying to be super-science-everything-mom."

"Well that, and apply better judgment to your next choice of fiancé?"

Carly leaned over and punched him in the arm. "Thanks for kicking a girl while she's flat on the ground." She wondered, not for the first time, what universal quirk of fate dealt her the genes to feel attracted to Todd, but not Dev, the dorkiest and funniest guy she knew. Most women swooned at his British accent.

His hand landed gently on hers. "Truly, I'm sorry he turned out to be such a wanker." He leaned back and grinned. "Although honestly, good riddance. I never cared for him much."

"Truly? Now you tell me?"

Dev scanned her face. "Well, I'm not saying he's a psychopath or anything. I just didn't appreciate all the teeth when he smiled. Oh...or the fake tan. Hardly sufficient to yell stop when your bestie is determined to find her son a daddy." His cheeks pulled back into an I'm-sorry-but-please-don't-eat-me-alive grimace.

Carly poured their tea, and looked again at the blank spots on the walls. Dev had a point about the missing photos; Sammy would notice when he got home. Last night on his bedroom floor, she practiced a hundred versions in her head of how to tell him that he and Todd would never do another of their little fist bump—high five—side bump dances. And she still didn't know how to explain to him.

Sorry, kid, I know I told you we'd be a family in a new house, but your mommy is the queen of crappy choices.

"Dev, before I get Sammy, I need your advice. I'm getting deeper into this weird situation with Ryn Brennan, our new investor."

"Weirder than your fiancé being married to her?"

"Yeah, it gets worse. Paul just..." She paused to ensure she could say the next words without choking up. "He just shared he has cancer and asked me to step in as CEO."

Dev's eyes widened. "I'm so sorry, Carly. I know you two go way back."

"Thanks." She took another sip of tea, seeking to regain control before the tears came. Paul and Myrna had two young adorable girls who didn't deserve to lose their father.

"I feel like I owe Paul. I mean, to take the job, even if I doubt whether I have sufficient experience. But then once Ryn signs the deal...well, you get it, she'd be my number one advisor and board member."

Dev steepled his hands in front of his chest. "A pickle indeed. It seems, my dear, one is best served by splitting these two conundrums apart. Let's start with the bigger question, are you the right person for the job?"

He stood and paced across the room. "I believe you're asking yourself the wrong thing. CEO is the ultimate multitasking job, so no one is qualified for everything involved. I wasn't qualified for a single company I launched. Despite your abysmal lack of self-confidence, you have many strengths, including enough smarts to recognize when you lack experience and ask."

"Gee, thanks. I guess?"

"You know I say it from a place of adoration. But here's the rub. A lot of what's involved in the job is making the team believe in the art of the possible, even while you yourself are racked with doubt. That's the real question. Can you believe enough to convince a whole team, your funders, the press, your customers to follow you?"

Carly sighed, loud enough for Dev to hear. If CEO

success depended on abounding self-confidence and making convincing presentations, she may as well admit defeat before she started.

"And Ryn?"

"You may not want to hear this, but honestly, I think she could be your ally. As in the best person to ensure your success in the role."

"Really?" If roles were reversed and Carly was the wife, she'd pray never to meet her husband's other woman again.

"She has high stakes in this game. From what you've told me, the amount her firm is investing isn't some small deal. The success of your company could well make or break her fund. Plus, she's a successful female VC. You don't achieve senior leadership level without keeping it all-business. I fully expect she'll deal with you as CEO without letting your personal history get in the way."

Carly rolled her eyes. Keeping it all-business was hardly her experience yesterday at Sentra. But if she intended to take the job, what choice did she have, other than to reach out to Ryn and mend fences?

At least if their meeting went badly, she could always rely on Dev to give her advice on next steps.

"And with this, my dear, I must away. I'm afraid I have lots to finish before I leave."

"Another business trip?"

"Mmm. Not exactly."

"Dev?"

"Well, I know the timing is abysmal with the Todd news and all, but I agreed yesterday to go East for a while. Heading to Cambridge for three or four months. I'm helping a friend get a new analytics startup off the ground."

Carly's stomach plummeted. If she took the CEO job, her best advisor would be gone for the entire first critical months after she started in the role. Without him, who'd prevent her from making god-awful decisions?

His eyes crinkled. "Stop looking so glum. You underestimate yourself, my protégé. You are ready to fly from the Dev advice nest. Trust your gut and stop second-guessing every decision, and you'll be fine. Plus, we can always do video calls."

Trust your gut? The same gut which told her Todd would be a perfect stepdad. And also six years ago, that Kyle had changed enough to have a one-night stand when she met him in Los Angeles, almost ten years after making the smarter choice to leave him.

She made her voice lighter than the doom closing in along the ceiling. "When are you leaving? Up for a goodbye movie night?"

"Sure, not for a couple of weeks, but it's going to be kind of crazy, which is why I'm home, getting a head start on packing up some boxes to ship."

She hugged him goodbye and closed the door. Leaving in two weeks. Easy for Dev to declare her ready to leave the advice nest, but he was throwing her out headfirst.

She checked the time to judge how long she had before leaving for Sammy's pickup. Tomorrow she'd email Ryn and arrange a meeting, but for the next twenty-four hours she needed to focus what little energy she had left on him.

She walked to the kitchen, grabbed the shears, and opened the drawer with the picture of Todd and Sammy at the beach. This part of Todd's lying she couldn't get her head around. She'd have sworn his affection for Sammy was real.

Maybe she'd start and end their conversation by telling Sammy how important, how perfect he was. And make it clear Todd leaving was her decision. Sammy hadn't been discarded, like her parents gave up on her.

She fingered the photograph. Severing this photo, leaving only half of Sammyville, felt as if the serrated edge dragged across her own heart. No matter what she did, she couldn't prevent her little boy from being hurt.

Chapter Seven

Dark tables sat in rows, extending onto the patio of Half Moon Bay Coffee Roasters. Ryn ducked inside the café and shook out her jacket from the drizzle which had started during this afternoon's sessions at The Ritz-Carlton.

The only other patron, an elderly gentleman, engaged in an energetic debate on local politics with the heavily pierced barista. Ryn waited by the bar for a pause in their discussion. It was past five in the afternoon, but this was the first time she felt capable of eating, with the dregs of this morning's hangover and the memory of her horrific conversation with Carly last night still lingering.

At least she had kept it together during the panel and the rest of the conference. When an institutional investor approached her at the end of the afternoon, she worried he intended to correct her on a fact she overlooked while coasting through the last session. Instead, it turned out he'd been convinced to double-down on health tech and wished to invest a large amount in her new fund.

Normally she lived for triumphs like this. She'd ride the success high for days. But all she could think about was what would happen after Todd arrived home tonight.

When the conversation paused at the bar, she

ordered a cheese panini, half-wishing she'd accepted Kim's invitation for a post-conference drink. Kim might have advice on how to thread the needle of closing the deal with BioLarge while minimizing the indignity of working with Carly Santos. But as a colleague, how dimwitted would Kim judge a woman who'd let herself be fooled like Ryn?

Instead, she slunk to the rear of the café, wishing she kept in better touch with her friends from college. She'd give away the rights to her best investments for the type of friendship where you could rehearse a difficult conversation like this evening's with Todd.

She imagined making him sit at the dining table the instant he walked in the door. When she demanded answers, his face would change from happy-to-be-home, to confused, then denial, then hopefully acceptance because he'd been caught.

Movie highlights of moments from a marriage she'd believed better than most played in her mind. The way he paired his socks and hers after laundry, nestled together in the drawer. How he'd leave early for the airport and detour to her office to deliver coffee with a goodbye kiss. The morning she aced her first IPO and stood in the lobby flabbergasted as delivery after delivery of flowers filled the lobby. Every woman on thirty-two floors of the building wondered what she was celebrating that day.

So what were those grand romantic moments, a head-fake? Or perhaps he meant them then, and she had been blind to how their romance withered in recent years.

Last Thursday night, she sat at home, working on the next morning's keynote, when Todd bounded in the door, a day early returning from Vegas. He pulled her to her feet at the dining table, and she knew he'd closed the contract for his latest apartment development. But even though they kissed, and she opened the good whisky to salute his accomplishment, when he returned from his shower and caressed her thigh, she still finished her prep work. Only the next morning, when he left for his co-working space in San Francisco without their usual morning coffee together, did she realize how much she'd slighted him.

The barista delivered her latte and sandwich, and Ryn angled toward the corner of the café, hoping it might open space for the old lonely gentleman to restart his conversation on politics.

She shook her head. Why the sudden projection of loneliness onto someone she'd never met? She suspected her mind played tricks on her, making her scared enough to stick with Todd, no matter what he said tonight.

After so many years of knowing she didn't need marriage, she'd been surprised how much easier life became with the right partner. She often wondered why Pops never dated after Mom died. She suspected it was because his loneliness came with a side of guilt. Guilt at pulling Mom away from a life she missed in San Francisco, which turned into depression after she died.

Ryn rubbed the scar on the inside of her right elbow where the bone protruded after she broke both arms at the ranch. She'd hoped to work on planning her eleventh birthday party that day, but Pops had been so down—about Mom, about money, about everything. For the fourth morning in a row, he didn't eat breakfast.

He'd complained about the fence poles Jack

neglected to fix, and she knew finishing the job would cheer him up. Plus, driving the skid steer loader wasn't difficult. Jack at sixteen and Adrian at fourteen had maneuvered it for years.

If she closed her eyes, even in this café, she could relive the terror of the moment when the pole lifted above her, and the loader tipped and cratered over the edge of the riverbank, slamming her head to one side and the other as it flipped, then rolled, and ejected her against the boulders of the embankment.

A week later when Pops wheeled her out of the hospital, she left in Aunt Dusty's car, not the ranch pickup. But even if Pops wasn't well enough to raise her in those following years—and still looked away today whenever Ryn swept her hair behind her ear as Mom used to do—she never doubted he wanted her to feel loved. Pops would be heartbroken when he heard she had no choice but to restart life on her own.

Ryn pulled out her phone and looked at the time. Four hours before Todd said he would be home. Right now he'd be waiting in the airport lounge. He liked to get there early and enjoy a peaceful drink before his flight.

She reconsidered the scenario where he arrived home tonight and she'd quiz him. Thank God her stomach had calmed enough to eat, because peppering him with questions made no sense. If Todd had become accustomed to lying, why did she expect him to suddenly start telling the truth?

Ryn shivered. She saw it now. He always had the right words. She remembered the time she didn't want to splurge unnecessarily and booked a cheaper room for their vacation at the Shangri-La in Paris. For a second, the way Todd's brows furrowed when the receptionist said they'd be on the lowest floor with no view, she'd thought him angry, but instead he touched her shoulder and asked if she could find them croissants, while he talked to the hotel manager. By the time she returned he'd charmed the lady in the impeccable mauve skirt suit, who seemed honored to show them into a suite overlooking the Eiffel Tower.

That was a hundred percent Todd. He always got what he wanted and left you convinced it had been your idea.

Ryn picked up her phone. She had a better plan, now. One which didn't require them to share a house tonight, because if he kept taking her for such a fool, she might be tempted to roll over and strangle him in his sleep.

Last week, in a gnarly negotiation, she suspected a business partner of a complicated form of revenue fraud. She printed every one of the company's financial statements, laid them out in the conference room and confronted him with the facts. The papers covered the entire table.

She loved the idea behind that company, but from the man's evasive answers, the problem was not an accounting mistake. She terminated their partnership immediately.

This was how to approach her conversation with Todd. Lay out the facts and hope he decided to come clean. She doubted anything he said could convince her to give him another chance, but maybe, in talking, she'd gain some understanding of where they'd gone wrong.

The photo of Paul Alexander and Carly at the Sentra office was saved on her phone. At the time, she couldn't avoid taking the shot without it becoming obvious she had a problem with the deal. Now that image could provide the evidence to shove across the virtual table at Todd.

She could leave and make this call in her car, where she'd parked two blocks away in the rain, but she liked the quiet in this almost empty café. And being in a public place would help keep her calm.

She posted the photo on Sentra's Twitter account with a congratulations message to Paul, then composed a text for Todd and attached the same photo.

—Look who I met yesterday—

She hit send, placed the phone on her lap, and waited.

She finished the last sip of her latte. Small dots moved on the phone screen…Todd typing.

—Your BioLarge deal closed. Congrats!—

The photo didn't have BioLarge written on it. Which meant Todd knew his mistress intended to pitch his wife.

Did it give him a sick pleasure knowing they'd be in the same room together, both of them oblivious? She imagined squashing his smug face into the glass wall of the airport lounge.

Ryn grasped the sides of the phone to steady her fingers and texted.

—Yes. Your mistress is quite impressive—

He'd better call. She put in her headphones and sat with her stomach roiling, the veins on her temples throbbing, to see if he'd choose telling her the truth, when offered the chance.

She waited.

One minute, two minutes. Everything in the coffee

shop had quieted. As if the ambient soundtrack and lighting dimmed in anticipation.

When she was about to pick up the phone and call him, it rang.

"Hi, baby. What's this? Some kind of Thursday-afternoon joke?"

Are you kidding me? "I know, Todd."

"What are you talking about, my sunshine?" His voice was too sweet, like pancakes when the top flips off the syrup bottle and half pours out at once.

"I know. About you and Carly, the affair. I saw your texts."

The line went silent, but only for an instant. Long enough to lie when it had apparently become second nature.

"I'm not sure why you'd be reading my texts, but you must have misunderstood. If you're talking about Carly Santos, she's a friend, has been for a while. We meet up from time to time. I've been helping her with company paperwork. Filing stuff."

Surprising for his voice to sound so credible. From the assured tone, it was as if he himself believed what he said. His confidence made her want to trust she'd been mistaken, believe that her fill-the-office-with-flowers, bring-me-toast-at-midnight man still existed.

But the despair seeping through her stomach lining reminded her of months of texts with secret dates, stay-overs, days at the beach. Adrenaline coursed through her arms, pulsed in her neck. In a heartbeat, she crushed her empty coffee cup and threw it in the garbage can near her table.

"Exactly how dumb do you think I am, Todd? You expect me to buy you were assisting a person *in a company I'm funding* to prepare for a meeting with me, and you didn't consider it worth mentioning?"

"Well, yeah...I mean yes, I should have told you I'm helping her, but lately we've not been making time for each other. You'll like Carly. As I said, she's a LinkedIn connection. Oh right, yeah, you met her in your meeting. Isn't she cool?"

Two strikes, already. The man spun out lies like a spider on speed.

Ryn's whole body tensed, the muscles in her arms and chest tightly tied, waiting to see if she could master the part she now had in mind. She placed her phone on the table to stop it from shaking on her legs.

"Listen up, Todd, because I will hang up after I say this." Impressive how in control her voice sounded. "Here is how this will work. My rules, my time. You break the rules and we're done. And I mean divorced-done. Finished, without further conversation."

She paused to breathe. She might well be offering Todd what he wanted, a divorce and the chance to leave her for Carly, but their marriage was already ruined.

"Baby, I don't know what you think you saw, but you're overreacting. If you—"

"—Stop right there." He didn't get to cheat, lie to her face, and then paint her as such a sucker.

She held up her hand, traffic-cop style. Although she faced the wall in the corner of the café, and she'd been careful not to raise her voice, it must look strange if the old guy or barista watched her from behind.

The line became quiet. She imagined Todd standing frozen in the airport lounge, even if she'd never seen him not gesticulate while he talked.

"You are not coming home. Not tonight and not in

the coming weeks. I'm sure you have enough clothes in your suitcase to survive. I don't care where you go. Find a hotel. Go to *Carly Bear's* place." The idea that he had a whole system for handling clothes between their houses made her stomach turn.

"Baby, that's not how we work things out. I think if we just get together and—"

"Enough." She raised her hand again, and this time her voice rose to match. She turned to check if the old man and barista observed the Todd and Ryn daytime drama. They stood together at the counter—staring.

"We're done." Ryn moved to cut off the call.

"Wait. Sorry, baby, this is crazy, but go ahead, I'll listen."

She lowered her voice to a whisper. "Do you even want a chance to tell me the truth? Because I'm pretty sure you don't deserve any more chances."

Ryn turned back toward the wall. She didn't know why she hadn't hung up by now. How could it hurt so much to say the next words? *Goodbye Todd.* From here on out his conversations would be with her divorce lawyer.

She drew in a breath, trying to understand why her heart accelerated now, when their conversation, their marriage, was almost over.

"Todd, I need an acknowledgement you aren't coming back to the house."

"If that's what you want Ryn, but please just give me a chance to meet and explain."

"You just had your chance to tell me the truth. Three chances, in fact, and there's no such thing as a fourth strike." When he didn't say anything, she kept talking, "It's too late, I think we're finished."

I think? Her voice sounded weak, as if her heart fought her, still wanting to believe, to grant him more chances, when her head knew she should do no such thing.

"Ryn, baby, I'm telling you, this is all a big misunderstanding." His tone remained too sweet, cajoling, as if convincing the front desk lady at a hotel to upgrade his room, not asking his wife of ten years for forgiveness. He still wasn't taking this seriously.

"I mean, I did mess up here, but please give me a chance to explain why." His tone had turned to pleading. "Just one chance? We have too much of a good thing, please don't give up on us yet."

Threads of regret tugged inside her chest. At least he admitted he messed up. Perhaps she expected too much, too fast. After all, what type of person doesn't give their spouse even a single opportunity to explain themself? Possibly the same heartless woman who dials a stranger and calls her a slut.

She heard a noise like a door swooshing behind her and spun around. The barista must have ducked into the back, and the old man had left.

"Ryn, I love you. And I know you love me. And you're not the kind of person who just gives up."

She pushed on her chest. He was right: a part of her desperately wanted him to give her an amazing, mind-blowingly logical excuse. No matter how unrealistic. The only explanation was that false hope must be her heart's reaction to imminent loss, the mental equivalent of trying to hang on by your fingernails when you know you're on the edge of plummeting off an emotional cliff.

"One meeting. I will consider granting you a single

meeting, no more. At a time and location of my choice."

She knew he couldn't provide any excuses for lying, but perhaps if they met in a week or two, after he absorbed he'd been caught, she could at least learn why he chose Carly over her.

"And don't take this to mean I'm not serious, Todd. Come home at any point before I agree, and we're done. The only talking you'll be doing is with my lawyer. Do you understand?"

What the hell? She clearly wasn't as strong as she thought. Offering him another chance wasn't likely to lead to anything other than more fury and disappointment.

She hung up the phone and removed her earphones without waiting for him to respond.

****

Despite the rain, after she reached her car, Ryn chose the slower ocean route to San Francisco. She navigated the tight curves, glancing every few minutes toward the grizzled ocean beyond the cliffs.

Forty-five minutes later she reached the end of the coast road, but instead of heading home, she turned toward Ocean Beach. No way she could face returning to their house yet, with tainted memories jeering at her from every corner. An image flashed of the office full of framed photos of them signing the paperwork on deals on which they'd supported and celebrated each other. How many of their last years had he been seeing Carly, supporting her, too?

She drove along the beach for a mile before turning into the parking lot, facing the waves. This spot had always lured her during her darkest moments. Not a picture-perfect California beach, but a place of isolation, with fog on good days and howling storms on the worst ones. She came here after Simon stole the leadership of her fund from her grasp, and fifteen years ago, when she abandoned her first job when her boss, Grant, tried to force himself on her.

The weather was more horrid than in Half Moon Bay. Even the surfers skipped this storm. She parked in front of the wall and lowered her head to the steering wheel while the wind threw sand against the sides of her SUV. Beyond sheets of rain on the windshield, dark waves crashed on the beach.

She'd always thought a trauma like this, discovering your loved one was not who you believed, would hurt in your heart, but it didn't. Instead, a hole gaped at the bottom of her stomach, as if someone had taken acid and carved it away, until nothing remained but emptiness.

She closed her eyes and let herself imagine walking out into those waves, avoiding all the pain of the coming months. For the first time she empathized with the thousands who stood near here on the edge of the Golden Gate, faced the skyline of San Francisco, and vanquished their problems with one poetic dive.

She wouldn't do it, of course. As Pops used to say—*she was built stronger than average*—also his justification for why he found it acceptable to send away an eleven-year-old.

She'd always believed that little phrase, embedded in her psyche, helped her source the motivation to fight others' biases, to prove she and other women were worthy of being included. Now it also assured her of something new. No matter how the meeting with Todd went when it happened, she refused to allow him to steal her self-respect.

Chapter Eight

Sammy swept his fries back and forth in the ketchup on his McDonald's tray, his eyes wide.

"So what I'm saying, honey, is even though Todd loves you, he and Mommy aren't going to be together anymore, so he won't be hanging out with us."

It was unusual for them to visit McDonald's right after school like this, but she didn't want to have this conversation at their apartment, surrounded by emptiness. Last night after talking with Dev, in a supreme act of avoidance, she'd taken Sammy to the movies instead of home after picking him up at the babysitter, but he still noticed the missing photos by this morning at breakfast.

Sammy's brows met in a confused frown. "But he'll come and see me. Sometimes?"

"Um, no. I'm afraid Mommy doesn't want him to visit."

"But why?"

Carly's phone jingled in her backpack. No doubt another unknown number, because her office knew she'd only be away for an hour. This morning Todd had filled the entire lobby with sunflowers and daisies, but nothing would melt her resolve to never talk with him again.

"Well, sweetie, Todd told some big lies, and we know how important it is to tell the truth."

"And that's why he can't be part of our family?"

Carly's chest tightened at the word family. "Well…yes, that's one reason. Lying to people you love is not good."

This wasn't exactly how she intended the conversation to go, but at least it was a positive life lesson.

Sammy pushed most of his ketchup-covered fries back into the paper packet, uneaten. She passed him napkins across the table. Perhaps she should have agreed to his request for KFC. That restaurant was only another five minutes' drive, but fried chicken smelled like Wednesday movie nights with Todd. Right now, she couldn't stand the stink of the stuff.

Sammy held a French fry like a pen and drew a circle on top of the paper.

"Have you eaten enough?"

He continued drawing without looking up.

"Sammy, it's rude not to answer me." *Great job, Carly, like chastising is what he needs right now.* She softened her voice. "You do understand this is between Mommy and Todd? It has nothing to do with how much either of us love you."

Sammy squirmed in his seat.

"Honey, what's bothering you?"

"Mommy, are there…different kinds of lies?"

"What do you mean, sweetheart?" She tried to guess where his five-year-old brain could be taking this.

He wiped his hands on a napkin in a motion reminiscent of Lady Macbeth. He obviously believed he'd done something wrong. Perhaps Sammy even believed he was responsible for Todd leaving. If so, she needed to address it.

"I did break the toothbrush."

"What?"

He spoke through a lock of curls which had fallen over his face. "I'm sorry, Mommy."

She struggled to connect the full-blown remorse in his expression and his crumpled posture with any memory of a toothbrush. Maybe he meant the kid's electric one they replaced after it broke over a year ago. Did he tell her he didn't break it? She didn't even remember.

"Sammy, are you worried I'd ask you to leave, like I did Todd? For lying?"

He continued staring at the table. When his gaze raised to meet hers, the tears in them broke her heart. She couldn't believe how badly she'd messed this up, too.

She jumped to her feet, circled the booth, and lifted him into her arms. He wrapped his legs around her waist and snuggled her shoulder, but she gently pushed back his head, so he heard her.

"Sammy, you and I are different. You are the most important person in all the world to me. I'll always love you, no matter what you do." She inhaled his aloe Superman shampoo. "We are already and always will be a family, and families don't ever give up on each other."

At least she'd told a kind untruth. Hopefully, he'd never learn otherwise. The only person in her family who didn't give up on her was Uncle Remy. Even today, not a single one of her other uncles or aunts or cousins in Los Angeles would talk with her, out of allegiance to her parents. Apparently, none of them considered family allegiance extended to her, or their new cousin.

She hugged Sammy so hard she had to force herself to let go. She held his hand from the front seat the entire drive to the after-school babysitter, wishing she could rewind the clock and start their conversation again. But she knew better than anyone: In this life, you didn't get a do-over. You just lived with the consequences of your screw-ups.

****

After dropping off Sammy, and giving him four more hugs, Carly reached the front door of the BioLarge office building five minutes late for her four-o'clock project meeting.

At the back of the lobby, Todd stood at the desk, his face lit with the smile of a televangelist, chatting casually with Sandra, BioLarge's marketing manager.

Carly's heart leaped to her throat before she resolutely set it back in place. He was married, for God's sake. *How dare he turn up here?*

Sandra smiled; her cheeks flushed from whatever compliments Todd had clearly thrown her way. "Hi Carly, your charming fiancé and I have been chatting about you. All good stuff, of course. I tried calling."

Carly gritted her teeth and walked past the flowers filling the lobby. "Thanks for trying to find me, Sandra. I can take it from here."

Once Sandra left, Carly stepped behind the front desk, placing a foot of hardwood between her and Todd. Through the lobby's glass wall, they were visible to every employee sitting at desks on this side of the office.

"Why are you here? There is nothing for us to talk about." She hissed the words but kept her face even in case anyone watched them. This morning she'd given Paul her definitive yes on the CEO job, then emailed Ryn to suggest they meet. But the mess with Todd was between her and Ryn. As the company's new leader, Carly didn't want every employee learning she'd been conned by a cheating liar.

Todd's expression transformed from televangelist smile to repentant sinner. "Carly-bear, I messed up beyond belief, but you at least owe me a chance to explain. Just come outside with me for ten minutes."

A flush of anger warmed the back of her neck. She owed him nothing, and yet, despite the sinner's hunch, Todd's gaze held the same quiet confidence as over two years ago, when they met at her favorite coffee shop while she stood in line with Sammy. As if Todd knew better than she did how this encounter would end.

Well, this time she would not succumb. She lowered her voice to a whisper, stepped around the desk, and made what she hoped resembled a good-natured gesture of pointing toward the door when wrapping up a conversation.

"Todd, there is nothing to explain. This is my workplace. You need to leave."

"I'm sorry, Carly. I didn't want to come here, but you won't answer my calls. Yes, I made a huge mistake, but if you won't come outside, then"—his volume had risen so that her closest team members turned and looked at them—"we can have our conversation right here."

God damn him. She understood his threat: talk with him, or he'd make a scene in front of everyone. Even now, he continued playing her. She had no choice but to go outside. If she gave him five minutes, and made it clear they were over, then maybe she'd never see his deceitful face again.

She waved down Sandra, asked her to push back the meeting, then marched, with Todd trailing her, into the small garden behind the building along the waterline—visible only from the CEO's desk and the rear conference room—all while cursing herself for allowing him to manipulate her.

She sat stoic on the picnic bench, staring at the water, and let him talk while pacing back and forth. She refused to let any of the words sink in. It hurt too much to hear more lies, even if, compared with the confidence she perhaps imagined in the lobby, his lowered voice now sounded contrite, as if no longer sure she'd forgive him.

"Carly, I'm sorry, truly, sorry. From the first day I met you, I meant to tell you the truth, but like I said, I let too much time go by, and then I wasn't sure if you'd forgive me. I can't lose you, because I do love you. You have to believe me…"

She glanced up from the bench. Todd's blond hair flopped across his left cheek in a way reminiscent of Sammy when he looked through his locks.

A memory returned of Todd kneeling at Sammy height the day they met. Todd spent several minutes talking to him and glancing up at Carly, as if she and Sammy were the only people who mattered in the world, before he offered to buy her a coffee and Sammy a hot chocolate. He was the first person she'd dated who didn't just tolerate that she had a son, but appeared to want the full package deal.

"Carly, I know the timing didn't work for us, meeting while I was still married, but the longer I waited to tell you, the more I realized I risked losing you both when I did. And I couldn't bear it, because I knew, right from the day I ran into you and Sammy in Low Grounds Café, that we were soul mates."

Soulmates. The term stung. How could this married liar pretend to know what the term meant?

She stood and whirled on him, her cheeks and ears flaming. "You really don't get it, do you? Two years. Two years, Todd. You don't accidentally forget every single day for over seven hundred and thirty days to tell someone you love you are married. And you certainly don't propose! Do you seriously have no conscience?"

His face crumpled, and he lowered to the bench beside where she now stood. "You're not hearing me. Leaving Ryn is hard for me money-wise, but I would have worked it out. I had every intention of fixing it, of getting divorced. I meant to tell you, because you and Sammy are my future. I know this sounds weird, but for you, I was going to do the right thing. I just ran out of time."

He reached for her hand, the contrition in his eyes absolute. Her chest burned with the desire to believe, but it was too late.

"It wasn't just me you hurt. How could you do this to Sammy? He loves you."

Todd thought mere words were enough to justify what he'd done. He believed forgiveness was owed to him, purely because he made the request. This must be how her parents felt when she returned home and asked for their forgiveness, hoping they'd allow her back into their lives, just because she asked.

She'd changed by then, and maybe Todd intended to change now. Perhaps if he'd made the harder choice and told her the truth, they might have stood a chance. But she could no longer take the risk. As her dad once told her, *You no longer deserve to be part of this family.*

Carly brushed off her sleeves and jeans, imagining the dust as whatever remained of her feelings for this man.

She'd never misjudged anyone as much, not even Kyle. One night six years ago in Glendale, she let herself believe the clean-cut Kyle in a suit, who listened in awe as they chatted about the decade they'd been apart, had become a new man. But she was wrong. It didn't take longer than the next day sober to realize clean-cut and well-spoken didn't mean Kyle wasn't still dealing, just that he moved up the supply chain.

Carly raised her gaze from the dirt to the man in front of her now, claiming he wanted to become a better man. Behind his shoulders, through the building's windows she saw the conference room fill with engineers carrying notepads and laptops, gathering for their rescheduled status meeting.

"Todd, it doesn't matter what you say. The truth matters to me, and after so huge a lie I could never trust you. And I can't, I won't be with someone I can't trust." *Or further risk my or my little boy's heart.* "It's over. Please don't ever call me or come here again."

She turned, leaving him standing by the murky water, her heart aching, and walked through the building's rear door without looking back.

Chapter Nine

"I understand. Yes, of course. I support your decision and wish you the very best and speediest of recovery." Ryn hung up with Paul Alexander.

She paced to the floor length windows of her office, drumming her fingers on her thighs. He'd just updated her on his strong recommendation to appoint Carly Santos as the new CEO of BioLarge. Not only did Ryn now have no hope of minimizing interactions with her but, as her board member, how could she play the role of the woman's closest advisor?

Sure, Todd's lying wasn't exactly Carly's fault, but that didn't mean Ryn could sit across the table and stare into the face of his betrayal.

She leaned her forehead against the cool glass and massaged the back of her scalp. She'd backed herself into a corner. In her tweet yesterday from the coffee shop she publicly committed to the deal with BioLarge. At this point, even if she wanted to, she couldn't back out.

Outside, lights flicked on across the city below, a string of firecrackers bursting over the buildings in Chinatown, North Beach. This morning's email from Carly requesting a meeting suddenly made more sense. Next week was Thanksgiving, but the week after BioLarge intended to hold their next board session—the first meeting where they'd be together again. Carly likely wanted to clear the air before they met with others in the room.

She studied the city at dusk. Standing here looking out over thousands of offices and restaurants filled with San Franciscans—each the center of their own story—usually helped her realize her problems were insignificant. Even with her marriage disintegrating before her eyes, she still had money, and a successful career she wasn't about to mess up. Although something increasingly didn't make sense about Todd's lying. If he truly wanted Carly over her, why didn't he just leave Ryn, divorce her?

"You're planning on the six-thirty ferry, right?" Ryn turned and saw Keisha's head and shoulders poking around the door frame. "Todd called to check."

Ryn froze. She'd made it clear she needed him to stay the hell away from their house until she was ready to talk.

She walked behind her desk and focused on a stack of papers to avoid glowering at Keisha. She didn't know better than to answer him. Ryn hadn't told her anything was wrong in her marriage. She and Keisha were friends, but she was also Keisha's boss, and sharing your possible, yet unconfirmed, divorce counted as letting your personal life seep inappropriately into work.

Ryn unclenched her jaw. "Okay, thanks, Keisha—have a good night."

She slotted her laptop into her briefcase, and texted Todd, before leaving for the boat terminal.

—*You better not be home? I told you I need time*—

Their house in Tiburon with its view of the bay and the morning soundtrack of gulls and yelping sea lions had always been her refuge; right now, from him.

During the thirty-minute ferry ride, she called her brother Jack, who lived an hour away in Palo Alto. Todd hadn't answered her text. She might need Jack's help to boot him out if he was there after she drove home.

****

When Ryn pulled onto her street, the lamps in the living and dining rooms of her house were lit. In the driveway, a bright purple van emblazoned *Gourmet Dining Delivered* was parked next to Todd's Mercedes and in the windows upstairs, people moved around in her kitchen.

A rush of blood pulsed in her ears. God dammit. Not only did he ignore her request to stay away, he let people inside without her permission.

Todd must have watched for her, because the moment she parked he came outside and descended the stairs. He held a bouquet shaped package, wrapped entirely in brown paper and his lips were set in that deal-winning smile which lit his face to the tips of his hair.

Ryn jumped out of her SUV and slammed the door. Did he really think he could charm her so easily?

They came head-to-head midway up the steps, and he leaned in to kiss her cheek. She inhaled Dior Homme and L'Occitane soap, and pain pulsed along the sides of her temples. That scent was her husband, her friend, the same thoughtful man who brought coffee to her office, just to see her. But the poised determination of his stance—the same charm that convinced even the testy lady behind the DMV counter—reminded her not to trust him. She turned away before his lips made contact.

Todd dropped the smile. "I'm sorry. I know you'd have preferred I ask first, but give me an hour. One dinner is all I'm asking. I promise I'll leave right after, if that's still what you want."

"And what if I want you to leave now?"

"Just look inside before you decide." He shifted the wrapped bouquet, so large in his arms that it obscured part of his face. "I realized today how odd it is I've never gifted you flowers in your favorite color, so I decided to set this one thing straight, if nothing else. Come see…" He placed the package into her arms, turned, and jogged up the stairs.

Ryn unstuck the tape, peeked inside the paper, and flinched. Bright blue roses.

She remembered loving these once, but only for an instant. She'd seen indigo roses in the Ferry Building Marketplace and researched them online when ordering bushes for the garden. But she'd learned blue roses don't exist. To create them you took ivory ones and drowned them in artificial coloring.

Apparently, she shouldn't doubt those who say the universe sends you signs. Her fingers brushed an insincere petal, and she leaned in and sniffed. No aroma. The color looked so vibrant, yet her chest ached. These were fake, another lie.

She looked at where Todd waited on the top step. He stood with a palm against the door and the half-grin of a tech billionaire ready to pull the curtain on his big product reveal.

Ryn climbed slowly. Perhaps listening to whatever excuses he offered wasn't the worst idea. She had already ninety-five percent decided she could never trust him again. Closing the remaining gap might not take more than thirty minutes.

When she reached the top, Todd flung open the door, and stood back so she could step inside.

The house bursted with more blue roses. Dozens covered the mantel. Garlands crept around the backs of every chair. The coffee table moaned under the weight of another monstrous arrangement.

Worse, a lattice had been installed at the edge of the dining room, as if set for a wedding, the roses spread so thick they smothered any light from the streetlamps outside the windows.

The effect was nauseating, as if the house choked to death from the enormity of lies it contained.

Todd moved past her and stood under the lattice. He looked as if he were about to launch into a speech. Behind him dishes clinked as two women prepared food in the kitchen.

She couldn't breathe in here. Ryn rushed through the lattice, avoiding Todd by turning to one side, nodded at the caterers as she passed them, and emerged outside into the bracing air on the deck.

She grasped the wooden bannister and leaned over the edge, watching the gulls circle the harbor. Did Todd seriously think this outrageous gesture removed his need for an explanation? Apparently, he believed the solution to gaining her forgiveness was to transform their living room into a zombie rose garden.

Fingers touched her back.

She spun around, and Todd handed her a glass of wine, then recoiled at her expression. "Listen, Ryn, I'm not an idiot. I know this doesn't fix anything, but I needed to show you how much giving us another chance matters to me. I want us to rebuild, find out where we, I mean I went wrong, because I'm taking responsibility for this. I made a massive mistake, but don't you think we have something too good to just throw away?"

He reached for her hand, and she took a step backward toward the deck railing. She had believed they shared something special until this week. They were the perfect partnership, different and separate, yet happy together: like their pairs of socks nestled together in the drawer.

She set her wine on the ledge and leaned against the bannister, suddenly tired beyond what coffee could solve. If she could, she'd rewind time to four months ago when they took that spontaneous trip to Sedona and stayed in their cabin ordering room service, catching up, and making love most of the weekend.

Todd continued talking, as if afraid that if he stopped, she might just declare them done.

"Ryn, what I did is inexcusable, but it's over with Carly. The truth is I was a coward. Once I let it go on so long, I became terrified if I told you, I'd lose you. You are the most impressive woman I've ever met, and I admit I made the hugest mistake, but I can't imagine my life without you as my wife, my friend, my partner."

Some slice of her heart begged her to believe. Didn't everyone ache to be wanted as he claimed to need her? The tightness in her lungs told her how much she longed for it to be true.

She stared into his eyes, judging his genuineness. Would she even know if he was still lying?

A scent wafted from the kitchen. Caramelized

onions. Todd stopped talking and scrutinized her face, waiting for a response. She hated how well he predicted her reactions, especially now when she questioned whether she knew him at all.

"I'm sorry, Todd, but it isn't so simple."

"Ryn, I know I was weak, but let's be honest, we'd become more distant with all the travel. You and I, we didn't talk as much, feel as close…"

For a second she considered the truth in what he said, before seeing his words for the gaslighting they were. Displace the guilt and blame her as the cause of his decisions. *Well, hell no.* He didn't get to trample on her self-respect.

"How dare you imply this is all my fault? You traveled as much as I did." She didn't even need thirty minutes.

His expression changed as he recognized the finality of her decision. The familiar drop of his head to the left, his right hand coming in and sweeping away his bangs. His eyes weren't only disappointed—like when she said she couldn't take time for a last minute cruise earlier this year—but wretched.

He crossed to one corner of the deck and crumpled, squatting on the floor, his hands in his hair. "We had so much, and I ruined everything. There's nothing I can say to fix us, is there?"

Fergus appeared and brushed against his legs, but Todd ignored him, rubbing at his forehead with his palms. Gentle sobs racked his shoulders, and his head dipped toward his knees.

Ryn stood in place. Normally Todd was even-tempered, logical. He didn't indulge in emotional theatrics. She'd only seen him cry twice: the day she accepted his marriage proposal and last year when his uncle Brian died.

Was this wretchedness what happened when you understood you'd ruined everything beyond repair? Because it sure felt that way to her.

She took a step closer, placed a hand on his shoulder, and the meter dipped to ninety percent. She'd also believed they had a special partnership. Was she truly ready to just throw them away?

She extended an arm and pulled Todd to his feet.

He rubbed a hand across his nose, backhanding away the tears. "Thank you. I thought maybe one day, after we patch things up, we could return to Sedona? Learn to appreciate each other properly, again?"

After we patch things up. He looked so pitiful, yet his choice of words remained hopeful, even confident.

A book she read last year on negotiation tactics explained one way to spot a liar was when their body language didn't match their words. And here, with Todd, everything felt out of synch.

He reached for her fingertips. "Tonight, I promise I won't force you to choose. But I have one request, a favor. It's Thanksgiving next week, can you please wait before telling your family? Give us a chance to decide how things end up between us before we let everyone else in?"

Thanksgiving. She picked up Fergus and nuzzled his fur against her cheek.

This time last year Uncle Brian passed away. With both Todd's parents dead, only he remained to make the funeral arrangements in Connecticut. He'd looked similarly pitiful then, dabbing away tears as he explained how he didn't mind attending the funeral alone, because she shouldn't miss the holiday with Pops and her brothers.

She'd never even met Uncle Brian. It made a hell of a lot more sense that Todd spent the holiday with Carly.

"Todd, where did you go last Thanksgiving?"

His eyebrows raised, as if insulted she'd ask. "You know where I was. I had to organize everything for the funeral."

She studied the droop of his mouth, the misery in his eyes. His sorrow at her disbelief so credible. And she didn't believe a single tear.

She stepped back, then again, as the magnitude sank in. He invented a funeral for a family member because he preferred to spend the holiday with someone other than her. The fake tears, the extent of planning, the lies built upon lies. The level of deception took her breath away.

The remaining doubt gap slammed closed. She could never love a man who showed her so little respect.

The caterers shuttled dishes into the dining room, but she refused to sit and eat across from him. She walked inside to request they pack up and leave.

"Ryn, I'm imploring you, be the better person among us. You can still choose to rise above this. To save us."

She turned away from the caterers. Todd had bent on one knee, his head bowed, under the blue rose arch. He held a velvet box, opened to display a platinum necklace with line engravings that matched her engagement ring.

Her face burned. Around the dining table the two

ladies in aprons froze in place.

"Ryn, I'll happily admit a thousand times how wrong I was, I'll repeat it until I breathe my last breath. Just grant me the chance to win you back, to reset the clock, and earn your trust again."

To win me back? She scrunched her eyes, and in her head she heard the sirens, screams, clangs of a game show. How massive a dupe she'd let herself become. To Todd, this was no more than a competition, with her as the grand prize.

The realization slapped her. To him their marriage had never been more than a game. He probably never admired her as he said. Never enjoyed spending time together. She'd been nothing more than the "successful wife" required to be on his arm for the doors he wanted opened.

Even tonight made up part of the same contest. *Prove you can win back your wife after everything you got away with.* For all she knew, he was running the exact same play on Carly.

"Get the hell out of here." She lunged forward, grabbed the velvet box from his hand, and threw it through the patio doors. It sailed past the deck and over the railing.

A wisp of confusion crossed Todd's face, as if he hadn't considered a scenario where she wouldn't forgive him. He turned and stared after the box. The neighboring lot where it landed had long unkempt grass. Impossible for Todd to find it in the dark, but who cared? Let him search, if it mattered to him.

She marched to the front door and held it open, standing half in, half out of the house. She'd damn well plant herself here until he left.

Todd joined her inside the doorway. A dark purple vein pulsed on the side of his neck against his white shirt. A mark of outrage she'd seen only once, the time a competitor stole his hugest real estate deal.

She softened her tone, hoping to calm him. Just because they were over didn't mean they couldn't stay civil. "Todd it'll be okay. Why don't I call a lawyer tomorrow, and we can work things out amicably?"

His lips set into a snarl. "*Amicably?* When you're the one just giving up on us. You really think I'm going to make this easy on you, Ryn? This is my house, too. And I'm coming home on Wednesday when I get back from this trip." The bite in his words completed the sentence *whether you like it or not.*

Ryn crossed her arms and pulled her coat tighter across her chest, the ice in Todd's stare chilling her lungs. She likely didn't have legal standing to prevent him staying in a house he half-owned, but his comment drove home what she suspected: she'd better find an excellent lawyer, because nothing in this divorce would be easy.

Todd stepped through the doorway. "Think carefully about how a divorce will affect your position at Sentra. You've worked so hard to achieve senior partner. Do you really want to screw it up now?"

Her heart paused for a second before she watched him turn, stomp toward his Mercedes, and back out of the driveway. She hadn't put serious thought into the logistics of divorce, other than berating herself for caving ten years ago when Todd insisted they didn't need a prenuptial agreement. But surely her job at Sentra couldn't be at risk?

She waited for his car to turn the corner at the end

of the block before bolting both locks.

In the kitchen, she asked the caterers to pack up and showed them out, then grabbed a black garbage bag and wrenched the blue roses off tables and the backs of chairs, her whole body jittering, as if she chewed her way through an entire package of coffee beans.

Now she considered it, yes, she owned venture investments at Sentra in her name, and no prenup, so they'd come into play when they divided their worth. But they mostly kept their finances separate, and Todd owned considerably more assets than she did. His real estate business had gone from strength to strength in the last five years, in part through introductions to her damn connections.

In the morning she'd find a first-rate divorce lawyer. And she'd return Carly's email and set up a meeting for next week, before Thanksgiving. If Ryn's divorce risked messing with her position at Sentra, she couldn't afford any other issues muddying her promoted role.

She ditched the garbage bags, bustled into the kitchen, and peeked inside the containers of food the caterers left.

Tomorrow she suspected the implosion of her marriage would truly sink in, but for tonight there were worse ways to commiserate than drowning your sorrows in two people's share of cheese fondue, sea bass with caramelized onions, and crème brûlée.

Chapter Ten

The coffee shop that Keisha suggested for the meeting with Carly was on Ryn's route home, near the Larkspur commuter ferry terminal.

She leaned over the railing of the boat's upper deck and let the wind toss her hair while the commuters below fought against the rocking floor, jostling to be first in line when they docked. Ryn might look disheveled for the meeting but this second—after signing the final paperwork to fund BioLarge this morning—letting go, if only for an instant, felt good.

Below her jacket, she rubbed her fingers along the line of her collarbone. A pain had lodged under there this morning when she met with her new divorce lawyer. As if the revelation of every way she misjudged Todd were a Band-Aid she'd ripped off, but now the wound just sat there oozing, reminding her she had no control over how long it took to heal.

She removed a mirror from her handbag, fixed her hair, and applied fresh Power Mauve lipstick. She tried to picture a moment, two or three years from now, when she'd be among the top five VCs in the valley and Todd would wonder why he'd been stupid enough to mess with her. The image refused to render in decent resolution. Whenever she imagined the future on her own, all she could summon were images of her house, empty and cold, while Todd lived happily with Carly, or whoever fell for him next.

She let the first level of passengers exit the ferry before descending the stairs and walking to the café.

A few steps from the door she stopped and shook out her hands. Carly might have been smarter when she suggested making this a phone call, but Pops always said apologies were best made in person. And God knew she owed Carly a proper apology, especially now they had committed to working together. Todd had tossed them into the worst kind of snake pit, and one of them needed to offer a ladder so they could both climb out. Ryn set her lips in what she hoped came across as a neutral smile before opening the door.

Inside the café, a long line of people in coats and scarves snaked around the edge of the room. In the center, three huge communal tables were packed, racked along each side with remote workers typing on their laptops, their faces side-lit by the flashing lights of an oversize Christmas tree.

Ryn blinked, taken aback by the throng, and the strands of multicolored lamps swaying over her head. This place was the opposite of what she needed for a private and delicate conversation with Carly, more like a Christmas parade through the Istanbul bazaar.

She searched the crowd, wishing she knew of any other cafés nearby. Carly's wavy brown hair rose above an armchair, one of a pair set beside a fireplace. From this side, with the firelight caressing her soft curls and the plaid shirt highlighting her ample chest, she resembled a sexy country star. Beautiful, but still approachable.

Ryn scrunched her eyes, trying to wipe from her retina the image of Todd's fingers stroking those soft waves. No matter how often she told herself that the details of what happened between him and Carly didn't matter, now that Ryn was divorcing him, her subconscious had not caught up. At this second, it spooled a cheating Kama Sutra reel with snapshots of them in every sexual position.

She shook her head to clear the latest image before approaching Carly. Even if she desperately wished to know whether Carly was still with Todd, today would not become a repeat of her lack of control during their meeting at Sentra.

She walked up beside the armchair and cleared her throat.

Carly jumped up, leaning down just in time to straighten the small table and catch her cup from falling. For a second, the flash of terror in her eyes said Ryn was the snake in Carly's own personal hell-pit.

Well, I guess I earned that.

Carly's expression morphed into a circumspect smile, and she stretched out a hand. "Sorry, Ryn, you took me by surprise. Thanks for agreeing to talk."

She shook Carly's slightly damp palm. "Well, these are some pretty unusual circumstances."

Ryn flagged the server, placed her order, and took the second armchair. The brown leather squeaked, then puffed out air as she sat.

She forced a smile. "First off, congratulations and welcome to the Sentra portfolio of companies. It isn't every day you close such a big funding round."

Carly glanced away, then at the ground before she answered. "Thanks for taking a risk on BioLarge." She sank back into the leather chair, looking as if she wished it would swallow her. She must realize no CEO described their own company as a risk to its biggest investor.

"I'm sorry, what I meant," Carly said, leaning in to meet Ryn's gaze, "is thanks for moving forward, what with the *unusual circumstances*, as you called it." She smiled as she spoke the last words, a real unreserved smile this time.

"Listen, Carly, I only take calculated risks with positive probable outcomes." Ryn's tone sounded synthesized, like a computer processing text to speech. She breathed out. "What I mean is, your technology is unique. You and Paul should be proud of what you've built."

The server delivered Ryn's coffee, and she drank a few sips to calm herself before restarting the discussion. "Carly, I wanted to meet in person to apologize. The way I acted in our last meeting was out of line. And I said things when I called you which were shameful. That's not normally how I'd behave, but I jumped to the assumption you knew Todd was married, and that wasn't fair."

Carly picked up her mug and stared into it. "Thank you." She paused, and her gaze flitted toward the ceiling as if she intended to say more, then changed her mind. "So, you heard about Paul?"

"Yes, terrible situation. For the company's future I hope he recovers fully."

Carly's eyes widened. Ryn must have come across as a cold-hearted bitch who cared only about return on her investment. This conversation was a verbal tightrope.

She pulled her gaze away from Carly's dark chocolate eyes, so much more alluring than her own steel gray, and stared at the table as she continued. "Again, I'm sorry. I didn't mean that. What I intended to say is it's truly awful." She grasped her hands in her lap, to keep from saying anything else so insensitive. "From the times we've met, Paul seems like a nice guy, in addition to a great CEO. He has kids, right?"

Carly's eyes flickered with sadness. "Yes. Two girls. Eight and ten. This morning they made him a get-better-Daddy collage and brought it to the office." Her voice hitched. "We're all struggling."

Ryn shifted in her seat and sipped her latte to avoid meeting Carly's gaze. She'd run through everything she came to say.

She noticed Carly's pale knuckles wrapped tight around her mug. Naked nails, no polish. Todd's texts said she loved to cook with those hands. And their warmth…

"Anyway, the reason I asked to talk," Carly said, her tone pushing more confidence, "is I want to be sure we can work together. I mean, if it's too difficult, I believe there is another choice. Simon Atherton could replace your position on our board?"

Ryn put down her coffee. This wasn't an option. To her boss, quitting on a board seat because of a personal conflict confirmed the type of remarks he frequently made about female execs. Idiocies she and Todd used to stand on the deck, watching the seagulls, and laugh over. *Women are too emotional for senior leadership. Can't keep the drama out of the office. Well, except for you, of course, Ryn.*

Bailing from the BioLarge board because of Carly would be equivalent to telling Simon she couldn't close her next deal because of her period.

She filtered the acid from her tone before responding. "I honestly don't think that's our best choice. Simon is..." She paused. How did she explain? This wasn't vaguely how she expected this conversation to go.

She couldn't badmouth her own boss, but given he objected to Sentra investing in Carly's company, he'd likely be even more of a jerk in board meetings than usual. And Carly was a female CEO. Not only did it put Ryn in an impossible situation, telling Simon why she needed a substitute—but didn't Carly understand he would be the last person she wanted?

Carly looked at her backpack on the floor, as if getting ready to leave.

Apparently, she expected Ryn to simply say yes, quit the board of her top investment, and Carly would never have to see her again.

Ryn's chest burned at the injustice. For all she knew, Carly was still in a relationship with Todd, too. She could be heading home any second to use those unmanicured hands on him.

The Kama Sutra film returned, the images reeling faster, making her dizzy.

"So, what do you think? There could be some advantages to just switching in Simon..." Carly's voice was hesitant, and before Ryn could stop herself she cut the woman off.

"Please tell me you're smart enough to not still be sleeping with my husband?"

Chapter Eleven

Carly jumped to her feet in the café, her chest thumping with the same need to flee as when she opened Ryn's note at Sentra. "How dare you? I would never…"

Ryn had no right to imply she would shack up with a married man. This time she'd made the right decision, despite hurting Sammy, and yet Ryn assumed she was nothing more than a dirty mistress. She grabbed her backpack, hoisted it over her shoulder, and turned toward the door.

Fingers grabbed her arm from behind, then nails dug in.

"Wait."

Carly spun around and glared at her. "Let me go, right now."

So much for Ryn's earlier apology. Why on earth had she imagined she could work with this dragon-lady?

"Oh God. Oh shit." Ryn released her fingers and held both her hands upward. "I can't believe I just did that." Ryn's tone held desperation, and her gaze roved around the coffee shop.

The software developers in hoodies at the nearest table stopped typing, their fingers poised over their keyboards, and stared at them. Ryn's nail prints stung on Carly's forearm.

"I'm so sorry, this is just…it's the craziest situation and…" Ryn slumped in her chair. "Since last week I can't get anything right." She talked not to Carly, but the battered leather of her empty armchair: "You know, they just started with the pumpkin spice lattes and now it's two days to Thanksgiving, the stupid Christmas lights are everywhere, and my husband is in love with a more beautiful woman who…who…" Ryn stopped, as if realizing her words made little sense and looked up, but her gaze focused on Carly's hair, as if embarrassed to look her in the eyes.

More Beautiful. Carly took a breath. Anything but true, although how surreal to live in parallel realities. Only fifteen minutes ago, she'd studied Ryn after she arrived, with her perfect lipstick and light sparking off her auburn hair and wondered what led Todd to cheat on someone who looked like the "everything together" star of a movie set in Manhattan. Although apparently not so together, after all.

Slowly, Carly sat back in her chair. She could afford some pity. It must be humiliating for Ryn to hold a conversation with her husband's mistress. If Carly were the scorned wife, she'd be assessing every word, every wrinkle, every roll of flesh, wondering what she lacked.

She pulled on her plaid shirt, checking no cleavage showed, and spoke in a low voice, so they weren't overheard. "To answer your question, I don't ever expect to see Todd again. I'd never knowingly have an affair with another woman's husband."

"Thanks for saying that, although don't think I fail to understand he's the one at fault here." Ryn scrubbed at her eyes and shook her head as if overwhelmed. "I still barely understand how this could happen to two smart women."

"Me either."

Ryn raised her eyebrows and they sat in silence.

Carly couldn't think of anything to say next. Perhaps she should tell Ryn that Todd still sent flowers twice a day. Ryn hadn't said if she'd decided to divorce him, but she should know. Although that'd likely make her feel even worse.

"Again, I'm sorry," Ryn said. "This is the complete opposite of what I intended for this meeting." Her tone was despondent. "My only goal today was to clear the air before next week's board meeting and apologize. But I guess, if you want Simon instead of me, let's talk about it."

"Sure. Although I have one other related question. I heard from Paul that you proposed another candidate." A man who would hopefully still be plan B for CEO, if Carly didn't pan out.

"Craig Wells, yes."

"I just wondered why Sentra didn't push for him over me? He has considerable experience." And for Ryn, choosing him would have avoided working with Carly.

Ryn's jaw loosened in what looked like relief. Perhaps she hoped Carly might change her mind on taking the job. "Well, you're right about the leadership experience…"

She paused and focused on the hanging lamps, as if debating how much to share, then looked at Carly and frowned. "Honestly, Craig would be much easier for me as CEO, but,"—her tone turned to one of resignation—"you are a better choice for the company. If you ask around, you'll find out he has an unforgiving leadership style. Seventy percent of his last executive team quit."

Carly's stomach turned over. "So, to put it bluntly, you're saying he's awful?" Another reason she just needed to succeed. There was no plan B.

"I don't believe those were my exact words." Ryn's lips lifted into a smile which said yes-absolutely-that's-what-I-meant. "Let's just say he and Simon Atherton have a lot in common in the level of respect they show to their executives in board meetings, in particular women."

Perhaps, in an alternate universe, she might have liked dragon-lady.

Ryn's brow furrowed again. "Carly, what you need to understand is I made a huge bet, staking my career and the reputation of my new fund on BioLarge. Even if it's tricky working together, we both want you and your company's success. Despite our rocky start—which I want to apologize for again—I supported Paul putting you in the CEO job. It may not feel like it, but I'm actually on your side."

Carly pushed on the knot in her stomach. Tricky working together seemed like an understatement. "I'm aware everything about this is odd, Ryn, but thank you for being honest. About Craig, and Simon."

Ryn gave a half smile which carried no joy. "Well, by this point, don't you think Todd's served up enough dishonesty for all three of us?"

Carly glanced at her shoes. Ryn couldn't be more right. They were both better than the circumstances he dumped them into. So long as they steered away from the personal and focused on professional topics, there was a small chance they could still make it work.

She met Ryn's gaze, slowly nodded, and matched her smile. "Why don't we try one board meeting and see how it goes?"

They left the café and said goodbye in front of the Christmas tree in the window. Although Ryn held her car keys, she stood rooted to the spot. "Carly, I know this is awkward, and you don't have to answer, but can I ask you one last question?"

Carly's shoulders tightened, but she nodded.

"I just wondered…were you, by any chance, with Todd last Thanksgiving?"

Images flashed from last year. The night she threw Todd out of her apartment in early November after he shared that he didn't intend to join her and Sammy for the holiday. They were engaged, so why prioritize a vacation with his friends in Hong Kong over spending time with her?

After calming down she explained over the phone at midnight how lonely every holiday made her feel, without any family. When Todd ended his trip early and arrived on Thanksgiving Wednesday—laden with five different types of candy, mini pumpkin decorations, and a massive turkey—she had to ask Sammy twice to stop jumping on the sofa. She remembered pausing during cleanup after dinner on Thursday and realizing that, for the first time, she hadn't called her parents only to have them not answer. The three of them were enough.

She closed her eyes a second to absorb the pain. *How on earth did Todd explain being away from his wife on Thanksgiving?*

Ryn must have read Carly's answer from her face, because she blinked several times, her fists clenched, before she pivoted and walked away.

Dammit. A line of muscles tightened along Carly's shoulders. Just when they'd reached a detente. It wasn't as if she kept Todd away deliberately.

"Ryn, I'm sorry, but it's not like I had any idea…"

Ryn turned and waved over her shoulder with a sad smile but kept walking.

Carly buttoned her coat and strode in the opposite direction, right as a ferry pulled into the dock. She watched the shuffling mass of humanity head up the gangway and wondered how many of them lied to their loved ones.

She rubbed her forearm where Ryn's nail indentations still stung. Her wanting to know about Thanksgiving was understandable. She certainly shouldn't trust Todd to tell her the truth.

Chapter Twelve

Ryn lay awake in the king bed she used to share with Todd, staring at the gray ceiling. She asked herself the same question for the hundredth time: how was it possible she hadn't seen through Todd's deception?

Everyone knew how men like Simon behaved in their personal lives. For God's sake, the whole office gossiped last year after he took his mistress on vacation and set her up in a ski condo opposite his wife and kids. So how had Ryn, with a million reasons to know better, let herself become the type of woman who didn't see past the lines her husband fed her?

She rolled left, then right. Perhaps with some fresh air and horseback riding she'd sleep better in Carmel Valley this weekend. Even if she'd be haunted by Pops' disappointed tone when she called and told him last-minute that she wasn't joining them in Montana for Thanksgiving. He sounded hurt, but although she'd already told Jack about Todd, she couldn't stand the extra inquisition from Pops and her brother Adrian.

She had always been the successful one in the family, the one her brothers teased about having such a clear life plan, despite being younger than them. She needed more time before she could deal with their pity.

She sat up in bed. Same as the last few nights, no more sleep would be coming, so she got up and dressed. Might as well get to work early, given she intended to take a half day. Her duffel sat at the foot of the bed, and she added her toothbrush, thankful she packed last night. She needed to be certain of leaving before Todd returned from his business trip.

She placed the bag by the front door, then ran back for a jar of Nutella and a spoon, and stuffed them in a side pocket before driving to the office.

A few hours later, she'd finished her work for the day and took a last look at her inbox, when Keisha stopped by, wearing a V-neck shirt in a bright orange and brown print with matching head wrap. "I've had about enough, have you?"

"Heck, yes. Ready to catch the Larkspur ferry to Hayward, Keisha? By the way, did I tell you yet how much that top suits you?"

Keisha shook her head. "Yes, you complimented the shirt twice already and honestly, you're never going to let the ferry thing go, are you?"

A year ago, Keisha had convinced Ryn to hire her—despite not having the graduate degrees held by most junior venture capital employees—during three weeks of morning conversations on the seven a.m. passenger ferry from Larkspur to San Francisco. She only admitted months after starting at Sentra that she drove two extra hours and took the ferry purely to secure uninterrupted time and impress Ryn during the ride.

"Nope, validates my best hiring decision," Ryn said. Turned out Keisha had more savvy in a single braid than any of those Harvard MBA frat-boy types who filled this office. Ryn gave her a broad smile. "Just give me a sec to pack up, and you can lock up behind me."

Ryn closed her laptop, and her wedding ring glinted, catching the midday light. She still wore it to avoid questions at Sentra that she couldn't answer until she found a resolution to her divorce. Especially since she'd have to admit that ten years ago, she rolled over like a puppy when Todd said a prenup insulted him. *I mean, Ryn, it's like you're planning for us to not work out.*

She and Keisha walked to the office front door, near the elevator bank. Perhaps Ryn should tell her about the divorce. Keisha wouldn't judge and with so many lawyer meetings coming up, Ryn would appreciate extra help to juggle her schedule.

"To your earlier point on the shirt," Keisha said, fiddling with the lock, "the reason you've never seen me wear this outfit is I wouldn't with Simon here in the office. Let's just say life would be easier if you were in charge…"

Ryn stopped and faced her before pushing the elevator button. Was Keisha saying Simon didn't appreciate such a bright ethnic outfit or that he was racist? Possibly correct on both counts. When it came to wearing anything more interesting than staid gray suits, her boss was an equal opportunity jerk.

She leaned in and gave Keisha a hug. "I know I've told you this, but you have no idea how much your help at Sentra and your friendship mean to me."

After the holiday she'd update Keisha on splitting from Todd. Once she had more time to live with the idea, and it didn't feel so humiliating to admit out loud.

****

The traffic ground to a halt, gridlocked on the piece of Highway One around Carmel. Ryn sat in her SUV and drummed her fingers on the steering wheel, ignoring the wedding ring taunting her.

The entire two-hour drive, the same question stuck in her head, like a plane circling SFO airport, refused a landing because of fog. She still couldn't understand how Todd fooled her like he did.

In retrospect, she recognized the tactics he'd used to manage her suspicions, like the surprise Kauai vacation he sprung on her two years ago.

Earlier that week she'd questioned why he traveled more often, and had less time for her. Suddenly on Friday, instead of dinner in the city, he drove them to the airport. She remembered sipping champagne in first class, floating on the excitement of the helicopter trip and other activities he'd booked for their weekend. Until his next words hit as if the plane itself had dropped. *We need to talk.*

She set the champagne aside and listened while he explained the problem was her. She'd been so focused on work lately, less emotionally available. *But it's okay Ryn, I know this trip will help us rekindle our flame.*

Looking back, she saw the truth. That trip was nothing more than a masterful diversion tactic. It must have been around the time when he started seeing Carly. And Ryn fell for it.

She hadn't truly absorbed—until this week, explaining to her lawyer why she didn't have a prenup—that it may not only be the last two years he'd played her. Which meant she'd swallowed his lies not weeks or months, but for a decade.

A car cut in front of her in the line of traffic, and she raised a hand to vent her fury on the horn, but stopped before honking. A case of road rage wouldn't provide answers to why she'd let herself believe a man who apparently held a masters in manipulation. Or why he picked her as his target.

It was already late afternoon by the time she arrived at the resort she'd booked for the long weekend. For years she'd admired advertisements for this place, California's closest experience to a dude ranch, and a better alternative than sitting at home, moping.

After being shown to her adobe casita, she rummaged in her bag for the Nutella and settled with the jar and a spoon on her patio, set between two thick trees, overlooking the horse corral.

She closed her eyes and sank into the smooth swirl. The velvety taste always took her back to sitting on the hay bales in the loft above the barn with Mom, savoring their latest contraband.

Nutella was hard to get in a rural area back then, and Pops called it a frivolity. At first, after moving to Montana, Mom convinced friends in San Francisco to send her jars, but when that supply dried up, she placed stealth orders with a store for delivery. On weekends, when Mom worked wedding photography gigs, Ryn's job was to stalk the mailbox. She could still feel the adrenaline rush of her special mission. She'd watch from her bedroom window, making sure Pops worked in the field behind the house, then sprint across the lawn to the mailbox, and sneak any right-sized packages into their special hiding crate in the barn.

Ryn slowly ate another spoonful and smiled. She might have lost Mom at ten-years-old, but the best conversations about French food and Indian palaces, and Mom's dreams of travel, and believing in who you are, took place above their barn. As far as she knew,

Mom never admitted to Pops the decadence of their secret Nutella parties.

Ryn glanced at her wedding band and sighed. She understood the connection. Todd never asked her to give up on her dreams. Unlike her two engineer boyfriends in college, who believed if they stayed together long enough, she'd do their laundry, or the tech billionaire she'd dated for about a minute before he asked her to leave her job, Todd never expected her to redesign life around him.

Behind the horse corrals, the last threads of light receded under the horizon, and as they disappeared the sky darkened to a deep blue. It was time to get rid of this damn wedding ring.

Ryn drew a bath and grabbed the small bottle of lotion sitting beside the shampoo and conditioner. She slathered her finger with half the bottle. Removing this ring might not be so easy, given she hadn't taken it off in months.

Easing herself into the tub, she pushed on the ring, and wondered what it meant, not attempting to remove it until now. She'd already paid the lawyer her retainer. Clearly, she intended to divorce. And yet she hadn't admitted to Pops, or her brother Adrian, or even Keisha today that her marriage had failed.

She held her breath and slid under the water, remembering the exact day she first understood failure was not an option.

Six long months had passed since she moved to Aunty Dusty's in Billings with two broken arms after the skid steer accident. Staying with her aunt made sense when Pops explained he and her two teenage brothers couldn't care for an eleven-year-old girl not capable of bathing or showering by herself. But both her casts had been removed months ago and Pops visited less and less. She'd even started a new school.

But when she proudly told him she'd been selected by her new teacher to lead the schools' mathlete team, Pops declared he'd drive four hours to Billings and stay the entire weekend, so he'd see every minute of her team's two-day performance.

On Saturday morning she stood, clicking her heels in the school door, waiting for him to pull up in the pickup truck. Pops didn't arrive until after the competition started, but she spotted his white hat in the back row when the teams were given their challenges. She peered along the aisle, checking whether he still looked sad. Tomorrow, after he saw how well behaved she'd become, she would ask him straight out to come home.

When she looked back, her team already scribbled on their answer sheets. She'd missed one of the first clues. And so the rest of the competition continued. Mr. Mac, her teacher warned that most kids were older than her, but she didn't realize it would be this difficult. By the middle of the first afternoon, her team had been eliminated.

They ate an early dinner at Applebee's. After Pops asked her about school and her new friends, he stood up before Aunt Dusty even finished eating. "Well, folks, someone needs to get up and feed the horses tomorrow," he said, putting on his hat, and turning it an inch.

He couldn't be leaving already. If she'd succeeded in the competition, he planned to spend all weekend. Before he disappeared out the door, she jumped up from the table, a sinking feeling in her stomach, and pulled on his sleeve.

Tears blurred her eyes as she searched for the words to explain that, if he let her come home, she wouldn't be a bother or make any more stupid mistakes, like with the skid steer loader.

Pops saw her tears, and cringed, as if embarrassed for her to show so much emotion in public. He patted her on the back. "It's okay honey, you did great. You're younger than most folks in the room today. And most of them are guys. Keep working at it and you'll improve by next time."

She wiped her nose, and swept her hair behind her ear, ready to argue her case. But before she got a word out, Pops met her gaze and answered the question she hadn't even asked. "Soon, Kathryn, but first your Pops needs to feel a hundred percent better and himself again, which is not yet."

Her chest cinched tight, and she struggled to take a breath, then another. He didn't want her. Jack and Adrian didn't need to win at math or enter tournaments to earn a second day of Pops' company, or live in their own home, but she did.

Ryn couldn't hold her breath any longer under the bathwater and rose to the surface. She'd remained in the tub so long the water had turned lukewarm. She stood, snatched a towel, and wrapped it around her before dousing her ring finger with another layer of lotion.

Recently she recast her memories of those years living in Billings with Aunt Dusty. During their weekend in Sedona, she and Todd sat around the fire and discussed what they'd change if they could turn back the years. For Todd, he regretted not spending more time with his Mom and Dad in Connecticut before they died.

For Ryn, her biggest regret remained her relationship with Pops. She wished she had the skills, when younger, to talk about how hollow he felt without Mom, instead of thinking he lacked in affection. Thanks to time, distance, and a little therapy, she understood now that the only difference between his love for her and her brothers was timing—and the fact only she grew up to look like a replica of their mother.

She'd told Todd she considered it a gift to have learned resiliency and the importance of demonstrating your value with real concrete achievements, because ever since then, she'd never stopped having to prove herself.

She left the bathroom, opened the patio door, and listened to the night birds on the branches outside. For her, nothing had been easy as birdsong. She'd fought every inch of the way through an undergrad math degree, and clawed her way up the wall to senior partner, demonstrating at each nail hold to Simon and the others, that she was more than qualified. She'd worked to prove herself to every man in her life.

Well, every man except for one.

Ryn closed her eyes as the truth sank in. This was how he successfully manipulated her. Todd gave her admiration from the day they met at the 30 Under 30 cocktail party. Unlike Simon, unlike Pops, she never needed to fight for his respect.

A sob stuck in her throat. She pushed harder on the ring. The damn thing clung as stubbornly to her finger as she'd clung to her perfect perception of Todd.

He made her believe he valued her for who she

was, without a struggle to earn his love, and of course it was all fake.

She should have recognized life never came so easy. She knew from being the only girl in her family, in the university class, the boardroom. You had to fight for every shred of respect.

With the towel still wrapped around her chest, she lay on the bed, but sat back up as tears choked her. She didn't know if she cried for the loss of her marriage, the years she spent failing to convince Pops to let her come home, or because she couldn't remove this stupid piece of metal binding her to a ten-year mistake from which she may never recover.

She let the tears run over her cheeks and onto her chest as she pushed and pulled and twisted at the ring.

It budged a millimeter on her finger.

She jumped from the bed, ran to the bathroom, and poured the last of the lotion over her hand. It turned another millimeter.

Finally, the stupid thing decided to stop reminding her what an idiot she'd been to believe anyone could love her unconditionally, as Todd claimed, no changes needed.

The ring twisted one more time and clanged on the casita's flagstone floor. She flopped onto the bed and continued to cry.

Chapter Thirteen

"But Mommy, my tummy does hurt. I don't want to go to school."

Carly glanced at Sammy in the rearview mirror. Judging from the quiver in his lower lip, she had about thirty seconds before he burst into tears.

On any other day she'd pull the car over and they'd talk about how feelings are just temporary, but no time today, not with her first board meeting in an hour. As a new CEO, less experienced than most, today her board members, including Ryn, would be assessing whether she understood and had enough confidence to guide the business.

God, I understand the fake tummy aches. Life is tough, and you want to stay with Mommy and go to the office again.

Waiting at the traffic light, she cursed her lack of planning when she fired her babysitter over Thanksgiving. Otherwise she could have dropped him off, just for a couple of hours. Not like she had any choice. When she returned from meeting the StackTech journalist in San Francisco last week, the lady was smoking pot and chatting on the phone outside the front door, paying zero attention to Sammy. And Carly'd believed hiring a grandma type would be a safer bet.

She checked again in the mirror, where Sammy theatrically clutched his book against his gut, and her own stomach churned. Brock Gordon, that journalist, was another reason she couldn't take Sammy to the office today and risk him running around the desks during the meeting. It wasn't her fault their interview went off the rails after Brock hit on her, but it was critical to leave a good impression with Ryn and her other board members today, in case his article took a negative slant, as she suspected it might.

She pulled into the school parking lot. She'd never turned to the bribery page of the parenting manual, but once he saw his friends, Sammy was usually fine.

"Tell you what, if your tummy still hurts by lunchtime, I'll come get you," Carly said, turning to the backseat. "Maybe we even get ice cream after school, if you make it all day? But I need you at school this morning, okay?" *Even for two hours. Just let me prove to them and me that putting me in the CEO job wasn't a mistake.*

Sammy's lips stopped twitching, and his chubby cheeks lifted into a smile.

"Choclit?"

"Yes, chocolate." If a promise of ice cream worked, then the stomach pain had to be a fake.

She took his hand and guided him into the building. Yes, she'd resorted to bribery, but the crying dam had been on the brink of opening. Or was that what everyone told themselves the moment before they threw out their principles?

She gave him a peck on the cheek before handing him to his teacher. The second her board meeting ended she'd check on him.

Driving toward the office, she rehearsed the questions she expected to be asked, and reminded herself of Dev's advice on making a good first impression. *Just remember you're in charge and don't show any fear.*

She parked in the lot outside the low rise BioLarge office building, entered the front door, and froze. The lobby brimmed with baskets of crimson roses, chrysanthemums, and gerberas. She'd called the florist and requested them to stop, but they refused to listen. The twice daily deliveries from Todd had already outgrown the front desk and spilled into the corners and floor along the glass walls. Stupid, stupid of her, forgetting to have these removed before Ryn visited today. Would she instantly guess Todd sent them?

Carly's chest clenched tight as it did whenever she passed the arrangements. This morning, for a glorious second after she woke, she imagined returning to her prior world, one where Todd loved her, and they would create a family. Then, like every day, she plunged back to reality once the drowsiness cleared. Walking past these arrangements reminded her of the type of man she'd chosen; someone who, even after he'd been caught, believed her weak enough to forgive if he launched a campaign by floral proxy.

She grabbed a card off a recent arrangement, and crossed the large open office-space, dodging around the expanding mish-mash of cheaply purchased desks, and deposited it into the wastebasket. With any luck, from the abundance of red, Ryn would assume the flowers were part of their holiday decor.

Carly moved to the conference room and made sure everything looked ready. Today she would give smarter answers to her board members than she did yesterday, in her first all-employees meeting. She toyed with the arrangement of coffee cups, remembering how terribly she handled the conversation when Derrick, her head of testing, questioned her decision on their launch date.

She'd been in the middle of presenting the new product schedule when he stepped forward from the crowd, his arms crossed. "Carly," He spoke as if explaining to a little girl. "You do realize we have no control over the timing of our FDA approvals? Killing ourselves to achieve May doesn't make any sense."

She squeezed her hands together before answering. A good CEO didn't let an employee challenge her authority in front of her whole team.

"Yes, Derrick, I am well aware how the FDA approval process works. But, as I explained, May is the date we must achieve to manage our cashflow. End of story."

End of story? She'd responded like an irritated parent who didn't want their teenager to borrow the car, not a CEO full of quiet confidence.

She stepped back from the console table in the conference room, where she'd arranged the cups in a neat line. No time for meditation, so she took ten deep breaths. Next time Derrick disrespected her she needed to summon her courage and talk with him. She wasn't the type to quit just because one meeting went badly, but she hadn't expected the stark loneliness of knowing she alone held the team's future in her hands, and she might not be enough.

Ryn walked around a corner in the hallway, wheeling a carryon suitcase. For her sake, she hoped Ryn dumped the scumbag. Carly pushed on her stressed stomach and stepped up to greet her.

Ryn stood at least two inches taller, despite Carly wearing the highest heels she owned. She'd heard tall people carried more authority, and today she needed every inch of respect her five-foot-three, plus four-inch pumps, commanded.

Carly showed her to the conference room. From her composed demeanor, Ryn hadn't noticed Todd's daily flower torture when she entered the building.

"How are you doing?" Ryn's voice sounded hesitant, similar to their first moments in the coffee shop as if she were really asking about more than business.

Carly layered as much confidence as she could muster into her voice. "All right, considering. Preparing for the product launch is keeping us on our toes." She pointed at the suitcase. "Heading out of town?"

Ryn smiled, as if relieved for the conversation to stay work-centered. "Just a short trip. I'm closing a deal in Los Angeles. Possible new exit strategy through acquisition for a company I invested in three years ago."

Ryn took a seat and Carly fetched Blake and Neil, her other two investor board members who waited in the lobby.

When everyone settled and Oliver, BioLarge's Chief Finance Officer, had also joined them, Carly offered the group refreshments. As she moved toward the coffeepot, Ryn frowned at her, then in a manner so slight as to be imperceptible to the others in the room, wagged her finger. A second later she stuck her hands under her legs and looked away, as if berating herself for reacting.

She objected to Carly serving coffee. *Why, because*

it's beneath me as CEO?

Carly plonked the coffeepot in the center of the conference table. If this was Ryn's version of supposedly being on her side, it wasn't helpful.

You're in charge. Don't show any fear. She walked to the projector and started the meeting.

After initial updates, she presented the proposed launch plans. "The latest schedule has us looking at May." The best part of this plan entailed Paul's health hopefully improving and him being back at work in time to handle the bigger media events.

"May? Don't you think that's too late?" Blake Cushings asked, his tone friendly. With his lemon-striped Ralph Lauren polo, he more resembled a preppy Stanford student than a billionaire investor in his early thirties.

In contrast, Neil better fit the stereotype of a bald middle-aged tech executive after too many company dinners. His buttons stretched on his shirt when he leaned in. "I agree, we need sooner."

Ryn drummed her fingers beside her laptop as if debating whether to side with Carly or the other investors. "Well, I believe May is the latest we can go without the delay in revenue affecting your runway, Carly." She finished with a reserved smile that seemed to say *I'm trying to help.*

Blake slammed the table. If it were made of wood, his hand might have made a crashing sound, but instead it slapped on the cheap Formica.

"I got it! South by Southwest in March. Know the organizers personally. They're launching a new med-tech focus next year." He gave a satisfied grin. "I'm pretty sure I could swing a keynote in the main tent."

Carly tried to think rationally, despite panic taking hold of her chest and throat. The South by Southwest trade show was massive. Thousands of people. And only CEOs presented in those humongous keynotes. Yesterday she failed to inspire confidence in an employee meeting of less than a hundred people she knew well. No way she could pull off a keynote.

Ryn smiled, clearly liking the idea. It probably didn't cross her mind that a CEO might have such crummy speaking skills as Carly. Ryn turned to her. "What do you think? Strong launch venue. Instant awareness pop."

It sounded like a terrible proposition to her. Was it only knowing she'd present in front of thousands that made her stomach threaten to throw this morning's granola up her throat?

No, something else didn't work. The timing. They didn't stand a chance of having final FDA clearance before March. And announcing an unapproved product wasn't wise. She heard Paul's voice in her head saying, *Hell, no, bad plan.*

Carly coughed twice to prevent her throat from freezing. "I'm sorry, but the FDA approvals won't be complete before then…"

She stopped when Neil glared across the table. "I understand your hesitation, but you need to think like a CEO, here, not a scientist."

Ryn turned and glowered at him, but when she faced Carly again, her furrowed brow only relaxed a little. Obviously, she believed March to be the right answer, too. And Ryn specialized in med-tech so surely she'd know best.

Perhaps there was a market dynamic here that

Carly didn't understand. As a scientist by background, it wasn't as if she had experience with these types of decisions. And her fear of such a huge venue could be clouding her judgment.

Blake held up his phone. "So, do I call in the favor? Yes or no?"

She stepped back from the table. *You're in charge. Don't show any fear.* Even if to her a March launch felt like committing her company to jump off a cliff running, her board members had more experience.

She spread her feet in a confident stance. "It sounds like a great opportunity we shouldn't miss."

Neil sat back and crossed his arms. An I-knew-it grin transformed his face, and he gave Blake a high five.

Ryn rolled her eyes at them, then smiled at Carly with approval, as if she'd just helped her younger sister through a difficult homework session.

Carly sank into her chair. How would she explain to a hundred employees who believed a May announce was too early that she'd committed them to March?

This was either a smart decision she didn't understand, or she'd made the worst type of rookie CEO mistake: allowing Ryn and the other board members to bully her into a decision that suited them.

They covered a few more topics, including Oliver's presentation of the financials, before Carly wrapped up the session.

After the others left, Ryn stayed behind. "Not too bad for a first meeting." She poured herself more coffee and grabbed the handle of her suitcase. "Can you walk me out? I need to talk with you about the lobby."

Carly swallowed. So Ryn did guess about the

flowers.

They reached the front of the building, and before Carly spoke, Ryn spun around the glass box of a lobby, in a surprisingly playful gesture.

"You know, Carly, at moments in there you looked as uncomfortable as I used to feel in that kind of meeting. Like with the coffee. Just a tip: never volunteer to become subservient, especially in a room full of men. And, let me help you on something else..."

At least she seemed to have empathy for Carly's struggle to appear confident in the meeting. Ryn gestured at the nearest basket. "As much as I appreciate the winter garden look, after today's discussion on reducing costs, it's not a good idea. Gives board members the impression you aren't being frugal with company funds."

Carly blinked a few times and took a breath, trying to calm her pulse as they stood surrounded by crimson flowers. She'd chickened out of telling Ryn about these last week. Now she had an opening and should tell her—if only in a spirit of solidarity. Plus, Ryn may already think they spent more money than necessary, unless Paul had explained how they got a special deal on this office park by the water, after a friend's company went bankrupt and couldn't fulfill their lease.

"Ryn." Carly's throat tensed. "I need you to know I'm not spending our money unwisely. The flowers they're, well...Todd sent them."

Ryn's eyes widened.

"Like I said when we met, it's over," Carly hastened to add. "I blocked his number, but he keeps sending these stupid things..." Her voice sounded pathetic, as if she had no authority over the situation.

"Believe me, I tried to get rid of them, but he won't stop."

Ryn's gaze swept from the desk covered in baskets of red gerberas and roses to more on the floor, and chrysanthemums up against the glass walls. She burst out laughing.

Carly looked from Ryn to the flowers, unable to source any words. Nothing seemed funny to her, and yet here Ryn stood, cackling.

Ryn shook her head, as if trying to absorb the scene around her. "The creepy bastard, begging me not to give up on us. At first, before I saw through him, I beat myself up, thinking—what type of woman gives up on her marriage so easily? But at the exact same time, he's busy trying to convince you?"

"I, uh...yeah." This was the man she'd chosen, one whose lies only kept getting deeper and creepier.

Ryn kicked a basket of scarlet chrysanthemums across the lobby as if it were a football. "Thank God I decided to divorce his sorry ass—and I suspect you also deserve a lot better."

Carly forced her shoulders downward from their tensed position. Perhaps Ryn had reason to laugh. The flowers were ridiculous. And if she could see the funny side, maybe Carly could, too.

"You couldn't be more right." She gave Ryn a smile, picked up two of the baskets, and sent them skidding across the floor to join the one Ryn kicked into the corner.

She would get rid of this garbage and fix the delivery problem. She'd never heard of placing a restraining order on a florist, but if that's what it took to stop the stalking by floral delivery, she'd darn well file one.

After Ryn left, Carly allowed herself a chuckle as she returned to her desk. She'd feared Ryn's anger, but of course a smart woman like her had already decided to ditch a man who'd proven to be a serial-liar.

Carly checked her phone.

Oh no. She'd had it on mute and missed four calls and two voicemails during the meeting. All from Sammy's school.

Chapter Fourteen

Carly inhaled into downward dog position. For once, the wooded glen behind her deck wasn't calming her. She'd taken ten minutes to center herself because already the article by Brock Gordon, the journalist at StackTech, had published. And it was a hundred times worse than she imagined.

She shot a glance under her arm through the patio door to Sammy, who played inside on the living room rug. Miraculously, his stomachache cleared within minutes after she collected him from the nurse's office two days ago. She took him to work with her yesterday, and he'd returned to school this morning without complaint.

She needed to remember his life had been turned upside down, too. If she wasn't dealing well with breaking up from Todd at thirty-five, her five-year-old couldn't be expected to *just get over it*, either. She moved into cross-legged mediation position and waved at him inside.

Sammy stood up, holding the Millennium Falcon model Todd gave him a year ago, and glided the starship toward the gap she'd left open in the patio door. "Can we go now? Will this be in the movie?"

She touched her fingers to Uncle Remy's gold cross for strength. Until Thanksgiving last week, when she suggested they settle on the sofa and watch *Star*

Wars, that toy in his hand had been a long-forgotten gift, dusty on the top shelf in his bedroom. She couldn't explain to Sammy, who'd scrambled up the shelves with delight as soon as the movie ended, how seeing that starship in his hand pinched her heart.

"I don't know, little guy. Give me fifteen minutes to focus on a work thing, and then we'll go see the movie?" She knew taking the night off to see the new Star Wars with him wouldn't fix everything, but it might make them both feel a little better.

He shrugged and flew the toy back across the living room toward his bedroom.

Carly finished her yoga and moved inside to call Dev again for advice. If he asked, she didn't even need the printout on the dining table to remember the words of Brock's article.

The recklessness of BioLarge's new CEO, talking launch plans without a secured date for FDA approvals, demonstrates naïveté and foolhardiness. A scientist with no financial background, Ms. Santos lacks the leadership depth and charisma to introduce a successful market-changing venture of this type. However, worse is her decision to put patients at risk by releasing an unproven medical technology.

She took a deep breath and counted out her exhale, while the phone rang to voice mail for the third time. None of the article was true. Well, at least not the part about their technology putting patients' lives at risk. She might not yet have a plan for how to announce in March, but they'd never release their product before it received final FDA clearance. Although now those words were out in the world, people would assume they were true, and BioLarge's product posed a danger to patients.

Entire companies and careers had been destroyed by lesser articles, but she wasn't about to allow seven years of her, Paul's, and the whole company's work to be put at risk just because she screwed up her first interview as CEO.

Dev often talked of going on the offense, and she intended to fight back. She just needed advice on what a good plan contained—perhaps a blog post, talking points for her board members—but she suspected Dev must be in flight, because he hadn't answered in the last thirty minutes.

She picked up the article and scanned it again. Even if Brock's facts were wrong, his assessment of her as inexperienced was correct. Her first mistake, indeed naïve, was believing his email request for a product interview, and not better researching his cut-throat CEO articles.

She had second thoughts the minute she walked into the restaurant and he turned and grinned as if their meeting were a date. It wasn't until he finished his second drink and asked at least five times why she declined to join him in one, that he finally got beyond chitchat and posed real questions.

"Have you considered what you'll wear for your company's big launch?" he inquired with a smirk, as if referring to her choice of dress for a movie premiere.

She knew better than to answer. She'd heard other female CEOs got conned into talking outfits, and then journalists would write they were more focused on fashion than business results.

"I'd prefer not to answer that." She dug her teeth into her lip. She wouldn't lose her temper at this journalist who pulled her away from her little boy on Thanksgiving week, even if he sought to bait her with questions he'd never ask a male CEO.

Brock placed his elbows on the table, clearly annoyed at her non-response, but the move also brought him within inches of her face. She jerked back and repositioned on the bench of the booth. From that point, the interview had gone downhill, with every second question a trick one, until she decided to end it, and stood to leave.

"Would you like a preview?" Brock asked. "As a gift, given it's the holidays. I'd be open to meeting again to share a draft. Say, Saturday night?"

Until those words, she'd truly missed that he was hitting on her. But as inexperienced as she might be, she still knew journalists never gave previews.

When she turned to put on her coat, Brock reached for it first, then held it up. As she inserted her arms, he grabbed her hips from behind, and exerted pressure to turn her in a too-close dance pose.

She'd dissected that interaction several times since last week, trying to decide whether she overreacted when she elbowed her way free and ran out on him. She knew she bruised his ego, but hadn't imagined he'd take it out on her in his article.

Carly shivered and turned on the heating in her apartment. It seemed sleaze-bag men were drawn to her. Kyle, Todd, now this guy. Did she send out homing signals saying, *Pick on me, I don't deserve better?*

She considered calling Paul, but he expended so much precious energy helping her prepare for the board meeting. It was more important for him to focus on his health. Plus, he'd ask why she didn't consult him before the interview. She thought she could handle a simple product conversation.

Clearly she was wrong. And now she needed someone to whom she could admit she caused the negative slant. Even if Brock's behavior had been out of line, every quote in the article including *no comment* were actual words she said.

Her board members would never understand that part of why she messed up the interview was Brock had it in for her, after she turned him down. Well, except perhaps for Ryn. As a woman she must have suffered men like Brock. She might even have empathy for how being propositioned puts you on edge, leading to mistakes.

She considered whether calling her might reinforce Ryn's perception—after stepping in more than once at the last board meeting—that Carly needed help to do her job. Then again, she did need help. Desperately. She smiled, remembering the way Ryn kicked the flowers around the lobby. Ryn likely wouldn't be fazed by this type of disaster.

Sammy ran back into the living room and bolted for his coat on the dining room chair. "Can we go, now?"

She promised they'd go tonight, but that was before this article. Now she didn't know what she'd been thinking when she asked for fifteen minutes. She couldn't just head off to the movies while her company burned.

"I'm so sorry, honey, but I'm afraid Mommy needs to work tonight. I know I said we'd go today, but we'll see it on the weekend instead, okay?"

Sammy's disappointed pout told her everything she

needed. This was the true cause of his phantom stomach aches. Not only had Todd disappeared overnight, but she kept disappointing him, too.

"I'm sorry, little guy, I know it sucks, but how about after I'm done on the phone, we bake chocolate chip cookies together, instead?"

She walked over and swayed her hips left, to start a version of Todd's side bump—fist bump—high five Sammy so loved, and confirm their new plans. He responded with a half-hearted hand raise and a *whatever* shrug, as if he didn't want to risk getting too excited by anything she promised.

Her heart tugged, and she pulled him in for a long hug. How did anyone juggle being a CEO with raising a small child? As a mom, her son was her first priority. As a CEO her company supposedly came first. If there were an award for Worst CEO of the Year or World's Worst Mom, she'd be in the running for both.

While she dialed Ryn, Sammy returned to sit on the living room rug and played with Todd's Millennium Falcon.

Chapter Fifteen

Ryn's boarding pass fell to the floor as she juggled handing it to the gate attendant while answering a call. She leaned and grabbed it, holding the phone against her ear with her shoulder. "Oh, hi, Carly, what's up? Not a great time. I'm about to board a flight home."

"So you haven't seen the article?"

"I'm sorry, no context. What article?"

"It's a piece on BioLarge. It hit the wire an hour ago—well, actually it's more on me as CEO. By Brock Gordon at StackTech."

Brock Gordon? Ryn stopped walking along the gangway for a moment, then started again when the man behind her grumbled. Carly should be smarter than to give a guy like Brock an interview. He was Silicon Valley's closest equivalent to a tabloid journalist, known for doing full-blown character assassinations of prominent execs.

"How bad is it? Give me a second." Ryn stowed her suitcase and located the headphones in her briefcase. She took her seat, searching for the article on her phone. "I only have a few minutes. Were you just calling to give me a heads-up?"

"Somewhat. But it's more…shoot, I'm sorry, I'm not sure how to say this. You remember how you said last week you're on my side? Well, I need to call in a favor already. I'm afraid the interview wasn't my best work. Well, actually, it's pretty awful."

As Carly talked, the StackTech website loaded and Ryn skimmed the worst lines.

Reckless.

A decision to put patients at risk.

A level of incompetence reserved for those who did not earn their jobs through skill.

Now she understood why Carly sounded as if she'd been pummeled, although Ryn still couldn't fathom why she agreed to an interview with Brock.

"I understand you're about to take-off," Carly said. "But when you land, would you be willing to help me?"

Ryn paused before responding, imagining how she'd react if Brock wrote a similar smear piece on her. The content would differ, of course. For Ryn, he'd interview colleagues, who'd refer to her by all the B words: Brash, Blunt, Bossy, a Bitch. All things she'd heard before—the last two starting in school when she insisted her mathlete team enforce a strict practice schedule—but she'd never been called incompetent. To be told you're not worth the space you're taking up in the world must really sting.

"Of course, I'll help." No way an article like this could be deserved two weeks into the job. Sure, Carly might have looked hesitant at various points in their first board meeting, but not more than normal for a first time CEO.

"Carly, okay, first thing take a deep breath. Yes, this is bad, but I've seen worse." *Barely. And never this early in a company's life.* "I'm sorry, I can't do much to help until I get off the plane, but let's meet after I land."

Carly's end of the line went momentarily silent.

"I know this is awkward, but might it be possible to

146

come over here…you see—"

"Carly, I'd prefer we didn't."

Ryn had never visited any CEO's private residence. Far too awkward becoming friendly if later she needed to fire the same CEO or shutter the company. She even declined party invitations. Not to mention Carly's place might be littered with trappings of Todd.

"It's just, my son. I can't leave him alone and I'm afraid I don't have a babysitter tonight…"

Ryn stared at the phone. Carly having a child didn't fit the CEO profile, so it hadn't crossed her mind. She tapped on the screen with a fingernail, the burn of frustration rising in her chest. Todd didn't just replace her, but took on a child, too?

The flight attendant walked down the aisle, raised her eyebrows, and pointed at Ryn. She had about thirty seconds to finish the call.

Negative press like this would snowball by tomorrow morning. And she could not afford for the most promising investment in her fund to be flushed down the toilet because of bad media coverage before they even launched.

"Text me the address."

"Okay, I'm sending it now. Ryn, um, thank you."

She switched off her phone and opened the inflight magazine. If she were honest, no matter how awkward it might be visiting Carly's place, a small part of her appreciated an excuse to delay going home.

When she'd returned from Carmel Valley, Todd was back in the house. And although they both now talked with lawyers, neither of them had offered to move out. They'd circled each other in silence in the hallways for two nights, like boxers preparing for who'd throw the first punch.

****

Two hours later Ryn pulled up to Carly's block at the back of the apartment complex. The spot was peaceful with the balconies overlooking the wooded valley. Not ritzy compared to her own home, but at least Carly didn't have to worry about a not-yet-ex-husband sharing her space.

Ryn took the concrete stairs to the second floor. She imagined Todd climbing these same steps, hundreds of times. On the landing, she studied the *Friends and Good Wine Welcome* doormat, expecting a flash of jealousy, if not a repeat of the Kama Sutra reel. Instead, disgust snaked under her skin. Disgust at the effort it took for him to successfully deceive them both: the planning, the inventing of excuses, meetings, backstories. Exhausting to consider the level of duplicity required.

She knocked, and Carly opened the door at once. She wore sweats, lip gloss, and a burgundy Stanford University sweatshirt with what looked like flour on it.

A recurring thought resurfaced, along with a pain that dug under Ryn's breastbone. This domesticity was what she lacked. She'd never be the woman who made dinner, then slid on some lip gloss, and welcomed her husband with warmth at the end of a long day.

"I'm sorry about the outfit," Carly said, taking in Ryn's own suit, heels, and scarf before gesturing to come inside. "We were baking."

Ryn scanned the apartment as she entered. Photos of Carly and a small boy with curls, ranging from toddler to kindergarten, filled the mantel and the bookshelf. Not a shot with Todd, anywhere.

To one side a compact dining area connected through a breakfast bar to an equally tiny kitchen. On her other side, toy trucks covered half of a multicolored shag rug in front of a worn sofa and behind it a patio door and deck overlooked the woods beyond. Small, but homey.

Ryn shook her head, trying to clear the competing thoughts invading every inch of her skull. She couldn't believe Todd was about to take on a son. When she brought up having children, he always said it would be selfish, unless they could both set aside their careers enough to make them a priority, even if it meant adopting by the time they were ready. She'd had her doubts, but having a child wasn't a decision only one of them should make.

And yet Todd apparently chose a mistress with a kid. She couldn't stop herself from wondering if perhaps he belonged to Todd.

No, she was being ridiculous. Those photos showed Carly's son must be in kindergarten, too old to be Todd's if they'd been together two years. And why now, among all of Ryn's stupid gullible decisions, would she let her brain start second guessing the smartest one, not having to put a child through her upcoming divorce. She knew how it felt to lose a parent; two parents, in some ways.

"Can I get you something?" Carly stood in the middle of the rug and played with the small gold cross around her neck, a gesture more fit for a chastised child than a resilient CEO. Or more likely nervous because Ryn was here, her gaze scouring the apartment.

Ryn settled her gaze on one spot, so she didn't look

like she was snooping. She picked the mantel behind Carly's head, then realized she now studied the photo of her son standing by a beach, with a uneven edge on one side.

Carly handed Ryn a printed page and gestured to take a seat. She sat opposite Ryn, then jumped back up. "I'm sorry, I didn't offer you anything to drink. I have soda, tea, coffee, wine, juice?"

"Yes, you did, thanks." Ryn gave what she knew must be an awkward smile. "Truly, I'm fine." She glanced over the printout and placed it on the coffee table. She'd read it twice already on the plane.

Their problem was that patient safety had become a fiery topic in the Valley after another startup's medical device resulted in four deaths, last year. The investigation revealed the CEO encouraged the company to cheat on their lab results.

Carly left for a moment and returned from the kitchen. She carried a plate of cookies studded with tiny colored chocolate chips. She placed it in front of Ryn, swaying from foot to foot, as if valiantly prepared to slay the dragon, even if unsure which weapon to wield.

Well, she was right about one part: you didn't win against bullies like Brock by ducking and taking cover. This article would toss lighter fluid on the same media frenzy about patient safety. Unless they handled it right, press like this could kill BioLarge before their product saved a single life.

"Please sit," Ryn said. "The first question I have is why did Brock target you? No insult, but so far you and BioLarge are unknowns, not worth the ink, so to speak. And you must have known his reputation, so why even meet with him?"

"Truthfully?" Carly sat, and her shoulders hunched slightly forward before she answered. "It was my screw up. He emailed me about an interview, and because I knew StackTech wrote product pieces, I didn't do my homework on Brock's other CEO—"

A small child, perhaps four years old, had crept around the corner and observed them from under long chestnut lashes. Ryn's heart slowed as she took in his shy smile, tiny hands. Even though she knew the timing didn't match, she couldn't help but search for Todd in him. She studied the boy's wide brown eyes and cinnamon curls cascading over his ears, and he observed her in return. There was no resemblance. This child had nothing in common with Todd's green eyes and brash blond highlights.

She rubbed her chest. The path not taken. In two years, Carly wouldn't be dreading a world where she sat alone in an empty house. Unlike Ryn, she prioritized having this child over her career. Or rather, she'd done both, which Ryn never believed to be truly possible. It's why she hadn't pushed when Todd said it was unfair to raise a child while they were both in such high-intensity jobs.

She focused on the article printout for a moment, gathering her thoughts. Sitting here, on the inside of Carly's life, was even weirder than she expected.

"Sweetie, you're supposed to be asleep." Carly's voice carried no reprimand. The boy walked over and leaned against her side. In one hand, he held a toy spaceship. "Sammy, I'd like you to meet Ryn. She's helping Mommy with some work things."

Ryn extended a hand and Sammy inched back against his mom.

"I'm sorry, he's just sleepy," Carly said, ruffling his curls.

Ryn smiled, racking her brain for what to say to a tired kindergartener. She zeroed in on the toy. "What's that in your hand? A starship?"

Sammy perked up, thrust the spaceship proudly into the air and flew it toward Ryn for her to see. Behind him, Carly's gaze rose to the ceiling, and her hand tugged on the underlayer of her hair, as if watching a train wreck in slow motion.

Sammy grinned, and he turned the spaceship to each side, showing Ryn. "It's the Melania Falcon. It was a present from Todd." He swung it back toward Carly, and she gave him a taut smile.

Ryn's chest tightened. Of course, Todd bought the child gifts. Even if Sammy wasn't his, a ready-made family must have been part of the attraction, part of him choosing Carly over her.

She blew out a breath. Not helpful thoughts right now.

Sammy alternated between scrutinizing Carly's face then Ryn's, as if trying to understand whether he'd said something wrong. Ryn wondered if he understood her relationship to his mom, then shook her head at her own silliness. What a caring kid. His concern more likely came from knowing that talking about Todd upset his mother.

Carly gathered him up into her arms in a bear hug. "It's okay, sweetie-pie." Her face flashed a mix of melancholy and frustration as she patted his back. "You need to go back to bed, though, so Mommy and Ryn can keep working, okay?" She set him on the floor and took his hand. "Say good night to Ryn."

"Night, Mommy's friend."

Ryn chuckled. This kid was adorable.

They were already halfway across the room when Sammy stopped and ran his cuteness back toward Ryn. He stopped by the plate of cookies on the coffee table. "Do you like them?" His eyes opened wide, as if waiting for the verdict from a food critic.

Ryn tried not to laugh. As much as talking with Carly felt like walking a trail where you couldn't see how far away the edges of the cliff were located, this little guy brought a breath of fresh air. She picked up a cookie and took her first bite. "Wow. These are scrumptious. Thank you, Sammy, for sharing."

Carly disappeared into the bedroom with him, and Ryn took another bite and realized the cookie indeed tasted delicious. She finished the whole thing and chased a few crumbs around the rim of the plate, then stood and walked to the patio door. A heavy rain had started and pelted the wood of the outside deck, splashing back every time it hit the wooden planks. Todd giving Sammy gifts tilted her world a peg further off balance. Playing the role of substitute dad couldn't be more at odds with the man Ryn believed she knew.

Carly returned to sit in the armchair and Ryn took the sofa, unsure of how to restart their discussion. They both stared at the cookie plate on the coffee table.

Ryn considered bringing up Sammy's comments, trying to make some kind of Han Solo joke linking Todd and *Star Wars*, but none came to her.

Carly's gaze met hers. "Did you ever suspect? Like consider maybe the signs were there, and you didn't want to see them?"

Ryn pressed on her chest. This question of how she

didn't see through Todd's game was still a struggle.

"Honestly, no, I never suspected. Although it's hard to admit. Not spotting any of it makes me seem so gullible."

Carly gave a slow nod, without losing eye contact. "Gullible. Exactly how I feel." She pulled on her hair. "Both Todd—and now add this Brock situation."

Ryn nodded. She saw the connection. Neither should have happened to smart women, like them.

"I think maybe that's why I'm struggling with the specifics of a 'fight back' plan," Carly said, picking at the chocolate chips in one of the cookies. "I mean, my experience is you can't change a bully, only escape them. And I actually said the stuff Brock quoted, so I can't exactly deny my own words..."

Carly shared the story of their meeting at the bar. When she described Brock grabbing her from behind around the hips, Ryn's stomach twisted, and bile rose in her throat. She understood the sense of helplessness when you stood up for yourself, refused to let a man abuse his power, then still got caught in the backlash of him feeling rejected.

She blinked, reliving fifteen years ago in the hotel corridor with Grant, the head of her first venture firm. He planted a hand on either side of her bare arms in her black shift dress, pinning her to the rough wallpaper, his face so close she could smell the rancid mix of his cigars and ginger scallops from their business dinner.

If you know what's good for your career, you'll be in my suite tomorrow morning for breakfast. His words were vague enough that she'd never be able to accuse him of anything other than requesting a meeting, but his voice left no confusion. It carried the triumphant hunger of a carnivore who'd already cornered his kill.

She'd never forget the disappointed head shake from Marilyn, her boss and mentor, when Ryn gave a lame excuse the next week for resigning.

She stood and strode across the many-hued rug to the dining room, then turned back to Carly. "You know what? I'll take some wine if it's still on offer."

Carly returned from the kitchen with an open bottle of red and two glasses. She poured for them both, and repositioned herself in the armchair, looking uncomfortable. No wonder she believed she didn't have a chance against someone like Brock. It had taken Ryn years to understand, when she became a boss, that she had a third choice other than quitting or greeting Grant in his bathrobe for breakfast. Marilyn would have fought for her. Twenty-three-year-old Ryn was just too naïve and scared to give her the chance.

She leaned over and tapped Carly on the shoulder. "Sit up."

"I'm sorry?"

"No one punches back from a slump." Ryn smiled to make sure her tone didn't come across as harsh. Carly was correct that neither she nor Ryn could fix a Brock or a Todd, but when it came to dealing with the aftermath of an article like this, Ryn had experience and influence. Neither of them was powerless.

"First off, you're right," Ryn said. "This guy's a bully. Also a primo jerk, pond scum, or any other term you wish to apply. What I'm guessing is you don't know he did the same hatchet job on Cyndi Adler, the CEO at CryoBarn last year. Congrats, you're officially in the big leagues."

Carly's smile seemed to pull up her shoulders.

"The big leagues, eh? I guess I can live with that." She stood and grabbed a few sheets of paper from the small table in the corner, the backs of the pages covered in kid scribbles. "Let me walk you through my thinking so far, and perhaps you can help me fill in the blanks?"

After thirty minutes, they'd documented a plan. Tomorrow, Carly would blog on patient safety, then call the FDA assuring them BioLarge would never launch without their approvals, and they'd coordinate between BioLarge and Sentra Ventures to answer calls from the media.

Carly leaned forward from her chair and pushed up and down on the balls of her feet, as if ready to tackle the first plan elements this very night. She stood and walked Ryn to the door. "Thank you for helping me. I recognize none of this must be easy for you, especially coming here…and I appreciate you doing it, anyway."

"You're welcome." Ryn caught her cheeks rising into a smile, surprised to realize she meant it. Helping Carly cope with the same issues she'd overcome in the past was actually satisfying. She reached to hold Carly by the shoulders, then thought better of it and let her hands fall to her sides. Even if tonight she'd learned they shared more in common than a company, they were still colleagues.

She settled for tapping the sides of Carly's arms. "You're gonna do great tomorrow, but one last thing before I go get soaked. I'm afraid journalists are pack animals. Expect more articles after the first one hits."

"You're saying hold my head up during the day, but stock in good wine and romcoms for the evenings?"

Ryn gave her a warm smile, thinking of Nutella, her own comfort serum. "Exactly."

They shook hands, and Ryn descended the stairway to head home, pondering how much her perspective had changed after only an hour in Carly's world. How much harder must it be, to tend to her grief, when a child dealing with his own watched her every word and move.

Ryn had assumed the heartbreak cut deeper for her, because she was married. But with Sammy to raise, Carly might actually have the worse half of the Todd breakup.

****

Ryn jogged from the front door of Carly's apartment building to her SUV, and ducked inside rapidly to avoid the rain. She texted her brother Jack in Palo Alto, in what had become a ritual over the last few days. Each time she returned to the house and didn't know if Todd would be there, she alerted Jack first.

—*Heading home now*—

She connected her phone to the stereo, then remembered she wanted to suggest to Carly they touch base tomorrow, once the full impact of the article became clear. She composed a quick text and Carly replied.

—*Yes, let's talk late morning*—

What she needed for the drive home was power music. The image of how she left Carly, head raised high, ready to go into battle tomorrow, made Ryn want to stop nursing her misery and source her own courage. The promotion she'd worked toward for years would be announced in two weeks, and she would relish every minute.

She selected a playlist she'd created at the ranch for moments when she needed strength in the coming months, one which contained her favorite "screechy woman" music, as Todd referred to it. She'd named the list Songs Todd Despises, before laughing at what the acronym stood for.

She drove with care in the pouring rain. Pools of water reflected the lights at each intersection. Tiburon Harbor looked choppy and gray in the moonlight, and rain obscured the lines of large houses, stacked above each other to the peak of the hill.

As she drew nearer to home, no lights showed outside the house. She pulled into the empty driveway and exhaled. No lights on inside, either. Tonight, she could relax and not face the tension of the two of them circling each other.

She exited the car and grabbed her suitcase, using the other hand to hold her suit jacket over her head against the rain. She always left the light on outside the front door, but tonight the steps were unlit, the bushes along the path casting shadows. Todd must have turned everything off when he left. Hopefully, he remembered to feed Fergus for the last two nights, as she asked. If he refused to move out, he could at least be helpful.

She reached the top step in the dark, rain running off the sides of her jacket, and pulled out her phone to use as a flashlight. She intended to turn on every lamp in the house, throw the STD playlist on the stereo, and crank up the heating.

The beam from her phone caught a silver shimmer on the door. A fancy new door handle. With a fancy new lock.

What the hell? Her head buzzed like an elevator with its doors stuck between *You've got to be kidding me* and *The bastard locked me out of my own house*?

She shook out her jacket. Hard to imagine what kind of jackass would do this to his own wife, but she knew the answer. The same type who lied for years. With blood steaming the inside of her ears, she checked under the rock where they kept a spare key—just in case—before inspecting the door again. Two dead bolts.

She threw her suitcase against the wall, tossed her jacket on top, and scraped the water off her face. So much for circling each other. The fight had begun.

The rear doors were locked too, and she considered climbing up on the roof overhang to see whether an upstairs window might be ajar, but she wasn't that athletic, and she didn't need broken bones from falling off a slippery building. Her suit pants and blouse were soaked.

Her suitcase slid around in her hand as she rushed down the steps back to her SUV. She stashed it inside, and threw herself into the driver's seat, her ears still pounding. With no lights on, the bastard clearly wasn't even here. Which left her two sucky choices: abandon her house and drive to Jack's an hour away, or contact a twenty-four-hour locksmith to fix this and let her in.

She shivered, and her teeth chattered. Apparently, fury could only warm you so long. She was too damn drenched and tired to wait an hour or more for someone to arrive and change the locks. Jack's home would work for tonight and she'd return tomorrow after work. She slammed the car into reverse and the taillights caught a flash of white behind her in the yard beside the street.

She pivoted in her seat, trying to see it in the dark. She couldn't read the letters yet, but the white square hung from a T-shaped post.

Like the shape of a...FOR SALE sign?

She reversed until she sat in front of the sign, which had a Realtor's photo and phone number on it. This became more unbelievable by the second. They were both on the house title so, for sure, neither of them could list the house for sale without the other's permission.

She remembered the chill in Todd's words the night he filled the place with blue roses. *You really think I'm going to make this easy on you, Ryn?*

She entered the Realtor's number on her phone, then straightened her thoughts enough to realize it was her lawyer she needed to call. She sent a quick text to Jack first, so he knew to expect her.

—Todd changed the locks, and the f-ing bastard decided to sell the house while I was gone—

Now her lawyer. Ryn's head throbbed in rhythm with the phone trills as she sought to compose a coherent voice-mail message, but she could only utter half-sentences. "The house...and For Sale sign...and locked me out...and joint owners...so how could he sell?" The vocalizations of someone who sounded as if she no longer had her thoughts or her life together.

She hung up, wondering if she should leave a second voice message or write a clearer email later tonight when a text arrived.

—So sorry. Want to come back over here?—

Back? Ryn squinted at the phone. She hadn't seen Jack in person since before Thanksgiving.

Oh shit. Her stomach dropped toward the floor mat. She'd texted her last message to Carly.

She took a breath. Perhaps returning wasn't the worst idea? Carly's place was fifteen minutes away. A

160

safe location to call her lawyer and perhaps change her mind and wait for a locksmith.

A second text arrived as she cranked up the car's heating.

—I have more wine :-)—

She shook her wet sleeves inside the car. Man, what was she thinking? Even if she enjoyed helping Carly, the most important lesson she'd learned in her career was to keep your personal and professional lives separate. Carly couldn't take her seriously as a role-model and advisor if it seemed like Ryn might be falling apart. She couldn't turn up at her home looking like a jittery drowned squirrel.

She pulled up Jack's number, told him she was coming over, then texted Carly to thank her for the offer, but she'd be fine.

Chapter Sixteen

Carly hung up, bit down on her lip and spun her chair toward the window, so her team in the open-plan office didn't see her frustration.

She and Paul had just finished brainstorming how to answer their distributors. They originally promised to partner with BioLarge, but this morning wrote saying they wanted to cancel their contracts. She and David had found no good answers.

It wasn't only Brock's article yesterday that prompted their partners' decisions. This morning had transformed into the exact media nightmare Ryn predicted. Carly's phone lit with alerts every time another news site released a similar story. Every article contained the same mistruths. Six in total so far. And it wasn't yet midday.

She turned her chair and scanned the office. This should have been a regular Friday. Instead, because of her poor judgment in agreeing to the interview with Brock, every team member manned the phones, trying to convince partners, doctors, hospitals, and FDA officials that BioLarge would never release an unapproved product or put patients at risk.

Most of her board members had called with variations of the same advice. *Don't worry, it'll blow over.* What a stupid metaphor. Which would blow over: the negative press coverage, or the company, which felt to her like a boat on the brink of capsizing.

In thirty minutes, she had another meeting scheduled with her largest distributor, and needed to convince them not to bail on BioLarge, but what could she tell them? StackTech was the most-trusted news source in the valley. Of course, people would believe the media over anything she said.

Her phone flashed, and Carly almost groaned aloud. Not another article?

When she glanced at the screen Ryn's number appeared. Carly took her phone to the conference room for privacy.

She kept her voice professional. "Thanks for checking in."

She'd apparently overstepped her bounds last night when she suggested Ryn come back to her apartment after Todd locked her out. That much had been clear from Ryn's curt response.—*Thanks. Sorry I texted you by mistake. Heading to my brother's*—

"How's it going over in damage-control HQ?" Ryn asked.

"As to be expected. Just don't tell me it'll blow over or any other storm-related metaphor." Carly noticed the edge of defeat in the low pitch of her voice. She'd better exorcise the crushed tone before her distributor meeting. She pushed herself to sound more upbeat. "Seriously, we're coping okay. The whole team is pitching in, and the press panel you suggested is booked for Wednesday."

"Yes, but that's not what I was asking. How are *you* doing?"

Carly let the silence sit for a few seconds. Four hours ago, after a full thirty minutes of meditation this morning, she'd arrived at the office fueled with coffee, ready to fight for her company's future. Until Ryn asked, she hadn't realized how much the burden of carrying forced optimism for an entire company, was wearing her down.

"Truth be told, I've had better days. I'm trying to stay positive for my team, but I'm aware I don't have answers to the big question journalists and my distributors keep asking—exactly when our approvals will be complete."

"Of course, you don't. Just fake it."

"Sorry?" Was Ryn suggesting she lie about an FDA approval date over which she held zero power?

"What I'm saying is on a day like this, you're bound to feel as if everything is falling apart. The team takes their cues from you. My advice? Don't lie, except on one thing—fake the confidence until you don't have to."

Just fake confidence. Maybe she could pull that off. Surprising how Ryn's tone seemed so calm, given last night she discovered Todd was selling her house from under her. "What about you, Ryn? How are *you* doing?"

"Super busy today. Among other things, I'm getting a lot of calls from the press about an investment I made in a certain biotech company."

Carly splayed her hands on the conference room table and pushed her fingers into the wood. Ryn's tone wasn't biting. Good that she could joke about the situation, but clearly, she didn't want to get personal. If opening up didn't swing both ways, then Carly had enough to handle here.

She heard Ryn breathe, followed by honking in the

background. "The truth is I'm juggling, but badly. I'm in the car, fitting an unplanned visit to my lawyer between two meetings I can't get out of." Ryn rushed her next words. "And more important, I realized this morning I didn't properly say thank you when you asked me back last night."

Carly smiled. Ryn didn't mean to be abrupt. The woman was coping with a world of crazy and she'd still found time to call her. "Well, if I can help...you know you can ask me, right?"

Ryn sighed, surrounded by more traffic noise. "Thank you. You know, sometimes when we talk, I feel like...kinda like all the right words escape me. But thanks for last night, and well...just thank you."

For what? So far, Ryn kept bailing her out.

They finished their call and Carly welcomed the two distributor executives who'd insisted on meeting with her. The man and woman in black suits had brought copies of several of today's articles and placed the printouts in a stack on the conference room table. After initial pleasantries they launched into the core of what they wanted: to cancel their agreement with BioLarge.

"After today's press," the man who'd introduced himself as head of sales asked, "why should we believe BioLarge's technology will release next year, when these articles say you won't be ready, or worse—you might release an unsafe product?"

Carly took a deep breath, and faked her thousandth smile of the day.

"Well, first, let me assure you we would never release any product which isn't fully compliant with approvals. Those parts of Brock's and the other articles are"—she stared at the pile of paper which sat accusingly in the table's center—"simply incorrect."

What they'd written exceeded incorrect, it was an outright lie. But Ryn warned her last night to avoid using emotional language in these discussions. She kept her tone measured. "In fact, I reached out to Chris Holmes, the head of the FDA this morning"—their eyebrows raised, and she continued—"and I intend to invite him to the keynote we are presenting at South by Southwest in Austin next year."

She hadn't invited Chris Holmes to Austin yet, and she had only managed to talk with his assistant so far, but why not? It proved they were in good graces with the FDA. In fact, if she included the head of the Mayo Clinic and several other prestigious hospitals too, it would show her faith in their launch. She'd make the extra calls today.

"Of course," Carly continued, "I'm sorry to hear you may no longer be part of an elite group of distributors working with our unique technology. I wouldn't wish for you to miss out, but I'll honor your decision. Bob in our finance department can draw up the amendment to terminate our business together before you leave."

Let's see if fake it works. She stood and picked up her phone from the table with an assured smile, ready to end the meeting.

The sales VP stood before she reached the door. "Wait. One moment Ms. Santos, we may have been a little hasty…"

Fifteen minutes later she hid a genuine smile when she showed them to the lobby. They'd accepted her offer of attending South by Southwest as her special guests, with an understanding they'd wait until then before making further decisions. Which was a great plan, except for Carly's complete inability to talk in front of a crowd without freezing. *Way to bet everything on a keynote you have one hundred percent probability of screwing up.*

Ryn's idea made sense in theory, but at some point didn't faking it become reckless captaining, if you actually hit the iceberg?

She crossed the office again and her team studied her, measuring her face as a real-time barometer of company mood. In response she gave a confident I'm-not-concerned smile.

Halfway across the office she stopped by Kiran, one of her engineers, and propped herself on the corner of his desk. Earlier, she'd given him some ideas and asked for his help on shortening an already tight schedule. "How's it coming?"

He pointed at the larger of his two screens. "Been working it all morning. If we double our contractors, and hire a new testing service for smaller code updates, I found a way to save us almost a month."

She resisted the urge to kiss her geeky testing engineer on top of his balding head.

A shadow loomed over Kiran's desk from behind her. "It won't work, Carly."

Similar to during the all-employees meeting, Derrick pronounced her name as a sneer. "The articles have a point. We shouldn't be committing to launch dates we can't control."

She turned toward him, hands on hips. A competent CEO didn't allow someone on her team to constantly undermine her. In fact, if Derrick weren't pivotal to achieving their schedule, she would have fired him by now.

She pointed at the only conference room not visible from the rest of the office, the one where Paul held difficult conversations with employees. Now, she needed to be the leader. She barked her words, drill-sergeant style. "Conference room. Now."

She closed the door behind them and folded her arms. "We've talked about this several times. If you have doubts, we need to address them privately, not in front of the team."

Derrick sat, turned another chair toward him, and put his feet on it. His cheeks lifted into the same smile Todd wore the day he turned up here; the sneaky grin of a man who refused to accept he'd been caught. "I honestly don't know what you're referring to, Carly.

Well, not this time. As Ryn said, Carly had joined the big leagues now. She straightened, so she towered over where Derrick sat. If she was strong enough to ignore the everyday twist in her gut that said she'd never deserve better than a Todd, she was strong enough to demand respect from this man, too.

"Derrick, listen carefully because I will not say this twice. In the past months there have been several incidents where you showed an unacceptable lack of respect..." She delivered the first of four examples, but from his blank expression, she couldn't tell if he even listened.

Her phone flashed on the table. She quickly checked it, assuming one more press article, and noticed the number of Sammy's school.

Dammit. She was living the CEO-Mom version of Groundhog Day. Her gaze bounced from the phone to

Derrick and back.

"I need to take this." She stood and left the room.

Derrick leaned back in his chair and watched through the glass with a smirk while she called the school and the nurse explained Sammy ate no lunch and had a fever.

She turned away from Derrick's gaze, so he didn't see her struggle. No worse day than today to abandon the office, with the press situation room next door. But she didn't have another choice.

She re-entered the conference room and told Derrick they'd pick this up later. He rolled his eyes then stood to leave. The answer to whether he'd been listening was *apparently not.*

Carly clenched her fists before heading out the door. She'd never have taken the CEO job in addition to being a mom, if she'd understood the impossibility of doing both well.

Now Derrick would take her leaving mid-conversation as more proof she could be treated like a pushover—the type of woman who let men like Todd, or Brock, or Derrick, get away with whatever they wanted.

****

Thirty minutes later, Carly dashed into Sammy's school and smoothed her hair before entering the nurse's office.

Sammy huddled on the sofa curled in a small silent ball, only his curls showing to the rest of the room. She leaned over, swept back his hair, and held her hand against his forehead. This was no fake tummy ache. Her baby indeed had a temperature. She'd never seen him this pale, except for last year when he caught the flu.

"Any idea what he has? I came as soon as I could." She hadn't noticed anything wrong at breakfast.

The nurse gave her a withering look. "I think you should make time in your busy schedule to see a doctor."

The warmth of a flush rose up her neck. She grabbed Sammy's belongings. What gave other people the right to judge her parenting? She'd never be perfect, but she did her absolute best.

She drove them straight to the doctor's office. While they sat in the waiting room, with Sammy leaning against her side, her phone flashed another news alert—and a hit of guilt. She stroked Sammy's cheek. If she were honest with herself, she'd been preoccupied this morning, reading the first news article. She could easily have missed his fever.

At least they'd reached Friday afternoon, which meant she could spend the weekend taking care of him, but starting tomorrow, she needed a whole squad of backup child-care options.

She wrapped an arm tight around Sammy and read the latest headline from the largest of the San Francisco newspapers, saying a silent thank you that—as hellish as today had been—having Ryn on her side, and knowing what to expect, had helped.

She stopped reading by the third line and stared at the cheap plastic artwork on the doctor's wall. This article said the company's best chance of survival was removing her as CEO. And part of her still wondered if they were right.

Chapter Seventeen

The orange locksmith van already waited in her driveway when Ryn turned the corner onto her street.

Finally, Friday, although she found it difficult to get excited for a weekend, when it meant sharing space with Todd. Her gut churned as she remembered her lawyer's advice this afternoon. She'd sat in Ms. Lindsay Baxter's leather-and-walnut divorce emporium and listened while her lawyer informed her that—according to the State of California—until Ryn officially gained possession of the house she did not have the right to deny her husband access. Justice is blind and all, but also hellish unfair if she was supposed to just hand him back a key tonight.

The law wasn't Lindsay's fault but the way she delivered the news, in such unsentimental nasal tones with her half-British accent, Ryn wanted to reach across the desk and strangle her own lawyer. Sure, she could move to a hotel, but why should she be the one to leave?

The white FOR SALE sign caught her eye when she turned into the driveway, conspicuous against the brown fence lining the front yard. Ryn pulled up beside the locksmith's van, her calves jittering over the pedals, as she remembered her lawyer's ominous answer to her first question during their meeting. "We're both on the deed. So how could he list the house without my permission?"

Lindsay rubbed her chin. "Well, under normal circumstances you'd be correct. You didn't sign him over a power of attorney at any point, did you?"

Ryn didn't think so. She greeted the locksmith and while he worked, she racked her brain, trying to recall every time she signed anything. Surely she'd remember such an important document? In her recollection they completed only one power of attorney, five years ago. She had traveled to Ireland for a conference, and Todd needed to sign their final mortgage refinance documents on her behalf, but it had only been short-term.

She stepped away from the whirring noise of an electric screwdriver, the hairs on her arms standing straight. All day a question sat in shadows of her mind: What if Todd had prepared for this moment for years?

She could have signed papers without noticing, if he slipped them among the pages of a different document, like those papers before she left for Ireland. Her only priority for tonight was get back inside the house and go through the remaining document boxes she hadn't taken to her lawyer's office in case she missed something.

The whirring stopped. The locksmith stood by the open door, writing a bill. Ryn paid the man, entered, and bolted the door behind her. Usually when she walked into this marble entryway, she took pride in the accomplishments which enabled her to live here, with the massive living room windows overlooking Tiburon and the bay.

Tonight, navy shadows crept up the walls, gathering behind each ornament and statue. She shivered. The downside of the glass frontage. No matter how much she cranked up the heat, this house always felt chilly.

She turned on every light and scanned the matching tones of ivory and steel-gray wallpaper, the white furnishings, the monochrome prints. In comparison to Carly's apartment, full of warmth and love and a rainbow rug, Ryn finally understood the snark during her brother Adrian's visits from San Diego—*My darling sister, you know they sell paint in colors other than Snow Queen White at Home Depot?*

She refused to take décor advice from a man who wore leopard-print loafers with plaid Bermuda shorts, but suddenly the high ceilings and picture windows seemed not stylish, but cold and sharp-edged. Apparently seeing your life through divorce goggles altered everything.

She threw on a pair of jeans and a sweater, and skipped dinner. She needed to rapidly locate those papers. Todd couldn't enter the house unless she gave him the new key, but he might well turn up later.

Her feet pounded on the steps to the garage, where they kept their document boxes. She'd already given every bank or investment statement and their house purchase folder to her lawyer. From what Ryn remembered, nothing but receipts for Todd's business and large electronics purchases remained.

As she carried the last box up the stairway and added it to the pile in the cavernous living room, the contrast with Carly's place wouldn't budge. She wondered who'd really been happier: Carly in her messy, homey apartment with all the love of her cute little boy, or Ryn, working here alone most nights. She didn't know exactly who she'd been trying to impress with this ice-white show house.

She emptied the first two boxes and splayed the papers across the pristine Persian rug. Perhaps she didn't want to fight to live here after all. So long as she got half the proceeds, selling didn't have to be a sign of Todd winning so much as letting herself move on.

As she worked through the papers, Fergus prowled along the corridor from the bedroom and jumped into a box. Todd must have put out food for him; otherwise he would be meowing up a storm. She stopped and petted his neck. At least in there he wasn't in her way, unlike when he lay across her fingers on the keyboard.

After forty minutes she'd flown through all but one box. She shuffled through the last sheaf of papers and discovered a slim white envelope. Inside she found another copy of the documents she'd been hoping for; their mortgage refinance from five years ago. She spread the pages, spotted the notary's seal, reread each line, and sighed in relief. Of course, she hadn't accidentally signed a document giving over her rights. This document clearly showed a duration of one week, when she visited Ireland. She slid the entire envelope into her briefcase.

The doorbell rang. She looked up and Todd's hips stood behind the glass panel in the front door.

Shit shit shit. Now, did she let him in or invite a standoff?

She should have better quizzed her lawyer for specifics on what happened if she didn't open the door. He'd locked her out for twenty-four hours, so she couldn't imagine she'd lose any rights if she told him to return tomorrow.

Todd took several steps back to better see her. He'd wanted that stupid glass-paneled monstrosity of a door installed after they moved in, and she hadn't realized until too late that it was unsafe. Strangers could see their living room from outside. From his angle now, watching through the glass from above her head, the papers spread across the living room floor were on full display. He could also see her sitting here, debating what to do.

She jumped to her feet and stashed her briefcase behind the sofa. The rest of the boxes contained nothing she needed.

He shouted through the door. "You letting me in or not?"

She considered not. Ryn shook her head. "I'm busy. Come back tomorrow."

Todd took a step back from the door. He wagged his finger, as if dealing with a bad-tempered child, and pointed at the glass, then took off his leather jacket and wrapped it around his fist.

He intended to shatter the glass? He seemed too calm, but his face said he meant business. She doubted he'd do it—and weren't those panels double paned?—but according to Lindsay she needed to grant him entry, anyway. The debate was only today versus tomorrow.

Perhaps if she let him in tonight, they might reach a temporary truce and just sell the place. It's not as if either of them benefited from a key-changing death-duel where they both kept a locksmith on retainer.

Ryn took out her phone and poised her finger over it, ready to quick dial emergency services if needed. She walked slowly toward the door and opened it.

Todd pushed past her and entered the living room,

mumbling as he proceeded into the kitchen. "Ten years…first sign of conflict…she just gives up."

Really? Sure, at this point the law couldn't carry her away from him fast enough. But in which alternate universe was he entitled to be mad at her?

He returned with a glass of whisky and sat on the sofa. Ryn walked to the opposite of the room and stood by the marble-topped bar. "You have a lot of nerve being upset at me." Her tone was as calm as she'd hoped. "Luckily for you, I'm considering going ahead with the house sale as part of our divorce. It's a good idea to separate our assets and sell as rapidly as possible."

Todd pointed through the window at the FOR SALE sign outside in the darkness and his face broke into a grin. "Oh, I think you'll find I already did."

Sold without her signature? Impossible. She'd been gone only two nights before the sign went up. Plus, her lawyer would have found out when she talked with the Realtor today. Todd was bluffing. Ryn forced her gaze into an I-see-right-through-you stare. He didn't get the pleasure of scaring her.

"At least the sale got your attention." He stood and strode toward her, his eyes not flashing the anger she expected, but glassy, impenetrable.

She stepped backward toward the bar to put more distance between them. The marble was hard against her back, her hands chilled against the stone. Perhaps she should have lied and told her lawyer Todd had a history of violence, so the court gave only one of them access to the house. She didn't know for sure that a brutal history wasn't one more thing he'd hidden.

He leaned in close and placed his hand on the bar

next to her. "You still don't get it, do you, Ryn? I'm your husband. You're *supposed* to forgive me. For better, for worse." The pores on his nose, inches from her face, smelled of her moisturizer.

He placed a hand on her other side, and memories of helplessness rushed back. Grant pinning her against the wall, his breath against her ear, her blood rushing so fast it pulsed in her wrists.

Except this time, she wasn't helpless or twenty-three years old.

She bulldozed through Todd's arm, registering his flash of surprise. He might want to appear intimidating, but he was the same man she'd slept next to for ten years. The one who worried about his love handles and borrowed her wrinkle cream. He might be an unbridled liar, but she refused to show the fear he clearly wanted, no matter how much her legs shook inside her jeans.

She stomped to the far side of the rug, placing a mini barricade of document boxes between them. "You need to back the hell off. Yes, we are getting divorced, but we can still choose whether to keep it classy." Well, that or she sawed off some of his body parts.

She piled one box onto another. A useless gesture, but it helped her catch her breath. "Me, I'd prefer we close things graciously." A contested divorce involving her Sentra assets was only a little less bloody than the hacksaw option, but only one resulted in a life sentence.

She grabbed her briefcase from behind the sofa. Leaving for a hotel might be smart, but if she left tonight, Todd would believe he'd won. Not a good negotiating position. She remembered their guest suite had a lock. "I'm staying in the guest room."

"Sweet dreams."

She wheeled her suitcase to the spare room, bolted the door, and lay on the bed, waiting for her breathing to calm. A few minutes later, when she'd centered herself, she opened her laptop and emailed Lindsey Baxter. Her lawyer needed to know Todd claimed the house had been sold, even if he was likely bluffing.

Now that she had opened her inbox, she dashed off a few email responses. She wondered how Carly felt, after a complete day of press torture and considered calling her. But with two phone calls in one day, she might think Ryn was checking up on her. Instead, she copy-pasted "I have complete confidence in Carly Santos and the team at BioLarge" several more times into emails asking if Sentra Ventures intended to stick with their investment.

Music drifted from the living room, seeming to get louder as she listened. The catchy tune—half rap, half ballad—sounded familiar. She recognized the melody of their wedding song, the one she and Todd selected for their first dance. A rap ballad was an unusual choice, but it brought her closer to him, knowing he understood her desire not to become a cliché, like couples who danced to Jason Mraz or Bruno Mars.

She rubbed the pain in her chest. How conceited she'd been to judge her marriage better than others. The words of this song felt different now. She'd never listened through the lens of being locked into a relationship with a man you no longer loved, but the lyrics were spine-chilling. Sure, the singer said he'd never let his woman live without him. It never crossed her mind that perhaps he meant it literally.

The boom boom bass-line increased again in volume. The music wasn't only getting louder, but nearer. Todd must have placed the portable stereo right outside the guest room.

She rose from the bed to shout at him to turn it off, but paused with her hand on the door handle. Todd's goal could be to force her outside the room. She looked through the narrow gap between the door and the frame, trying to judge whether he stood waiting on the other side. A tiny slice of the white wall...and a shadow.

She lay on the floor and peered through the crack above the carpet. The stereo's black rubber feet were six inches away. Next to it, Todd's shoes walked away toward the bedroom.

He stopped. His feet turned back toward her door and she held her breath, waiting to see if he returned.

Ryn rolled her eyes and chastised herself for the ridiculousness of lying on the carpet, hiding in her own house. She stood up, making no attempt to be quiet. She was a grown-up professional woman, not an actress on the edge of being disappeared in a "What happened to Ryn?" suspense movie.

The same song restarted. Todd must have set it to repeat. No one could sleep with that racket. Time to quit here and find a hotel. Even if leaving might be exactly what he wanted.

A toilet flushed on the other side of the wall in the master bedroom, which meant Todd no longer stood in the corridor in front of her. If she intended to leave, now would be the moment.

She flung open the door, ready to yell at him to back off. The hallway was empty. She bent, grabbed the stereo, yanked it inside her room, and secured the lock. Heart pulsing, she stood with her back against the wood, and turned off the music. *Great act of bravery there, Ryn.*

She wedged a chair against the door. As if she needed more confirmation, they couldn't continue to share a house, even for one night. She remembered what Carly said yesterday. *You can't change a bully, only escape them.*

That decided it. Tomorrow morning, she'd pack a bag and find somewhere else to live. Likely a hotel to start, while she searched for a temporary apartment, but she'd sleep on the floor of her nieces' room in Palo Alto before she suffered a second night locked in her own guest suite.

She sat on the bed, her pulse still surging too fast to sleep. If there were a television in here she'd flick through random channels or search for a lighthearted movie like Carly suggested, because she sure as hell wasn't going out to the kitchen for Nutella.

She reconsidered calling Carly. It couldn't hurt to touch base with her. Or for Todd to hear Ryn on the phone and understand he didn't succeed in scaring her. She'd be going about her business, having a regular phone conversation.

She texted Carly asking if she could talk and she called right away.

"Hi, Ryn, thanks for checking in again."

"No problem, I just wondered how the rest of the day went." She realized she whispered, like during nights at Aunt Dusty's when she spoke quietly with her school friends, for fear of waking her.

"Well, I wanted to say your advice, the fake the confidence thing, really helped. Thanks."

Ryn raised her volume to show Todd everything was perfectly normal, if he listened. "I thought the answers in your blog post were quite thorough. A good balance of setting facts straight and a non-defensive tone, as one should in these situations."

"Um, is everything okay?"

"Yes, indeed."

"Are you sure? You sound...I dunno, different."

What was Ryn thinking? She didn't want to hold this conversation for Todd's benefit. She walked into the en-suite bathroom. "I'm sorry. Just a weird situation here at home tonight." She closed the door and ran the water, ensuring they weren't overheard. "Carly, I do genuinely want to know how you're doing. Today must have been one hell of a day. You were worried for your team. Feeling any better by the end of it?"

"Yes, although I had to leave early because Sammy has an ear infection. He's running a terrible fever."

"Oh no..." Ryn remembered the kid's sweet grin last night. *Night, Mommy's friend.* "I'm sorry—he must be miserable."

"Yeah, and not so easy being out of the office. Especially since I have so much prep before this press panel on Wednesday."

"Can I help?" Ryn remembered the sense of satisfaction when she left Carly's apartment yesterday evening. And the warmth. Odd to feel safer and more at ease there than in her own house.

"Yes, actually. I realized in a couple of press calls today I need tips on how to avoid saying 'no comment' when you cannot give a direct answer."

"Ah yes, you mean how to avoid sounding either clueless or like you're hiding something? You know what, how about if I come over and help you prepare for those kinds of questions. With Sammy being sick, I could even bring dinner?"

Carly didn't respond immediately and Ryn mentally kicked herself. Did she have so few friends that, when trapped in her guest room, or stuck alone in a hotel for the weekend, the first person she sought comfort from was her husband's ex-mistress? "I'm sorry, that was—"

"—A great idea," Carly said. "Let's do it tomorrow night. You bring food, I'll supply the wine. That means I can spend the day focused on Sammy. How's eight o'clock?"

"Great. I'll see you then." Ryn hung up. From the pause before Carly answered, did she want her to come over or feel forced into it? Ryn hadn't offered her another choice, for example, meeting on Monday at the office. Her normal practice of keeping work relationships at arm's length was so much easier.

She left the bathroom and returned to the bedroom, listening for Todd's next trick.

****

Ryn woke to the rumble of a car engine. Above her head a gray ceiling met ivory-striped wallpaper. To her left the portable stereo sat silent on the bedside table.

The last thing she remembered was lying on her back, trying to guess Todd's location in the house. She must have fallen asleep, because here she lay, fully dressed, on the guest bed.

She sat up and listened. Outside her room, nothing but the squawking of seagulls. The car must have been him leaving. She opened the door and padded across the living room rug to peer at the driveway. Todd's Mercedes had left, and it was not yet eight o'clock. Sometimes he worked Saturdays, so he could be heading to the San Francisco ferry, on his way to his favorite co-working space on Market Street. Or he might have driven to the local café in Tiburon for coffee, which meant he'd be back in ten minutes.

She ran toward the master bedroom and grabbed two large suitcases. Hopefully, she had enough time to pack most of her clothes.

After yesterday, she no longer pictured her future here. It wasn't only Todd playing music to stop her from sleeping. This shrine to success used to be home, but now it felt like part of her past, a role she once played in an upscale movie no longer showing. Staying meant volunteering to continue playing the victim-heroine.

She opened a second suitcase next to the first, throwing in blouses, and scarves. Her phone buzzed where it lay beside the cases on the bed, and Keisha's face flashed across the screen.

Calling on the weekend meant a problem at Sentra.

"Keisha, I'm sorry, not a good time."

"I hear you, but Simon wrote another blog post. Twitter is going crazy…"

"I'm really sorry. I need to call you back later." The fallout from whatever ignorance couched as insight Simon had written now would have to wait. First, she needed to leave and double-check that the papers she found last night from her Ireland trip matched the ones she already gave her lawyer.

Wait. The document boxes. She left them on the living room rug last night. The same rug she walked across five minutes ago to look out the window and verify Todd had left.

She hung up and rushed into the living room. The

ivory rug was spotless. Empty. This must be why Todd played the music. It wasn't a petty act of revenge to prevent her from sleeping, but a ploy to keep her confined in the guest room while he piled the boxes in his car. *But why?*

She sank, and sat cross legged on the rug, pressure rising in her chest. Without coffee her brain moved at syrup speed, but Todd's motivation for stealing a bunch of his business receipts didn't add up.

Unless he had something to hide. Who knew what connections he feared her making with the remaining papers if she'd taken more time to scrutinize them. The pressure in her chest expanded again and she pushed on her ribs and forced herself to exhale. Enough of playing defense. She needed to know what Todd had truly been up to.

She poured food into Fergus' automatic feeder—she'd come and get him in a day or two, as soon as she found a place which allowed pets—and loaded her cases into the car. After driving three blocks she pulled over and called her lawyer's cellphone.

"I know it's the weekend, but I wondered if your firm has a good detective on retainer?"

Chapter Eighteen

Carly tucked a blanket around Sammy, where he sat on the sofa watching a cartoon on his iPad. She leaned in and touched his forehead. At least his fever decreased since yesterday, even if he'd only eaten half the tomato soup she made.

"Almost bedtime, buddy."

"But I've been sleeping all day." He looked up with a pout but didn't stop his video.

She raised an eyebrow and he paused the program. "It's almost over. Can I finish it?" His face lit with a pretty-please grin which gave her hope he might be better before the press panel on Wednesday. Just in case, she'd arranged today for three new babysitters, each with great references, to come over tomorrow, on a Sunday, for interviews.

"Okay, only until it ends." She still had enough time to put him to bed and change her dirty shirt before Ryn arrived. She tidied the coffee table, waiting for SpongeBob to finish his latest adventure.

The show ended, Sammy switched off the iPad, and the doorbell rang. Ryn? If so, she had arrived twenty minutes before Carly expected her. Even with everything going on, the woman still had it together enough to arrive early?

Carly opened the door with the tomato soup stain from Sammy's dinner still smeared across her right shoulder.

Ryn stood surrounded by four bags, one of them too large for food, unless it contained half a pig. "I got us steak, but then I realized I didn't know if you were vegetarian, so I added Thai. But then I wasn't sure if you enjoyed spicy, so there's a Chinese dish, too. Sorry, the steak's likely cold." She rapidly closed the door behind her, as if desperate to lock out the outside world.

Something was wrong. A simple text would have told her Carly's food preferences. And from the way Ryn stood with her back against the door, she was clearly upset. Carly grabbed three of the bags and headed toward the kitchen. Last night Ryn admitted on the phone there had been a weird situation at home, but perhaps it was too personal to inquire exactly what happened. "Everything okay?" she asked, taking the less invasive route.

Ryn followed her to the breakfast bar. "Let's just say, after the last forty-eight hours, I desperately need some wine." She sat on a stool, then continued in a rush. "Truth is, today has been hellish. I moved out, and now I'm staying in a hotel in Sausalito. But can you believe I spent five hours calling temporary apartments, and there aren't any who'll take pets? Apparently, they all consider a single feline to be a destructive Freddie Krueger. I mean, what the hell, when did everywhere become so anti-cat?"

"I'm so sorry, that's gotta suck." Carly gave what she hoped came across as a sympathetic smile, opened a bottle of Pinot, and poured them both a glass.

Ryn glugged, not sipped her wine and Carly smiled. It reminded her of herself when life turned upside down. Except for their first meetings, Ryn gave the impression of being better organized, more confident, more together in general than her. Hard not to wonder if all the women Carly admired for seeming like they navigated life gracefully—like those at Sammy's school who effortlessly juggled the carpool line with charitable board positions and jobs at law firms—were another case of *just fake it*.

She glanced at the sofa where Sammy thought she hadn't noticed him start a new show while hiding under the blanket. She'd always been more of a dog person, but Ryn helped her a lot in the past few days. Perhaps her apartment could survive taking in the cat?

Ryn raised her glass and took a slower sip, this time. "Sorry to rant, I just needed to tell someone. To be honest, except for the cat thing, leaving the house behind is probably positive." She replaced the glass on the counter and looked up at Carly. "When I got back in, every picture on the wall reminded me—what was the word you used the other night?—how gullible I'd let myself become. And then I thought about your wise words that you can't change a person, you can only escape them. That's when I realized staying there meant fighting a battle I didn't even care to win."

"Um, I'm glad what I said was useful." Flattering that Ryn found Carly's words helpful. *But wise?* She leaned into a cupboard and grabbed plates and silverware. She couldn't even compose what to say next. *Good call. At least you got away from him* sounded condescending when Ryn just lost her home.

"Well, hello again, Sammy. I didn't realize you were in there." While Carly's back was turned, Ryn had moved from the breakfast bar to the living room. She crouched at sofa height, holding the largest of the bags.

Sammy sat up, pushed off the blanket, and shook Ryn's hand, grown-up style, while staring at the half-pig sized plastic bag.

"I hear you've been sick?" Ryn said. "I brought you something to cheer you up, but mostly to say thank you for sharing your cookies and your mom last time." Ryn looked at Carly in the kitchen for approval. "That is, assuming your mommy says it's okay?"

Carly nodded, praying Sammy wouldn't spot the red wine and ask why they drank Mommy juice. Ryn was different tonight, more open, but Carly still didn't need her chief investor thinking she tackled her challenges by swigging pinot every night.

Ryn pulled from the bag a massive box with a Transformers truck inside and handed it to Sammy. His eyes lit up, and he slapped his cheeks the way he did when overwhelmed. Thankfully, instead of giving Ryn a slobbery tomato-soup-kiss, he jumped off the sofa, bowed a quick thank-you, and ran out of the room with it.

"Wow, thank you." Carly grinned. She suspected he'd return any minute to show off the rest of his matching collection. Gleeful chatter erupted from the bedroom, proving her wrong. The new truck must be staying to be introduced to Bumblebee, Inferno, and Optimus Prime.

Ryn beamed as if she'd closed the deal of the century. "Guess Transformers are a good choice then?"

Carly's chest warmed. How thoughtful of her to consider Sammy, and moreover to have noted the exact type of toy he loved. She laughed for the first time all week. "Oh, you have no idea how much you nailed it— not just for him, but my own mental health. He's been carrying around that dang starship Todd gave him for a week. It's like a constant reminder of the gullibility you mentioned, but instead of empty patches on the wall this one stalked me from room to room."

Ryn gave a wide-mouthed laugh and raised her glass. "Well, good riddance. To him and the starship. Maybe it could accidentally get lost under the table in a restaurant if Sammy ever remembers it again?"

Carly raised her glass in return. "Indeed. Speaking of restaurants, should we eat before it gets cold?"

Thirty minutes later they'd finished dinner and a bottle of wine between them, opened a second, and Carly gathered pages of notes on deflecting difficult questions. Apparently the trick to avoid answering a difficult question with *no comment* was to flatter the person asking, then answer on an entirely different topic.

"I know you're still worried about next week," Ryn said, "But for what it's worth, I predict the press interaction will go much better, this time. Don't forget Brock wasn't your average interviewer. His whole schtick is to burn female entrepreneurs."

The wine must have made Carly a little light-headed, because an image flashed of Brock standing at the bottom of a pile of wood. She sat atop the stack, tied to a wooden kitchen chair, and in his hand he held a foot-long match. She rubbed her palm across her face.

Ryn watched her over the half-empty food cartons with a confused frown, as if figuring out whether she missed a joke.

"I'm sorry. Strong mental image of Brock attempting to burn me at the stake."

Ryn reached over and patted her hand in a way that

could have been patronizing, if not for the smile spread across her cheeks. "Good. You're not letting the douchebag supreme get to you. I find it helps to make light of these things."

Make light? Carly raised an eyebrow, and they burst out laughing. She realized she grinned from ear to ear. It felt good to let loose. Especially with Brock as the butt of their joke.

Sammy ran around the corner from the bedroom. "Why were you laughing, Mommy?"

"Just a grown-up joke about a not-so-nice person, honey," Carly responded.

"Yup, a nasty man who wasn't nice to your mommy," Ryn added.

Sammy crossed his arms, with a pout. "You mean Todd? Well, I don't like him either."

She looked at Ryn to judge her reaction. Silence filled the space between them for a second before they both chuckled.

"You are so beyond right, honey." Carly excused herself and took Sammy to the bedroom. She settled him to watch one more show, even though it was past his bedtime.

When she returned, Ryn had taken the bottle of pinot and their two glasses into the living room.

Carly refreshed their wine before sitting. "Do you have younger siblings? Just seeing you so relaxed around Sammy, and how you nailed the exact gift…you seem like a natural with kids."

Ryn had been smiling a second ago, but now blinked rapidly, as if trying to avoid reacting to a difficult topic. *Way to go, Carly. Ask her about children mid-divorce.* "I'm sorry, never mind, that was

190

insensitive."

"No, it wasn't. It's just…" Ryn rolled her eyes toward the ceiling. "Remember I said part of why I realized I didn't want to stay in the house was what you said about escaping?"

"Yeah?"

"Well, the other part came from seeing you with Sammy." Ryn ran a finger around the rim of her glass, her gaze now melancholy. "I mean, we're both in a similar situation ending our relationship with Todd, but when I saw the two of you together it brought home that physical things—like a house, for example—are just that. Stuff you can win or lose, but also live without. Whereas, post Todd, you still have a little boy who loves you. A family. It's difficult for me to admit, but it's obvious in many ways you made smarter life choices."

Carly's breath stuck in her chest. How could Ryn be so right and yet so very wrong?

Smart life choices? It was because of her bad choices that Sammy's grandparents still refused to acknowledge his existence, and BioLarge now flailed, purely due to her misjudgment. And yet Ryn also had insight. Even if, in this moment, Carly couldn't find the time she wanted to dedicate to Sammy, they were still the best tiny family in the universe.

She gave Ryn a warm smile, tingling with the realization that sometimes another person brings the exact perspective you need. "Thank you. Although, you give me too much credit. You know, I don't even remember exactly what I said the other night about escaping, but I can guess why I said it. My ex-husband wasn't among my smarter choices. Let's say not the type you'd welcome meeting in a dark alley. When I finally left him, I ended up in my early twenties without an education or any money. Or even moral support, until my Uncle Remy stepped in and bailed me out." And now, to Ryn's point, she had an entire new family, and her chosen close friends and colleagues to be grateful for.

"Speaking of which, would you like us to take your cat, at least until you find somewhere?"

Ryn smiled, although her eyes stayed sad. "What a lovely offer, but I don't intend to lose Fergus. I suspect I'll need his company in the next few months. I just need to find an answer soon."

Carly stood and tidied up the boxes and plates in the dining room. Dev's place would be empty soon. Suggesting he rent his apartment to Ryn would be a much bigger help than taking care of her pet.

"Got any more of those amazing cookies for dessert?" Ryn asked.

While Carly walked to the kitchen, she pondered whether to suggest Dev offer his place. On the one hand, tonight she'd seen a more open Ryn, but on the other it would still be awkward with her living just across the landing. The woman was practically Carly's boss.

She glanced at the kitchen clock. Ten more minutes and she absolutely must put Sammy to bed, especially being sick. But first she hoped to address another work topic. She still hadn't admitted to Ryn that she'd done the equivalent of committing her company to jump off a cliff when she invited everyone to her keynote. Might as well be now, in the more relaxed environment of her living room, than the office.

"So…" Carly twirled her wine stem, after returning with the cookies. "There's one more company thing I need to share. About the launch keynote in March."

"Yes?"

"Paul may have neglected to mention this, but I think we have a risk there. You see, I'm crummy at public speaking. I mean, not just a little stammery. More like get me in front of a big hall of people and I melt down entirely."

She glanced up to judge Ryn's reaction, and found her smiling. "I see why you'd be worried, but CEO stage fright is not unusual: Warren Buffett, Richard Branson, lots of others. Believe me, no one will be judging you on a scale of eloquence from Abraham Lincoln to Obama."

"Richard Branson has stage fright? Maybe there's hope for me yet."

Carly smiled, but guessed her unease must show across every inch of her face, because Ryn's eyes brimmed with the same compassion as earlier, when Carly shared her history with Kyle. "Listen, we all have parts of our job that don't play to our strengths. This isn't something I'd normally share—in truth, I haven't told anyone other than Todd—but you know how VCs are supposed to effortlessly reject investment proposals, because it's just business?"

"Yeah?"

"Well, with a few entrepreneurs, like you, the genuine idealists passionate to change the world, I hate rejecting them so much I'd excuse myself from the meeting and go to the bathroom."

Carly squinted, trying to balance the compliment with her lack of understanding. Ryn suffered from gastro issues?

"On the way, I'd grab the flask from my drawer, and in the bathroom, I'd slug two shots of tequila for strength, then write how shitty I felt on a piece of paper on my desk and stuff it into a jar—before I told them I'd decided not to fund their company."

"Really?" Ryn had indeed dropped the *just fake it* façade tonight, because Carly could no more imagine her throwing an entrepreneur off a building than slugging firewater in a bathroom stall. She met Ryn's gaze and gave an understanding nod. This successful woman, who managed millions, at times felt just as vulnerable as her.

Ryn's lips met in a wistful smile. "Yup, truly. Although I'm afraid these days I don't need the tequila, because I've evolved into an investing machine." She chuckled in a way that seemed forced. "A machine unencumbered by emotions, or a husband and family, who on pitch day Mondays, can easily reject six to eight teams."

Her eyes were so full of regret Carly wanted to reach out and hold her hand, an entirely inappropriate gesture, and tell her what Uncle Remy used to say: it's never too late to become the person you want to see in the mirror.

Instead, she raised her glass. "Thank you for sharing. I guess we do the best we can to cope with what life throws at us?"

Ryn clinked with her, strong enough to send red wine spilling onto the coffee table.

Carly grabbed a cloth from the kitchen and mopped up the spill. She wondered, having consumed this much wine, if Ryn still intended to drive home. Carly glanced at the clock while rinsing the cloth in the kitchen sink. She didn't want to kick her out, but Sammy had been up an hour past his bedtime.

Ryn entered the kitchen and placed the empty wine bottle on the counter. "You know, Carly, for the keynote, if you'd like, I'll personally commit to help you rehearse in the evenings in the run up to it. As often as it takes."

"Wow. That's really nice of you." Her instincts said to accept Ryn's generous offer. And if Ryn wanted to help Carly, why wouldn't she do the same and propose Dev's apartment?

"Why don't I tidy up the food while you put Sammy to bed?" Ryn must have noticed her glancing at the clock.

Carly grinned. "Okay, that's great. Then maybe, when you're ready, we can call you a car?"

Ryn nodded and Carly headed to the bedroom. Sammy sat on top of the covers, leaning against the wall, nodding off. But he still wouldn't allow her to skip his bedtime story. When they settled under the blankets, he picked his favorite book. He looked up at her, those chestnut eyes wide, even when sleepy. "Mommy, is Ryn like the donkey and you're the chicken?"

A dull thud-thud sounded in the living room—Ryn tidying up?—and it took Carly a second to refocus on the question. Sammy must mean she always felt scared, fearful of how one more mistake might ruin everything for them. Deep for a five-year-old.

She noticed the image he pointed at on the first page and chuckled, remembering she had it reversed; the chicken in the story was proud and the donkey afraid. "You mean are we different, but still friends, like these guys are"—she tapped the picture in the book—"by the end of the story?"

"Well, duh, Mommy." Sammy rolled his eyes and Carly chuckled. Strange to realize she actually liked the idea of her living next door. Although, she didn't know if Ryn would feel the same way.

"You know, little guy, I don't know yet. Let's wait and see what happens."

Sammy snored before she reached the end of the book. When she returned from the bedroom, Ryn wasn't in the kitchen. Instead, low voices came from the dining room.

She turned the corner and found Dev sitting at the table with Ryn, chatting as if he'd been catching up with a long-lost friend. He beamed a teeth-forward smile at Carly, "I can't believe, when you talked about Ryn, it never once occurred to me we'd met earlier. Twice, in fact, at startup events when she was at her old firm. Although I didn't make the connection between Ryn and Kathryn."

Carly stepped up to them and smiled when Dev poured her more wine. This felt surreal, to realize they knew each other, but also fun. "So this makes my task easier."

"What's that?" Dev asked, as he walked around the table and pulled out a chair. Before Carly sat, he hugged her close and whispered, "You didn't tell me the wife in your little love triangle is quite ravishing."

She jerked away, embarrassed that Ryn might have heard Dev's comment, but she seemed relaxed, calmly sipping her wine on the other side of the table.

"Wait until you hear what we were talking

about…" Ryn said.

Dev returned to sit in his own spot and finished her sentence. "Tips to help you with your stage fright. Including the age-old 'imagine your audience naked.'"

"I find that it helps to mentally add bows, too," Ryn said, smiling at Carly. "In a rainbow of colors. Then when someone in the audience asks a question, I remember he's the guy with the mustache up top and the pink polka-dots down below."

Ryn and Dev laughed loudly, and Carly joined in, amused to see the way Dev's head tilted toward Ryn. She wasn't his usual type—brunette, busty, and lacking in IQ—but Carly couldn't help but notice the genuine smile he offered.

"Speaking of getting naked…" Dev said, facing Ryn again with a mischievous grin.

Carly almost spit her wine on the table. If he indeed flirted, he was being unusually unsubtle.

"…perhaps you can settle a point on which my best friend here"—he pointed a thumb at Carly—"refuses to give me the time of day. I keep telling her the best way to get over heartbreak is climb back on the horse."

He took his phone out and pulled up a photo. "A friend of my sister's. He's a scientist, like Carly. Worthy of a date or not?"

Carly glowered at him. Did Dev have to embarrass her? Perhaps she and Ryn were becoming friendly, but they needed to work together, and the situation still felt raw.

Ryn took the phone Dev offered, but her smile disappeared. She side-glanced at the screen, before handing it back. "Cute, I suppose, but I suspect, from our earlier conversation, that Carly and I both have higher-order priorities than dating."

She gave Carly a small smile and a nod, and Carly nodded in return. Nice answer.

"So, Dev," Carly said, "what I wanted to say is it's good you came over. I know you weren't going to bother renting your place, but I may have found the perfect tenant." She raised a palm toward Ryn. "She's responsible yet fun, trustworthy, and travels with one well-behaved cat."

Ryn's eyes widened, clearly surprised by the suggestion. Dev leaned in across the table with a grin. "Well, sure. Anything for Carly. Plus, I mean you're both divorcing the same jerk, right?"

Ryn's mouth opened, but she said nothing for a moment. Her gaze focused on Carly, not Dev. "That is, why, it's the nicest offer, but..." She stared at the tablecloth, a small frown creasing her brow. "I don't think it's a great idea." She squeezed her fingers together on top of the table. "You know, investor impartiality and so on..."

"Okay, never mind, just a random thought." Carly's voice carried a note of disappointment she hadn't intended. Although seriously, *impartiality?* Perhaps Ryn should spend more time worrying about the husband trying to sell her house from under her and less about those just trying to help.

"And saying that, I should probably get going." Ryn turned to Dev. "Is the offer of a ride still open?

"Sure. Ready to go?"

"Yup. And, Carly, good luck with the press thing on Wednesday. I know you're going to knock it out of the park."

Carly said goodbye, closed the door behind them,

and tidied away the wineglasses. Goodness, she struggled to understand Ryn. Carly would have sworn earlier tonight, with her being so vulnerable, she needed a friend. Guess that was one more misjudgment.

Chapter Nineteen

The tingly dry taste of stale red wine lingered on
Ryn's tongue when she woke on Sunday. She smiled,
remembering last night at Carly's place. They say you
can judge a person by the friends they choose, and
during the drive back Dev had been charming, and
made her laugh most of the way. In an alternate
moment, she might be drawn to those long lashes and
that wry British sense of humor.

She threw her head back on the pillow. God, it had
been good to open up to Carly in a way Ryn would not
normally risk doing with colleagues. She laughed more
last night than in months.

The one part she'd change was Carly's
disappointed expression when Ryn turned down her
offer of Dev's apartment. Why had she instantly
rejected the offer? She'd dismissed the idea of them
being neighbors without even considering it. Which
made limited sense given today she faced the
unenviable task of sneaking back into her own house—
hopefully avoiding Todd—in order to feed Fergus.

She dressed, left the room, and took the elevator to
the hotel restaurant for breakfast. When she declined a
third cup of coffee, it hit her how insensitive her answer
to Carly must have sounded, talking about impartiality.
She'd never questioned the wisdom of her first boss's
advice to draw a hard line between her professional and

private lives. But she and Carly were well past those type of boundaries even being relevant.

When Carly admitted her terror of public speaking, Ryn had truly wanted to help. She deserved to conquer her fear. Pops might have said Ryn was stronger than average, but Carly must be the most resilient person she'd met. She'd left an abusive ex, created a family by herself, and founded a company destined to save thousands, if not millions of lives. And she just spent her Saturday night preparing for a work event, with her sick son in the next room.

If anything, Carly's achievements showed that keeping personal and professional unconnected was a pipe dream, because she'd become valuable, in a way Ryn didn't know if she could ever be.

As she headed back to her room to grab her car keys, she considered whether the belief she'd inherited from Pops—you're *stronger than the rest of us*—had influenced her in ways that were not so positive. What he meant during her teen years was don't rely on him to be there to love her. Find your own happiness, because depending on others makes you weak. But she never agreed with his perspective.

The hundreds of women she helped with advice to find funding or succeed with their companies weren't weak. Just as Carly wasn't weak because she'd asked for help. Quite the opposite; she demonstrated true bravery signing up for something that terrified her.

But apparently, a part of Ryn still believed in offering, but not accepting help. She couldn't think of another explanation for not giving Carly's proposal even a second's consideration. When she stepped back to think on it, living next door to someone who gave a damn about her sounded pretty good.

Luckily, she knew exactly how to make it up to her. Ryn had scheduled another event on Wednesday morning, but she'd cancel it and attend the press panel to show her support.

She texted Carly and said thanks for last night, and called a taxi to go pick up her SUV. Then she said a quick prayer that while feeding Fergus, she wouldn't have to face another showdown with Todd.

Chapter Twenty

The walnut paneled door to her lawyer's office opened and Ryn shifted in her seat in the waiting area. Lindsay declined to say on the phone why she insisted Ryn meet at the most inconvenient time: the middle of a Tuesday afternoon.

In Ryn's experience with corporate lawyers only bad news required an in-person visit. Was it possible the detective already learned something in only a few days?

A man wearing thick glasses exited her lawyer's office and took a seat opposite her. Likely another heartbroken spouse completing his divorce paperwork.

Ryn turned her attention to her laptop and juggled the next set of email responses. After spending time with Carly on Saturday, she'd decided enough with the shame and this morning she took Keisha out for coffee and let her know about the divorce. Thank God she did, because Ryn couldn't risk telling Simon that Sentra's assets might become involved, so Keisha had offered to cover for her this afternoon, as if Ryn were at any other off-site meeting.

The door swung open again and Ryn's heart beat a few strokes faster. Lindsay nodded at the man across the waiting room and motioned for Ryn to enter. She took the seat opposite her lawyer's desk and listened while she reviewed the disclosure process, explaining what papers needed to be filed in which order. Lindsay's accent, part harsh Boston, part fake British English, still grated on her. As if her lawyer had attempted to rid herself of her original twang and instead ended up sounding like an actor in a cheesy British comedy. "As I said last time we met, we filed papers disclosing your assets and asked Todd to do the same..." This review of material they'd previously covered couldn't be why she needed Ryn to come so urgently.

She studied the room, which smelled of musty papers and heartbreak. Two boxes of Kleenex sat within reach on either side of the expansive desk. Ryn felt luckier than most who'd sat in this walnut hellhole and grabbed for those tissues. No matter what, she remained one of the most respected female leaders in the Valley. Her phone buzzed, and she glanced at the incoming text. Keisha sharing that she intercepted Simon on his way to Ryn's office.

"Ahem."

Her lawyer stopped her lecture and waited for Ryn to pay attention. She stashed her phone under her thigh on the chair. "Sorry about that. Just work stuff." Her behavior might be rude, but couldn't Lindsay just get to the point of this meeting? This must be how it worked when someone charged by the hour.

"Ms. Brennan, what I'm trying to make you understand is we may have issues, a reason not to believe Todd's disclosures on his assets, if and when he submits them."

No shit, Sherlock. "I agree. That's why I'm hoping the detective will figure out what we're missing. Is there any news?"

A flash of annoyance crossed Lindsay's face. She turned to the table behind her and grabbed a stack of red, green, and yellow folders. "I'm going to assume you understood what I explained so far because it's important context."

Ryn considered how impolite it would be to grab the folders off the desk, rather than wait for what promised to be a lengthy explanation, but her lawyer's hands rested on top of them. "These are from the investigator. And I'm glad you requested we assign him, because this is among the more unusual situations I've encountered."

Issues. An unusual situation. Why could lawyers never speak plainly?

Lindsay handed her the yellow folder. "This is the original power of attorney you gave me from five years ago, when you refinanced your house."

Ryn opened the folder, recognizing the same document she signed giving Todd power of attorney during her Ireland trip. She scanned the pages. The dates showing it lasted only a week were highlighted in pink.

Her lawyer pushed the green folder across the desk. "This, on the other hand, is the power of attorney used to list your house for sale. I know the Realtor, and she's meticulous with her paperwork. She had no problem providing me with a copy, as your lawyer."

Ryn flipped through the second set of documents. The text on the pages resembled standard power of attorney language, similar to the first document. No, wait a minute, the exact same…except for the date.

She spread the two sets of papers across the desk and glanced from one to the other. Her signature had always been a scrawl; no two were ever alike. But the signatures on these documents were identical, down to the out-of-place ink dot hovering above the last 'n' in Brennan.

How underhanded. Todd altered the dates to list the house for sale without her permission. She swallowed, trying to source saliva for her dry mouth, before stating the obvious. "This one's fake."

"You didn't sign this second document then, Ms. Brennan?"

"Of course not. That's my signature, but you can clearly see they're the same document with the date changed."

The lack of emotion in Lindsay's eyes reminded Ryn of her own poker face during difficult contract negotiations. Not letting your emotions show must be a useful skill set for divorce lawyers, too. She swallowed again. She suspected that, similar to herself, lawyers became calmer as conflict escalated.

If so, her lawyer had terrible news to deliver.

"This is where our problem starts," Lindsay said. "This power of attorney was not only used to put your house up for sale. It has shown up in other transactions."

Ryn's stomach twisted. The red folder, still on her lawyer's desk looked fuller. It held several documents. Multiple *transactions.* She glanced around the office, wishing she had water, but not wanting to delay discovering what was in there.

"Take a few minutes to review those to get a handle on the situation, and I'll come back with the detective to answer your questions."

Ryn nodded but didn't speak. She couldn't wait a

moment longer to see what they'd discovered. The second Lindsay left the room, she grabbed the red folder and flipped it open.

The first set of papers was the same fake power of attorney, but with a different date, this time used for a loan against her house. She read the amount and blinked a few times, expecting to find that in reading too fast, she accidentally added a zero.

This represented the entire equity in their home. If this loan was outstanding, there'd be no value left to split between her and Todd. After their divorce she'd have nothing other than the assets tied to her job at Sentra Ventures.

Surely, he couldn't borrow money against their house without her permission. She leaped to her feet, her blood firing, and chest burning. But where would she go? The answers were coming momentarily. She sat and breathed into the panic.

This couldn't be right. Todd didn't need extra money. His business had grown so rapidly he struggled to onboard employees fast enough. He took frequent trips to Nevada to keep up with the expansion of new development projects. Although now she knew at least some of those trips were only an excuse to stay with Carly.

Oh shit. She struggled to focus her vision on the door her lawyer had left ajar. What if nothing Todd told her about his business had been true? It wasn't as if they combined their taxes: with her complicated investments, they'd always filed separately. And his company was private. Sure, she'd met his accountant a couple of times, but it wasn't like she had any reason to inspect his company's profit and loss statements.

How could she have been so stupid? In reality her perception of his stellar success was built only on what he told her, plus a few tweets and press releases. His business wasn't growing in leaps and bounds. For all she knew he was drowning in debt. Or bankrupt.

She rifled through the rest of the papers, the throbbing of her heart threatening to overwhelm her focus. The next pages contained five different real estate transactions, all in Nevada. All through corporations listed with Ryn's name.

Using her name to buy properties. What the hell was Todd up to?

Her lawyer reentered with the man wearing thick glasses from the waiting room. "Ms. Brennan, meet Mr. Hopper."

Ryn had always imagined detectives in leather jackets and jeans, not a crisp suit and tie. He took a chair, next to her, and launched into a description of his qualifications, his time helping the FBI. Now she understood, he was a forensic accountant: the type who specialized in finding hidden assets.

"The key to my methodology is I start by looking at shell companies…"

"Mr. Hopper, thanks for the explanation of your approach." Ryn struggled against the blood pounding in her eardrums to hold her polite voice. "But can we please talk about what these documents mean. How screwed am I here? Can Todd take a loan against our house without me agreeing? Do I now own property in Nevada?"

He leaned in toward Ryn, kind lines creasing his forehead. "Ms. Brennan, I understand your concern, so let me explain. What you are looking at are deeds for several development projects in Las Vegas. From what I've found so far, after researching with the Clark County registrar this morning, you were on the title of four apartment buildings. I also found documentation showing you were on the advisory board for two larger developments. I've not had much time, so I cannot promise this to be a complete list."

Ryn flipped through the papers again. "I own these?" Maybe he had good news to deliver after all.

"I'm afraid not," said Mr. Hopper. "Each of these properties was originally purchased in your name, but you've since been removed from the titles. However, I fear the larger problem is these transactions have the hallmarks of a straw buying scheme."

"Straw buying? Isn't that a type of..." The pounding in her chest sped up. She hesitated to say the word *fraud*. As a venture capitalist Ryn managed other people's money for a living. She couldn't afford to be implicated in financial wrongdoing. The slightest whiff of impropriety would be enough to demand her resignation as a venture firm partner.

"Yes, it's a type of fraud where the identity of a person with good credit is used, sometimes without their permission. Often with the goal of requesting mortgages or driving up the value of new-build properties."

Fraud.

Ryn's breath froze in her throat. She feared an exhale might mean accepting what Mr. Hopper said. The blood took over her vision, the room blurring. If Todd's fraud was discovered, if she became associated with it, she'd lose her reputation. Her assets. Her career.

A whirlwind of every inch of her own stupidity

assaulted her, tearing at the inside of her head, her ears, her chest. This was why Todd picked her. It wasn't only her connections in the Valley. She had assets, great credit, and a reputation to leverage in his deals. The perfect persona to front a fraudulent real estate company.

Now she understood why he took every document that might lead her to one of his companies. "Am I at risk here? I mean, for criminal charges?"

The detective gestured toward Lindsay. Legal advice was her domain, not his, but from the way he straightened his tie and glanced at the door, as if his turn had come to leave, the answer must be yes. Ryn pushed back and stood, stumbling from her chair. The walnut-paneled walls threatened to close in and swallow her.

Lindsay said nothing while the detective headed out the door, and closed it behind him as if they'd rehearsed this moment. She sat behind her desk and studied Ryn's face, measuring her response to the news. Perhaps her wording earlier had been deliberately vague because she wanted to see Ryn's reaction. Meaning her own lawyer thought her a criminal?

"Ms. Brennan, I need to ask you, and you can be brutally honest with me because we have attorney-client privilege. Were you aware of these transactions?"

"No. Absolutely, positively not."

"Please sit. I didn't think so, but I still needed to hear you say it."

Ryn staggered backward, but shook her head, refusing to sit. Lindsay left and brought a tray with a pitcher and poured two glasses of water while Ryn calmed her urge to storm out. She downed half the glass and paced away from the desk, then returned, trying to organize the question mayhem in her head. Could she be found guilty of fraud even if unaware Todd used her identity?

For sure, she'd lose her job in a heartbeat if this came out, whether guilty or not. And after giving up her house, her job was all she had left. Did she spend her entire career building a reputation that might vanish in an instant?

"Are you absolutely sure it's fraud?" Ryn asked.

Her lawyer refilled her glass with a sympathetic smile. "Please sit down."

Finally, the microdose of empathy Ryn wished she'd possessed since their first meeting. She hired Lindsay Baxter because her references described her as efficient and unsentimental, someone who never backed away from a fight. But Ryn never imagined the fight would be for her reputation. Or to stay out of prison.

"I recommend you contact a criminal defense attorney. Here's one I trust." Lindsay pushed a business card across the table. "He's a colleague at another firm, but we can work together."

Criminal? Ryn sat, picturing herself on the witness stand in front of a full courtroom. *Ms. Brennan, did you or did you not own these properties? Is this or is it not your signature?*

Her lawyer pointed at the card. "Hiring additional counsel is a defensive measure. I discussed the details with Mr. Hopper regarding what he found in Nevada, and we can't yet, with certainty, prove it's fraud or even what type. That's why I want your permission for him to keep digging. Also, the longer you can avoid your husband being aware of what we've discovered, the better." She replaced the documents in their folders on her desk as if to wrap up their meeting.

That's it. Welcome to the possibility of losing your house, your job, and going to jail, Ms. Brennan. *Appointment over?*

Ryn had to exercise restraint not to scream her next words. "Of course Mr. Hopper has my permission to search for more, but I need to understand the next steps. Do we alert the police? But then…if this investigation becomes public, you do realize I'll lose my entire career?"

"I'm afraid that exceeds my purview as a family law specialist. Talk to the criminal attorney, but unless he differs, I think we'd benefit from letting Mr. Hopper gather a fuller picture. Also, on the topic of your house…" Her lawyer continued to explain that if they received offers, Ryn might want to consider taking one and paying off the loan. The other option would be to take on a court case with the mortgage company and prove the loan illegitimate.

She focused on a silver handle on one of the drawers behind her lawyer's desk. A court case with a mortgage company sounded like an expensive and losing battle.

At this moment only Ryn, the detective, and Lindsay knew of Todd's fraud. She worried that continuing to investigate might increase the risk of it becoming known more broadly and Ryn losing her job. But then, what other choice did she have?

****

Outside, Ryn's thoughts circled as fast as those gulls over the parking lot. Perhaps she should proactively talk to Simon, given that the firm's reputation could be at risk from any association with fraud; especially true once Ryn became senior partner next week, with more control of their funds. And her lawyer advised her to avoid telling Todd she knew. But if she ran into him just once at the house feeding Fergus, he'd read it on her face.

She drove toward the office, her brain stuttering, scrambling, swirling. A screech of tires to her left told her she'd driven through a red light.

She pulled into the nearest parking lot and grasped her shaking hands together. How dumb to worry just three nights ago that living next to Carly would mean her personal and professional lives colliding—when her career already teetered on the precipice of ruin because of the man she'd been fool enough to marry—and she just wasn't aware.

Carly might be the one person in the universe who'd understand how Ryn got herself into this fiasco, because Simon sure as hell wouldn't. He hated anything that put Sentra's reputation at risk. Best case, he'd ask her to step back from the senior partner job and take a leave of absence. Worst case he'd demand she quit the firm immediately.

She leaned her head on the steering wheel, trying to catch her breath. She was stuck. She couldn't come clean with Simon, or even tell the authorities, until she understood the details of what Todd had done and how deeply she'd been implicated.

The only elements she controlled in this situation were getting more legal help and making sure she moved somewhere fast, so she didn't risk running into Todd each time she returned and fed Fergus. If she'd just accepted the offer to move into Dev's place, she wouldn't even be worrying about the second one.

If Carly welcomed her as a neighbor, she had no reason not to say yes. All her carefully constructed approaches to keep her life in order had already failed. So what was she trying to protect herself from? Friendship?

She hated what that said about her. How pathetic that the person she believed a month ago she had every reason to hate was now her closest thing to a friend.

Chapter Twenty-One

Carly sat in her car in the parking lot of the Santa Clara Marriott, where the press panel started in fifteen minutes. A more experienced CEO might be in there working the room, meeting and greeting the attendees. But Sandra, her marketing manager, recommended not arriving too early to avoid being cornered by the journalists before she gave her presentation. So instead, here she sat, reliving last night's nightmare.

In the dream, she'd been onstage for this panel, with journalists arranged in rows in front of her, but when she looked up from the podium, instead of facing twelve people she stood in front of thousands. The room had morphed into the massive conference hall for the South by Southwest keynote in Austin. And she stood frozen onstage, with no inkling of what she just said or what came next. Half the audience sniggered and those in the front row took furious notes, documenting whatever idiocy she had uttered.

The sheets were drenched in sweat when she woke at five, convinced she'd made an irrecoverable mistake when she bet the company's future on the Austin keynote.

She took a breath and banished the you're-a-fraud banshee screaming in her ear. How would Ryn deal with a big goal like recovering from BioLarge's terrible press? *One step at a time.* Like she said on Saturday,

Carly had every reason to feel good about today's panel. She knew the answers to the most likely questions, and she'd studied the profile of every journalist. If anything, she risked sounding too rehearsed, as if she over-cribbed an online dating profile. *Hi, you must be Matt and I believe you're from Milwaukee, went to Northwestern, write on the topic of med tech, and enjoy experimental theatre and fondue.*

A hand rapped on the window and Carly jumped in her seat.

Ryn stood next to the car, wearing a navy suit, red scarf, and a thrilled-to-be-here grin. Carly lowered the window. "I thought you had another thing you needed to be at today?"

"I did, but you're more important. I reckoned it couldn't hurt to offer a little moral support?"

Carly opened the door and exited the car, a warm tingle spreading across her chest and shoulders. She hugged Ryn. How kindhearted of her to cancel an appointment and be here, just for her.

When she stepped back, Ryn looked inside the car, as if confused. "I'm sorry, are you waiting for someone? Aren't you starting at ten?"

"Yes, but avoiding getting cornered."

"I hear ya. Well, let's go in together."

"Can't hurt for the journalists to see me walk in with one of the best-known investors in the Valley, right?"

Ryn's eyes crinkled, clearly flattered by Carly's words. "Probably not. But truth is I don't think you need me. I just wanted to see you meet my prediction of doing great."

They walked in side by side, matching strides

across the expansive lobby. When they pushed through the double doors of the Grand Pacific ballroom, Carly relaxed her shoulders. The room setup was nothing like the combative White House press conference she imagined. Instead, four tables were arranged to form a small square in the center of the hall. As they walked across the sea of beige carpet, she made a note to thank Sandra for the more casual setup, even if this cavernous ballroom, with its glistening chandeliers, better fit an awards ceremony than a small question-and-answer group.

Ryn took a seat on one side of the square close to Sandra, while Carly made her way around the tables, greeting each journalist by name and making small talk using the profiles she'd studied.

The three doctors she'd invited sat on the presenters' side of the square. She moved along the row, greeting each of them, praying Derrick was wrong in the email he sent this morning—copying the entire company—where he questioned her decision to include them. As medical experts who didn't work for BioLarge, she wanted the doctors to explain how they'd applied the technology in their hospitals. But after Derrick's email she realized that could also be a problem: they didn't work for BioLarge. When she called Paul to ask his opinion, he agreed that inviting them was a risk because she couldn't control what they said under pressure.

"Nice suit." The voice came from behind Carly. A whisper but weighted with sarcasm.

She turned to face Brock Gordon's self-satisfied smirk and her stomach clenched. He hadn't been invited.

She searched for Sandra who handled the invites. She circled the table, handing out information packets. Carly took a breath before turning to Brock. He would *not* derail her. She prepared for this panel, and she knew her stuff.

"Please take a seat." He'd just have to sit and listen like any other journalist.

She pivoted back toward the doctors, but as she turned the edge of her heel caught on the carpet. Her palms landed with force on the back of Dr. Nichols, an elderly cardiologist from Reno. He pitched forward, and his water glass tipped over his papers, the floor, his lap.

Everyone around the table turned toward the commotion. Carly straightened and checked to see whether her heel had broken. No, it hadn't. She was just a klutz. Dr. Nichols shook the water off his pants and Sandra ran up with a stack of napkins. Carly bent over him. "I am so sorry. My heel caught on the carpet. Are you all right?"

He turned and gave her a kind grandpa of a smile before he took the napkins and dabbed at his pants. "It's really okay, dear. Shall we get started?"

From across the table Ryn mouthed *Are you okay?* and Carly smiled back, then patted kindly Dr. Nichols on the back. "I'm fine if you are."

She walked to her seat, the entire group watching each of her steps. The panel hadn't even begun, and already she reinforced the journalists' impression that what BioLarge's reputation needed saving from might be its CEO.

When she reached her own seat alongside the doctors, Sandra walked up and whispered in her ear.

"I'm sorry, he swapped in for the other journalist I invited from StackTech, without asking. But everyone's here, so we should start."

Carly arranged her papers and looked across the table. Brock had taken the open seat directly opposite her. *Just great.* What did Ryn call him again the other night—oh right, douchebag supreme. Beyond rude of him to turn up without an invitation, but it fit the profile.

She started her presentation and completed the product overview section without stumbling once. This was her domain, the tech side. When she looked up, Ryn gave an encouraging smile, then without her hands lifting from the table, an ever so subtle double thumbs up.

Carly turned and introduced the first expert speaker, a middle-aged cardiologist with salt and pepper hair, who reminded her of George Clooney. "Let me present the renowned Dr. Gregory Dolan from the Mayo Clinic, who will share his experience with the clinical tri—"

"Ahem." A hand tapped the table opposite, interrupting before she could hand off to Dr. Dolan. Her stomach dropped. Brock raised his arm straight up in the air, with the same smirk.

He lowered his hand and leaned toward Carly. "Okay but seriously...too much blah, blah, blah. Of course, your product is wonderful. It probably slices bread and drives your car, too. Welcome to Silicon Valley. You can't finish your piece without covering the question everyone wants to know. How can you be talking launch if you don't know exactly when you'll receive your FDA approvals?"

She squeezed her hands together under the table. Launch timing was the one question she had practiced how to avoid answering. She just hadn't expected it to come from him again. She snuck a quick look at Ryn, who nodded toward Brock, then rolled her eyes heavenward, as if to say: *Here he goes again. Douchebag supreme with extra cheese.*

Carly leaned in across the table, mimicking his aggressive stance, but with a polite smile instead of his scowl. "As I said during my presentation, it's the FDA, not any Silicon Valley CEO, who control the timing of clearance and approvals for medical devices. The most important thing is patient safety, and I'm sure you understand why none of us wants to rush that. So it's not a question I can give you a definitive answer on today."

She didn't wait for his response. "With that, let me reintroduce Dr. Dolan to start our field presentations and share his experience on the clinical trials."

A few minutes later Brock leaned in again, his gaze focused on Carly, not the doctor. He started to raise his hand, clearly intending to cut off her guest, again.

She waited for the end of the doctor's next sentence before stepping into a gap. "Brock, just a reminder for you and everyone else that we've allowed plenty of time for questions at the end, so please hold them for that section of the agenda." She gave a smile and a regal nod to the room, then wiped the beads of sweat behind her neck.

Brock scowled at her, but the rest of the journalists took notes on what the doctor explained. He would look like a total jerk to everyone in the room if he interrupted again.

Before the conclusion of the doctor's presentation Brock stood, grabbed his bag, and headed out the door, passing surprisingly close to Carly's side of the table and glaring at her. A vague waft of whisky hit her as he strode by.

She breathed a huge sigh of relief and noticed Ryn's smile, too.

They continued with the presentation and finished the question-and-answer session. She thanked the journalists and was about to thank the speakers when Dr. Dolan interrupted her. "If you don't mind, there's one thing I came here to say today that I haven't yet shared." His eyes saddened. "Part of why I volunteered my hospital to participate in the trials is I lost my wife because of cardiac problems four years ago. She was only forty-seven."

Carly's chest twinged. Forty-seven. Even younger than Uncle Remy.

"I bring up her death not for sympathy, but because she had a highly unusual heart condition, and if BioLarge's diagnostic tool had existed back then, we would have been alerted in time." He rose up on his toes and leaned forward. "So when I see articles in the press arguing about the wisdom of a CEO pushing to bring a solution to market that could have saved her life, you cannot imagine how much that infuriates me. It doesn't matter whether their final product approval arrives in March, October, or three years from now. What matters is when it's ready and approved, it'll prevent deaths like my Maggie."

He sat, and Carly watched him dab delicately at his eye with his shirt sleeve, wishing it were appropriate to walk over and hug him. She looked and noticed Ryn's eyes had softened, and she subtly rubbed the back of one hand across the top of her cheek.

Carly blinked away the moisture in her own eyes and offered up a proud smile. In the past months she'd lost her sense of perspective. Her inspiration for this technology came from not wanting others to be stolen so young from their families. Years ago—before agreeing to become CEO, or the Austin keynote, or before she even met Todd—she'd been all about the science. When did she let that change?

After Carly thanked everyone, Ryn approached while she gathered up her papers.

"I know you're probably anxious to tell your team the good news, but can we talk, just for a minute?"

They returned to the lobby and took a seat on a sofa next to the massive hotel-sized arrangement of calla lilies.

Ryn leaned in toward her. "First off, you should give yourself more credit. I'm amazed how nothing fazed you in there. Maybe try to box the memory for the next time you feel nervous about speaking?"

Carly chuckled, sensing that same tingling in her arms, gratitude that Ryn had gone out of her way to come here and support her.

"You know I wasn't once tempted to say no comment? I owe you for the coaching on Saturday. And for the offer on the keynote help, which I definitely want to take you up on."

Ryn glanced at her stilettos for an instant. "There's something else. This isn't easy for me to admit, but I think I made a mistake on Saturday night."

Carly's shoulders tensed. A mistake? In offering her help? Ryn had perhaps decided them spending so much time together wasn't a good idea.

Ryn's face broke into a slow smile. "If it's not too late I would very much like to accept your offer and move into Dev's apartment. I would love the pleasure of being your neighbor."

The pressure in Carly's shoulders released, replaced by a wave of warmth. Dev was right that she should listen to her gut more often. Asking Ryn on Saturday hadn't been the misjudgment she assumed. No more so than inviting the doctors today. They stood and hugged to seal the deal.

When Carly reached her car after waving goodbye to Ryn, she stashed her backpack on the floor of the passenger side, then thought better of it and grabbed her phone. If she intended to start trusting her gut, it told her a certain decision couldn't wait any longer.

Derrick's email to the entire company this morning had not only knocked her confidence, but she'd wasted brain cycles unnecessarily worrying herself leading up to this panel. She remembered what Ryn called her the other night. *An idealist with a passion to change the world.* She deserved people on her team who felt the same way and supported her.

She dialed the number for Tyrone, her HR manager. Before returning to the office, she asked him to meet at a café and help create a plan to fire Derrick.

Chapter Twenty-Two

Ryn looked up from her laptop and took in the line of cypress trees and the valley behind Dev's apartment. Outside the sun glinted off the copper railings. If she hadn't woken up each of the last few mornings petrified of a knock on the door about Todd's fraud, and dreadfully missing Fergus, she might enjoy staying here.

She glanced at the shelving unit where the fake power of attorney papers sat in their same colored folders. It was Saturday already and since Tuesday her detective had discovered squat beyond those documents. Absolutely nothing she might take to the authorities and prove her innocence.

She slammed a fist on the dining table, then winced. Her promotion would finally be announced next week. She expected to be overjoyed at this moment, yet how could she be, when her involvement in Todd's fraud loomed over her: a cloud of hail ready to pummel her upgraded professional reputation into the pavement.

She stretched her fingers and rubbed her hand, wondering how long her lawyers expected her to wait, her career in limbo, while the investigator kept looking. Weeks? Months?

A loud knock sounded, and she jumped. The police?

Her heart clamored to escape her chest. She gulped in air, but her constricted lungs refused to fully exhale. Too much obsessing over the Feds banging down her door, apparently, because she acted like a crazy woman. The knock was almost certainly Carly. They planned to use this free afternoon, after she dropped Sammy at a birthday party, for their first keynote rehearsal.

Ryn placed a palm on the back of the front door and collected herself before opening it. Carly smiled from the other side. She carried a tray from Starbucks with two cups. "One nonfat vanilla latte for you, and a chai for me."

Ryn stepped back and held open the door. "How did you know what I wanted?"

"Remember when we met in Larkspur at that coffee shop? You can call me pedantic, but I like remembering drink orders. Shows the person mattered enough for me to pay attention."

Ryn led her to the dining table where she'd prepared a tip sheet with ideas on stage fright and speaking at large audience events. In return, she suspected Carly could teach her a thing or two about showing you cared for others.

"Where's the cat?" Carly glanced around the room. "How's he settling in?"

Ryn cringed. She'd consoled herself that Fergus was an outdoor cat, but she had now become the universe's worst pet mom.

"Ryn, are you okay? Did he run away?"

"No, nothing like that. Just beating myself up, because, well, truth is he's still back at home. I'm so grateful to be here now, that I've been delaying the Tiburon trip to fetch him in case…"

225

"Afraid of running into Todd?"

Ryn stared at her nails. "Yeah. Pretty much." Carly must think her a coward, not to mention a terrible person, for not yet retrieving her own cat. But so far only her two lawyers and the detective knew of Todd's potential fraud, and telling anyone else, even Carly, posed a risk they recommended she avoid.

"Okay then, let's go."

"Sorry?"

Carly put her arms back into the sleeves of her jacket. "Let's go. Right now. Or actually, first, have you checked his Twitter? Maybe he's not even in town?"

Why hadn't Ryn thought of that? Likely because she never followed Todd's Twitter. She'd always considered it a bunch of business deals he'd brief her on later, anyway. Although she did give her detective the details, in case she missed something.

Carly already held her phone in her hand, searching. "Well, yesterday he was in Henderson, Nevada. Look: a ribbon cutting on a new apartment complex."

She held up the screen, which showed a photo of Todd with local officials and Ryn's pulse quickened. That could be one of the complexes her name had been involved with. And why would Todd fake her name on deeds unless he was doing something illegal? Perhaps she should tell Carly. It wasn't as if Ryn always listened to the advice of her conservative lawyers at work.

The screen scrolled under Carly's fingers as she read more tweets. "Nothing today, but if he had events in Nevada late yesterday, don't you think it at least decreases the chance we'd run into him?"

"I suppose. Although it's only a two-hour flight from Vegas. He might have returned this morning."

"Tell you what, it's not more than a forty-minute round-trip to Tiburon. Why don't we just go over there? We could drive past at speed. If his car's there, we hit the accelerator and keep driving. If not, I play lookout while you grab Fergus."

"But what about your rehearsal?"

"Will you even feel settled until we sort this out? I've got over two months before D-day. Isn't Mission Impossible: Save Fergus Edition more important for today?"

Carly started singing the Mission Impossible theme tune. "Dun-dun, dun-dun…" and Ryn felt a little giddy. Her chest loosened its hold on the fear it had been clamped around all week. Describing the trip as a mission to jailbreak Fergus sounded ridiculous, but Carly was right. The chances were good Todd hadn't arrived home.

They locked the apartment, left in Carly's car, and twenty minutes later turned the corner onto Ryn's street. Carly sped up her Honda to fifty miles an hour, and Ryn watched for her house as they flew past gardens and mailboxes.

"It's this one coming up with all the glass and the FOR SALE sign," Ryn said. "But don't slow down."

"Nope, not slowing. Just promise me you won't take this Mission Impossible idea too seriously, and duck and roll," Carly said, chuckling. "We'll loop back and drop you off if the driveway is empty."

A flash of white sign and gray concrete told Ryn no one was home. She glanced through the rear window and checked that Todd hadn't parked his Mercedes on the street either. She turned to Carly in the driver's seat. "Yes! I think we're a go. Now let's pray he doesn't come home while I'm in there."

Carly pulled around the corner at the far end of the street, where they weren't visible from the house. She stopped in front of a play park. "Where's the best place for me to watch from?"

They agreed on the opposite end of the road, the direction from which Todd normally approached when driving up the hill from Tiburon.

"But what if he recognizes you?" Ryn said. Carly's car wasn't an unusual brand, but she'd still be obvious, sitting at the end of the street, if he arrived.

"Yeah, that might be a bit ugly... I'll park behind another vehicle, so the license plate isn't visible and stay ducked below the windshield."

Ryn clasped Carly's arm before they started off again. "Thank you." Coming here was the type of thing only a true friend would do for you.

Carly dropped her in front of the driveway and drove away while Ryn rushed inside, thanking her luck that Todd hadn't seen a reason to change the locks again after she left.

In the house, everything was still. No heating running, so likely he hadn't returned since yesterday.

"Here Fergus, tshhh, tshhh, here, Fergie..." She called for him while she located his food, accessories, and carry bag, then walked through each room and looked on the deck, but no sign. She hadn't thought this far ahead. Normally she just put out food and Fergus came to her.

She started looking under furniture. The weather

had turned chilly enough that he shouldn't be outside. Todd wouldn't have taken him, just to spite her, would he?

She walked to the bedroom. A text from Carly jolted her before she had a chance to search under the bed.

—*All okay?*—

—*Still looking*—

As Ryn finished typing a familiar paw tagged her leg. Thank God.

Slowly, she bent and let Fergus come to her. He loathed the carry case, which meant a trip in the car, normally to the vet.

She heard a noise at the front door, and held her breath. Her pulse raced. Had she secured the bolt when she entered? Todd could have driven up the hill from the opposite direction and Carly missed him. Fergus squealed when she plopped him into the carry case, pushed hard on his head, and zipped it. "Sorry buddy. We need to scram."

She threw the bag with his supplies over one shoulder and headed out the back patio door. From behind the house she texted Carly—*Meet me at the park*—

She crept along the side of the building. She'd make a terrible spy because Fergus squealed so loud inside the vented bag that if Todd stood near the front entry, he'd already heard them.

She hid at the front edge of the house and peeked around, ready to make a run for it if needed. Her chest relaxed. The FedEx truck sat behind the driveway, and a man in a cap waited at the front door.

She jogged up the steps, signed for the package,

grabbed it, and ran along the street as fast as she could, rounding the corner still running. When she reached the car, she threw the duffel in the back, jumped in the passenger seat with Fergus and the envelope on her lap, and Carly took off immediately. The poor cat must feel as shaken as she did.

When they reached the highway, Carly turned and offered her a high five. "Nicely done. And hello, Fergus, nice to meet you. I'm guessing he'll be happier once we stop moving?"

"Yes indeed." Ryn put her hand in the carrier, and petted him. He wouldn't stop whining until they got out of the car, so during the drive she treated Carly to highlights from her Songs Todd Despises playlist, in part to drown Fergus out. As they sang along to P!nk, Beyoncé, and Gypsy Cowgirl, Ryn considered how many fellow women had walked this same path back from heartbreak that she and Carly were treading.

They reached Dev's apartment, still giggling and singing along with the lyrics about being just fine without him, long after the music stopped. Ryn opened the carrier and stroked Fergus. "How about I make us some tea after I settle him?"

Once he calmed and investigated each corner of the new apartment, Carly sat in the living room and reviewed the notes on speaking tips while Ryn waited in the kitchen for the kettle to boil. She opened the FedEx package: a PIN code reset for a bank account. She took a photo and emailed her detective. The day Todd stole the documents, she downloaded past statements for every bank account and credit card she had access to. This was a new one from which she'd scrape a full history, just in case it became useful at a later date. For example, if she were investigated by the police.

She returned to the living room with the tea, dread pinpricking her arms. One more bank account she didn't know about...one more thing she'd missed. "Carly, I just...well...I want to say how big it was for me, you offering to come to the house, helping me like that."

"It was kind of fun, wasn't it?" Carly said with a snort. "Slinking down behind the steering wheel might be the closest I get to playing a secret agent this lifetime. But seriously, you seemed pretty freaked out when I got here." She paused and studied Ryn's face. "And to be honest, you still look kinda uneasy. Are you sure everything's okay?"

Ryn glanced at the yellow, green, and red folders on the shelf. Carly had proven when she offered Ryn this apartment and again today that she wanted to support her. She was the last person in the world who'd put in jeopardy the investigation into Todd. She would want to help.

Ryn ran across the room, grabbed the folders, and threw them on the coffee table before she risked changing her mind. "These are why I was, and honestly still am, freaking out."

Carly flipped through the papers while Ryn explained what the lawyer and detective had taken her through: The fake power of attorneys, purchasing properties in her name, how there might be more, but they didn't know for sure how many or why he'd done it.

At each new revelation Carly repeated the same words. "Oh my God. I am so sorry." She looked at the pages once more. "Seriously, oh my f-ing God. Who would do this?" She leaped up, walked to the kitchen, washed her hands, and then returned, as if she either needed time to think or wanted to wash off the taint of Todd. She sat beside Ryn. "This is hard to absorb. But I'm sure there's a way out. What are you thinking as next steps?"

"That's just the problem, not much I can do. My lawyer advised for now to let the detective continue his investigation. But if this leaks, I'll lose my position at Sentra."

"Oh, boy. Again, I'm so sorry, but you know what this proves?"

"How screwed I am?"

Carly touched her arm and met Ryn's gaze, as if to say *I don't know how, but it will be okay.* "Of course not. This is what good lawyers are for. No, what this means is we should stop letting him make us feel gullible or worthless."

Ryn squinted at her. Didn't this say the exact opposite? She hadn't seen any of it coming.

Carly explained, "You know how we thought there were signs, stuff we missed? Well, there probably weren't. Todd really is a con man. I mean, like a professional." Carly whistled. "No wonder neither of us saw it. This isn't just about cheating. He does this for a living."

Ryn exhaled and took a sip of her tea. Nothing was any more resolved than ten minutes ago, but her shoulders felt lighter. As if she wasn't alone in this impending disaster.

She placed her hand on top of Carly's. "Thank you, truly."

After a moment, Ryn stood and picked up the notes from the table. "You still want to practice?"

"I'm not sure I could focus now after all this excitement." Carly grinned, as if struck by genius. "How about you come with me and pick up Sammy from his party, and we all go see the new Star Wars movie? I've been promising him for a while."

Chapter Twenty-Three

Rough waves slapped the concrete wall that ran along the garden behind Carly's office. She paced the waterline, preparing for the nine o'clock meeting with Derrick. She'd expected the birds to calm her, but instead they frenzied around the feeder, jostling each other off the ledge, and her mind kept repeating the same question. Even if her gut said firing Derrick was the right thing to do, what if her team didn't see it that way?

Ryn told her last night even the most experienced CEOs second-guessed their firing decisions. Still, the rest of her team might see her choice as a lack of leadership, that the only solution she found for an unruly employee was telling him to leave.

She unlocked her phone and texted Ryn. Her promotion would be announced today, and Carly understood how deep her angst ran about Todd's fraud.

—*Good luck with the announcement. Don't forget what a smart woman advised me. JUST FAKE IT*—

—*Thanks. Good luck with D too. Be strong*—

Carly moved to the picnic table where she could see Derrick's arrival through the window in the empty conference room.

She studied the geometric beauty in the pattern of frost on the bench. This was the exact spot where she sat and listened while Todd repeated—even after everything he'd done—that they were soul mates. As if he ever understood what the term meant. There had been no frost on the ground that day, but she remembered pulling her jacket closer, feeling a hundred times colder than now, and wondering whether she'd ever deserve the true warmth of love. Not the fictitious kind filled with Todd's false promises, or her parents' type of love with the impossible expectation that she turn back time, but acceptance of a person as they are, complete with their history and flaws. Like the type of honest warmth she felt developing with Ryn over the last weeks.

Carly looked up and spotted Alfie, their office complex's security guard, enter the conference room, scan the surroundings, and leave. She'd asked for his presence this morning because of Ryn's other tip: A person like Derrick, who felt entitled to say whatever he wanted, might overreact.

She just needed to have faith; and trust in her decision. All of Ryn's other advice had been good, even if Carly had laughed out loud a few nights ago when she opened one of Ryn's cabinets looking for a mug and discovered no less than ten containers of Nutella. Apparently she used that stash for consolation in the same way Carly meditated, or Sammy ate chocolate ice cream.

She looked again toward the building. Derrick waited in the conference room.

Carly pushed back her shoulders and put on a smile before opening the building's rear door, then removed it. *You don't smile while firing someone.* She spotted Tyrone, her HR manager, in the corridor, motioned for him to follow her, and they entered the room and sat opposite Derrick, who once again put his feet up on the chair.

"Please tell me someone brought caffeine. You know I'm not my sparkly self this early in the morning, right?" Derrick registered Tyrone's presence for the first time, with an incredulous stare.

"No, I didn't know that." This time Carly made no attempt at covering the edge in her voice. "I scheduled this meeting because I'm letting you go. This is your last meeting here. We've prepared a package of documents you will have an opportunity to review at home, and if you sign them, you will receive payment as outlined. We thank you for your service, but as CEO I have to make the best staffing decisions for the health of the company."

Carly breathed. She'd delivered the exact words she prepared: not too specific, not too vague. She hated giving Derrick money as he walked out the door, just for signing a waiver, but this was standard practice in the industry because it helped protect the company from being sued.

Derrick's brows met in the middle. "And what exactly have I done that is not in the best interest of the health of BioLarge?" His voice rose enough that those at the closest desks behind the flimsy wall could likely overhear.

Carly hardened her expression, channeling Uncle Remy's words on why she struggled. *A failure to believe you're worth better...that's what's preventing you from going after your dreams.* "The attitude you display toward our team members is not a fit with the kind of employee BioLarge needs. Tyrone will arrange a time for you to clean out your desk." She walked across the conference room and opened the door. Tyrone would finish explaining the paperwork.

"And what if I don't agree, or want my things right now?" Derrick jumped to his feet and moved toward her, his voice menacing, the exact tone of Todd the day he turned up in the lobby. Tyrone stood, too, and put a hand on his shoulder. Derrick shook it off and advanced toward Carly, clearly intending to pin her into the corner, beside the open door.

Be strong. Ryn wouldn't stand for being threatened in this way. Carly needed to finish this, even with the door open and every word she said echoing into their open plan office. She took a step toward him. "Derrick, you're being fired because we have an amazing team here who believe in saving lives, and you provide neither the caliber of skills or teamwork needed to be part of that. I do not expect to see you here again."

She pivoted and strode through the door and around the corner, her pulse charging, before taking a breath. Behind her she heard the conference room door shut—likely Tyrone trying to settle Derrick and smooth things over in the wonderfully calm way he did—and realized she stood right in front of Kiran's desk.

She'd just fired his boss, overheard by the entire team.

Kiran looked at her over his two computer monitors, his expression bemused. He grinned, then clapped, slow, before gaining momentum. Behind him the other engineers in the testing area chuckled, and one joined him in clapping.

Carly slowly shook her head, taking in the entire testing team, smiling back.

Mindy, an engineer who started working for Kiran

two months ago, walked over and slapped her on the back. "Well done. You are so right. We can find someone better. Maybe already have them in house, eh?" She turned and looked meaningfully at Kiran.

To one side along the corridor, Derrick scowled, then shook off Alfie's arm as he was escorted toward the building's rear exit.

Kiran reached to shake her hand. "You know I'll support whoever you hire, but that was well overdue. I thought you'd never unchain us from that deadweight."

Derrick stopped before the exit door. He clearly overheard Kiran's comment, but Alfie placed a hand on his back, pushing him outside.

Carly rubbed her eyes. She couldn't believe she hadn't realized her team also hated Derrick's attitude. Perhaps most of the decisions she'd wasted energy second-guessing—just like this one—were actually time she could have focused on Sammy.

Kiran gestured at the line of screens. "Sorry to break up the party, Boss, but we've got a launch coming up, which will be much easier to plan without the extra negativity around here." He spun around and high-fived two employees behind him, then turned toward Carly. "Okay, if we all get back to work?"

"Of course. Back to work it is." Carly grinned and walked to her own desk, by the window. She intended to research an inspired idea for a little celebration tonight with Sammy and Ryn.

Chapter Twenty-Four

—Good luck with the announcement. Don't forget what a smart woman advised me. JUST FAKE IT—

Ryn reread Carly's text and set her phone aside. She leaned back in her office chair and studied the poster of John Wayne. *Courage is being scared to death, but saddling up anyway.*

Carly was right. Ryn didn't have a choice other than faking pleasure and excitement at the release of her fund. She'd imagined this day announcing her as a senior partner would be special. She'd glow with pride as she talked to journalists, and tonight she and Todd would enjoy a celebration they'd planned for years: opening the most expensive whisky they found in the specialty liquor store and saluting a decade of hard work to get here.

Her chest tightened. *Just be patient, Ms. Brennan:* what her lawyer said earlier this morning, when Ryn called her. She still debated whether to come clean with Simon about Todd's possible fraud before today's press event. But telling him almost guaranteed losing her new position. And she'd worked too long and fought too hard, to sabotage it now.

"Hey, Ryn?" Keisha walked into the office and took a seat across the desk. "Are you all set with the presentation? I need to print copies before the press arrive."

Ryn took a breath before turning her laptop for Keisha to see. "Yes, except for this last page. I need the final okay on the thirty percent number for our diversity focus."

At the word our, Keisha grinned. A year ago, during their morning ferry rides, they'd talked about how the playing field for startups had not been created equal, and the difficulty for minority-run businesses to secure funding. This passion was why Ryn convinced the firm to hire her: Keisha wanted to do more for the world than calculate a funds' Total Value to Paid-In Capital. And now that Ryn had become part of the senior leadership team, she could use her clout and convince the firm to invest in more worthwhile opportunities, starting with focusing thirty percent of their investments on diverse and female entrepreneurs.

"We're finalizing it in the partners meeting in a few minutes," Ryn said. "How about I send you the presentation now, and I'll text any changes before you print?"

"Sure, that'll work." Keisha lowered her voice to a whisper. "Is your cat settling in? Any updates on Todd the Terrible?"

Ryn fake-chuckled. Keisha didn't know quite how spot-on her wording was. Even if Ryn realized she had no reason to hide from Keisha the ups and downs of general divorce-landia, including moving, she hadn't told her everything. She wouldn't put Keisha in the position of being aware of Todd's fraud, because to know the firm's reputation was at risk and not speak up would be a fireable offense.

"Honestly, I'm starting to wonder if I'll ever escape him." This much Ryn could say with a hundred percent truth.

She pushed on her lungs, trying to exhale the now familiar panic. If his fraud were revealed, no one in this industry would have empathy for a woman who put her own job on the line by choosing a con artist for a husband. And if she lost her reputation, her career, she wasn't sure what remained. She'd be just as worthless to the outside world as Todd had left her feeling inside.

"Okay, email me the presentation," Keisha said. "I'll watch for your text."

Ryn waited a moment after she left, centering herself. She glared at the Feelings Jar on her desk. Since she and Carly started talking in the evenings, Ryn had barely used it. *Seriously*, stuffing paper in a pot hardly fixed this stupid stalemate with Todd.

She reapplied her lipstick before heading along the corridor. All five senior partners, including herself, intended to roll straight from this meeting into the press event.

Once they all arrived in the conference room, Ryn spoke first. "Let's finish our conversation on the diversity funding proposal before any other business." She pulled up the page in the press presentation. "I'm intending to use the thirty percent number and make the point on how our firm is different from others: more open for minority and female entrepreneurs to approach."

She noticed Simon didn't look at her, but stared out the window. Avoiding eye contact?

Bob, another partner with wavy white hair spoke up. "Well, you made a passionate case last week about lady entrepreneurs having higher company success rates, and yet a harder time finding funding…"

"Great. We're set then?" Ryn flipped off the screen and looked around for approval from each partner at the table, hoping the tremor in her voice didn't betray the knowledge this program might last longer at Sentra than her.

Even if she only made it another month, this diversity focus could still be her legacy and help other female entrepreneurs, like Carly, or Keisha as the future generation, who struggled to get great ideas funded.

Bob shuffled his papers, as if embarrassed. "What I was going to say is, although you made an interesting point, after we discussed it this weekend at the club…"

The club as in Simon's golf club? They'd discussed the proposal without her there to participate in the conversation.

"Yes," Simon broke in. "My recommendation is that for now, we limit our exposure to the less educated. Keep our funds centered on where the smart money is. We have other topics on today's agenda, so let's table this and loop back in a few months?"

The less educated. Simon believed women and minorities had a lower chance at success, completely the opposite of every data point in the proposal package she gave them. Not to mention beyond sexist.

On second thought, his comments were entirely consistent with every asinine belief he'd ever voiced. Ryn crossed her arms, then uncrossed them, realizing her stance provided a visible sign of trying to cork the mix of frustration and fury fizzing in her chest.

How the hell could she walk into the press conference in a few minutes and act thrilled to be announced in her new role, when she now suspected she might be nothing more than their token woman here. The one person Simon could point to and say *No, we're not biased—look, one of our partners has breasts.*

There was no other reason for him to go behind her back and make a decision without her. So much for her extra clout as senior partner.

She stepped away from the conference table. She didn't intend to give up on this idea, but sometimes you won the war by losing the battle. She needed to tackle the other partners individually, without Simon, and see where they really stood on her proposal. Perhaps they'd accept less than thirty percent, but that was for another day.

"You know what, guys, I need a few more minutes to update something before the press conference. Why don't I meet you in there?" She left quietly, resisting the urge to kick the garbage can beside the door on her way out.

Ryn returned to her office, wishing she knew a different solution than to walk away. She left rather than confront them. Exactly like when she quit her first job after the problems with Grant.

Keisha would be so disappointed. Ryn sent her a text.

—Please remove the page on diversity focus. Will explain later, I promise—

On her desk the Feelings Jar promised temporary relief. She just needed to control her anger long enough to announce a promotion she no longer believed gained her anything more than a title. She tore off a scrap of paper, scrawled—*assholes all of them*—and shoved it inside the jar.

Chapter Twenty-Five

Deep breaths. Ryn stood on the deck of Dev's apartment and inhaled the forest air. This afternoon's press conference had been an unmitigated disaster. Unable to discuss her diversity focus, she'd looked incompetent when journalists pummeled her, seeking to understand why she'd claimed, in her pre-release materials, this fund would be different from the myriad of others in the world.

In truth, it wasn't any different. Unless she convinced the other partners to accept her proposal, her new fund—Sentra V—represented just one more set of fat cats seeking the best investment returns. The worst part of the afternoon had been her realization, as the journalists kept pushing and pushing for answers, and she became more and more evasive: she sounded exactly like Simon.

She inhaled again but struggled to fully exhale. With every breath she'd taken in the last weeks, it felt like air had stuck in her lungs, failing to escape, and now pushed against the inside of her chest. As if not only had she lost control at work, and with Todd, but of her entire life.

She glanced inside and checked the time on the dining room clock. The only rituals that maintained her half-sanity were standing here inhaling the forest air, and the comforting rhythm of rehearsal sessions with

Carly, and Sammy as their little helper. They were scheduled to meet again any minute.

She walked toward the front door. When she opened it, Carly stood by Sammy who had one hand raised in the air as if about to knock. Ryn scooped him up. "Well, hello, Sammy, have you come to help Mommy practice again?"

She placed him on the floor, and he grinned. "No, we're…" he looked at his mom and pronounced the next word with care and an even wider grin "celebrating!"

"That's right, honey." Carly hugged Ryn, then stepped back, breathless. "I did it. I fired Derrick. And you got your promotion, so I figured we should do something special to mark the moment."

"Well done. So it went okay, then?" Ryn noticed the paper grocery bag by Carly's feet.

"Better than okay. I wanted to tell you the whole story in person. And I have a surprise." Carly picked up the bag and placed a folder, likely her presentation notes, on Ryn's dining table before Sammy scampered ahead of her into the kitchen. She pulled a different piece of paper—what looked like a handwritten recipe—from her purse.

There was a lightness in Carly's step, and her curls swayed over her shoulders as she bounced around, pulling items from drawers and cabinets. Since the day they met, Ryn hadn't seen her this cheerful.

Carly pulled two cartons of milk and a packet of coffee from the bag. "I wasn't sure if you were set on nonfat so I brought both but believe me whole milk will be better." She gestured toward the rear of the kitchen and Sammy climbed on a chair and opened the cabinet.

Ryn pointed at the regular milk and grinned when Sammy grabbed one of the jars of Nutella. "What exactly is going on here?"

"The other day you mentioned how much you miss the café in Tiburon where you used to go for Nutella lattes."

Ryn nodded. Not a chance she'd visit there now and risk running into Todd.

Carly held up the jar Sammy had passed her. "Well, I swung by this afternoon and convinced a barista to give me their recipe." She smoothed the handwritten sheet of paper on the countertop.

Tears lumped in Ryn's throat. How amazing of Carly not only to have listened when she talked of how Nutella reminded her of Mom, but plan something special like this.

Carly picked a pot and asked Sammy to pour in the milk. "Anyway, I wanted to do something nice for you to say thanks. After you helped with Derrick, and everything else. Because you were so right that I needed to give myself more credit."

Ryn sat on the stool by the breakfast bar. "I do remember saying that. Possibly more than once."

"Dev said something similar, before I took the CEO job, about trusting my own decisions. And then today it was like God, or whoever is up there, sent me a direct message. If I hadn't been so busy angsting over the consequences of firing Derrick...my life would have been a heck of a lot easier. You know a few of my employees actually applauded when I came out after doing the deed?"

"Like a scene in a movie?"

"Not quite as corny, but same idea."

Ryn reached across the countertop and gave Carly a high five, and Sammy ran around the counter to claim his, too. She raised both hands for a double.

"Mommy's happy because she's a good boss," Sammy said.

"Yes, she is, little guy. And a great mom, too, right?" Sammy nodded vigorously and Ryn pulled him into her lap.

Across the countertop, Carly wiped a hand across her eyes to stop her tears. She grinned back at them.

"Listen, I know today must have been hard for you, what with all the Todd stuff," Carly said. "But it doesn't mean you can't still celebrate. You worked a long time to achieve this level, right?"

"This is the most thoughtful thing anyone's done for me in a long time." Ryn closed her eyes for a second, pulled Sammy in closer on her lap, and breathed in. His hair smelled of cookie dough and comfort.

Sammy squirmed. "Wait, we baked Nutella cookies, too." He jumped off, ran, and grabbed them from the paper bag.

Carly relayed the details of firing Derrick, including her decision to promote Kiran as his replacement while she whisked the milk. She made the drink, grated chocolate on top and passed it across the counter.

Ryn took a sip and it warmed from her scalp to her knees. She leaned back on the stool, closed her eyes, and sank into the nutty chocolate. In her frazzled state after today's announcement, Carly knew exactly what she needed.

She used to consider Todd thoughtful—even if she

now knew it as fakery—but in the last month, it had become clear Carly was the kindest person she knew. "You know you're a better person than me?"

Carly stopped drinking and stared at Ryn as if a spaceship had landed behind her in the dining room. "I'm sorry?"

"The way you remember the details that make others happy. Or consider your team first, which is why you struggled with the decision to fire Derrick." Ryn took another sip and grinned at Sammy who sat on the sofa enjoying his own Nutella and milk drink, minus the coffee. She leaned in across the counter and spoke more quietly "Or the way the guy over there looks at you as if no one in the universe could feel more loved. And this…"

Ryn lifted her cup and took another sip. "For me, this taste will always seem as if my mom is standing next to me, patting me on the back, and telling me it's all going to be okay." And maybe, somehow, it was. Ryn exhaled, and the pressure holding her chest hostage since the day at her lawyer's released an inch.

"Well, me being a good person is certainly not what I tell myself every time I screw up, but thank you." Carly walked around the bar and pulled Ryn into a hug. "That might be the nicest thing anyone's said to me in years."

When Carly stepped back from the hug, a thoughtful look crossed her face. "You know, I sometimes think losing Todd means I lost my family all over again…but I didn't. Sammy is my family, and so are my friends. Like you."

Ryn smiled again. This holiday she would finally enjoy seeing Pops and her own family, without Todd.

"Carly, I was just thinking about Christmas. What are you and Sammy doing next week?"

She would swear Carly sighed ever so quietly. "The usual. Fun but small. You'd be welcome to join us."

"No, I have a better plan. Why not join me, my nieces, and Pops, at my brother Jack's in Palo Alto? I can tell you Jack makes a mean turkey and normally does crabs too, given it's the season."

Sammy perked up on the other side of the room. "Crabs? Like at the beach?" He looked pensive for a moment. "But will Santa know where to go?"

Ryn laughed. "But of course. How could Santa forget you? I suspect he'd deliver your presents at home as usual, and you can open them in the morning, and maybe even a few from your Auntie Ryn, too. Then in the afternoon you can cause a riot with my nieces running around the kitchen making the crabs talk. How does that sound?"

In response, Sammy bounced up and down on the sofa and Ryn laughed again.

"Guess that's a heck yes," Carly said.

Ryn glanced at the folder Carly placed on the dining table when she arrived. "I know we're celebrating, but did you still want to show me your latest keynote revision?"

"Yes, not letting up now." Carly picked up the papers she brought. "How could I miss out on a session of the Ryn torture chamber?"

Ryn chuckled. In their last rehearsal—after she realized Carly knew the words so well she now sounded rehearsed—Ryn had suggested standing on a chair. Every so often she'd poke Carly from the side to upset her balance and make her start her sentence again, sounding less like she read from a script.

Ryn pulled out a chair by the dining table, then turned to Sammy. "We can use your help again, but first, if you search in my bedroom, I suspect there may be a new game hidden in there if you look carefully."

When the knocks and bangs of him hunting for the toy started in the other room, Ryn pointed at the chair.

"One more thing, while he's momentarily out of earshot," Carly said. "Your advice has been so good. Would you be willing to give me your take on something else?"

"Always."

"This one's more personal. Dev keeps texting me—okay, to be honest haranguing me—about going on a date with another friend of his, so I wanted your opinion. Do you think I should even consider it? What with everything else going on?"

Ryn sat on the sofa and gathered her thoughts. New ground for them to talk dating, although she didn't see why Carly shouldn't.

"Also"—Carly playfully twirled a lock of her hair—"Dev seems to ask an awful lot of questions about you, whenever he calls…"

Ryn shook her head, smiling. She'd shared with Carly that Dev texted her several times since she moved in, under the pretext of checking in on the apartment, which to her seemed like text flirting. But even if Ryn wasn't yet ready to consider a new relationship, Carly deserved every ounce of happiness she could squeeze from life. "I say why not? Even if work is crazy, life needs to continue. For both of us. Can I see this fine specimen Dev believes is worthy of you?"

"Carly grabbed her phone. "Sure. If only for kicks. I haven't even looked at his email."

She unlocked the screen, found the message, and handed the phone to Ryn, without even glancing at the photo. "You look first. Give me a rating—one to ten?"

Ryn peeked. Her lips quivered, but she stifled the laugh. The man in the photo had a can of Blue Ribbon in his hand and wore a stained white T-shirt. Above his beard sat a trucker hat with a picture of a fish with a hook in its mouth, a big bloody grin, and the words *Get Hooked*. This must be Dev's idea of a joke; perhaps on both of them if he expected Carly to share the photo.

"What's so funny?" Carly asked, leaning over her shoulder.

She saw the photo and burst into peals of laughter. Ryn joined in, so hard a jagged pain stuck in her sides. This specimen belonged on a fishing boat in the Delta, not on a date with a smart, caring woman like Carly.

"Oh, for goodness' sake." Carly raised both palms toward the ceiling. "Guess Dev doesn't actually have a date. He's always pushing me to laugh and take myself less seriously."

"Well, it worked didn't it?" And apparently, Ryn had been correct in her initial assessment of Dev's wicked sense of humor. Perhaps, in a few months, after he got back to town, she'd consider returning his text flirtations.

Carly walked to the dining table and mounted the chair. "Rehearsal time. Anyway, Fish Hat Fred is clearly not my type. Even if Dev considers him quite the catch."

Ryn groaned at the quip, and positioned herself next to Carly, within poking distance. "Well, he may not be your next Prince Charming but at least there's plenty more fish in the sea?"

This time Carly groaned, even louder than Ryn. "Let's get focused here." She scanned the first page of her notes, then handed them back to Ryn and started. "Welcome to the largest technology breakthrough in cardiac diagnosis…"

She had completed only a few lines of the first section when Sammy roared back from the bedroom with a huge grin, holding the new Star Wars game Ryn had bought.

He paused halfway across the living room, likely realizing he almost missed out on his role as chief paper holder. "Wait for me!" He sprinted toward his mom's chair, but failed to stop soon enough and slammed into the edge.

Carly wobbled left, then right, arms flailing, as the chair teetered on two legs. Ryn jumped to catch her. The chair tipped and Ryn hit the ground first, the air thrust out of her when Carly landed on her chest. Ryn wheezed, failing to catch her breath.

Carly attempted to sit up, but her elbows dug further into Ryn's ribs, and she yelped. Instead, Carly leaned over to one side and looked back at Ryn over her shoulder. "Are you okay?"

Ryn grabbed her side dramatically, staring at Sammy. "Ay! No. I think I'm missing a rib."

Sammy's brows furrowed in concern, until Ryn could hold it no longer and burst out laughing. He grinned and piled on top of them with a scream.

Ryn's chest shook at the bottom of the pile, still struggling to breathe for laughing so hard.

Chapter Twenty-Six

Red velvet curtains loomed over Carly's head and to both sides. She tapped her microphone and peered down from the stage to where Ryn stood in the aisle.

Ryn arranged this extra Christmas gift for Carly. She'd called in a favor with a friend to let them rehearse the keynote here, in this massive San Francisco theater, during their January dark season. Today would be their last of four sessions.

"Hang on a minute. One more thing," Ryn shouted. She turned and walked toward the rear doors.

Carly scanned the sweeping curve of empty red velvet chairs. Thanks to Ryn's help she already knew her speech, and in their practices on this huge stage she'd become used to looking down at the audience and the way the lights dazzled unless you fixed on a point in the first rows. But in little more than a month, the seats in Austin wouldn't be empty.

She took a deep breath. Right now she needed positive thoughts. From the moment she fired Derrick in December, everything had improved. Her team was happier, the press articles mostly supportive, Paul's health was improving, and since the joy of Christmas at Jack's—the first Sammy relished with other kids—he miraculously hadn't experienced a single tummy ache. Even if she wasn't working fewer hours, including him in their evening rehearsals at home, as paper holder and prompter, made him feel less neglected.

She looked toward the far end of the aisle, trying to understand what took Ryn so long. Chatter and shouts carried from the velvet-paneled lobby, as if a large crowd waited to enter. Had Ryn double-booked their last rehearsal?

The doors launched open and a crowd of twenty-somethings in jeans and hoodies flooded the aisle, jostling toward the front in groups. Tens of them filled the first rows and heckled the stage.

"Already boring!"

"Come on, entertain us!"

What the heck. Where was Ryn?

Carly spotted her sitting in the third row among the students. At least today she smiled. Last night, Carly wished she could offer more than hugs when Ryn shared she felt as if she were stuck in quicksand and slowly sinking, just waiting for the final moment of suffocation to arrive. Today was the last day of January and she'd not received any news from the detective's investigation.

Carly lifted both hands in a stage-sized shrug. She shouted toward Ryn over the heckling. "What is this?"

The microphone picked up her raised voice, and it reverberated around the theater.

Ryn stood and pointed at the rows in front of her. "Say hi to your audience. Recruited from City College for the high price of free beer. I told them I'd double the budget if they make you forget your words."

Carly shook her head. *Really?* Another of Ryn's torture tactics. When they moved from their apartments to this bigger venue, she'd changed from poking Carly's side to testing her focus by throwing balls of paper.

Last week she'd shared a video with Carly that showed, although her voice carried confidence, sometimes her body language betrayed her.

For example, when she repeatedly squeezed her hands together, then walked a few steps to the side, a nervous pattern the audience watched play out, stride by stride, until she reached the far edge and looked as if she wanted to jump off the stage and run for her life.

She inspected today's audience. Ryn passed out stacks of paper and each student scrunched up sheets, turning them into a personal arsenal of paper balls.

Carly tapped her microphone again. Might as well get this paper-throwing, student-heckling ordeal over with. She'd need a glass of chardonnay at the wine bar Ryn had suggested for lunch after they finished.

"Okay, I'm ready. Turn up the lights." She moved to center stage. "Welcome to the presentation of the largest technology breakthrough…" She continued, getting into the swing of her speech before the first ball hit her. Then a second, and a third.

"You're off center!" a student yelled.

Carly glanced around the sea of hundreds of empty seats in the curved theater, then froze. Paper hailstones pelted her. In less than five minutes she'd walked to the edge of the stage, almost behind the huge golden ropes that held back the curtain.

"Look up!" Another ball landed at her feet. She'd been staring at her shoes again.

She looked into the theater to see who last spoke and the stage lights blinded her. Darn it, she knew by now not to stare straight at them.

Where was she with her lines? Thirty-odd faces

stared at her. Even as college students, they'd likely do a better job at staying center stage and looking at their audience.

Just like in her nightmares, she'd forgotten her next sentence. Her hands trembled, and she squeezed them together, then remembered this was exactly what she needed not to do. No one threw paper.

The theater remained silent except for her own breathing echoing across the microphone. And the accelerating thud-thud-thud of her heart. The students had earned their beer because she was stuck.

"Imagine them naked! With bows on." This time Ryn's voice sailed above the crowd, but Carly couldn't laugh, because forgetting her lines and freezing, when the real event loomed so close, wasn't funny.

Ryn edged out of her row and came toward the front, ducking a few balls that took flight as she walked. She spun back to the students. "Stop it with the paper for a minute, okay?" She shouted at the back of the hall, "And turn the lights off, please?"

When she arrived below the stage, she flashed Carly a smile, although the tightness of her forehead didn't match. "Let's try something different. I'll sit there in the center." She pointed behind her at the seats along the aisle. "Just keep checking for me. If you see I'm not straight ahead, you've moved too far from the middle. No big deal, just walk back and reclaim center stage. And if you forget your lines and freeze, I want you to pause, take a few deep breaths, then talk only to me, ignoring everyone else in the audience until you get your momentum back. Got it?"

Carly turned away from the students and hid the flush burning her cheeks. She grabbed the skull at the bottom of the tattoo on her forearm. Those tips worked for Ryn, who was used to being onstage, being articulate. But not for Carly. If she froze in front of a tiny audience of students, why believe she'd be any better in Austin?

She wouldn't even be in this jam if, in that first board meeting, she'd found the gumption to push back. Her hands caught on the underneath of her hair. Best to stop now. Let the students leave with the double beer money they'd earned.

She turned and faced the front of the stage. Ryn stood, waiting patiently. She gave a half-smile of encouragement and waved as if she had no cares other than Carly succeeding with this rehearsal. Which couldn't be farther from the truth. Ryn had lost her house, and she stood on the edge of possibly losing everything if Todd's fraud came out. And yet she wasn't sitting at home, wallowing in her past mistakes. She'd chosen to spend time here every Wednesday, and several nights a week at Carly's apartment, helping her.

Ryn somehow courageously kept going, even without knowing the final outcome.

Carly looked at her student audience. Her whole team at BioLarge depended on her to give Austin her best shot. If Ryn could face the possibility of losing everything with such grace, then Carly could survive struggling onstage for forty minutes of her life.

My invention, my presentation. She walked to center stage, and squared her shoulders. "Turn the lights back on. I'm starting from the top."

The students showered her with paper balls, which landed at her feet. The microphone caught her laughter.

Chapter Twenty-Seven

The hostess in the wine bar seated them by a window, where sun filtered through the blinds, painting broad stripes on their table and the wooden floor. Outside, trams rattled on Market Street, passing the entry to the theater where they'd just rehearsed.

"How are you feeling?" Ryn asked.

"Glad you'll be at South by Southwest, but in all honesty…" Carly stopped, and her gaze focused on their glasses of chardonnay on the table next to the salads. "Eighty percent chance I'll wish we'd chosen a lower-profile launch, but I'm gonna give it my absolute best shot."

Ryn sipped her wine, debating how best to help Carly see that even if she forgot her words in Austin, it didn't matter. She came across as genuine, and idealists always shone on stage.

Ryn wished she understood why, despite Carly's gains in confidence and skill, when she faltered—like this morning—suddenly, her expression said she questioned not only what came next, but her very right to be up there delivering the message.

"Let me ask, what's the worst thing you think might happen? Because to me, so long as you don't faint and get carried offstage on a stretcher, it's clear what people will remember is how passionate you are about your mission of helping doctors save lives."

Carly rubbed the back of her neck. "The worst? I pace beyond the edge of the stage, dive off, break both legs, and become a never-ending Internet meme?"

Ryn forced a laugh, trying to lighten the mood.

"No, in all seriousness," Carly said, "the worst case is I say something stupid that tanks the company, the board sees me for who I am, and removes me as CEO."

Sees me for who I am. Why was Carly talking as if she were the con artist?

Ryn studied her flushed cheeks, her friend's gaze stuck on her wineglass, and finally she understood. Those were gestures of shame. She'd assumed Carly worried the audience in Austin might misjudge her product and her company, but perhaps that wasn't it. Did she fear they'd be judging *her*, and she didn't measure up?

"You've already proven you're an awesome CEO, and your team loves you. At this point, why be afraid of anyone judging you?"

Carly gave a sad smile. "I could ask you the same, my friend. Why are you turning yourself inside out over something becoming public that Todd did, not you?"

Ryn rapped her knuckles on the table. *Doesn't she get it by now?* Every person Ryn worked with would see her as the type of docile, brainless, woman who let herself be duped into letting her name be used for fraud. Worse, the people who'd experienced her lack of camaraderie and warmth at the office might even judge her guilty.

"You know why. I could lose my entire career."

"Yes, and—? You've told me more than once in the past month how the old boy's venture club—as you dubbed them—gives you no respect…"

The door of the wine bar opened, and Ryn shifted on her chair in the draft. Carly had a point. Ryn losing her reputation hurt the most; imagining colleagues who looked up to her before, now laughing in the lunchrooms. But was her fear of being judged—in this case by a set of men she claimed not to give a damn about—really so different from Carly?

She sighed. "Maybe you're right. Perhaps none of it matters. The keynote, my career...even Todd screwing us both over."

"Huh?" Carly looked at her as if she'd stated air wasn't required for breathing.

Ryn shook her head, struggling with how to explain what she suddenly understood. She'd spent her whole life so angry, battling to prove herself each step of the way; from the first mathlete tournament to vying for this last promotion.

"You know, I always believed if I performed better than the guys people would eventually recognize my value. Then Todd left, I got the promotion and—setting aside the fraud bombshell—for a person who never wanted to marry, I should be happy to finally achieve the career level I always sought. And getting divorced shouldn't matter so much, right? Because my value didn't come from being someone's wife. And yet it does matter. I never felt as worthless as the day I realized he'd chosen you over me."

Carly leaned in and touched her hand. "But, that's not what happened..."

"I know. Well kind of, in the logical side of my brain, at least. But the thing is...now I look at you and BioLarge where it's a much bigger purpose, saving millions of lives, as you say in your speech. I guess what I'm saying is you're a caring leader, an awesome mother, a great friend. Whether you fall off the stage or ace it, keep your job or quit, those things are bigger."

Carly smiled, pressing her fingers to her lips, and a tiny thread tugged inside Ryn's chest. A recognition that the same things couldn't be said for her.

Ryn glanced up from studying her wineglass and caught Carly staring through the window, her nose wrinkled as if a skunk had walked up and sprayed their table. Ryn followed Carly's gaze, and blond highlights bobbed into view outside the window frame. Irrationally, her chest tightened; a memory of stubble, Dior Homme, and L'Occitane mixed with longing for a companionship that never really existed. Todd stopped straight in front of them.

He stared first at Ryn, then Carly. The flash of disbelief, then fury, passed so fast it was almost indiscernible. He blew his hair off his face, threw his shoulders back, and his expression shifted to one of disdain, as if he pitied his poor wife and mistress commiserating over white wine. Although he remained glued to the same spot on the sidewalk.

She glanced at Carly, who continued to glare though the window.

Todd turned and strode toward the restaurant's front door.

Ryn jumped to her feet. For more than a month she'd succeeded in not letting on they'd discovered his fraud. The last thing she wanted was to talk with him now. But if he headed inside the restaurant, she didn't really have a choice. Perhaps she could scrub any trace of fear from her expression by sourcing pure anger.

Carly grabbed her arm. "Don't."

"At a minimum, I can demand the jerk respond to my lawyer's proposed settlement." Ryn stomped toward the front, working to compose her expression into regular how-dare-you-cheat-on-me anger. Before she reached the door, Carly caught up and linked an arm through hers.

When they arrived at the glass panel, they peered through the wine bar's logo, but he wasn't on the other side.

Carly pulled open the door, and they looked in both directions on Market Street. Todd's back was straight ahead. He strode away, and ducked behind a trundling tram, just before it came to a stop, hiding him from view.

"What now?" Carly asked.

Ryn gave a small shake of her head before returning to their table. No point in chasing him. She knew it would be unwise for them to talk, so no reason to force it.

They sat in silence for a moment, staring at the now stationary tram which had blocked Todd's exit. Not so shocking for them to see him here, on the busiest street in San Francisco. He used a co-working space only four blocks away.

And yet something wasn't right.

Ryn's thighs trembled against the wood chair. Why should it matter if Todd learned the two of them became friends? But his expression, so full of disdain, as if he understood something she—or they—couldn't possibly know...

"Ryn, are you okay?"

"I'm honestly not sure. Did you see his face? He's not even pretending to be a regular person anymore."

"You think he'd deliberately leak the..." Carly's voice lowered to a whisper, "the f-word?"

Ryn rubbed her eyes. Could he somehow be setting her up to take the fall? "I honestly don't know... I can't see how it's in his interest to incriminate himself. But then, when I turn it over in my head, nothing makes sense. Like why keep stalling on our divorce paperwork? You'd think he'd want it over, but my lawyer made him a proposal where I don't ask for anything in his companies, and he's ignoring it. And then, there's the question of you."

"Me?" Carly's teeth dug into her lip.

"Todd's a professional con man, so what was his angle in your relationship? You're not a secret billionaire, right?"

"No, I don't think that's it..." Carly crossed and uncrossed her legs, then flagged a waiter and ordered water. The distress in her eyes said she had a theory, but wasn't yet ready to share—or perhaps admit it?

After the water arrived, she took a sip and glanced outside, as if ensuring Todd hadn't returned. "Okay, this is going to sound weird, but I've had the same question since the night you shared the fraud. Like, if Todd is all about the game, what game was he playing on me?"

Her voice dipped to its lowest volume yet and her face twisted. "...and I think it's something to do with Sammy."

Ryn joined her whisper. "Sammy?"

Carly continued, scanning Ryn's face. "I keep remembering the first moment I met Todd. He knelt at Sammy's level in the café, chatting with him before Todd even looked up and introduced himself. I always assumed loving Sammy was a path to me, but…"

She squeezed her hands between her thighs, before looking back at Ryn. "Every conversation I replay, even the day he turned up at my office to argue for another chance; it was always me and Sammy, the package deal, as if he really wanted a son."

"I don't know what to say. Everything else we've talked about matches, down to exactly how he manipulated us, but with this…"

Ryn sat back in her chair, a little dizzy. It made no sense. The Todd from Carly's stories, those with Sammy, sounded like a different person.

She pressed on her chest bone. What did it matter whether Todd was pure evil or evil who wanted a ready-made family? This shouldn't even still hurt. Perhaps what pained her most was accepting she'd let herself be manipulated throughout her child-bearing years. If she hadn't fallen for his con, she might have chosen to be a mother by now.

She straightened in her chair, knocking over her wine glass. Luckily, it didn't break but rolled toward Carly's plate. "Honestly, I don't understand why I'm surprised by anything. The only thing I'm sure is that I never knew him at all."

Carly inspected the glass for chips, then righted it. "Maybe neither of those Todds are real." She glanced at her phone. She'd need to pick Sammy up from school soon.

"Hey—before I go." Carly stood and removed a brown paper bag from her backpack. "I have something for you. Weird timing now, with us running into him, but I found this in a shop in Sausalito last week and got us each one." She handed Ryn the bag and stood, twisting her backpack straps, as if afraid the gift might not be appreciated. "I figured it apt for us both, as a sistership of survival."

Ryn pulled out a tiny wooden plaque with flowers painted on either end. In the middle a quote was printed across the wood in cursive. She ran her finger along it. *It is better to have loved and lost than live with the psycho for the rest of your life.*

She laughed, a comfortable warmth settling on her cheeks. She met Carly's gaze and smiled. "It's perfect, the exact sentiment I need. And may I add it's better to stay single—you know post-psycho escape—than end up with a Fish Hat Fred?"

The tinge of relief in Carly's answering laughter told Ryn how uncertain she'd been about the gift. "Couldn't agree more on both counts. Figured I'd hang mine on the bedroom mirror—to remind me before I tackle each day."

"I can imagine mine next to the Nutella jars," Ryn said, laughing. "That way I see it every time I open the cabinet." She stood and pulled Carly into a hug. "Thank you. This is exactly what I needed to hear today."

Carly met her smile. "I'm heading out, but first listen to me. I know it's seems hopeless lately, and I'm sure seeing Todd didn't help, but don't lose faith. My Uncle Remy used to say two things: It's never too late to become the person you want to see in the mirror, and you're already as strong as you'll need to be. I know it feels hard right now, but when it comes to strength, you have more than any other woman I know."

Ryn smiled. If anyone else told her she was stronger than average, like Pops used to, she'd second-guess manipulation or at least a veiled insult, but not with Carly. She meant it. As she watched Carly swing onto Market Street, the fullness in Ryn's chest reminded her of Sammy's delight with his gifts on Christmas day.

She held the wooden plaque to her chest. Ryn had friends in college, and work friends she'd held at a distance, but never someone who appreciated her like this. Not for what she'd achieved, but for who she was. And she had enough strength to survive whatever Todd threw at her next.

Chapter Twenty-Eight

Ryn finished giving an evasive answer to an entrepreneur's question and studied the faces of her audience in the Zidera Hotel ballroom. She cracked her knuckles under the table, wishing she had mustered a more convincing response. She'd been asked whether her fund's focus on diversity was nothing more than tokenism. *Of course, it is.* After a month of trying, she'd only gained agreement from the senior partners to set aside a measly five percent.

After the session finished, Simon approached while she noted a few follow-ups on business cards. "Great turnout." The smug smile said he believed the full house of entrepreneurs—driven by her calls and tweeting—had been his achievement. "Want to join me for a quick drink next door before you head out?"

She paused, finding no reasonable words to say she'd rather gouge her eyes out with the pen in her hand than spend time in the Zidera Bar.

Her distaste came not only from the idea of spending a minute more with him. For years she'd been obligated to attend this place—the Silicon Valley version of an old boys' club—and network with fellow VCs. But it was demeaning, the struggle to impress a room full of older men who were more interested in patting themselves on the back and celebrating their latest deals with bottles of Opus One and later in the night, baby blonde Ukrainian escorts.

She intended to turn Simon down when the realization struck. He and the partners at Sentra might not give her the respect she merited, but in this bar, among the up and comers, she would now be the big dog in the room: the senior partner others sought to impress. She'd earned the right to see the view from the other side of the glass ceiling, if only for one glass of sauvignon blanc.

"You know what, sure. I've never been a fan of the Zidera, but perhaps this evening can convince me otherwise."

They walked along the corridor from their meeting hall. When they turned the corner into the bar, she did a double take. Instead of the scents of whisky, shoe leather, and ingratiation, giggles and champagne floated over the crowd.

From across the room Neil Kendrick, a fellow VC from the BioLarge board, waved them over. "Fancy seeing you here, Ryn. I wouldn't have expected this to be your scene."

Not her scene? *This is a VC haunt, and I'm a damn VC.* Clearly, despite the promotion, Neil still didn't think she belonged. Although now she studied the room full of high-heeled mules and blow-out hairstyles, it more resembled a wedding than the usual old boys' club. She glanced around, searching for signs of a special event.

When two women in bandage dresses stared at her, and with a flutter of eyelashes, turned possessively toward the two men in their group, Ryn understood. She'd heard rumors, but never visited on a Thursday evening. Tonight was Cougar Night. Despite its name, not a place only for older women. More like *The Bachelor*, Silicon Valley edition.

Ryn's toes curled inside her pumps. Long before meeting Todd, she'd decided never to submit to the humiliation of venues like this: where women were treated as prime cuts, on display to be ordered up by a man with money. Worse, Simon and Neil probably knew exactly what they'd find here, tonight. Perhaps her boss even wanted to see how she'd react, or put her in her place. She rolled her eyes and picked up her briefcase from under the table, ready to go home.

Near the bar's entry, the crowd parted, and the gaze of several women and a few men turned and took in the person sauntering though the center of the bar, granting charismatic smiles to those on each side as they stepped out of his path.

The blond highlights he touched up every month gleamed under the light, and his gaze found and focused only on Ryn. She used to imagine those green eyes as pools of deep water at the base of a waterfall. Right now, they resembled an incoming Arctic ice storm.

Oh shit. Seeing Todd in San Francisco near his office could be a credible coincidence, but this sure as hell wasn't. How did he even know she'd be here? *Oh right, her tweets.*

In one hand he clutched a large manila envelope. Court papers? Perhaps his goal was some type of showdown in the middle of this bar, surrounded by her venture colleagues? He strode toward her group, glowering as if he intended to toss over their high-top table.

Ryn cursed the coward in her who hadn't admitted

to Simon her assets at Sentra might become entangled in her divorce. Humiliating for it to become known here that she had no prenup, in front of everyone she needed to respect her as a strong, fierce leader.

She noticed an exit through the archway on the left and calculated whether she could make it out of the bar before Todd reached their table. *Maybe.*

No time to make excuses. She dashed across the room, directly crossing his path.

The arch shadowed over her head as she passed through, and Todd followed, his breath now inches from the back of her neck. Before she reached the exit door, he grabbed her arm.

For an instant, her mind fed her a lie. After seeing her with Carly yesterday, Todd decided to sign the proposed settlement Ryn's lawyer sent him months ago. Delivering the documents here was just a last childish act to embarrass her.

She spun and faced him. The Joker-esque twist to his smile said she couldn't be farther from the truth. He didn't come here to concede anything.

He thrust out the envelope, with the entire room watching them. "That is a proposed divorce settlement, one which I know you *will accept.*"

Her heart beat several strokes faster. Nothing he proposed in that you-will-do-as-I-say tone of voice would be worth considering, yet ants crawled inside her skin. His voice carried not the fear of being exposed, but the confidence of a deal he'd win. She ignored the envelope and strode out the door before he could say anything further within earshot of her colleagues.

With him on her heels, she kept her pace along the wood paneled corridor toward the lobby. Although now she was mere steps from the front door, she realized she lacked an escape route. The hotel parking had been full earlier, so she picked a spot on its far side. Now if she didn't stop and listen to whatever Todd had to say, he'd follow her across the empty parking lot.

She stopped before the sliding doors, which whooshed open, and faced those arctic eyes, shivering in the draft. "Just talk, so we can be done here."

Todd dangled the envelope from two fingers. "Don't you want to know what's in here?"

She muttered under her breath. "No more than I want to stay married to you."

"Inside that envelope is a document that outlines everything—you'll give me seventy percent of your assets and pay me alimony for five years. Oh, and if you ever find yourself in a position to testify against me once no longer my wife, you'll produce another chunk of cash as a lump sum. Compensation to defray my legal costs."

He pushed the document into her hand and Ryn jerked back, her pulse pounding in her wrists, as if it wanted to escape that overconfident grin as much as she did.

"I'd never sign that." She laughed, as proof he couldn't scare her, but her head spun. The fraud must be real, or why worry about her testifying? And yet he possessed enough negotiating power to not seem concerned. She shivered again. They were already selling the house. What else could he threaten to make her sign such an uneven divorce agreement—except perhaps her job?

She fought to control her breathing, so he couldn't tell he had her spooked. "Are you done now?"

"No, I haven't explained option B, which is if you don't sign what's in that envelope, I will file papers tomorrow morning insisting on detailed outside valuations of every one of your portfolio companies."

Ryn's blood surged as she finally understood his leverage. He'd make her work life hell by insisting Sentra disclose information on every company they'd invested in.

At least he'd laid his cards on the table. She grabbed the envelope from his hand and marched past the line of Teslas and Porsches flanking both sides of valet parking. A quick glance back confirmed he'd remained in the lobby, where he glared after her.

She pulled out her phone, as she always did before walking across a large empty parking lot. Her footsteps pounded as she sped up, jogging toward her car.

Of course, Todd found a way to play dirty. Simon would be furious with Ryn for leaving Sentra vulnerable to legal demands by not telling him about her divorce before they put her in charge of the new fund. He'd never have made her senior partner if he knew that risk existed. But at least now they'd already announced her in the job. And the valuation information Todd wanted was semi-public. It'd be a hassle to collect and disclose it for every company they'd funded, but if Ryn minimized the work involved, she could perhaps convince Simon it was manageable.

She rounded the corner toward her SUV and glanced back one more time, making sure Todd hadn't followed her.

Fuck. He strode right behind her. He must have come out the hotel's side door.

Why was he still following her? He'd said all he

needed. Ryn fled toward the car, her lungs burning, cursing the shadows and quiet of the parking lot when inside the hotel had been full. The SUV unlocked with a beep and the blood pumped in her wrists and throat as she threw her briefcase past the driver's seat and jumped in.

Like hell would she consider signing away everything to this man who'd lied and broken her heart, but at this second, she feared more for her safety.

Todd ran the last few feet, swung in and grabbed the door before she closed it, the stubble on his chin quivering with a rage she'd seen in flashes, but never like this, fully unleashed.

"Let go." Her voice sounded as shaky as her legs under the steering wheel, less a match to his anger and more petrified child.

"Not until I finish explaining."

"I'll call the police." This time she shouted, holding her phone above the passenger seat.

He leered around the edge of the door, inches from her face. "I'll be done before they arrive. But hear me out. It's rather fun."

She started the ignition, ready to slam the accelerator. Too bad if she pulverized his toes or screeched out of the hotel driveway with him hanging off the side.

"But, Ryn, you haven't let me tell you the best part. Now that you're a senior partner—congratulations by the way, always knew you'd do it—I will also make a claim on your income. Which means I will need Sentra to disclose their carry percentages, their management fees, their ownership structure, so my experts can calculate my share of your future earnings."

The breath left her chest, along with any hope of convincing Simon not to fire her. He would never give out the confidential information Todd had listed, including Sentra's carry, the percentage each senior partner got paid on deals. A regular person didn't even know to ask for such data, virtual gold dust in the venture world. Todd wouldn't have known either unless she herself had explained the benefits of being a senior partner.

"Got your attention now, did I, dear wife? Oh, I almost forgot the most important part. You call off your stupid little gumshoe detective. And the proposal is take it or leave it. I'm not soliciting edits from your lawyer." He stepped back and released the door, his grin transformed to full Jack Nicholson Joker triumphant.

"Go to hell." She hit the accelerator, pulling the door closed before rounding the corner to exit the parking lot, and roared toward the freeway's on-ramp.

No wonder Todd sounded confident. He'd waited for her promotion to make his play. *You expose my fraud, I take your job.* She raced around the curves of the freeway, her hands shaking, pulse pounding, and vision blurring, and a gap widened in her heart.

Big brave Ryn. Cleans up Simon's crap at work, negotiates billion-dollar deals, but when her husband uses his legal rights to threaten her, what does she say? *Go to hell.* Now she was no better than divorce clichés.

She didn't even know if she wanted to convince Simon to cooperate. She'd be helping Todd claim money he didn't deserve to keep a job that didn't deserve her.

She clutched the steering wheel hard, and struggled to catch her breath. In reality, she didn't have another choice. If she left Sentra—once it became known she'd put the firm's confidentiality at risk—no other VC firm would hire her. And certainly not with her divorce not final, meaning Todd could lay claim to a new firm's assets.

If he did what he threatened tomorrow morning and filed papers on Sentra, not only would Ryn lose her job, but she'd become unemployable.

Her whole career she'd ensured every investment had an exit strategy: If a company didn't go public as planned, then it could be acquired or merged, or its assets sold. But she didn't have a backup plan for her own life.

She wove in and out of traffic on the way back to Marin, counting the seconds until she could talk with Carly and ask for help, her breaths speeding as fast as the dark-light-dark shadows of the poles passing on the bridge.

Chapter Twenty-Nine

Carly checked Sammy snuffled in the bedroom, which meant he'd entered deep sleep, and responded to Ryn's text.

—*Yes, come right over*—

She returned to the living room and opened the front door, so Ryn wouldn't need to knock.

While she waited, Carly rubbed the tense muscles in her shoulders. Since they ran into Todd yesterday, she couldn't shake his expression, not only anger but a certain ambivalence: *If I'm going down, you'll burn in hell with me.*

When Ryn arrived, they sat at the dining room table, and Carly did her best to follow as Ryn rattled through Todd's threat and how she'd lose her job, her career, her everything.

"All my fault…knows about the detective"—Ryn heaved several short breaths between her words—"and threatened disclosures on Sentra. And none of this, I mean, I'm the idiot who didn't insist on a prenup."

"Why don't I brew us some kava tea? It's calming and helps with focus, and maybe we can start again from the beginning?"

Ryn rolled her eyes, stood, and paced across the room toward the window.

A few months ago, Carly would have worried she'd upset her, but not now. Now she knew Ryn so well her angst ran in her own veins. "You do want my help, right?"

"Yes, I'm sorry. It's just it'll take a hell of a lot more than a cup of tea to get me out of this mess. But my way sure as hell isn't working because my brain is a mustang stampede. So let's do it your way. Tea it is."

Carly stood and touched Ryn's shoulders. "If we're doing it my way, I have a better suggestion, if you'll trust me?" She put on the kettle and when she returned Carly lowered herself and sat cross legged with her back against the sofa. She gestured for Ryn to follow.

"You know," Carly said. "I used to get worked up regularly. I'd tell myself everything was hopeless and why even try and fix my mistakes, when the universe seemed determined to make sure nothing went my way. That's when Dev taught me meditation. I'm still not great at it, but most mornings it helps me at least find gratitude for my blessings. And when something hits me sideways, I take some time and source the strength to tackle it."

Ryn sat awkwardly on the floor next to her. "Okay, this is a first, but I trust you. Tell me what to do."

"We're going to sit here and breathe for ten minutes, focusing on different parts of our body in turn. It will seem long, but I promise it'll help clear your head."

Carly breathed in and exhaled, then again, and led Ryn through a short version of what she knew by heart from her guided recordings She'd meditated twice already today, the second time because, right after she dropped Sammy off late, an FDA memo arrived, confirming her fear their product approvals would not be final by the presentation in Austin. With the help of a short meditation in the garden, she'd focused enough to work with the team and develop a new plan for what to say onstage.

When they finished, Ryn breathed out a huge sigh.

Carly patted her shoulder, stood, and made the tea. When she returned with the teapot and two mugs, Ryn, who still sat on the floor, opened her eyes again.

"You were right, thank you. It didn't solve anything, but look—I can at least talk coherently, now. My head still hurts, but you made me realize I never just stop like this." Ryn seemed to be breathing normally now, and boosted herself onto the sofa.

Carly sat close to her. "So tell me again why Todd asking for information from Sentra is such a problem?"

She listened as this time Ryn explained her possible responses to Todd's threat, which included signing his proposed agreement, or convincing Sentra to hand over a subset of the data Todd would legally demand, but not too much, while she waited for the detective to complete his investigation.

"But what probability do you put on him actually discovering more?" Carly asked. "I mean it's been what—two months?—since he found those fake power of attorney docs."

Ryn pulled her knees in close to her body on the sofa and rocked back and forth. "Honestly? About zero percent. I think, by now, Todd's hidden stuff well. If the detective was going to find anything, I'm pretty sure it would have happened already."

"Well, obviously you can't sign the agreement Todd gave you," Carly said. "He's asking for practically everything you have left. Not to mention the not testifying thing."

"Yeah, I suspect it's not even legal." Ryn nodded at the envelope she brought with her, which sat on the dining table. "I just decided. I'll give it to my lawyer, but I'm not even opening it."

Carly shook her head, refusing to accept that Todd had Ryn cornered. "Well, it sounds to me like your best hope is convincing Simon to cooperate, but slowly. Like you said, try to wing it by giving Todd only a subset of the information he asks for, and just pray the detective finds out more soon." Even Carly recognized she'd used all three—wing, hope and prayer—in her last words.

"And why would Simon give any information when he could just fire me?" Ryn lowered her head to her knees.

"Maybe you underestimate how much he needs you?" Carly asked.

Ryn looked at her through her fingertips. Based on what Paul had told Carly of the ruthlessness of venture capitalists, it sounded unlikely one would prioritize a partner's personal issues over the confidentiality of their firm.

"Well," Carly said, "you still lose nothing by talking to him before Todd files papers. I mean Sentra will find out soon, anyway."

"Indeed." Ryn grimaced. "If they haven't already figured it out from Todd coming after me in the bar at Zidera. It's a long shot, but it doesn't seem like I have another choice. I'll talk with him first thing tomorrow."

The tension in Ryn's forehead said she didn't believe for a second her boss would agree to help.

Carly reached and patted Ryn's hand, wishing she could help more. "Sorry to bring you platitudes here,

279

but don't forget you're already as strong as needed. Even for this."

Ryn stood and gave her a grateful smile. "I sure hope you're right. Because you know those wooden Jenga blocks? Since the day I called Todd's hotel back in November, it's felt as if I pulled out the first block from a life-sized tower. I suspect once Todd files those papers on Sentra tomorrow, the whole damn thing is gonna come crashing down."

Chapter Thirty

Ryn's SUV careened into the Sentra Ventures garage, clipping the edge of the curb when she veered toward the first parking spot. It was only seven-thirty in the morning, but she needed to reach Simon and convince him to help, before he received Todd's documents or threats.

In the elevator, she practiced the arguments she discussed with Carly last night for why Simon should cooperate. First, she'd reinforce how valuable she'd become to Sentra, especially now as the leader of their newest fund, and then she'd promise a hundred percent of the work involved would fall on her. The problem was, to her knowledge, no venture firm had ever divulged proprietary data like this as part of a divorce—because, of course, no senior partner would fail to have a prenup.

The twenty-fourth floor sat quiet but for the hum of printers. Most days only Ryn, Simon, and Keisha arrived before eight. She peered left to verify Simon's office was still dark before heading to make coffee. As she walked along the corridor, low sounds of conversation came from the kitchen. The office must not be as empty as she believed.

In the break-room, Keisha sat alone hunched over a laptop, the screen blue-lighting her face, and a full cup of coffee next to her fingertips. The voices came from a video she watched.

She turned down the volume "Ryn, you need to see this. It's from a session in London this morning. A friend texted me because it's already all over the socials."

Ryn poured herself a cup from the pot Keisha had brewed. "I appreciate you being here so early, but can it wait until after I meet with Simon?"

Keisha stared at her without saying a word, but the quirk of her perfect eyebrows above the bright green eyeshadow said absolutely not. She turned the laptop so Ryn could see the screen.

The setup on the video with multiple women onstage resembled the panel Ryn did in Half Moon Bay last year. She recognized Leslie Lawler, who worked at Sentra two years ago as a junior associate, before she left for a job in London.

Ryn sat beside Keisha, so they could both see the screen. "One of those roundtables promoting female entrepreneurship?"

"Nope. It's a discussion hosted by public radio on sexism and harassment and how #MeToo has played out in tech. You need to hear what Leslie says."

"About Sentra?" God knows what stupidity Simon would be quoted as saying now. On certain days working here was like standing at the bottom of a cesspit into which he kept shoveling more excrement. Although interesting timing: this might be something Ryn could use today to remind him of her value, given every time she'd cleaned up after his verbal diarrhea.

Keisha forwarded the video and stopped at the midpoint. Her expression had been somber since Ryn walked in, but now an emotion she couldn't peg shone in her eyes. Relief?

She pressed play, and the interviewer posed a question of the panel. "We saw a new dynamic in Hollywood where women who'd been silent for decades spoke up en masse. A cleansing, so to speak. Would you say the same thing happened in the tech sector?"

Leslie answered with a sad shake of her head. "I'm afraid not yet. For sure, there are similarities in tech, in that it's essential to know how to dismiss sexist comments and come-ons with a half-smile, without engaging or making a powerful man angry. Or if that's just not possible, you quit your job before rejecting him blows up on you."

Ryn realized she nodded along.

"But frankly, some of us have had enough and are starting to speak out, damn the consequences. Let's take my own example from two years ago, when I worked for a firm in San Francisco. I'd be a partner today, if I'd just agreed to have sex with their sleazy lead Venture Capitalist any of the times he propositioned or grabbed at me. But I refused, so when a more senior role opened, and I still wouldn't screw him in order to get the job, I was fired."

Ryn's stomach clenched and her eyeballs burned. How was it possible she hadn't seen Simon for the harasser he was? Yes, he behaved like a jerk, a stupid frat boy who said insensitive things, but surely she'd have known if he stooped to the same full-on creep behavior as Grant, her first boss, who considered responding to his advances part of her job description.

But then, she didn't even realize Leslie was fired. Ryn had just believed Simon, when he told everyone she received a better offer in London.

She jumped to her feet and stepped back from the screen, her chest tightening as she ticked through every moment she'd vouched for Simon's stupid words, like onstage at the Women's Forum last year, shame smoldering in her stomach as she explained how he simply misspoke when he'd offhandedly stated female entrepreneurs didn't have the balls to make good investments.

She remembered the time a female CEO approached her saying his leering in meetings made her feel uncomfortable. Ryn offered to substitute for Simon on the board, but if she were honest, after that episode, wasn't what Leslie referred to further along the same continuum?

She scrubbed her forehead with the palms of her hands. She and Leslie might have worked together, but outside the office, Ryn barely spent any time with her. If she'd asked Leslie out for coffee, just the two of them—even once—she might have learned Simon behaved exactly the same as Grant.

She didn't even know why she'd been so distant. Carly had shown you need not quash emotional connection to be a good leader—quite the opposite.

Ryn turned toward Keisha, the shame of not acknowledging the truth about Simon before now driving her gaze toward the floor. "Why didn't you tell me?"

Keisha squirmed in her seat. "Honestly? Until this moment and the look on your face, I thought maybe you were aware."

Ryn thought back to the day Keisha said she wouldn't wear her V-neck printed shirt with Simon around the office. Her stomach turned over. How could she have been so dumb? Keisha didn't mean the ethnic pattern. She'd told Ryn directly, and she still hadn't listened. Keisha meant she'd never wear anything so revealing as a deep V-neck, for fear Simon take it as an invitation.

Keisha closed the laptop and the full impact of her relieved expression when she started the video sank like a block of iron in Ryn's stomach. "You, too, Keisha?"

Keisha's fingers moved across her mouth and she averted her eyes. The jerky movements and refusal to look up were all the confirmation Ryn needed.

Ryn sat again and stared at the table. She wanted to touch Keisha's hand, ask her to share what happened, but what did it say that she believed Ryn already knew? She'd convinced herself, because Simon never propositioned her, that there was a line between what a person said and what they did. But she had no reason to believe that, other than because she wanted to. Because it had been convenient for her.

The office front door near the bank of elevators opened, and the slip-slide of leather dress shoes echoed, heading away from them toward Simon's office.

She reached and laid her hand on Keisha's. "I am so, so sorry for not seeing it. I promise you I'm going to fix this."

Keisha's gaze rose and met hers with a small sad smile.

The footsteps stopped and changed direction, coming back toward them. Simon's voice roared along the corridor. "Ryn, are you here? We need to talk. Now." He must have seen the video before he left home.

She headed toward his office, trying to unpack the impact of Leslie's statements. If Sentra became mired in a defamation or harassment suit—the most likely scenario now Leslie had gone public—Ryn would be called to testify as the most senior woman.

And what would she say? That she believed her boss to be a regular-type-jerk, but if he forced himself on female employees, she'd been blind to it.

Ryn marched along the corridor toward his office. Leslie couldn't be more right about this industry. The room at Zidera last night—with women lined up to be treated like slabs of meat—was the encapsulation of its problems. Powerful men believing they were entitled to say, and apparently do, whatever they wanted. And by talking around Simon's comments on panels, half-justifying his disrespect of women, she'd been part of the problem.

They said you should never negotiate without a clear goal, and suddenly she had sharp clarity: She refused to let Simon continue getting away with this, and no longer cared a damn about saving her job.

She banged once on the door and entered his office, struggling to not immediately start screaming at him.

Simon stood by his oak desk holding a sheaf of papers covered in small font legalese; the tops of his ears rage-red. Her name and Todd's showed on the pages. Somehow, before eight in the morning, Todd already served him with disclosure demands.

"What the hell, Ryn?" Simon's tone was that of a dad who discovered his teenage daughter is turning tricks. With a jerk of his chubby fingers, he signaled her to shut the door, plunked himself behind his desk, and stared at her, eyebrows raised in incredulity.

She strode up, not bothering to close the door behind her. *Unbelievable.* She spent years letting this lowlife hold her future in his grubby hands. Simon didn't deserve an ounce of the power she'd granted him in groveling for his respect.

He pushed the papers toward her. "This firm cannot get involved in your divorce proceedings. Have you even seen what they're asking for? I will credit you're normally not like other women who bring their personal drama to the office, but how many degrees of stupid would you be not to have a prenup?"

She slammed the palm of her hand on the desk, inches from his fingertips. She would not be called stupid by this specimen of depravity.

"I'm not here about those papers. We need to talk about what happened with Leslie."

And the others. How many women did he threaten while Ryn refused to see the truth? Nausea rose up her throat as she considered some might have felt they had no option but to submit.

"Leslie Lawler?"

She pulled herself to full height, looking down over his pudgy cheeks and wrinkled forehead. "She didn't quit like you told everyone. You fired her."

"How is this relevant to our conversation?"

"Because you tried to force yourself on her and she refused."

For once, the great Simon, so full of bluster, seemed unsure how to respond. He rubbed the back of his neck and glanced toward the corridor. Other colleagues, now arriving for their eight o'clock meetings, likely heard her shouting.

Footsteps paused outside. Either to listen or for fear of walking past the open door.

"This is all a misunderstanding, and please lower your voice." Simon's own volume became the most quiet she'd heard. "It's more we came to an understanding after our interactions because it was too awkward working together."

"Too awkward because she wouldn't sleep with you." Ryn stomped around the desk and stopped inches from his beer belly. "You fired her because she wouldn't fuck you. Then paid her extra severance, made her sign an agreement, and keep quiet. How many others have you done this to?" *Like Keisha?*

She didn't expect an answer, but Simon's glare held more defiance than remorse. Just like Todd, the only thing he regretted was getting caught.

Ryn closed her eyes a second, fighting the instinct to ram him into the wall behind his desk. She might never forgive herself for her role as his enabler.

"You disgust me. No job is worth selling your soul to work with sleaze like you."

She pivoted and marched out the open door, past four colleagues who listened, slack-mouthed, in the corridor. No need to say the words *I quit*. It was obvious. Simon could up go in flames on a golf course as far as she cared.

She walked to the storeroom, grabbed two empty boxes, and returned to her office, tossing inside the few personal items she'd permitted herself at work—the John Wayne poster with a horse rearing up, her Feelings Jar—while she embraced the fury scalding the inside of her chest.

Fat lot of good the jar did her. If she had allowed

herself the kind of empathy and connection Carly nurtured, instead of stifling every emotion, she'd never have been so blind.

She stuffed a last stack of personal papers into her briefcase. Before leaving, she found Keisha and asked her to meet at a coffee shop in an hour, then walked toward the elevator with her two boxes, stacked one on the other.

She wanted to slam the glass lobby door and watch the Sentra logo shatter, but she wouldn't give Simon or the other partners the satisfaction of adding a point on the *women bring drama to the office* scorecard. Instead, she placed the boxes on the marble floor, then turned and closed the door behind her with a measured nondramatic click.

None of the other partners watching from the corridor offered to help.

She pressed the elevator button. It was not yet nine on a Friday morning, and she had no emails to answer, no prep work, and no meetings, because she just quit without a clue what came next.

Chapter Thirty-One

Ryn paced outside the café where Keisha agreed to meet her, the coffee she bought for them sloshing and leaking over the edge of the paper cups.

She didn't have any idea what she'd say to Keisha, but Ryn couldn't stay at Sentra after what she learned about Simon. Nor did she know how to keep her promise and fix it, now she had burned all bridges by quitting.

She stared at her reflection in the window; a deranged woman, her hair in disarray, the open briefcase over her shoulder overflowing with papers, and two coffee cups leaking onto her shoes and the sidewalk. And that's what people in the industry were likely to call her—deranged—after the way she screamed at Simon.

Yet what burned inside was not remorse that she'd likely kissed her career goodbye, but a mix of shame and crimson fury at not having seen through Simon before now.

Keisha jogged around the corner, out of breath. "Hi, sorry. Hard to get away. It all went to hell after you left. Simon is storming around barking orders at everyone, making sure they cancel your access and keycards."

"Sorry." This backlash from Simon meant Keisha needed to leave Sentra, as soon as feasible, especially as Ryn wouldn't be there to protect her from Simon's wrath.

Ryn pointed farther along the street. "I have a place in mind where we can talk in private." She handed Keisha her cup, and they set off along Market Street.

When they reached the door of one of the large banks, Ryn guided them through the open-air lobby and up a set of stairs. Keisha whistled when they exited into a rooftop garden, which looked as Ryn remembered, with a wide rose-brick plaza and intimate spaces on either side separated by concrete planters and hedges. The weather was chilly today, so they were alone, apart from a homeless man sheltering under a bench.

"Wow, how did you know about this place?" Keisha asked.

"Oh, a colleague at my old firm told me, and I used to visit every so often. Mostly when I needed a sanity restoration moment after one of Simon's rants." If only she'd thought to bring Leslie or Keisha here just once, and asked how things were going.

Skirting the bench, Ryn led them to sit by a sculpture on the far side of the garden. "I know this is hard, but can you please share more about...well, did Simon threaten...did he assault you?"

Keisha grimaced, but Ryn saw the strength in the clamp of her jaw. "At first it was subtle, you know, little things you're better off ignoring. A comment on my pants if I wore something tight, or my blouse—which really provided an excuse for staring at my cleavage. But I'd just joined the firm, and you had taken a chance on me, so I didn't want to cause a fuss..."

Ryn nodded. She understood what Keisha meant.

Not causing a fuss was why Ryn left her first firm instead of reporting Grant. But based on the way Keisha squirmed on the stone bench, she braced herself for worse.

"Remember the first week in December, when you traveled to Los Angeles? I was in the office late, around seven o'clock—" The too-loud beep-beep of a truck backing up on the street below interrupted her, and Keisha stopped, looking relieved for the pause.

"I was finishing the day delivering packages to each office. When I walked into Simon's, he called me over to see something. He sat behind his desk…" She stared at the ground, obviously embarrassed.

"It's okay," Ryn said. "You don't have to tell me if you don't want."

"No, it's all right, it's just awkward. Under the desk he had pulled out his, well, you know…his junk."

Ryn's jaw dropped and the rage in her chest burned brighter. Simon's behavior went far beyond what she experienced with Grant. Bile rose in her throat, wondering how the hell she could prevent his lumbering frame from backing any other junior associate into a corner of his office, the lunchroom, a hotel corridor.

"Oh, Keisha. What happened next?"

With a smile, Keisha put on a fake Southern accent. "I told him his Momma would be ashamed, slammed the door shut, and made sure he and I were never alone in the office again."

"Wow, you handled it great, but I'm so sorry you ever had to deal with that. Talking of which—we've got to get you out of there. In the last hour I drew up a list of alternate firms that have office manager roles. I'm not sure how much a reference from me is worth now, but I could still make some intros, help set up a few interviews."

Keisha gave a half-smile. "How do you know the partners at those firms are any different?"

Ryn studied the rose-colored flagstones for a second. In the background, passing trams screeched and whooshed past on Market Street. She owed Keisha an honest answer.

Grant, now Simon; taking advantage of junior women appeared more the rule than an exception. And she'd noticed none of the other male partners stepped forward to help or called today after she left.

Keisha had a point. Ryn couldn't know for sure if any firm she recommended would be better. This industry was populated by an army of Simon clones, who believed respect to be merited only if the speaker came blessed with a scrotum. And if Ryn herself simply opted out, walked away without doing something—anything—to fix the broader problem, she knew this chill in the air might enter her soul and lodge there.

"Again, I'm so sorry, Keisha."

Her heart hung heavy as she pulled Keisha in for a long hug. As they descended the stairs back to the street, Ryn racked her brain on how she—one single person—could fix any of this. At minimum, she should call Leslie Lawler. If she intended to sue Simon, Ryn could offer her voice and support. But what else? She owed Leslie, and the other women she'd failed, to do something more.

****

At three o'clock, Ryn parked on the hill leading to Cliff House restaurant, where she'd asked Carly to meet. She peered the length of Ocean Beach, which ran south for miles, and inhaled the sharp smell of waves hitting the seaweed.

The last time she visited this beach was after she confronted Todd, the day his lies had unraveled. Strange how everything she thought might end her in the last months—losing her house, her reputation, her promotion, and now her job—seemed petty compared to the magnitude of what she realized today affected thousands of fellow women.

She pulled up her collar to protect her face from the spinning sand particles whipping off the concrete sidewalk while climbing to the restaurant which sat on the cliff, jutting out over the ocean. She entered, found a table in the bar, and ordered two glasses of a red wine she knew Carly would enjoy.

Within a few minutes, Carly arrived and took a seat. "You quit?"

Ryn replayed the events of the day, ending with her conversation with Leslie Lawler, who said she always respected Ryn and appreciated her call, but wished she'd known two years ago that Ryn would have supported her if she came forward about Simon.

"Holy cow." Carly said. "I'd heard Simon was a bit of a jerk, but this is way beyond the pale. What an asshole."

"I wish it were only him." Ryn explained her hesitancy in recommending Keisha to another firm. "I mean, if I'm honest, when Leslie or I or Keisha speak out against Simon, we're only three people. Even if we are believed—and history says we'll be painted as vindictive women—it's an industry-wide problem. With a troop of Simon-types out there, taking one off the battlefield changes nothing."

Carly stared out the massive windows and watched the waves, looking pensive.

"You're right, Ryn."

"About which part?"

"The sexism in tech. It's been accepted for decades, so it's not a one-person problem, and it's not a one-person solution. It's almost as if someone needs to change the whole rules of the game, of what is and isn't acceptable behavior."

"You mean like a #MeToo for the venture capital industry?"

"Yeah, exactly, power in numbers. Some way women in our industry could outline what is no longer okay and stand up for each other...maybe like a hotline to call, get the type of support from other women Leslie felt she lacked?"

Ryn smiled, respecting Carly's ability to think through such a massive problem in its parts, like a true scientist. This was why she'd asked for her time this afternoon. "I love the idea of a more structured, public approach. Something that gives experienced executives who've lived with harassment when younger, like me, a chance to stand up for newcomers like a Keisha or Leslie."

Ryn's brain spun, analyzing the implications of such a massive industry-wide endeavor. "If I wanted to help...I mean, what do you think it would take? To pull off something like this?"

Carly's lips curved into a knowing smile. "Well, the first variable to solve in this equation is it requires a leader who can rally people. Ideally someone who's articulate and willing to put herself out there,

295

consequences be damned. Kind of like you described Leslie this morning. But probably someone more advanced in their career, perhaps a senior partner?"

Ryn shook her head and laughed, but her hopes were sinking. How could she be that leader? She, the person who'd stood onstage at entrepreneur's forums and talked around Simon's stupid sexist comments, had no right to speak for other women.

"Well?" Carly's smile said she waited for Ryn to catch up. "Know anyone?"

Ryn rubbed her forehead. Carly was right about one thing: taking on the boys' club of VCs required a person who no longer cared about their own position in the industry: someone in the unique situation Ryn now found herself.

"Tell me again that thing your Uncle Remy used to say?" Ryn asked.

Carly set aside her wine and met her gaze. "It's never too late to become the person you want to see in the mirror." She searched Ryn's eyes, as if questioning whether she could rise to the challenge. "And if you're willing to take this on, I want to help."

Ryn's stomach did a small somersault. Her gut told her she was crazy to even consider this; taking on the boys' club meant venture career suicide, a sure way to get herself blackballed from opportunities at all future firms. But the absolute belief in Carly's eyes and the warm flush radiating through Ryn's chest said she needed to try.

She placed both hands on Carly's. "Okay partner. Let's go fix an industry."

Chapter Thirty-Two

In the BioLarge lunchroom, ten women buzzed around tables and countertops covered with stacks of paper, furiously typing emails and making calls. Carly hollered from where she stood by the whiteboard to be heard over the din.

Ryn held the phone away from her ear and Keisha stepped away from working on their website. Carly waited until she caught the attention of everyone else in the room. During her previous conference call, they'd achieved a milestone. Three more female CEOs agreed to join their initiative, Equal Chances Silicon Valley.

When the chatter stopped, she erased the number forty-seven from the whiteboard and replaced it with fifty. The number of participants who had pledged—in the two weeks they'd been working around the clock calling contacts in venture capital and among tech startups—to share their stories and support other women.

Keisha and several others stood and applauded. Ryn clapped with her hands high over her head. "Three in one call? I swear Carly could rally snowmen to go on a tropical jungle tour."

"What can I say…" Carly lifted up on her heels, not hesitating to show some pride. "After a few slow days, we're gathering momentum."

"Erase that number!" Kim shouted from the

doorway. "I got us two more."

Since Ryn had introduced them, Carly had been amazed at how Kim—the most prominent female venture capitalist in Silicon Valley—consistently looked as if she walked straight off a Conde Nast Travel fashion shoot. Today she wore a printed silk coat in a bright green pattern which glided behind her black pants and stilettos.

"Well done." Carly grinned, removed the top, once again, from the marker, and updated the number of participants to fifty-two.

Kim swooshed across the room and beckoned Ryn and Keisha to join her. They huddled with Carly in a corner near the whiteboard.

"You will never guess one of our new supporters," Kim said, tapping Ryn's arm.

Ryn stared at her quizzically.

"Marilyn Walters—your old boss."

"Seriously? What changed?" Ryn asked. "I spent an hour at her office yesterday, and she basically tried to talk me out of the whole initiative. I believe her exact words were that 'taking on the old boys' club is equivalent to banging all our conjoined heads against a wall.'"

Kim smirked and pulled her coat in playfully around her legs. "Perhaps your words of wisdom finally sank in? Or she could have been influenced by my pointing out that, a month from now, she may not want to be the only senior woman in the valley who isn't participating."

"You really think it will get that big?" Ryn shook her head and turned to Carly. "Thanks for the help with getting us so many CEOs. You are much better connected than I am."

Carly stood straighter. She might never be the world's best public speaker, but every peer she talked to one-on-one had asked about, and been fascinated by, how her company's technology would help prevent heart attacks. After this much validation, it was time to accept that she had something truly important to say onstage—on behalf of BioLarge—at South by Southwest in two weeks.

Even bringing Sammy here in the evenings to work on Equal Chances hadn't been a mistake. He was thrilled to help with stuffing papers in folders and any other tasks she found.

"What kind of critical mass do you think we need for a public announcement?" Ryn asked.

Keisha spoke up. "A couple hundred, maybe?"

Kim nodded. "And going at the current rate, it may not take us more than another few weeks."

"Wow, faster than I expected," Carly said. "So long as we work around our Austin trip, that timing is fine." She'd been touched when Ryn offered to pay out of her own pocket, now she no longer worked at Sentra, to still attend South by Southwest. "The real question is what's our launch venue for Equal Chances? I mean, when it comes to hearing our message, it's not as if a man like Simon—"

Ryn interjected in a good-natured tone, "Or Grant."

Carly nodded. "—will voluntarily attend an event announcing an initiative to help women."

"Good point." Ryn stroked the side of her forehead, seemingly lost in thought. She walked into the center of the room and raised her voice. "Hey everyone, great news. At this rate, we should be ready to go public in a matter of weeks. Can you all start thinking of ideas for a good announcement venue?"

Carly followed the nodding heads and thoughtful expressions. Every one of these women, each from different companies, with busy jobs, had volunteered their time. She noticed those farthest from the whiteboard were distracted by someone outside the open door.

In the entry to the lunchroom, Brock Gordon, the StackTech journalist, stood watching them.

Carly's heart climbed toward her throat. She didn't know how long he'd been standing there or what he heard, but they weren't ready for this initiative to be written about in the press. The horror on Ryn's face said she feared the same: he'd leak their story. And Brock was the last journalist they'd want to have an advance scoop.

Carly marched to the hallway, and led him back toward the lobby, while she calculated a credible way of explaining the campaign room he just saw. Maybe she could pass it off as BioLarge planning for their launch?

She paused before the front desk. "What are you doing here?"

"I'm sorry for interrupting, but can you spare five minutes to talk? I owe you an apology." Brock's head dipped, the sheepishness of his posture a different man than when she last saw him at the press panel two months ago. "If now isn't convenient, I can come back another time."

Hard not to compare his humility to Todd, who stood at this same desk last year and demanded she make time for his apology. Carly touched her sleeve, debating her answer. Under the shirt, her skin was raw from the new butterfly she had tattooed a few days ago to remind herself that Todd represented one more learning experience, not a lifelong error.

She wanted to say no, and slap Brock in the same category as Todd forever, but something in the way he stood there waiting, giving her space, told her to listen. "Why don't we go for a walk?"

They took the path that skirted the Bay, running along the side of the office park, and after a few minutes he stopped, as if he'd worked himself up to speak. "I know this is probably unexpected, but I'm trying to make amends with people I've hurt. I've stopped drinking, not giving that as an excuse. What I did in my article about you was petty and unprofessional. I'm not expecting you to forgive me, but I wanted to apologize all the same."

Carly stared at the choppy water for a moment, her chest burning. She'd spent every minute of the last months battling the impact of Brock's article and the slew of others which came on its heels. She turned toward him, not sure what to say, but surprisingly, pity rose in her chest. She never imagined the arrogant Brock standing here in front of her, contrite, his gaze lowered toward the concrete.

She stroked the other butterflies that ran along her arm, now entirely covering the gun. She hadn't been without fault in this lifetime. She remembered the sinking sensation of standing on her parents' doorstep, once at nineteen years old and again at twenty-nine, when she believed they might be ready to forgive and move forward. Twice they weren't big enough to accept that a person, their own daughter, could change.

Brock's hair fell over his face, in a way that reminded her of Todd, but that didn't mean no man could grow or improve. Uncle Remy's smiling face, sitting on his rocker on the porch filled her memory, and a weight lifted from her heart. Like her, Brock might carry his history forever, but she understood that was the point of making amends, so you could forgive yourself and try to do better next time.

She turned and offered him a genuine smile. "I once had an uncle who taught me to believe in second chances. So I accept your apology, and wish you nothing but the best with the program."

Brock smiled in what looked like relief. "I know it's a long journey…but thank you."

As they walked back toward the office, they chatted for a few minutes about the difficulty of making those first few changes and Carly shared how she herself had rebooted her life more than once.

When they reached the lobby, Brock extended a hand. "If there's ever anything I can do to help you or your company, please let me know."

Carly stopped mid-shake, an idea striking. "Isn't your big awards ceremony for StackTech coming up soon?"

"Yes, week after next, why?"

She gave a sly smile. "I may have the perfect way for you to realign your karma with women."

****

A few minutes later, Carly reentered the lunchroom. It was getting late in the afternoon and while the babysitter would pick Sammy up at school, most of the volunteers needed to leave and collect their own children, or catch up on their day jobs.

She walked over to where Kim and Ryn chatted near the coffeepot, pulled up a chair, and joined their table.

"You are never going to believe this, but I think I just found us a launch venue." After summarizing her conversation with Brock, she shared her proposal to use the StackTech awards ceremony.

"That is just inspired." Ryn leaned over the table and air kissed Carly on both cheeks. "Everyone who's anyone attends those awards in case they're a winner, so we'll have them all in one room."

"And StackTech will obviously cover the event, so they'll likely write about us, too," Kim added.

Carly gave a quick glance heavenward. It seemed the universe had realigned. Or at the least, someone up there was on her side these days. If she hadn't listened to Brock, this wouldn't have been an option.

Kim stood. "I need to get going, but promise me you'll give it more thought?" She raised her eyebrows at Ryn in an expression of *come-on-you-know-what-I'm-saying*, which Carly didn't follow, then walked out the door, leaving the two of them.

"What was Kim talking about?"

"Anyway, I need to ask—"

They both spoke at the same time. "You go first," Carly said quickly.

"Now that it's just us, are you sure you want to be involved in the public part of the announcement? You've helped so much getting Equal Chances in motion, but it'll be difficult to work with Simon on your board once he sees you're part of this. And Sentra is still your company's biggest funder, after all."

Carly rolled her eyes, although Ryn was only

looking out for her. "Seriously? Every woman in Equal Chances will stand together when we go public, and you think I'd consider backing out?"

Ryn smiled. "No, but I felt I should at least ask…"

Carly waved a hand as if batting away a fly. "Don't worry about me. Meeting with those CEOs has done wonders for my perspective. You know, feeling like a fraud despite your success is a common thread among at least half of them? I'm starting to think questioning your competency is just part of being a leader. Kind of like the age-old Andy Grove quote on how only the paranoid survive."

Ryn's lips twitched. "Meaning paranoia is actually an asset?"

Carly laughed. "Perhaps. Certainly raises the bar on what we expect of ourselves. And I guess I'm finally ready to accept I'm not a half-bad CEO. If this initiative has shown me anything it's that—even if it shouldn't be true—knowing how to handle jerks like Simon is a core career skill."

"Go, you! I love this kick-ass Carly." Ryn paused for a moment before a small smile snuck across her cheeks. "Am I allowed to say how proud I am of you, without it seeming condescending?"

Carly put her hand over Ryn's, enjoying the glow in her eyes. "Of course, you are. And thank you."

They sat in silence for a second before Carly spoke. "What was Kim suggesting so cryptically when I walked up?"

"Oh, no big secret. She thinks I should create the same diversity fund I'd proposed to Sentra, but on my own, as a new firm." Ryn's eyes lit as if impassioned by the possibility, before her lips pinched. "I even considered it for about a minute yesterday. It's still a great concept, but I'm afraid it's a nonstarter. Even if I could raise the money—which will be near impossible once we announce Equal Chances and I become the Lazarus of Silicon Valley—there's still the whole Todd fraud thing, which could slam me sideways at any moment. Reality says I'll have to take a career break."

"God, it's just not fair."

"Well, I suspect I'll want to shoot myself every time I write him an alimony check. My lawyer says even though Todd has whole businesses in Nevada, we haven't been able to tie any assets to him instead of his companies, so I'll pay him an obscene amount every month if we ever finalize the divorce. But you know what?" Ryn's gaze focused on the square tiled ceiling, as if searching for words. "I thought leaving Sentra would be the end for me, but apparently the bottom cratering out of your life has a way of reordering your priorities. Like this." Ryn swept her hand toward the whiteboard showing their count of women committed to Equal Chances. "Or us. As friends. This is gonna sound like a cliché, but although I might have lost a lot, I feel like I've gained so much more."

Carly leaned in and held Ryn's gaze. She knew exactly what she meant. How far they'd both come together in understanding what truly mattered. Except the Todd piece still wasn't right. How was it fair that he got to move on, penalty-free, and keep playing his game on other women?

Carly's chest warmed as her frustration resurfaced. "Here's what I don't understand. Why—when we intend to read the riot act to the biggest names in tech—can't we catch the one guy who conned us both? I mean, are you sure your detective looked everywhere Todd might have held assets or be guilty of fraud?"

Ryn picked up the napkin beside her coffee cup and tore it into small pieces as she talked. "Nothing in Nevada, no joy in California, Connecticut, or New York."

"Nada in Oklahoma either? Maybe he wasn't so careful in his younger days?"

The resigned expression on Ryn's face transformed, as if Carly just declared Todd came from Mars.

One more lie. "Where did he tell you he was from?" Carly asked.

"Connecticut. He's always been super clear, talked about how his parents never left where they grew up. Although it's not as if I ever visited... *Holy shit.* This might be my first real lead." Ryn tossed the pieces of napkin on the table, almost bouncing out of her chair. "Are you sure? I mean, wait, why would he tell you the truth on this and not me?"

Carly broke into a grin. Oh boy, was she sure. "He didn't. You know how he uses Twitter for his business?"

"Yeah, real estate stuff."

"Well, I saw it in a tweet, but it got deleted. I remember because Todd was staying at my place—"

Carly paused and Ryn laughed. "Could that water be any further under the bridge?" She rapped Carly's arm. "Tell me!"

"Someone tweeted a photo of a football team, all smiles, holding their helmets. An old friend of Todd's sharing a high school anniversary of some type. I remember noticing his darker hair, before he got the highlights."

Ryn grinned back. Those carefully tended highlights had become a metaphor for his fakery. "And?"

"And when I joked the brown hair suited him, he turned a little crazy, ranting about how unprofessional it was, putting a high school photo on someone's work Twitter. He took his phone outside on the deck and ten minutes later, when he returned, he said it was taken care of. When I looked, the tweet had been deleted. And that's it. He stayed mad the rest of the night, but we never mentioned it again. It happened the first year we met. I'm so sorry, I should have remembered sooner…"

"You're sure it was Oklahoma?"

Carly laughed. "I remember thinking I couldn't imagine Todd with his manicured nails and fancy suits as a country boy. Plus, I guess my entire sphere of reference is the musical. The damn earworm of a song stuck in my head the entire next day."

Ryn whistled. "Okla-friggin-homa. By this point, nothing should surprise me. I suppose when someone lies to this magnitude it's like sick cows dropping poop. It takes a stretch to find where it all landed, and by the time you're done, you're not even sure you wanted to."

Carly looked sideways across the table, not quite understanding, and Ryn laughed. "Maybe Todd was right on one thing. No one outside Montana gets my stupid ranch jokes. Not even you."

Carly shrugged. "So you think the Oklahoma thing can help?"

"Are you kidding me?" Ryn's eyes danced. "My detective won't admit it, but clearly he's been stymied for months."

"Or it could be nothing." So far, Todd had anticipated Ryn's every move.

Ryn slowly stretched and took Carly's hand in hers. "Yes, but this is a place he never expected me to look because he didn't imagine the two of us becoming friends."

"Well, in his defense—neither did we," Carly said, picturing the cold, hard glare when Ryn passed the note across the table during their first meeting at Sentra.

Ryn guffawed. "I did say sorry for our first interactions like a million times by now, right?"

After they stopped laughing, Carly packed up her laptop and papers while Ryn, cheeks flushed, dialed her detective's phone number.

Chapter Thirty-Three

"The US Attorney in Oklahoma City confirmed a past investigation into your husband, but he wasn't willing to disclose details over the phone."

Ryn blinked hard, and shifted her cell phone, forcing her brain to bridge the dissonance between her detective's dull tone and the revelation he just shared. He sounded more like a dieter admitting defeat and ordering fast food: *I'll take the mega burger with large fries...and the US government first investigated your husband for fraud over a decade ago.*

"Can you hang on a minute?" Ryn set down the sheaf of handouts she and Carly were placing on each row of the long tables in The Ritz-Carlton ballroom. She glanced up at the StackTech awards banner that spanned the front wall. Her detective's timing was horrible. In less than an hour, she, Carly, and the team, would go live with the announcement of Equal Chances Silicon Valley.

She found her headphones, waved at Carly, and sat at the first table in front of the two massive video screens. "Okay, sorry, Mr. Hopper, please continue." She opened her laptop as he talked.

"Here's the thing, Ms. Brennan, I suspect the US Attorney might be more forthcoming if you, as his spouse, made an in-person visit..."

Ryn's head buzzed as her fingers flew over the

keyboard, pulling up a map. She and Carly would be in Austin next week. If she wanted to meet this US Attorney, how far was Oklahoma City?

Mr. Hopper droned in the same monotone. "Of course, if you'd prefer to cover my expenses, I could go on your behalf, however the timing is such…"

The map popped out her answer. A six-hour drive. Traveling to Oklahoma seemed like a desperate measure, a Hail Mary pass, but especially after today's event, it wasn't as if she'd have a job after the Austin conference.

"No, no, I'll go. I'm already planning to be near there next week."

Award attendees in business suits arrived at the back of the room, so she left her laptop, and exited through the patio doors facing the golf course. She walked across the flagstones toward the row of fire pits, hoping the phone signal held long enough to give her privacy. Despite the cold, sun streaks filtered through the cloud layer and the waves beyond the cliff reflected military blue.

"Mr. Hopper, I only have a few minutes, and I don't mean to pry into your methods, but how did you even find out about the investigation? Isn't this stuff confidential?"

"Well, the US Attorney there is an old friend. I simply assumed if real estate fraud is what we suspect your husband of today, perhaps he got a start in his home state, and put in a call. If you decide to go, I can help schedule a meeting for you."

"Yes, that would be great. Thanks so much for all the digging."

Ryn turned back toward the building. Beyond the

French doors, the ballroom had half-filled. Brock Gordon stood at the center of the room, between the rows of tables covered with navy and gold tablecloths and name cards, welcoming the attendees.

"Wait, Ms. Brennan, I have one more significant piece of information."

"There's more?"

"It sounds as if Todd involved a prior wife in his real estate transactions in a similar way. Apparently, her signature turned up on several documents that formed part of the investigation."

Prior wife? Ryn's stomach turned over. "He was married before?"

She sank onto the seating along the edge of the fire pit, expecting the adrenaline hit and pounding pulse of another huge revelation. But instead, her heartbeat rapidly returned to normal.

Mr. Hopper continued talking, and Ryn tilted her head and studied the clouds. She remembered sitting on the living room rug after Todd stole the document boxes, the pressure rising in her chest. And now finding out he used to be married: barely a flutter.

Perhaps she had depleted all her shock reserves. At this moment, if Mr. Hopper announced Todd was head of the Turkish mafia, she suspected she'd say, *Yup, makes sense.*

"I tracked down his ex-wife and talked on the phone to verify—"

"Wait, you talked with her? What did she say? Does she still live in Oklahoma?"

"Well, she wasn't very forthcoming. In fact, she hung up before I got in too many words. Her name is Ella Simmons, and she still lives in his hometown of

Weatherford."

Ella Simmons. Todd would have been in his early twenties when he left Oklahoma. She could be a childhood sweetheart he married in his teens, perhaps even his first victim. Although this wife succeeded with something Ryn had yet to achieve—breaking free of him. Ella might have advice for Ryn on how to prove she wasn't involved in his fraud.

The detective promised he'd send her contact information, and she finished the call, then checked the location of Weatherford on her phone. Only an hour drive from Oklahoma City.

Ryn walked back toward the ballroom, her stomach fluttering in excitement, tinged with dread. If she traveled to Oklahoma, Ella might not want to help. In fact, she may refuse to even answer the door, and Ryn had no guarantee the US Attorney would tell her anything of value. But if there was even a chance she could uncover one more layer of Todd's deception, she owed herself to make this trip.

She crossed the last of the flagstones and rapidly formed a plan. If Carly brought Sammy with her to Austin, the three of them could visit Oklahoma after the conference. And Ryn already knew the one person Carly might trust to watch Sammy while they were at the keynote. Dev had called yesterday and said he was considering flying from Boston to join them in Austin.

Ryn opened the patio doors and focused on the here and now. She glanced around the now full rows of chairs. While she might not succeed in catching Todd in his fraud, she could still hold many in this room, including Grant and Simon, accountable for their actions.

She nodded politely at the two men sitting closest to the door as she entered. They had no clue the rules of behavior in the Valley were about to be redrawn once her team unveiled Equal Chances.

She scanned the crowd of several hundred, searching for Keisha and Carly. Keisha sat in the back corner of the room. She leaned over her laptop, putting the last touches to the website full of women's stories of harassment and unequal treatment they planned to unveil during this presentation.

Ryn walked across the room and joined her. "Almost ready?" She peeked over Keisha's shoulder at the screen.

Keisha whispered back. "Yes, by the time you start your speech. You know these latest stories make our favorite Sentra exec seem tame in comparison?" She tilted her head toward where Simon sat in the front row, chest puffed out, as if he expected an award nomination.

Ryn nodded. "Yeah, I read every one. Made it quite clear how important today is."

She squeezed Keisha's shoulder and headed toward the front of the room, where Carly and Kim waited by a second laptop with a video conference on it, ready to be displayed on the huge screens, currently turned off.

She approached and touched Carly's arm. "We should start, but let's talk right after. I have Todd news."

Carly raised her eyebrows. "Way to keep a gal in suspense."

Ryn hustled to the technician beside the stage and attached the microphone to her jacket. This was likely the last time half the men in this room would look her in the eyes without wishing her dead. And if some had reason to feel threatened by their own behavior, their anger would be a sign her group had succeeded. When the Equal Chances team met for the last time before this announcement, they all agreed that, even if it wasn't realistic for Silicon Valley to change overnight, there was power in finally speaking up.

From the middle of the hall, where Kim had taken a seat in one of the rows of tables facing the stage, she gave Ryn a thumbs-up.

Brock took the stage and spoke first. "Starting shortly, we will have a ceremony to recognize impressive exploits in fund performance. But before we begin, there's a much more important issue in our industry that we need to address." He paused, looked over at Ryn and gave her an encouraging smile. "After this session, I'm sure some of you may wonder why I'm up here introducing this topic, and you'd have every right. But you see, all of us have space to evolve, and like me, some of us must. And this is why Ryn Brennan is here today. Over to you, Ryn."

She took a breath and climbed to the stage. Today was not about her, but for Keisha, and Carly, and every woman on the other end of the video call on the laptop screen.

Ryn smiled and pointed at the handouts on the tables. "For too long, this industry has had an imbalance. Just look around this room. How many women or people of color do you see in your row?"

She paused, allowing the audience to scan their colleagues and recognize that, in an audience of three hundred of the best-known venture capital leaders, each row contained less than one-person who might qualify.

"But I don't just mean that imbalance, which by itself is a problem. I mean an imbalance of power. An imbalance where junior women or minorities simply seeking progress in their careers are pressured to act a certain way, to dress a certain way, to speak a certain way, or at times to accept bigotry and sexism, a boss propositioning them, or outright *sexual assault.*"

When she paused on the last word, a murmur traveled across the room. Several venture capitalists peeked around, likely wondering if a colleague stood on the edge of being outed, Harvey Weinstein-style.

Other attendees studied their tables, avoiding Ryn's gaze. One senior leader in the fourth row even checked—no wait, played a game?—on his phone.

Ryn descended the stairs from the stage and continued her talk as she walked along the aisle. She stopped when she reached his row.

"Well, I'm here to tell you we've had enough." She slammed a hand on the end of the table and watched gaming man jump. "This industry has a wide and pervasive lack of respect for anyone in the minority, and it's time we gave you the tools and the incentive to fix it."

She walked back toward the front and remounted the stage. "You may think I am being dramatic—another lie of a stereotype we apply only to women, by the way—but we will give you a chance today to hear the stories of those who've been on the other side, and put yourself in their shoes, because we have gathered hundreds of accounts of sexism and harassment and intend to release them on a public website which will go live in a few minutes."

The murmur increased to a buzz as attendees

whispered to each other. Several men pulled out their phones, Simon among them. Ryn smirked, wondering whether they realized how guilty it made them look.

"Cool your heels with the phones, folks…we aren't here for a public hanging, but to offer you redemption." She walked across the stage and smiled pointedly at Simon. "Stories are powerful, and this is why we've decided to publish over three hundred of them. Anonymously." She'd swear a relieved sigh swept across the audience, but she didn't stop long enough for them to misunderstand. "Today we are announcing a new support network: Equal Chances Silicon Valley. You might know a few of the founding members. Could those in the room please stand?"

She paused and Kim and Carly and Keisha and Marilyn and every woman in the room stood, around twenty in a crowd of three hundred. In front of Ryn, Simon chuckled, obviously not feeling threatened. He must wonder how much impact a handful of women could make.

Ryn gestured to Brock who turned on the two large screens. They flickered for a second, then resolved into a video conference with live images of hundreds of women: three hundred and twenty-nine, to be exact. In the last days she had scrambled to find special video conferencing and screen-splitting software that allowed this many faces.

"Here are the women whose stories we have collected on the website, including my own. Every woman on this screen and in the room, and more you don't yet know, and soon an increasing network of men, too, will promise their support to anyone who feels cajoled, unfairly treated, or in danger. And that includes if they believe their career is threatened by behavior that will no longer be considered acceptable in our industry."

She paused, waiting for the audience to catch up.

"Equal Chances will focus on three areas. First, we will publish guidelines for those of you who need extra assistance understanding decent behavior. You've got a starter pack on the table in front of you. What those papers say is in the future you will hire a diverse crew that resembles the makeup of this nation. You *will not* invite or ask or cajole or threaten your crew into going on a date with you, making you coffee, getting your dry cleaning, and certainly not ever for sex."

From beside the laptop powering the video screen Carly grinned, and Keisha gave a wave from the back of the hall, meaning their website was ready. Ryn picked up the pace, wanting to get the next piece out. "Second, we now have a help line for women and minorities in our industry. Every person on the steering committee, and many more, have committed to be available to help; and will believe you. Third, the site is now live, and behind the firewall it has the name and details of every person featured in those three hundred plus stories. And if any among our industry cross the line into unacceptable behavior again, *it will* stop being anonymous, one story at a time, as soon as we feel forced to fix any ongoing abuses of power."

This time a true gasp lifted the room.

Simon put down his phone and stared at her, his eyes narrowed, as if she were the lowest of vermin.

His expression matched several other men in the front rows, including Grant, who sat with his jaw clenched, arms crossed, and glared at her. Ryn grinned.

This outrage was what she'd call success.

In the center of the hall, Kim stood and chuckled, clearly amused to see the shocked reactions from her colleagues. Ryn nodded to her, then Carly, Keisha, and the rest of the team who'd worked together and created this initiative, before she handed the stage back to Brock.

Together she, Keisha, and Carly marched out the rear door, their heads held high—*Charlie's Angels* style—as if waiting for the building behind them to explode.

The minute they rounded the corner, Carly grabbed Ryn and Keisha around the shoulders. "Step aside, Wonder Woman. Ryn, you are now officially my badass hero, and Keisha, you're the tech genius who made it all happen!"

Ryn laughed. "That works, I guess. Well, so long as Wonder Woman has a rocking team." She reached to squeeze Keisha then Carly's shoulders. "You are both amazing."

Kim jogged up to them, out of breath.

"And?" Ryn asked.

Kim grinned. "Brock started the awards ceremony already, but there are still a lot of pissed off men in there."

"Mission accomplished, then?" Ryn raised her arm, and they joined her in a group high five, before she pulled Carly aside. Assuming she agreed, the two of them had an Oklahoma trip to plan.

Chapter Thirty-Four

"And what would you like to drink, young sir?" The ponytailed flight attendant leaned toward Sammy in the window seat, enunciating over the airplane noise.

"Coke?" He posed the question to Carly, peering through his brown curls.

She smiled and swept the hair off his face. She didn't like for him to overload on sugar this late in the afternoon, but with Dev arriving from the East Coast tonight and joining them for the next forty-eight hours in Austin, he'd likely be happy to play games with Sammy and help burn off the excess energy.

She nodded, and while the attendant poured their drinks, she glanced at Ryn sitting beside her in the aisle seat. Carly couldn't imagine how she expected the conversation with Ella to go, after Dev returned to Boston, and they drove to Oklahoma.

"You sure you don't want us to join the Weatherford part with you on Thursday, instead of hitting the zoo. For moral support?"

"But, Mommy,"—Sammy grabbed her arm, spilling the Coke he'd been handed—"you promised." He grinned at Ryn, clearly needing to educate her on their plans. "We're going to see lions and tigers. In habitats."

Carly laughed. Habitat was his new word of the week, learned from the zoo's website.

Ryn reached over Carly and patted his hand. "Don't worry, your Auntie Ryn isn't going to torture you with an extra hour drive to the vast metropolis of Weatherford. Especially when I don't even know if Ella will be there."

Sammy wriggled in his seat while Carly mopped up the Coke spill. Perhaps it was best for Ryn to take that piece of the trip alone. Having Sammy with them on the doorstep would make it difficult for Ryn and Ella to talk. Carly picked up the earphones he'd dropped between his legs. "Do you want to see the end of your show, sweetheart? We'll be in Austin in an hour."

He started watching and Ryn pivoted in her seat and faced Carly. "Truly, it's okay for me to do that part on my own, but I appreciate the offer. You know what I still can't believe? After your keynote tomorrow, my schedule is full. Somehow, I'm more in-demand without a job in the last month than I ever was with one. There's a whole community of women who heard about Equal Chances and want to repeat it in other industries."

Carly chuckled. "I'm not surprised, but I'm proud of you, well, of us."

Ryn's nails brushed her lips. "That means a lot to me." She leaned toward Carly and their shoulders bumped.

"You know," Ryn whispered, "however this works out with Ella, I'm grateful. Without you, I'd never have known Todd was being investigated in Oklahoma or anything about this ex-wife."

Carly smiled, glad to hear Ryn so hopeful, even if the same thought kept dragging on her since Ryn shared the news of this other wife. No matter which way she spun it, Todd had almost taken Carly for a bigger fool than she realized.

She'd convinced herself his engagement to her was a ruse, but if he remarried once and kept it a secret from his next wife, then why wouldn't he have done the same with her? Perhaps there had even been others between Ella and Ryn.

Carly settled back into her seat and closed her eyes. Todd had been so diligent on planning their life together. Choosing colors for the wedding. Even discussing the backyard and decor of the house they'd purchase. His behavior made more sense if he wasn't just leading her on but intended to divorce Ryn and marry her. In which case she'd have become one more victim, stuck exactly where Ryn was now, tied to him and scrabbling to escape.

She rubbed the pain pushing against her forehead. At this point in her mental chatter, she normally reminded herself that Todd divorcing Ryn made no sense when he'd used her to front for purchasing properties.

Ryn interrupted her thoughts, leaning closer to whisper. "I get the distinct impression you are not in a happy headspace. Worried about my Ella visit?"

Carly played with her plastic cup of water on the tray table, her stomach already moving into its starter spin cycle. "Not exactly. Although I keep wondering if Todd's still in contact with her?" What might he be capable of doing to Ryn—or Carly—if Ella informed him they'd chased his past from another state, trying to catch his fraud.

"I mean, it's a smart move, talking with her, I'm just not sure how welcoming you should expect her to be. For all we know, she might have called Todd the minute your detective reached out."

Ryn sighed. She stretched her long legs into the aisle and retracted them before answering. "You could be right. But you know what?" She turned to Carly and smiled. "Maybe it's the residual high of launching Equal Chances, but I feel like we should move beyond being afraid of what he might do. And I can't help but believe this poor woman, this Ella, struggled exactly the same as me with her divorce. If anyone has advice to help me get disentangled, don't you think it's her?"

"Yes, or she's just one more naïve stooge who wasn't smart enough to see through him."

A sparkle of amusement danced in Ryn's eyes. "Seriously? Did you brand us both as naïve stooges?"

Carly groaned. "Sorry, you know that's not what I meant."

Ryn's gaze softened, and she laid a hand on Carly's arm. "We both know at this point that Todd didn't single either you or me out because we were easier to fool than average. He's a pro who can con even the savviest women." She winked and nudged Carly's shoulder. "Even you."

Her friend's faith warmed her, but Carly pushed on her swirling stomach, already more rattled than she'd like with the keynote first thing tomorrow. Perhaps she had a case of advance stage fright.

"Don't mind me. I think the nerves are just hitting—now the keynote's so close. You know, my brain keeps serving up a roulette wheel of alternate nightmare scenarios for what can go wrong, if I even let myself think about it."

"Like what?"

"Well, while I made breakfast this morning I suddenly thought: What if I drink too much coffee tomorrow, then get jittery onstage and forget my lines? So, maybe I'd better skip the coffee. But then what if I end up presenting through a pounding caffeine withdrawal headache? And the nightmares finish the same way, with me forgetting my lines and standing frozen onstage in front of thousands." Carly's chest tightened, and she closed her eyes then opened them, the image still so clear she feared she might wish it into reality.

Ryn touched her hand on their shared armrest. "You have every reason to believe you'll succeed tomorrow. I know with one-hundred percent confidence you'll be great."

A voice on the intercom announced they'd be landing soon, and Carly closed her eyes again and took two deep breaths, banishing thoughts of failure.

Chapter Thirty-Five

Carly waited with Ryn outside the keynote hall for Sandra, her marketing manager, who'd volunteered to bring her coffee. This was the plan Ryn and Dev laughingly invented over a few glasses of wine last night to combat one of her nightmare scenarios: coffee exactly twenty minutes before the presentation. Too soon for jitters to kick in, but not so late she'd battle a caffeine headache onstage.

The double doors opposite them opened and hordes of South by Southwest attendees charged out, plastic lanyards swinging around their necks. Sandra appeared in the crowd, fighting upstream.

The river of corporate logoed T-shirts parted enough for the closest group to eyeball Carly, and they nodded as if acknowledging she looked different from the throng. Hopefully, it was her keynote speaker lanyard, not because her cornflower blouse and black pencil skirt were a poor choice.

Sandra completed her crowd combat mission and handed Carly the paper cup. "Here you go. T minus nineteen minutes. Exactly as we planned."

Carly took a careful sip. "Thank you so much."

"See you in there? I must tend to our media guests." Sandra turned and immediately disappeared into the throng.

Ryn pointed at the cup. "Caffeine headache

averted?"

Carly shrugged. Regulating her coffee intake only left about twenty other things that might go wrong, including forgetting her words, tripping up, flubbing the statistics. Or she could take so many steps to one side that she exited the camera angle, like she did twice yesterday during the rehearsal, which took place in a room so big she had a hard time imagining them filling more than half.

Ryn turned to her. "Are you okay? You look really pale."

Carly attempted a real smile. She'd rehearsed today's presentation as much as any human could.

"Seriously," Ryn said. "I've never seen you this white, not even back when..." She paused and Carly wondered what she remembered. Perhaps their awkward meeting in the coffee shop. Ironic that today she was blessed with Ryn here to support her.

She breathed out, her stomach already in full speed swirl. "I'm fine. Just a massive case of pre-stage nerves."

Ryn reached for her hand and squeezed. "Hang in there. I have an idea, but it requires me to leave for a few minutes. Will you be okay?"

Carly nodded. "Yup, I'll go find a quiet place and meditate for a moment." She'd finish her coffee, then do a few breathing exercises, because she refused to let a case of pre-presentation jitters be in charge.

She left Ryn and found a bench around the corner. Two good-luck texts flashed on her phone, making her smile. The first—*go kill 'em*—was from Dev, who she'd left back in the hotel suite with Sammy. The other message from Paul said simply—*You can do this.*—

He'd already sent balloons with a card this morning, but nice to know he must be watching the clock in real time, thinking of her.

Carly took another sip of coffee, ready to settle into her breathing. Before closing her eyes, she noticed one of her board members, Neil Kendrick, chatted with someone in the crowd farther along the corridor, his eggshell bald patch glowing under the wall lamps. She last saw him at the Equal Chances launch glaring at her, right before she and Ryn left the room.

He turned toward her, and a smile of recognition lit his face. *Darn it.* She just needed a few moments to herself.

He strode across the forty feet between them.

"Ready to wow 'em?" Neil's demeanor seemed friendly, but she no longer needed to bend to the demands of every man who expected her attention. Right now, she had a right to politely demand time inside her own head.

She rose smoothly to her feet. "Good morning, Neil. I'm afraid I don't have time…"

His dismayed expression registered before the warmth on her chest.

Carly looked at her blouse. Multiple coffee smears spread across the top of her blouse, covering the cornflower blue. Could she even get those stains out before she went on stage?

Neil grabbed a handkerchief from his pocket and reached for her chest.

She jumped back, raising an incredulous eyebrow. Maybe they should have included dabbing at a colleague's breasts as behavior to avoid in their Equal Chances behavior guidelines.

"I'm sorry." He handed her the handkerchief, his face now a shade of magenta. "Are you all right? I just came over to say hi." He rubbed a hand across his hairline. He looked stricken, but she didn't have time.

She turned on her heel, adrenaline pumping, and headed toward the restroom. A quarter of the way across a massive hallway she stopped. Even if she used soap and water, she couldn't risk a damp shirt on video. It might become see-through.

Instead, she bolted for the front door of the convention center, running as rapidly as she could in heels, her breath already catching in her throat with the exertion. Thank God Ryn secured them a hotel nearby. For the last month Carly had wavered between the blue and crimson blouses. Fifteen minutes was just enough time to reach the hotel, change into the red one, and return.

If she ran. *Fast.*

****

Six minutes later, her breathing ragged after running two city blocks, Carly barged into her hotel suite.

Sammy and Dev were on their knees behind the coffee table. Silver and purple glitter covered Dev's shirt, Sammy's hair, his hands, the floor. A minimum of sparkle had made it onto the card over which they leaned. Carly read the start of C-O-N-G written in glitter.

Sammy looked up and his face fell, disappointed he hadn't finished, but in an instant his eyes re-lit and he charged toward Carly, arms held out.

"Mommy! Did you tell them how you're going to save people? Like Uncle Remy?"

She stepped back and held him at arm's length as sparkles flitted onto her skirt and shoes. *Great.* She had a backup blouse but not another skirt. *Fix the coffee, gain glitter.*

But who could be mad at this little face, so pleased to see her? Judging by the card and his I-love-my-mommy smile, at least one person had unbounded confidence. A warm tingle spread down her arms. Even after the last months, when she struggled to find time for him, Sammy still believed in her.

"Look," Carly said, pointing at her blouse. "Mommy spilled her coffee. Gotta change, but you keep going—I'll be back soon, okay?"

She pinched his cheek, took his glittery hands in hers and walked him back to Dev. On the other side of the room he'd plugged his laptop into the TV, which showed the live-stream of her keynote.

"Are you all right?" He gestured toward the bedroom. "Got a change in there?"

"Thankfully, yes."

Dev gave her one of his broad smiles. "Go get 'em, tiger."

She hustled into the bedroom, pushing Paul's helium balloons out of her way. They'd arrived first thing this morning with the sweetest card. *I know you're going to nail it, so why wait until after to send these? Congratulations, Paul.*

She glanced at her phone after changing shirts before leaving the hotel. She'd arrive right before her stage time, but at least with a clean blouse.

When she reached the convention center, her chest heaved. She slowed to a walk when she entered the main corridor. The massive doors to the main tent event—her keynote—were open and conference attendees streamed inside.

She entered and stood to one side of the doors at the back, almost doubled over, trying to catch her breath. This hall, now full of people, seemed so much bigger than during rehearsal. Thousands of chairs were arranged in regimented square sections, below eight massive screens, each bigger than the largest movie theater. She'd entered from the front yesterday, but from here she realized that everyone but the front sections—a half football field from here—watched only on screen. This was a set up for a rock concert, not a corporate speech.

She wouldn't have thought it possible for her heart to speed any faster after the run, but it pounded, drumlike, as if an entire band had hijacked her stomach and played thrash metal all the way up her throat. She put a hand against the wall and forced herself to stand tall in case any of the media entered and saw her back here, struggling to hold it together.

She tread slowly down the center aisle, past hundreds and hundreds of rows, the endless carpet swirling in a nausea-inducing gray-green pattern repeating every twenty inches. Green debris circling thousands of black holes.

Remember to breathe, Carly. That was another nightmare scenario: where she stopped breathing, lacked oxygen, and passed out, like one of those fainting goats that freeze from fright, then fall over sideways. By the time she reached the front, she'd started breathing so deeply, others must be able to hear her.

Dr. Gregory Dolan walked over, waving. "Carly,

I'm so impressed." He gave a just-look-at-this-place eye roll, then wrapped her in a hug.

Carly smiled, not sure if she could quite string words together yet. For him and the wife he lost, she would beat this panic. For now she just had to keep breathing.

Ryn rushed up to them. "Where were you?" She looked at Carly's change of blouse. "Oh, you're right— stronger choice for the camera. How are you feeling?"

Like I want to puke up coffee was not a CEO-like answer, so Carly just nodded. Journalists took their places in the front row, including two reporters Carly recognized as the science journalist from the New York Times, and the senior medical correspondent from CNN. These were in-depth experts who understood healthcare inside and out; in many ways, better than she did.

Breathe, Carly, in and out. She knew her stuff. She'd practiced this. She would succeed. Even if her body was staging a revolt, and she struggled not to hyperventilate.

Ryn's hand closed over her wrist. "We still have a few minutes. Come with me." She nodded at Gregory Dolan and pulled Carly toward the side exit. The set of Ryn's brows said *don't even think about arguing.*

They exited through a side door and reached a dark corner beside four phone booths. Ryn placed a hand on each of Carly's shoulders. "First off, I know it's petrifying. This venue is bigger than even I realized, but you are ready for this." Her voice carried calm, confidence. "Remember, I have a hundred percent faith in you."

Carly closed her eyes and breathed again. It was

calmer out here, away from the hordes readying themselves in the ballroom. Ryn's confidence soothed. And Carly was ready; she'd prepared for today. Her heartbeat slowed. She could pull this off.

Ryn bent around the booth, grabbed something, then returned. In her hands were two shot glasses.

Shots of alcohol? "This is what you left to fetch?"

"Tequila." Ryn held out a glass, and Carly remembered her story of taking a slug before rejecting entrepreneurs. "You don't have to drink this, but I recommend it. Not sufficient to get you drunk, but enough to support your rise to the occasion of giving the best CEO keynote at this conference."

Carly was surprised at being able to chuckle. "So this is how powerful women do things in Silicon Valley?"

Ryn arched an eyebrow she interpreted as *desperate times call for desperate measures.*

Carly grabbed the shot and downed it. The bitter burn of tequila flooded her mouth. "No lime?"

Ryn laughed and raised a hand to slap her back, then thought better of it. "You're gonna ace this, my friend." She handed Carly a bottle of water to wash away the taste. "Every person in that room came because they want to hear what you, Carly Santos, will say. Remember Plan B and Plan C?"

"Yup." Carly drank more water as the tequila warmed her. If she forgot her words and froze, Plan B involved calling her engineer onstage for the demo. Plan C was to find and focus only on Ryn until she got her composure back.

Specks of Sammy's glitter sparkled on her shoes. Carly remembered his grin in the hotel room. *Mommy,*

331

did you tell them how you're going to save people?

Sammy believed in her.

Ryn believed in her.

Paul believed in her.

Her entire team believed in her. She turned toward the hall's entrance. She was indeed ready.

"Don't forget I'll be in the fifth row in the aisle," Ryn reminded her. "I'm the stage's center."

Ryn put a gentle hand on her back and Carly turned and grabbed her into a hug. "Thank you for being here."

When she stepped back, Ryn's eyes shone. "You're beyond welcome."

They returned to the hall and by the time the technician finished attaching Carly's microphone, the band in her stomach had switched from thrash metal to upbeat jazz. Apparently, the tequila trick worked.

Carly climbed the staircase at the front of the stage and joined the moderator, visualizing Sammy's cheeky face with each step. The way he said *good luck, Mommy* before she left the hotel. She did this so other kids wouldn't lose their parents, grandparents, or uncles.

The moderator introduced her, and Carly walked to center stage. The lights blinded her, and she couldn't see past the tenth row, but that was an asset. She'd pretend those front rows were the only people she needed to address.

She pushed out what she hoped came across as a confident smile and located Ryn, exactly where she said she'd be.

Carly turned and looked at the video screen. This image broadcasted to the eight larger screens. Ryn was right about the red shirt looking more vibrant on camera. Dynamic, even.

She turned back to her audience. "Welcome to the largest technology breakthrough in cardiac diagnosis in the last two decades." Carly pointed at the image of a heart on the screen behind her. "Heart disease. Still, the number one killer of Americans, and the survival rate for heart attacks when they hit unexpectedly, outside a hospital, is less than ten percent…"

She talked for a few minutes, checked the audience for Ryn, and realized she'd crossed half the stage. Continuing with the presentation and breathing into the repetition of a pitch she knew by heart, she glided back to the center.

Ten minutes later, she'd reached the demonstration. She introduced her engineer and stepped aside, appreciating the opportunity to quench her dry throat.

After the demo, she finally relaxed a little. This part of the pitch on clinical results played most to her expertise. A few minutes into explaining the hospital trials, she noticed the journalist from the *New York Times* in the front row took furious notes.

She rechecked her location against Ryn in the center. *Darn it.* She was nowhere close. In her enthusiasm, she must have stopped checking how far she'd moved from stage center. She looked to her left.

Her feet stood six inches from the edge of the twenty-foot-high platform. One more sentence and she'd have been a goner. Below her a security guard wore a panicked expression, likely wondering whether her job included catching a falling speaker.

A glance at the screen confirmed Carly's fear. She didn't know how many steps ago she left the camera angle, but half the people in the hall watched footage of an empty stage. She took several steps right to reenter the shot. In the first row, Neil laughed, then waved. Was he laughing because she said something stupid? She didn't remember her last words before she reached the stage's edge. Maybe this was why the *New York Times* journalist took such frantic notes?

No. Stop right there, Carly.

Until now, the presentation had gone just fine.

She noticed two of the female CEOs she collaborated with on Equal Chances seated in the second row. They were smiling, not laughing. Carly might have been on the brink of stage diving, but she said nothing wrong. Now she just wished she remembered where in the speech she'd stopped.

She walked step by step to center stage, hoping she'd recall her last line by the time she arrived. When she reached the middle, she stared down the aisle between the chairs. *Dammit. Still no idea.*

The audience in the first rows looked up, perplexed, and the journalists no longer scribbled. The entire hall waited for her to continue. How long since she stopped talking? Twenty seconds? A minute, or more? It felt like forever.

Behind the first ten rows that she could see were hundreds more faceless attendees. Those at the back of the hall who'd witnessed her walk off camera for minutes on end, and now saw her back on screen—turned to stone in mid stage—were likely laughing their asses off.

The slow freeze took control of her throat.

She coughed, then again.

Still frozen. No speaking now even if she could

remember her lines.

She couldn't just stand here—like a mute snowman about to melt under the lights. She looked out into the first rows. Too late for Plan B, as the demo had finished. *Plan C it is.*

She scoured the seats by the main aisle for Ryn— *Focus on me*, she said—but where she'd swear Ryn had been, sat a man in a white hat.

A white hat with a picture of a fish and *Get hooked* written above it. An identical trucker cap to the one Fish Hat Fred wore in the photo Dev sent them. Ryn raised her head and gave her a toothy grin from under the hat, and Carly laughed.

She turned, glanced at the stage behind her, and saw her laugh beamed across eight massive video screens. In the front row, two journalists, several CEOs, and Dr. Dolan gave encouraging smiles.

Although her heart still pounded and her stomach spun, her throat was no longer frozen. She smiled, remembering Uncle Remy, and the phrase Ryn said helped her decide to launch Equal Chances: *It's never too late to become the person you want to see in the mirror.*

If Carly could survive Todd, create and lead a company changing healthcare, and co-launch an initiative like Equal Chances, then she could darn well finish one presentation. Even without remembering the words.

"You know what, I forgot where I was," Carly said with another smile. "But I'm sure you can appreciate what it's like to be up here onstage, in front of you all. Instead, let me tell you a personal story on why this matters, and why my team and I have spent over seven years working on this technology. My uncle Remy meant everything to me..."

Carly's throat caught, but she kept talking. "He was the funniest man in the world. A man who'd do anything for his family. At fifty-six years old, we lost him to a heart attack that could have been prevented with a simple operation. That's why I investigated options, talked to doctors about what might be possible to better diagnose cardiac arrest before it happens, and it's an honor to present our solution today. As a doctor I respect told me recently, it doesn't matter whether this product gets approved in three months or three years. What matters is when it's ready, we'll save thousands of lives like my Uncle Remy."

She looked for Dr. Dolan. He stood by the steps to the stage, a huge beam of a smile on his face. "I'd like to invite on stage Dr. Gregory Dolan—one of the cardiac specialists from the Mayo Clinic who worked with us on the clinical trials—and I'll happily cover anything I missed during our question-and-answer section."

Carly stepped aside, and while he climbed the steps, the audience applauded. Several of the first row even stood. She allowed herself to ad-lib the ending, and she'd still been coherent. Perhaps even charismatic?

She thrust back her shoulders before taking her seat for the Q&A section, a flush of pride tingling down both arms. She looked for Ryn, who grinned and raised the fish hat in her hand in a gesture of *brava*.

When they finished taking questions, and Carly dismounted the stage, Ryn rushed to the front and gave her a bear hug. "Girl, you killed it."

Ryn held up her phone where Dev and Sammy showed on screen, jumping on the sofa in the hotel suite among the balloons. Sammy held his congratulations card over his head and glitter floated everywhere.

She waved at them on screen, her breathing settling back to normal, and grabbed the fish hat from Ryn's hand. "Where on earth did you find this? Don't dare lose it. I want it as a souvenir."

Ryn gave a cocky wink. "You can locate almost anything online these days. But looks as if you're not done yet, rock star." She grasped Carly's shoulders, pointing her toward the long line forming along one side of the stage.

Carly stood straighter, summoned her brightest smile, and walked over to the line of people with questions. On the way, she dusted a speck of glitter from her skirt. Today, thousands of future patients had depended on her not to let them down. When she returned to the hotel suite, she'd share with her son that her success was powered by his belief in her, and a dusting of Sammy sparkles.

Chapter Thirty-Six

Miles of small towns, flat fields and spindly water towers sped by on Ryn's drive from Oklahoma City to Weatherford. She checked the rental car's clock: not yet ten a.m. Plenty of time to make the hour drive, hopefully speak with Ella, and return for her appointment with the US Attorney in Oklahoma City this afternoon.

In the last twenty minutes of driving she'd counted five grain silos. As each one blocked the sun, she tested different versions of what to say if Ella was home and opened the door. She'd rehearsed with Carly this morning, before dropping her and Sammy at the zoo, but all versions still sounded awkward.

Hi, my name's Ryn, and you used to be married to my husband. Can you help me?

Hello, I'm your ex-husband's new, well soon-to-be ex-wife, from sunny California. Any chance we can chat?

The city limits sign passed on Ryn's right, and she remembered when she was ten and would ask Pops questions about Mom, hoping to clutch at vanishing memories. *Kathryn, there's no point digging in the past, when it just causes pain,* he'd say.

Was that what she'd do to Ella today, cause hurt by digging in her past?

Conveniently, the radio, on which she'd found

mostly country music, wailed a song about *getting used to the pain*. She could see now how Pops' perspective, that emotional bruises were best not poked at, had colored her whole life. With Simon she'd thought it best not to share how he made her feel, even with the other women in the office, and she couldn't have been more wrong. And after discovering the truth about Todd, no matter how painful it was for her and Carly to face the heartache, weren't they better for having worked through it together?

Still, that didn't mean Ella wanted to relive whatever nightmare her divorce from Todd had been over iced tea with his latest mark. Ryn had left four phone messages now, and Ella had returned none of them.

Ten minutes later, she located Ella's address in a residential neighborhood on the fringes of Weatherford, wondering if the smarter plan would have been to bail on this whole endeavor and spend the morning with Carly and Sammy.

The red brick ranch houses on this street matched other roads she'd passed through in town, but Ella's house was better maintained. Violet pansies in long containers lined the front yard and a new SUV, the same brand as Ryn's, sat in the driveway.

A young girl, perhaps eight or nine years old, in a primrose sundress and blonde curls opened the door and watched Ryn walk up the path toward her.

"Hi. My name is Ryn, and I wondered if your mother…" She noticed a woman in the shadows of the hallway behind the girl and directed the end of the question to her, "is available to talk?"

The woman shooed away the child and stepped

outside, arms crossed. Chestnut hair skimmed her shoulders. Ryn would guess early forties, which fit with a late teen marriage to Todd. Her pink scarf and black dress seemed formal for a day at home. Perhaps Ryn caught her leaving for work, or another engagement. In which case, she had better make her point.

"Hi, you must be Ella? I'm Ryn, I called a few times. I wanted to talk with you about Todd."

Ryn extended a hand, but Ella's arms remained locked in place. She scrutinized Ryn's face, then glanced at her car.

Ella took a step forward off the porch, less than ten inches from Ryn, as if ready to point at the street and ask her to leave. "What's he done now? Is this about his business?"

She knew of his fraud? It made sense if she'd been implicated in the previous investigation, as Ryn's detective said. But the combative tone implied Carly could be right. Ella might still be in touch with Todd. Even protecting him.

"Um, no, it's more personal." Ryn replayed what she'd told Ella in her voicemails: only that she knew Todd from California, needed her help, and wanted to talk.

A neighbor in the adjoining garden stopped watering his plants and stared at them over the fence. Ryn offered him an awkward nothing-going-on-here smile. She lowered her voice. "Listen, I'm not with the police or anything. I'm simply in trouble and thought you might be willing to help. I'm sorry, turning up on your doorstep, like this, but I didn't know how else to reach you. Is there any chance we could talk inside?"

Ella studied Ryn's outfit, taking in her jeans and

blouse as if still deciding whether she actually were a cop. She must have decided not, because she stepped back and gestured at the open door.

"We'll talk out back."

They walked through a long hallway. Ella stopped and shouted into a room on one side. "Shawn-Michael, we're going out back."

As she passed, Ryn peered inside. A young man—no perhaps an older teenager—sat at a computer desk, his brown hair held back with a thin bandana. He turned and gave her a welcoming smile.

Ryn blinked several times, and her chest constricted, working the dates in her mind. If Ella was the same age as Todd, early forties, he could have had a son before he left for California, who'd be this age now. Ryn forced her feet to keep moving along the corridor. Carly mentioned that when she first ran into Todd, he seemed enchanted with Sammy. In some weird, warped, Todd-logic, did he regret leaving behind his own child and recognized a chance to rebuild a family he lost?

Ryn pushed on the pain in her chest before she exited through the back door. It still hurt to consider the years she'd lost when perhaps she could have built her own family.

The backyard was a gardening magazine cover. Patio seating covered with bright orange floral cushions and a wicker coffee table were set around a woven outdoor carpet. The smell of hyacinths mingled with fresh-cut grass from a neighbor's yard. Ella brought a jug of water and two glasses and poured for each of them. She pointed at a flower-cushioned seat and Ryn sat.

"That's my son, Shawn-Michael Junior, inside. He has a phone and will call the police in case you had any funny business in mind. And yes, I'm Ella." This time she extended her hand, and they shook. "So, how can I help you? All you said in your messages was that you know Shawn, I mean Todd, and need my help."

The name hit Ryn hard, freezing her lungs mid-breath. She grabbed for her glass of water. She needed a second: Todd and Shawn, same person...which meant the young man inside was indeed his son. Perhaps the girl his daughter, too.

Would she ever be done with the Jenga tower of revelations crashing down?

Ella must have registered her shock because her eyes narrowed, and she leaned back in her chair perhaps grasping Ryn hadn't come here about a business issue. "He was Shawn-Michael when he lived here. Todd is his business name. How exactly do you know him?"

The way Ella said *Todd is his business name* in present tense confirmed they were in contact. Which made sense if they shared a son. Ryn might be wrong to assume Todd conned Ella and an ugly divorce ensued. Maybe they were still friendly.

"No, this isn't business. It's a personal matter." She took a sip of water to calm her negotiation brain that worked every angle. In this moment, it calculated what Ella and Todd being in touch meant for this conversation. She'd gotten this far, but she may risk every word being repeated to him.

She took a deep breath, met Ella's widened eyes, and recognized the fear. Ryn was thinking about it all wrong. This wasn't a business negotiation. If she were truthful, Ella might take pity and help her, even if she and Todd were still friends.

"I'll be completely honest. Todd and I are getting divorced, and it's turned kind of ugly. Given your history with him, I thought you might be open to giving me some advice."

"What the fuck?" Ella jumped up, smashing her knee into the coffee table. Ryn's glass fell and rolled along the rug. Ella's hands raised halfway toward her head, then stopped as if frozen. She stepped back, then again, before lowering them to her sides.

She marched forward, her flushed cheeks inches from Ryn's face. "I don't believe you. You say you married Shawn in California? Then prove it."

Ryn stood. Acid scalded the base of her stomach as the realization burned up her arms and into her shoulder blades.

"You and Todd are still married?" Ryn's voice came out as a whisper, as if her vocal cords refused to apply normal volume to a scenario that, until moments ago, seemed unimaginable. Impossible.

She wasn't sure whether Ella heard her, because she spun away and placed her palm against the red brick of the house, leaning into the wall.

Pops' words taunted Ryn. *There's no point digging in the past when it just causes pain.* She'd waltzed into this woman's life and nonchalantly delivered her worst nightmare. The same evil trick fate played when Carly walked, clueless, into the meeting with Ryn at Sentra. She should have known better.

She stepped toward Ella. A million questions pounded inside her head. Were Todd and this woman legally married? If legal, did Ella have any documents to prove it? If they never divorced, bigamy would make

Ryn's marriage invalid.

She wanted to ask all the questions, then scream victory—finally Todd lost—but she couldn't because Ella stood two feet away, both palms against the wall, her head hanging between her arms. As if afraid that standing straight might make her legs give way.

Ryn understood that sensation. A rip tore in her heart for Ella. It might be better to know the truth and move forward, but she just shattered this woman's world.

Ella dropped one arm and turned toward her. "Is this some kind of sick joke?" The distress in her eyes said she knew it wasn't. She walked over and sank into a chair, her elbows on her knees, her fingers squeezing her forehead as if it might prevent the world from imploding.

Ryn remained standing, her head spinning through every sordid scenario that could make this even possible. When she'd researched cheaters, preparing to file for divorce, she read stories of men with alternate lives, bigamists who were married in other states. There were even databases where wives registered their state-line crossing husbands. But she'd thought it all so improbable, even after everything she learned about Todd.

She studied Ella crumpled in the chair. Any comfort Ryn attempted to offer would not console. Ryn knew because she'd been there. She remembered staring at the waves on Ocean Beach, nothing but emptiness in the pit of her stomach. Even if she'd learned that friendship soothed and grief lessened with time, nothing helped in those first few days, before she worked through the denial.

She walked over to where Ella sat. She wanted to share that even unimaginable heartbreak—the kind that shatters you in a hundred pieces and makes you realize you don't even want to put your life back together in the same way—could be survived. Ryn took a seat next beside her, channeling the empathy Carly had shown her in the last months as her own life cracked open. "I am so, so sorry."

When Ella raised her head and looked at Ryn, she shook. "Twenty-one years…we've been married, although I don't see him much these days, his business being in California. But he takes care of us." With the back of her hand she waved at the house, the well-tended garden, the playset with two slides and a climbing net.

Ryn sat back, speechless.

Todd's lies, his cheating she understood, the base act of a privileged man who thought his needs came above others. But this she couldn't absorb: He supported his first wife and family the entire time she'd known him?

Ella said twenty-one years. Ryn must have been right about them being high school sweethearts. Shawn-Michael Junior had to be Todd's child. But the girl? She couldn't be over ten or eleven. "Are both your children Todd's?"

"Yes, Shawn-Michael Junior's eighteen, big hopes for going into business like his dad." Ella's volume became so quiet Ryn had to lean forward. "He's well now, thank the Lord. For years, with his condition, we were in and out of hospitals. Priscilla has one more year of middle school."

Condition. Maybe Todd hadn't wanted to abandon

them because his son was ill. But then he still left, moved to another state, and remarried. Ryn's vision blurred at the edges, as it had at her lawyer's office, when she learned of his fraud. Nothing here made any sense. Todd might have a warped sense of morality, but supporting his family here for twenty years didn't fit into the neat sociopath box she'd filed him in.

Ella sat without moving, evaluating her. They likely wore matching expressions of disbelief.

"Where did you say you know him from?" From the sharp edge in Ella's tone, denial had kicked in.

"We met at a business networking event in San Francisco." *How is that even relevant?* "I'm sorry, what I mean is we were...we still are...married ten years."

Ella's face crumpled. "I think you should go." Her gaze darted everywhere, as if she feared the house, the yard, the whole town might evaporate.

Ryn needed marriage documents, details on Todd's involvement in real estate, whether he used fake powers of attorney with Ella's name, too. But she didn't have the heart to be that cruel. She imagined how she'd have felt if Carly demanded that kind of information during their first meeting.

"I'll go, but is it okay if I call you in a few days?"

Ella didn't respond but instead stood and walked through the back door into the house. Ryn waited, listening to the sound of a distant lawn mower, unsure whether to follow.

After a minute, Ella returned, her face pale white. She wrote on a pad of pink notepaper. "That's my cell number. Please never call my home again. Now go. Before my kids ask who you are." She pointed at a concrete walkway along the side of the house.

Ryn took the notepad, and wrote her own details. She touched Ella's arm, torn between giving her the privacy she deserved and being afraid to leave her. "Is there someone you can call?"

Ella glanced toward the house, her face panicked. Ryn touched her arm one more time before heading to the side alley. "If you just want to talk or even scream, please know you can call me."

She reached her rental car, drove three blocks, and pulled over. Children on bicycles passed as she leaned her head on her hands and steadied herself. Todd's marriage to Ella was great news, if he never divorced her. But right now she felt like a heartless monster for the way she'd flounced into Ella's neat magazine-cover life, crumpled it like a sheet of wastepaper, and set it on fire.

Tears rolled down her cheeks for Ella, who was only starting the steep ascent from heartbreak that Ryn had been blessed to make with Carly as her friend. She already knew they'd try and help this woman.

She wanted to call Carly and share the news, but this wasn't the type of revelation—that your former fiancé is a bigamist—she should hear over the phone. And Ryn needed to be at her meeting with the US Attorney in Oklahoma City in two hours.

She texted Carly and arranged a place to meet right after her appointment, then dashed off an email full of exclamation points to her lawyer and detective, asking them for an urgent investigation of Todd's potential bigamy.

Ryn turned her car toward the highway. She'd drive as fast as legal to the US Attorney's office and hopefully have a few minutes to spare before the meeting. If so, she'd call her lawyer and research how annulments worked.

Likely Ella already called Todd, so if there was even a small chance Ryn had received a magical get-out-of-your-marriage-free card, she needed to know how best to play it.

Chapter Thirty-Seven

Carly stood beside a bench in the playground, near their hotel in Oklahoma City. She watched Sammy spin, the white and red panels of the merry-go-round whirling together into one large, joyful, candy stripe.

She glanced at her phone. Nothing since Ryn's text saying she'd be here in twenty minutes: which she sent half an hour ago.

Carly couldn't resist peeking at her other texts and emails. Since the keynote, her phone had buzzed non-stop—messages from her team letting her know they were proud of her, press interview requests, new offers of funding for her company. This newest email contained a request from *Forbes*, who wanted to do a profile piece on her. She'd agree to this one because she loved yesterday's news article, which called her charming and approachable—*For once not a stiff CEO, but someone who seemed truly vested in patients, took the stage in Austin.*

Who knew that what she considered a weakness—her caring too much and lack of polish—could actually be an asset?

She checked on Sammy, who had moved from the merry-go-round to the slide, wondering what caused Ryn's delay with the US Attorney. Already, the sun edged below the top of the nearby buildings and Ryn's one cryptic text earlier only said—*I have huge news.*—

A screech of tires stopped at the curb behind her. Carly turned as Ryn jumped out of the rental car, holding a folder of documents and a paper bag, and beaming as if someone gifted her a lifetime supply of Nutella. Whatever she learned must be great news.

When she reached Carly, her face reset into an apology. "I'm sorry I'm late, but I had an opportunity to get my hands on these," she said, holding the folder aloft. "Then I made one small stop at the store." She placed the folder and bag on the bench beside where Carly stood and pulled her into a hug.

Sammy spotted Ryn and ran over. "Hi, Auntie Ryn, can we go to mini golf now?" Since he and Carly left the zoo earlier, he hadn't stopped talking about the family entertainment center Ryn proposed they visit this evening.

"When have I ever let you down?" Ryn asked, crouching at his level. "Don't worry, we're going, but can you play just a little longer, so Mommy and I have a few minutes to talk?"

Sammy's brows furrowed, and he stroked the side of his face as if considering his options. "Okay, I suppose. But only for ten minutes, no longer."

Carly laughed, enjoying the warmth of the day's last rays of sun as she watched him return to the slide. "Did you see that? Since when did he learn to do an exact imitation of me negotiating his bedtime?"

Ryn gave a chuckle, sat on the bench, and looked up at her. "Join me, because you'll want to sit for this one. Ultimately, it's great news, but before I tell you, remind me what happened the day before yesterday?"

Carly threw her a quizzical look before she sat, then broke into a grin. "You mean the part where the company I founded successfully announced a solution that's going to save thousands, perhaps millions of lives?"

"Yup. And later. Remember when you told me that all of us hanging out—you, me, and Dev—felt like the most family you'd ever need?"

The hairs on Carly's forearms rose in warning. Ryn was pumping her up...before what?

Ryn glanced around, checking Sammy's location, before she spoke. "You're never gonna believe this. Todd's still married."

Carly would swear her heart stopped, just for a second, before it restarted at twice the speed. "He never divorced her?" Surely bigamy was impossible in today's electronic world, with everything in every state connected.

"It's insane, right? I barely dared believe it this morning when I met Ella." Ryn's palm pressed to her heart. "Oh, the poor woman was as unaware as we were. I feel awful because I totally blindsided her."

"Wow." Carly's heart hurt, torn between sympathy for someone about to go through what they had, and a dragging sensation that confirmed her suspicions were right. Todd would have married her, too. Perhaps without divorcing Ryn. "But I still don't get it. I mean, how's bigamy even feasible?"

"Exactly what I asked the US Attorney. He said it's difficult in the same state, but in two different states it's possible if the states' records aren't connected, which they weren't more than a decade ago."

Possible in another state. A neutron smashed into another in Carly's brain. This was the missing jigsaw piece. Her mind sped through conversations with Todd after their engagement. Him saying how nice it would be to live somewhere more peaceful, less traffic. She remembered the article he sent her about how California schools were becoming dangerous, full of gang violence.

It was hard to believe she'd have fallen for it, but he'd already begun his campaign; showing her how great life in another state, outside of California, could be.

"There's something else." Ryn's face twisted, as if unsure how to deliver her news without distressing her. She tilted her head and nodded toward Sammy on the playset. "Todd has a son and a daughter with Ella. I can't explain it, but I think maybe he wanted to make up for what he missed out on with his own kids, or something. As in, your gut was correct…I think he did want you both, as a new family."

Carly studied Sammy's curls bouncing as he swung on the monkey bars beside a tiny girl in a blue jumpsuit. She tore her gaze away from his smile. Should this make her feel better, knowing her instincts that Todd loved her and Sammy were correct? She'd almost married a bigamist.

For a moment, she imagined Todd had succeeded, and they'd moved. She pictured her and Sammy trapped inside a new house, in an unfamiliar town where they knew no one. Would he have become abusive, like Kyle, if she tried to leave?

But that wasn't what happened. Both she and Ryn escaped. And life was good, with family enough.

She sat back and gave Ryn a smile. Sure, she could live in the past, beating herself up for mistakes almost made. But she refused to be that person any longer. She and Ryn were a sisterhood of survivors.

"You know how that actually makes me feel, Ryn? Overwhelmingly grateful—for us to be sitting right here, right now."

She glanced toward the monkey bars and Sammy jumped down and waved back. "Overall, this is phenomenal for you, right? I mean, with an annulment, won't you be totally free of him? As in not need to give him a single cent?"

"Yes, in fact, that's why I'm late. The US Attorney called in a favor with the folks in the county where Weatherford is located—to get me proof of his prior marriage. Which is one of two reasons I stopped at the store for these." Ryn reached for the paper bag and placed it into Carly's lap without opening it.

She peeked inside the bag: two mini splits of champagne, but no glasses.

"Go on," Ryn said with a grin. "Open them while I tell you the rest."

She opened the bottles, and handed one to Ryn, who raised it in a gesture of cheers. "Not only can I get an annulment, but do you remember saying last week how you wished we could declare an amber alert on Todd's highlights? Like anything to stop other women from getting conned by him in the future."

"Yeah?"

"Well, I have one better. The US Attorney said if I'll help, which of course I will, they'll suggest the FBI reopen the fraud investigation. I agreed to supply them with copies of every document I saved—Todd's bank accounts, credit card statements—any way I can assist with the case, assuming they pursue it. You can likely help, too, maybe even Ella if we can convince her."

"Of course." Carly realized she'd been grinning so broadly for the last seconds, her cheeks hurt. She likely looked manic to passersby, or Sammy, who now headed toward them from the far side of the playground. "So how do we celebrate? Should we upgrade pizza and mini golf to steak and champagne?

"Nah, let's make tonight about Sammy. Once my lawyer tells me I'm out of the woods for sure, then we can have a proper celebration. You, me, maybe Dev too, if he's back, so I can thank him for letting me use his place."

"Deal."

Carly raised her champagne in a toast, but Ryn spoke first. "Wait. Carly, I have one more thing to say. Don't think I'm unaware how much I owe you, here." Ryn leaned in and met her gaze. "Not just the Oklahoma lead, but you may never appreciate what it's meant to be my friend through all this crazy." Her eyes sparkled and a tear trickled down Ryn's cheek. She laughed, not bothering to wipe it away.

Carly felt a happy lightness, starting from her feet and lifting her chest, and she channeled it into a smile. Who'd have imagined Ryn, so mighty and perfect when they first met, would be grateful for her help, or Carly would be proud to offer it, to a true friend?

She set aside her mini champagne, and they hugged, long enough to hear each other's breathing.

"I feel the same way." Carly leaned back from the hug, picked the bottle up and raised it, trying not to let her voice quaver. "I think I have the perfect toast. It is better to have loved and lost—"

Ryn completed the phrase "…than to live with the psycho for the rest of your life. Never a truer word."

Carly leaned near Ryn's ear so Sammy, who had now joined them, couldn't hear. "And even better to take the jerk down!"

Chapter Thirty-Eight

The title company's low-rise office complex reminded Ryn of a strip mall. Sitting in her SUV, fifty feet from the entry, she skipped to the newest song—which Carly had suggested for today—on her *Songs Todd Despises* playlist, and rocked along to P!nk's *Blow Me*.

She shouldn't need to psych herself up for seeing Todd, after everything she'd learned. But spending thirty minutes in a room with him, for the first time since he hung off her car door at Zidera, gave her the chills.

He must wonder why, a month after her visit to Ella, she still hadn't filed for annulment.

She checked her makeup in the mirror, sat back into her seat, and sang at the top of her lungs. This time she had no problem following her lawyer's advice to *just be patient* and wait until the house sale became final today, before sharing any of her other news with Todd.

She picked up her phone and read Carly's latest text.

—Good luck. Don't forget to let him sign before you pull the big reveal—

Ryn smiled and texted the process server her lawyer had arranged to serve Todd the annulment papers at the end of this meeting.

—Ready to go in 30?—

While she waited for his reply, an email arrived. She responded to Kim and confirmed their lunch date, tomorrow. Kim hadn't given up on pushing Ryn to start her own firm. She'd even offered her help. But with practically every male power broker in the valley avoiding Ryn since the launch of Equal Chances, it still seemed such an uphill struggle.

The process server responded with a text confirming the location and Ryn laughed at herself as she exited the SUV. The US Attorney had granted her immunity from future prosecution for Todd's fraud, so she actually didn't know what she feared.

Even if she launched a new company and it didn't succeed, the prospect of public failure didn't seem as harrowing as it once had. Apparently, surviving trial-by-Todd-fire had liberated her to pursue what she believed in, and not give a damn what others thought.

Twenty feet in front of her, Todd pulled up and parked his Mercedes in the disabled spot by the door. His gaze met hers for a second in a clear challenge before he strode into the office with every bit of his usual swagger.

A caustic taste swirled in her mouth. The only thing disabled in that man was his capacity for basic human decency. Even his nonchalance today showed how little he cared how he'd hurt Ella, too. Ryn had talked with her four times since they met, but she knew Ella was still early in the same journey she and Carly traveled.

Ryn straightened her posture and entered the building, where a receptionist directed her toward a conference room. Framed posters of beaches hung on

357

one wall, and a bowl of apples sat in the center of the round glass table. Todd stood with his back to her.

The notary, wearing a coral pantsuit and carrying a massive stack of papers, walked in behind Ryn. "Have a seat, folks. I know this looks like a lot of paperwork, but it won't take long. The pages are marked with stickies for each place you sign." She passed half the stack to each side of the table.

Ryn sat opposite Todd, grabbed an apple, and rubbed it on her skirt, attempting to match his nonchalance.

For the last weeks, her lawyer cautioned her not to say anything that might provoke Todd into backing out of this sale, which freed them both from the debt he'd accumulated on the house.

She took a bite of the apple, which tasted of wax, and discarded it on a napkin, being careful not to look up. She kept her gaze focused on the stack of papers, so as not to give herself away too soon.

The notary folded her hands, looking uncomfortable. With neither Ryn nor Todd speaking, she couldn't fail to notice the tension crackling across the table.

"You know I'm only selling the house for my convenience, right?"

Ryn glanced up, expecting Todd to be staring at her, but he faced the notary, his neutral expression in conflict with the I-need-you-to-understand-I'm-in-control tone.

The notary jumped to her feet. "It's getting warm in here. Why don't I get us more water?" She grabbed the full pitcher and left the room.

Ryn ignored Todd and flipped through her papers.

She waited until he started signing pages before she risked a glance. He looked the same but for one thing: His highlights had grown out, and a hint of gray showed at the roots.

She returned to her documents, surprised by the tug in her chest. Fascinating that she could sit across from the man who'd turned her life inside out, conned her, made her lose her job, and she still had an ability to feel sorry for him.

Not because the fading highlights were a sign that not all was well with him, but because it had become clear he utterly lacked the human capacity for empathy. She and Carly talked endlessly in the last weeks. To marry multiple times, or con people at the level of hundreds of fake real estate deals and mortgage fraud—which she'd learned from the US Attorney was what Todd did—he had to be born without the gene that allowed basic human connection. And didn't missing that gene mean you could never get close enough with another human to experience real love, yourself?

Ryn paused and breathed into her gratitude before she continued to sign. She might have been a fool when it came to Todd, but at least she and Carly could experience the pain of loss, the angst and delight of falling in love again, and the warmth of friendship to see them through it all.

The notary returned with the jug of water, plus two lemon slices, and Ryn noticed Todd had reached the last page of his stack of documents.

She signed her last pages too, then under the table she hit send on the text she'd written for the process server before leaving her car.—*Anytime now is good*—

The notary finished taking Todd's fingerprint, and

he glared at Ryn, the dark purple vein on his neck throbbing against his shirt, as if it had taken extreme effort to harness that much rage inside one body during the time they were signing. This anger was more like she expected. Like her, he'd apparently contained himself until they both completed the documents.

The notary finished taking Ryn's fingerprint. "Congratulations, your house sale is complete. Let me make you both copies." She gathered the stacks of signed papers and left.

Todd stood, but waited until the moment the door clicked closed, then strode around the table toward Ryn. He loomed over her, the same threat in his eyes as the night he chased her in the Zidera parking lot, except this time she had nothing to fear.

"How does it feel now you've lost your house, and your job?" He pointed at her as if to call out a witch.

Ryn laughed. *Great?* Any sliver of sympathy dissipated the moment she saw those hard-iced eyes.

"I gave you a choice," Todd said. "And you rejected my agreement. You just had to keep digging with your stupid little detective. I know what you've been doing, searching for assets in my companies you can claim as yours, but you already lost. You won't get a dime."

She rose and stood face-to-face. "Why are you so angry? You conned me, but who wronged you? What made you this way?"

He stepped closer, now inches from her forehead, but Ryn calmly turned her back on him. She opened the door and exited toward the reception area where they'd entered, passing a man in jeans and a Grateful Dead T-shirt.

The man spoke behind her. "Todd Runyan?"

"Yes, and who the hell are you?"

She turned, and the man handed Todd an envelope. "Sir, that's a summons. The court date is specified inside." He turned on his heel and walked out past Ryn.

She smiled inside as Todd's gaze flitted from one side of the corridor to the other, as if calculating his next move, before he refocused on her.

"Guess you finally got around to serving me annulment papers then?" he asked, derision dripping from his voice. "Thanks for saving me the hassle of fixing my marital forgetfulness."

Ryn met his gaze. "Yes, indeed, annulment papers. And you're right on one point. By the end of May, it will be as if we were never married. So no, you will not be taking me for any amount of my venture holdings. In fact, you have no right to any part of me, and never did. And now that our house sale is final, I'll happily never hear from you again in this lifetime."

He scoffed. "I never needed your money, anyway." He half turned toward the conference room, then spun back, and barked his next words. "So why the hell are you still sniffing around in my businesses in Nevada?"

This time she let out a real victory smile. Turned out Todd using her persona for his deals in Nevada wasn't so smart after all. Not when it meant she could request copies of any document her name had been listed on, not to mention every credit card and bank statement she'd kept and now given to the FBI. And once she provided the contact information for Todd's accountant, he also saw the light and decided to cooperate with providing documentation.

"Oh yeah, that," Ryn said, entirely deadpan.

She told Carly last week it was just as well she didn't have a full schedule since returning from Oklahoma, because gathering information for Special Agent Wayne Richardson—who'd been assigned after the fraud investigation reopened—became a full-time job for the last few weeks.

She realized the notary had returned and waited in the corridor with their copies, standing three feet away from them.

"Did you want to give me those?" Ryn asked.

She took the papers and placed them in her briefcase before turning back to Todd. "You're right— I've been requesting copies of a significant number of papers and statements recently, but those weren't for me. They were for the special agent." She took a moment to savor the genuine shock in the rise of Todd's eyebrows. "Apparently by asking for documents with my access as your wife, I saved the FBI a ton of time dealing with pesky subpoenas."

And based on what the special agent told her, Mr. Todd Runyan—or Shawn Michael or whatever he wanted to call himself—would soon be heading to prison.

Chapter Thirty-Nine

Ryn waved goodbye to the young entrepreneurs from Baltimore and watched their rental car kick up dust on the ranch driveway. Only two months since she announced the launch of her own firm, and this company was the second she wanted to invest in, if she raised enough funds.

She winced at the metal-on-metal sound as she wheeled closed the barn doors. Introducing those young men to her animals had made her late for the picnic with Carly. It should be a relaxed affair, but as the guest of honor, she needed to get going.

On the short walk to the office suite, Ryn admired the golden shimmer of the hills surrounding her horse fields. She made a smart choice buying this property in Sonoma. Her firm already had a strong pull, with Kim lending her name as a founding investor, so entrepreneurs were willing to make the extra hour's drive past San Francisco. As for other venture partners in Silicon Valley who Ryn heard now called her *the crazy ranch VC*, she no longer cared. She actually quite liked the term. Maybe she'd rename the company Crazy Ranch Capital, and print T-shirts.

She hadn't been as smart when she admitted, in a magazine profile last month, that the biggest advantage of this location was having her animals next door. Normally she refused requests for barn tours from entrepreneurs merely trying to ingratiate themselves, but she couldn't refuse the young men she just met. Their company provided opportunities for city teens from low-income areas by matching them with employers. A perfect fit for her fund's mission of investing only in companies with social benefit, and the men themselves looked as if they'd never seen the inside of a barn.

Ryn laughed, remembering the thrilled expression on their faces when she rolled open the doors and her miniature donkeys, or minis asses as she referred to them—Simon and Todd—trotted up to say hello.

She climbed the office steps to say goodbye to Keisha, before leaving for the holiday weekend.

Inside, Keisha straightened the bright orange and yellow woven cushions on the lobby sofa, working around Fergus, who appeared to have decided the new couch was his domain.

Ryn stopped and admired the framed poster of Carly's *Forbes* magazine cover on the wall, as she often did. *Why Shy Can Spell Success in Medical Startups.* It wasn't her favorite title, but a jolt of pride hit her every time she saw her friend's wavy hair and broad smile on the wall. She might be the only person who understood everything Carly overcame to reach her success.

Ryn joined Keisha and helped her fluff the rest of the cushions. The best part of starting a firm was complete control to hire her own team. She remembered her nerves the day she took Keisha out for coffee and proposed she join as junior partner. She'd expected Keisha to at least make her sweat and say she wanted to think it over, in recompense for everything Ryn should have seen with Simon. Especially as Keisha received lots of offers after CEOs saw her work on Equal Chances, and Ryn couldn't yet pay as much as larger firms.

"I thank my lucky stars every day you didn't turn me down."

Keisha rolled her eyes and laughed. "To go where? You were the first person who took a chance on me. And I didn't even burn cash on ferry tickets this time."

"I know you said you've got plans, but are you sure you don't want to join us at the picnic?"

"Nah, like I said, my girl and I are headed to Monterey for a romantic weekend. Speaking of which, I should get on the road. We're the last ones here."

Ryn lifted the lid of the clay pot on the front desk, and hid her disappointment at finding it empty. When Keisha suggested giving every office visitor the chance to nominate a charity for the month, Ryn knew the perfect container.

She replaced the lid on what used to be her Feelings Jar. "You already chose?" This had become her favorite moment of the month: when the team got together and decided the charity. Although, to be fair, she'd been traveling most of June raising money. Today was July third already.

Keisha tossed back her hair and grinned. "The decision didn't require much discussion." She opened a drawer behind the desk and handed Ryn a slip of paper. "We all knew you'd want this one."

Ryn read the name. Keisha couldn't be more right. This nonprofit co-sponsored women through harassment cases. They'd become a partner organization to Equal Chances Silicon Valley, Austin, and now Raleigh. And one of their biggest grants supported the cost of Leslie Lawler's high-profile case against Simon Atherton.

She chuckled. Amazing how a little perspective helped reframe history. For years she'd been so busy stuffing emotions in that jar, she never stopped and asked why she had so many negative sentiments to stifle.

"Do you know how you can tell you've hired the best team, my friend?"

Keisha glanced at the cushions. "Please don't tell me it's similar taste in office decor?"

Ryn reached over and touched her hand. "It's when you're confident they'll go on to do greater things than you."

They hugged, and Ryn grabbed the box of beer from the office fridge before leaving for the picnic. Today was the celebration Carly promised once Ryn officially became single. The annulment became final over a month ago, but with everyone's packed schedules, they'd decided to wait for the holiday weekend.

****

Twenty minutes later, Ryn watched the sun sparkle off the rearing horse logo as she passed through the wrought-iron gates of the winery Carly had chosen. How àpropos. The iron horse reminded Ryn of the John Wayne poster she'd taken from her office at Sentra, which now hung above her bed, where she most needed courage if she were to take the leap into loving again.

On a grass hill above the sweep of vines she spotted Dev playing Frisbee with Sammy. She drove up the curved drive and parked nearby.

Green and purple blankets, white cardboard boxes

and Tupperware covered the picnic area. Carly, Ryn's brother Jack and his wife, and Paul Alexander and his wife, stood chatting beside a picnic table.

Ryn walked up to the group and placed her package of beer on top of the cooler.

"Paul, what a great surprise, it's been forever. I'm so glad you could join us." She gave him a hug. Carly suggested inviting him, so she could catch up with her friend outside of his limited hours in the office. He looked well compared to when Ryn last saw him.

"How does it feel to be back at work?" She'd heard from Carly he was in remission and worked two days a week.

"Great, although I sometimes wonder if my co-founder even needs me anymore," Paul said, nodding toward Carly. "My protégé has become so admired my returning as an advisor almost seems unnecessary."

Carly blushed and started opening plastic containers. She must know Paul was right. Ryn made a mental note to remind her later, just in case. It never hurt for either of them to bolster the other.

Ryn greeted the rest of the guests, turned, and waved at Dev farther up the sloping grass. From here, she noticed he played not only with Sammy, but also her nieces Jenny and Nicole, and two girls of similar age who, she'd guess, were Paul's daughters.

Her nieces barreled down the hill, and Ryn grabbed them in a three-way hug. "Happy Independence Day, everyone."

"Don't be silly, Auntie Kathryn," Nicole said. "Independence Day is tomorrow."

Carly laughed. "Well, actually for your Aunt Ryn, it's today. I told her many months ago that when it happened, we'd have a picnic and celebrate." She picked up the wine and poured a plastic glass to almost overflowing for Ryn.

Sammy arrived, his hand in Dev's. He beamed at Ryn. "Did you see what me and Mommy made?" He bounced on his toes, his gaze fixed on the largest of the plastic containers.

Carly sprang off the lid and displayed a massive chocolate and ivory cake. "Tell them what we created, Sams. It's in honor of Auntie Ryn."

He counted on his fingers. "It has Nutella, mer-ang," he checked with Carly to see if he'd enunciated correctly, and she nodded her head, proud, "and raspberries and choclit!"

Ryn peered into the box. This creation looked so perfect it would win one of those television bake-off shows. Well, except for one corner where small fingers had clearly swiped a taste.

"It seemed only appropriate," Carly whispered, with a conspiring smile, "given you've relied on Nutella for so many darker moments, to reframe it and ask your mom to join us in a moment of victory."

Ryn's chest tingled, and the touch of a breeze rustled over the warmth of her arms. She leaned in and gave Carly's wrist a squeeze. "Only you know how much this means, especially today."

Carly's cheeks flushed, obviously touched. She wrapped her own fingers around Ryn's and winked. "We make a damn good team, eh partner?"

She re-covered the cake and helped Jack open the other packages of food while Ryn looked out across the vineyard. Long lines of vibrant vines curved up the hills, dotted at each end with rosebushes. From this distance she couldn't tell for sure, but even this late in the season, she'd swear they were blooming. This was how roses should be. Outside thriving on a hillside. Not severed, and never blue.

She inhaled, trying to smell them, and she captured dirt, grass, sunshine, and something sweet, like honey. Carly picked the perfect spot to celebrate together.

The group settled on the blankets and Ryn caught Carly's eye as she opened what must be the last of twenty different boxes. "Seriously, you didn't need to prepare all this for me. Well, except for the cake. How did I not know that was missing from my life?"

First Nutella lattes, a cake, and this impressive picnic, all created as acts of love. Warmth radiated from the grass up Ryn's bare legs and across her chest and shoulders. She met Carly's gaze, hoping she'd understand her level of appreciation, and Carly matched her smile.

A few minutes later, Carly declared the picnic of the decade ready to eat, and the wine and conversation flowed.

"How's the new house coming?" Jack's wife, Cynthia, asked Ryn.

"Not quite open for visitors." *Understatement.* Ryn had put her energy and money into getting the office building ready, along with finding barn help. She occupied only two rooms of the creaky Victorian farmhouse—the bedroom and kitchen—until she could find time for renovations.

"Oh shoot. I'm sorry." Jack slapped his forehead. "I promised to come over last weekend and help fix the screen doors."

Ryn gave him an understanding smile. "It's fine. I

stretched Saran wrap over the door. The house has a long way to go, but I'm planning for a visit from Pops soon, and I'd love if you came before then, if you can stand the odd cockroach."

Dev's face scrunched in disgust. "You sure you wouldn't prefer a return to my bug and rodent-free apartment?"

Ryn blushed. The group likely didn't realize he flirted, but Dev had been living in his place for the past two months. And none of them knew, not even Carly, that yesterday she'd agreed to his persistent requests for a date. She'd tell Carly when they found alone-time this afternoon, and make sure dating Dev didn't cause issues, because she refused to risk their friendship.

"Making good progress with the firm?" Jack asked.

"Great. We've raised around thirty percent of what we need. Very little from traditional Silicon Valley, but after Equal Chances, I'm getting lots of interest from retired female execs who want to support the next generation. Still looking for more investors, though."

"Aren't you into investing in startups?" Paul asked, turning to Dev.

Ryn popped a deviled egg in her mouth, hoping the question might disappear in the flow of conversation. Dev was charming, found her jokes funny, and like Carly, kept trying to convince her to meditate. Even if they ended up not being a romantic fit, she didn't want business interfering with the chance of a new friendship. But she also didn't need a discussion of her dating life in front of the group. Not when she hadn't talked with Carly.

"You've been doing your homework," Dev said, without shifting his honey-brown eyes from Ryn's.

"What do you think? Wanna take my moola?"

He sure enjoyed making her squirm.

"We tend to look for a different type of investor. More, er…"

Now she couldn't think of an end to her sentence which didn't insult Dev. More rich? Less chivalrous? Less of a joker? She made a face at him, away from the others' line of sight.

Dev took pity and interrupted the questioning by picking up his plate and standing. He turned to Sammy. "I believe I owe you the rest of a game of Frisbee, young man and ladies. Shall we burn off some calories before we tackle the amazing Nutella confection?"

Ryn exhaled, and watched him rise and run toward the grass, motioning for the kids to follow.

Jack and Paul and their wives tidied up the Tupperware containers, behind the picnic table, leaving Ryn and Carly alone on the blanket.

Carly held up her wine. "Congratulations, Ms. Brennan, finally single. Here's to forgotten asses and new beginnings."

They touched plastic glasses.

"Any update on our favorite criminal?" Carly asked.

"The special agent told me last week they gathered enough to pass the investigation back to the US Attorney and press charges. Oh, and I know this may not shock you, they found one more wife, between me and Ella."

Carly rolled her eyes. "Seriously? We should start a dang Facebook group."

Ryn chuckled. "I'll fill you in later if you want. For today let's just enjoy the moment?" They'd discussed last week how the entire story had already started to feel surreal, almost distant to them.

"Talking of asses, when can Sammy come see them, again?" After helping pick out the donkeys from the shelter, he now considered them his own.

"Let's plan for this—" The Frisbee flew across their blanket. Ryn ducked, swept her hand, narrowly missing Carly's wine, and caught the disk.

Carly applauded, and Dev ran toward them and grabbed it. A few beads of sweat on the muscles of his arms glowed in the sunlight.

"Sorry to interrupt," he said, "but nice one!" He talked only to Ryn. "Are you by any chance a stealth world Frisbee champion?"

Ryn blushed before saying thanks. She turned her attention to Carly as he ran back up the hill.

"What was that?" Carly asked, her eyes wide.

Ryn stared into her plastic glass a moment too long.

"No way." Carly nudged Ryn with her elbow, her voice lowered to whisper-level. "You and Dev, really? How long?"

Ryn broke into a grin and took another sip of wine. She whispered too, not wanting to share this conversation with anyone other than Carly.

"Well, once he got back to California, he kept asking me in the funniest ways. Most recently a piece of artwork, because he said flowers were a cliché. First date is next Saturday, but only as long as you don't mind. He is wickedly funny..." She watched as Dev took a soccer-style dive to the grass for the Frisbee, "and athletic."

Carly smiled as if the Disney castle had been

plopped next to her on the hill. She rocked back and forth on the blanket. "Really and truly?" She grinned again, a flush crossing the lines on her cheeks. "I've never understood why Dev doesn't attract a higher caliber of women, because he's one of the good ones."

"It's early days, but good to know you're not worried about him breaking my heart."

Carly laughed. "I'm not worried about you. Or me. Clearly, we can survive anything."

They touched cups once more. Carly took a sip, put her wine aside, and flopped back on the blanket, staring at the sky.

Ryn lay back too, the sun caressing her legs below her skirt.

Carly sighed. "Who would have thought? My two besties…"

Ryn smiled and exhaled warmth. She'd never been described as a best friend by anyone other than Todd.

"Could you imagine us having this conversation last year?" Ryn asked.

"Are you kidding? You would have taken that Nutella cake, stuffed it down my throat, and held my mouth closed."

Ryn joined in Carly's laughter, flipping through her mental Rolodex of every advice session, every glass of wine, their road trip to Oklahoma, the launch of Equal Chances, and every discussion of heartbreak and second chances which brought them from there to here, lying in the sun. Best friends.

"I know I've said it before but thank you. For everything. I don't think I could have survived the last year without you."

Carly said nothing but touched her hand.

Ryn closed her eyes. A breeze rustled through the vines and over their blanket, whispering of new vintages and future possibilities. She'd swear she could smell the faintest scent of those roses.

Author Note

This book is fiction, and I took liberties in some areas, such as timing of the FDA clearance process and simplification of California divorce proceedings and venture capital job titles—in reality Ryn's promoted role would be known as general partner.

However, what's not fiction is the continued sexist climate in the tech industry. Many moments, drawn from real life, were toned down for credibility, but getting excluded from meetings, being pushed to smile more, different performance standards, cougar night, even being invited to 'bond with the team' at strip clubs, are experiences I lived as a female senior executive.

If you'd like to better understand the state of sexism and the pace of progress, I have a recommended reading list on my website, including *Reset*, a memoir by one of my real-life heroines, Ellen Pao, and Julian Guthrie's book, *Alpha Girls*.

As an author friend and mentor Laura Drake said after reading this novel, "I wish for the day that a young woman will ask her mother, 'This stuff didn't really happen to women of your generation, did it?' And the mother can truthfully say, 'Of course not, dear. It's fiction.'" Unfortunately, that day is not yet here.

A word about the author...

Lainey Cameron is an author of women's fiction and recovering tech industry executive. Her award-winning novel, *The Exit Strategy*, was inspired by a decade of being the only woman in the corporate boardroom.

A digital nomad—meaning she picks locations around the world to live (and write) for months at a time—Lainey is an avid Instagrammer and loves to share her travel tips and insights with readers.

Originally from Scotland, Lainey has a soft spot for men in kilts and good single malt whisky.

She's always grateful to you, the reader. Reviews mean the world to authors. If you have time, please consider writing one?

You can connect with her online and find extras, including Ryn's Songs Todd Despises music playlist, book club questions, and a travel guide to locations that inspired this book:

https://www.laineycameron.com/the-exit-strategy/extras